Thunder Road
By
David Donaghe

D1526188

Thunder Road
David Donaghe
Published by David Donaghe at Amazon.Com
2021 Amazon Print Edition

Disclaimer

All characters an events in this work are fictitious. All references to any motorcycle club are also fictitious. Any resemblance to real persons, living or dead is coincidental.

Table of Contents

Chapter 1
Chapter 2
Chapter 3
Chapter 4
Chapter 5
Chapter 6
Chapter 7
Chapter 8
Chapter 9
Chapter 10
Chapter 11
Chapter 12
Chapter 13
Chapter 14
Chapter 15
Chapter 16
Chapter 17
Chapter 18
Chapter 19
Chapter 20
Chapter 21
Chapter 22
In the Wind Sample Chapters
About the Author
Other Books by David Donaghe

Chapter 1

I woke up with a pounding headache that felt as if someone was up there busting up the joint with a sledgehammer. I couldn't even remember my name. My mouth felt like I had gargled with used Kitty Litter. I gazed about the room realizing that I lay in a hospital bed. I had an IV drip in my arm and EKG sticky pads on my chest. I felt the uncomfortable feeling of a catheter jammed up my Johnson. A thin hospital gown covered my naked bruised body. Gauze bandages covered my chest and my head. I noticed a USMC tattoo on my left bicep. *I must have been in some kind of accident*, I thought.

My gaze widened taking in the green-tiled floor, the blue walls, and the white curtains. The EKG machine by my bed beeped. Outside, I heard birds singing. The smell of medicine and pine-scented cleaner filled the air. Pictures of sea fairing vessels hung on the wall to my left, and a small television set hung on the wall in front of my bed. To the right of the TV, a glass door offered a view to the nurse's station in the hallway. Above the door hung a large clock, the kind they have in grade school with a white face and big black numbers. A motorcycle rumbled down the street outside, pain shot through my head and a chill shot through my body.

I squinted, clutching the sides of my head with my hands waiting for the pain to subside. Sweat cropped up on my forehead and my heart pounded. The pain faded. I saw a middle-aged man with dark hair, wearing a black suit sitting on a folding chair leaning up against the wall. I studied him for a moment. He looked familiar. Streaks of gray spiraled through his coal-black hair. Stubble covered his wrinkled chin. He scratched his hawk-like beak, turning a page, and seemed engrossed in the novel. I noticed a small scar on the cleft of his chin, his bushy eyebrows, and his middle-aged spread. Someone paged a Doctor Valentine. I heard a nurse laugh.

"Water," I croaked.

The man looked up, his eyes widened, he jumped to his feet, tossing aside the book, and sprinted to my bedside.

"Mike. You're awake!" he said and laid a hand on my arm. His hands felt warm to the touch.

"My name is Mike?" I asked looking up at the man.

The man patted my forearm, seeming overjoyed. "Yes. Mike McDonald. Don't you remember?"

"I don't remember anything. Who are you?"

"I'm Pastor Blackwood. You don't remember what happened?"

"I said I don't remember anything. Could you get me some water? My mouth feels like I gargled with cat piss."

The preacher grinned, handed me a bottle of water from a metal stand next to my bed and I sucked water through a straw. After soothing my parched throat, I looked at the preacher. "I guess we must be friends?"

The preacher couldn't seem to keep that silly grin off his face. "Yes. You are one of my closest and dearest friends."

He kept patting me on the arm with his hand and I paused for a moment studying the man. He seemed like your typical middle-aged Joe on the outside, but I sensed something deeper.

"What happened to me anyway?" I asked.

A sad expression shot across the preacher's face. "You've been in a coma for three months. I'd better get the nurse. We'll talk later after the doctor has a chance to check you out." The preacher spun around, heading out the door and I watched him through the window. He stormed across the hallway to the nurse's station and pounded his fist down on the counter to get her attention. I laughed; I was starting to like this preacher. Pondering the situation for a few seconds, I tried to figure things out. My name meant nothing to me. This preacher claimed to be a friend of mine, yet I didn't remember him. I had a banged-up body that had been asleep for the last three months. I must have been in the Marines at some time or another because I had the tattoo. Other than that, everything seemed fogged in like pea soup. I tried to remember, but a blinding white-hot pain shot through my skull and I let out a blood-curdling scream.

A young doctor wearing a green lab coat followed by a chubby Hispanic nurse came running into my room. The preacher followed at their heels and I let out another scream, sitting up in bed, and held my head in my hands.

"Take it easy," the doctor said sticking a needle into my arm. I let out another yell and began to hyperventilate. My head throbbed and felt as if it was going to explode. "Ride it out. The medicine should start to take effect in a few seconds."

The pain eased off, I felt light-headed and leaned back feeling the effects of the medicine. "Take it easy? That's easy for you to say. My head feels likes some monkey is up there using a Jackhammer."

The doctor smiled. "It's good to see that your sense of humor is still intact. All things considered, you're lucky to be alive," the doctor said. I breathed in the smell of Vodka on his breath.

"What happened to me?" I asked.

The doctor paused looking at my chart. "What do you remember?"

I shook my head. "Not a damned thing. Everything, before I woke up is a blank."

"Your memories will start to come back after a while." The doctor looked over at Blackwood.

Blackwood let out a sigh. "Don't sugarcoat it. Tell him." Blackwood stepped up next to the doctor and laid a friendly hand on my arm.

"You and your wife were on vacation. You were taking a trip on your motorcycle."

My heart hammered inside my chest and my breathing accelerated. "Did we crash? Is my wife all right?"

The doctor shook his head. "No. You stopped in at a little bar on old Route Sixty-Six and a gang of outlaw bikers attacked you. They beat you half to death, gave you some minor brain damage, shot you in the shoulder, and stabbed you. They left you for dead."

That was a mistake, I thought. "My wife? What happened to her?"

The doctor paused and looked down at his feet, so the reverend spoke up.

"They killed her, Mike. After they raped her." I saw tears form in the reverend's eyes. "She was pregnant. She wasn't far enough along for them to save the baby."

"I'll give you two a moment," the doctor said and left the room.

I felt numb. “Look. There’s no need for you to get all worked up about this. Shit happens. I don’t remember any of it anyway. It’s like it happened to someone else.”

“I’m so sorry Mike,” the preacher said.

The doctor and the nurse came back in and the doctor gave me a thorough examination.

“How bad am I, doc?”

The doctor shrugged. “For someone who’s been in a coma for three months, you are in good shape. You suffered some minor brain damage, you may have to relearn some motor skills and then there’s the memory loss. That should come back with time. You suffered some muscle atrophy. You’ll have to undergo therapy for that. You took a bullet to the upper shoulder and you had some ribs broken. Those wounds are healing.”

“How soon until you take this damned catheter out of me?”

“We’ll bring in a portable toilet to set by the bed. Tomorrow, if you are strong enough to get up and get out of bed.”

“I’m strong enough now. If a man can’t stand up to piss, he ain’t much of a man,” I said.

“Yes, well sometimes life knocks the strongest of us on our ass. Keep up that attitude, though. We’ll keep you on the pain meds for your headaches. For now, what you need is rest. Let your body recuperate. Tomorrow, we’ll see how strong you are and start your physical therapy,” the doctor said.

After the doctor and nurse left the room, Reverend Blackwood stepped up closer to my bed and I studied the man’s face. He looked concerned.

“Preacher what’s your first name?”

“Craig. Craig, Blackwood.”

“Well Craig, pull up a chair. Since my memory is a blank slate right now, I need some information. I need you to fill in the blanks. Unfortunately, it’s all blank space up here,” I said tapping the side of my forehead.

Craig pulled his chair up next to my bed. “What do you want to know?”

I took a pull through the straw taking a drink from a water bottle that one of the nurses left me. “How long have we known each other?”

The preacher's eyes lit up. "For about two and a half years. When you came back from the gulf, you started coming to church with Sharon."

"What church is that?"

The preacher leaned forward resting his hands on his knees. "Cross Roads Assembly. They call it the church on the hill. It's in Redlands California."

"I live in Redlands California?"

"No. You live in East Highland. It's a little town east of San-Bernardino."

I shrugged. "None of those names sound familiar to me. What hospital am I in?"

"You're in Saint Marie's in Victorville."

"What's this gulf you were talking about?"

"The Persian Gulf in the Middle East. You served in the war. You drove tanks. Saddam Husain, the president of Iraq, ordered his troops to invade Kuwait. Kuwait is a little country on the Iraqi border. The United States took action. The buildup lasted for several months. After the war started, it only took a few days for the US forces to drive the Iraqis out of Kuwait."

I nodded glancing at the USMC tattoo on my arm. "I take it, that I was in the Marines?"

"Yes. Say, Mike, I brought you a Bible when they first brought you here. I put it in the top drawer on that nightstand next to your bed. You might want to read it when you're feeling better."

I shrugged. "These scumbags that killed my wife. What's the name of their gang?" I asked.

The preacher leaned back in his chair and frowned. "They call themselves the Lost Souls. The name fits, but you don't need to worry about them right now."

"They raped and killed my wife. They shot me, stabbed me, and beat me half to death. They took away my memories. They took away my whole life. They left me for dead. That was a mistake."

The preacher sighed and said, "Vengeance is mine, says the Lord."

I smiled, but my fists white-knuckled the metal railings at the side of my bed. "Sorry pastor, but not this time. This time, vengeance belongs to me."

"You need to get well. You don't even know how to find those people or which ones to go after. I know Sharon wouldn't want this."

"I have no idea what Sharon would want. I can't remember. You wouldn't happen to have a picture of her, would you?"

The preacher grinned. "I sure do. I have a picture of both of you." He pulled a photograph out of his wallet, leaned over, and handed it to me. I looked at a photograph showing a young blond-headed Marine in his dress blues. He had his arm around a petite blonde-headed young woman. The woman's hair cascaded down her ample breasts and she looked beautiful, but I didn't recognize her. For that matter, I didn't even recognize myself.

"Can I have this picture?"

"Sure. Keep it," the reverend said.

I studied the picture that I held in my hand for a few seconds. The knuckles on my left hand gripping the railing of my hospital bed turned white. A red-hot cauldron of anger boiled up down deep inside of me. I know the preacher must have sensed what I was thinking because a look of trepidation crossed his face.

"If we're supposed to be buddies, tell me about it. What do we do? Hang out and stuff?" I asked.

The preacher ran his hand through his hair. "You and Sharon used to come over to the house for barbeques. You helped me build a hotrod." He showed me another picture showing him standing in front of a thirty-two Ford Coupe. He stood with a dark-haired woman. I don't know how I knew the car was a thirty-two Ford, but I did.

"That's a sweet-looking car. Who's the woman?"

"That's my wife Darlene."

"I guess I ride motorcycles. I take it that you do too?"

The preacher nodded. "Yeah, I have a Gold Wing a year newer than yours." He showed me another picture. This one showed him and his wife sitting on a maroon motorcycle with all the bells and whistles.

"What did I do for work?"

"You sell Insurance. I've been in contact with your boss at the agency. He says that your job is waiting for you as soon as you get better."

"What else?" I asked.

"You teach Sunday school at the church. You teach the teenaged class. The kids miss you. Everyone has been praying for you."

The nurse came in and interrupted our conversation. "I'm afraid I'm going to have to cut this short. Visiting hours are over. Mr. McDonald needs his rest," the nurse said.

The preacher stood to his feet and stepped up to my bed. "That's okay. I need to go home and spread the news. I can't wait to tell Darlene and everyone at church."

I reached out, took the preacher's hand, and studied his face for a few seconds. He looked thrilled by the fact that I had woken up. "Thank you, Pastor. All though I don't remember it, you must be a true friend."

"I am. It wouldn't hurt to pray a little if you get the chance, and read that Bible. Get those silly thoughts of revenge out of your head. My phone number is on the back cover of that Bible. Call me if you need anything. Any time, day or night. I'll come back tomorrow."

I nodded. The preacher and I said our goodbyes and I watched him saunter out the door. *He's a good man, but we'll have to disagree on that vengeance thing* I thought. A plan began to form in my mind. Then the Hispanic nurse came back into the room to give me some meds and broke my train of thought.

"You know that man has been by your bedside ever since they brought you here in the ambulance. He sits there by the door reading them cowboy books."

"He seems like a good man," I said breathing in the smell of her perfume.

"He cares a lot about you. I know that much," the nurse said and handed me a newspaper. "Here, they told me your memory was a might fuzzy. I thought you might want to catch up on current events." I looked at the newsprint before me and my eyes widened in horror. I couldn't read. I couldn't remember how.

"I'm sorry. I can't read this. I don't remember how." A tear tracked down my cheek.

The nurse let out a sigh and laid a hand on my shoulder. "Things are a little slow right now. I'll read it to you. What do you want me to read first?"

"Let's start with the date. What's today's date?"

The nurse smiled. "That one's easy. November third, nineteen ninety-three," she said.

The nurse read to me from the newspaper for the next half hour and I watched, trying to read over her shoulder. The words seemed jumbled, but now and then, I picked up a word here and there.

"You'd better get yourself some rest now, Mr. McDonald. You've had quite a day," the nurse said.

"What's your name?" I asked.

She grinned. "Elena Cortez."

"Thank you, Elena. Call me, Mike. They tell me that's my first name."

She laughed. "Okay, Mike. Why don't you get that preacher friend to bring you some of them cowboy books? That might help you with your reading."

"I'll do it, Elena." After the nurse left I reached into the drawer on the nightstand and brought out the Bible. I thumbed through the good book and my letters began to come back to me. The more I thumbed through the book, the more I picked up. *I must have liked to read*, I thought because I became obsessed. As I turned through the Bible, words began to come back to me. I found the passage where the Lord said vengeance is mine. I also found another passage that said those who live by the sword, will die by the sword. I grew tired and set the Bible on the nightstand. My headache lessened somewhat, but it was still there. I drifted off to sleep.

***

My dreams flowed like a movie in my mind consisting of jumbled faces that I didn't recognize. In one dream, I looked down a long dark tunnel; I heard people talking, a man yelled and a woman screamed. Their voices seemed far away and I couldn't recognize any faces. In another dream, I stumbled around in the fog and I kept hearing a woman calling my name, but I couldn't find her. I shivered, goosebumps formed up on my arms and legs; I let out a snort and woke up. My eyes darted about the darkroom, my heart thundered in my chest and I let out a shallow breath. Silence wafted across the room. Fear shot through me, and for a few seconds, I couldn't remember who I was or why I was in this dark room.

"Mike. My name is Mike and I'm in the hospital," I said to myself. That cauldron of anger that ignited earlier in the day flared up. *The ones, who did this to me, will pay.* I stayed awake for a couple of hours because my mind wouldn't turn off. *How do I find the ones that did this? When I do find them, how do I deal with them? I was in the military. I must be proficient with guns, but these sons of bitches need to die slow.* I felt guilty. Here I was thinking about revenge, but it was all about me. They raped and murdered my wife, but it's hard to grieve for a woman you can't remember.

"It's not for me alone. It's for you, too Sharon," I said to the darkroom. Sharon. The name seemed to roll off my tongue. I drifted off to sleep.

***

"Good Morning Michael," Elena said when she came into the room the next morning. The smell of her perfume filled the air. Michael. That caused a curious sense of joy to shoot through me. I looked up. Elena shot me a pretty smile and wheeled a portable toilet into the room. "How are you feeling today?"

"Like a warm bag of shit, but my headache is better."

Elena laughed. "That should lessen after I give you your meds. Doctor Valentine will be in, in a few minutes, to remove your catheter. We want you up and peeing on your own as soon as possible."

"It's about time, all though I can't say I'll look forward to the procedure."

She patted my shoulder. "It will be over before you know it."

"Yeah, well why don't you have him slide some bamboo splinters under my fingernails while he's at it."

Elena chuckled. "It won't be that bad."

An orderly brought me my breakfast: poached eggs, toast, and corn beef hash with a glass of orange juice. I took a bite of the corn beef hash and then looked for a place to spit.

"Good old corn beef hash: the human version of dog food. There are some things that I do remember."

Elena giggled. When I said the words, "dog food," something rippled through my brain. The image of a tan German shepherd flashed through my mind. My headache intensified for a few seconds and my heart thumped inside my chest. I finished my breakfast and the doctor came in a few minutes later.

"How are we feeling today Mr. McDonald?" Today his breath smelled of Bourbon.

I shrugged. "Like five pounds of shit in a three-pound bag."

"Care to elaborate on that?"

"My head still hurts. My side hurts, my shoulder hurts and this log jam you got shoved up my dick is as uncomfortable as hell."

Doctor Valentine smiled. "We'll take care of that shortly. He reached his hand under my covers and my hospital gown.

My heart did a drum roll. "Take it easy doc. I don't know you that well."

Valentine laughed. "Have you been watching TV? Are you catching up on your sports?"

"I haven't been paying much attention to the TV. I'm trying to remember how to read." A sharp pain shot through my groin, my hands gripped the sides of my bed, and sweat beaded up on my forehead.

"There we go. You should feel better now."

The pain in my groin dissipated. "You don't bother with foreplay do you doc? You go straight to the dirty deed."

"When a job needs doing, you should get 'er done," Valentine said. I laughed; the doctor checked me over and left.

"Do you feel the need to pee?" Elena said.

"Yes, I do. If you'll help me over to that piss pot I'll take care of business."

Elena helped me over to the edge of the bed, I moved my legs over and pain racked my body. My feet found the floor, Elena helped me up and I took a step. The touch of her left breast against my arm caused a stirring sensation to shoot through my loins. Sweat beaded up on my forehead. Huffing and puffing like a steam engine, I took three steps to the portable toilet while Elena held onto my arm.

"You might want to sit down."

I shook my head. "A man doesn't sit down to pee. There are something's you don't forget, coma or no coma."

Elena patted me on the back. "Some men don't have good sense."

I pulled out my member and let 'er rip. "Awe," I groaned feeling sweat relief.

Elena helped me back to bed, but I felt like I had run a marathon. She left the room and came back a few minutes later with an aluminum walker. "We'll start you out on this and then get you down to therapy tomorrow."

"You're a Jewel, Elena," I said.

The preacher came again that afternoon. He came to visit me every day that I was in the hospital. My reading increased by leaps and bounds. I read a few of the preacher's cowboy books. There was one I enjoyed called the Mojave Kid's Last Ride. I felt stronger each day, but the therapy was brutal. I had to learn to walk all over again. The therapist made me do several types of exercises to increase the strength in my legs and upper body. I didn't know what pain was until she got hold of me and by the end of the week, the nurse took away the portable toilet. I remember my first trip to the bathroom struggling across the room using the walker. When I entered the bathroom, I stopped staring into the mirror. I looked into the eyes of a stranger studying my reflection.

I had short blond hair, what I considered a good-looking face, and a small scar on my left cheek. I noticed faint traces of what had once been a tanned muscled body. A trace of Indian and Irish ancestry showed through. My high cheekbones and strong jaw seemed to be the most prominent features of my face. I turned from the mirror, sat down on the toilet, and sighed. "Finally, I get to take a shit in private," I said to myself and all seemed right with the world.

I woke up in the middle of the night after a nightmare a few days later. My pulse pounded in my veins and I let out a short little gasp. Silence filled the room, except for the ticking of the clock hanging over the door and the beating of my own heart. My head throbbed and a memory slammed through my mind like a runaway freight train.

***

CHAPTER 2

Tick, tick, tick. I looked up at the clock over the door; its unrepentant ticking was starting to drive me bananas. *Three PM. Two more hours and I'm out of here.* I clicked the print button on my computer printing out the insurance documents. A faint trace of perfume wafted across my desk. The scent was Channel Number Five. I recognized the fragrance because it was one of Sharon's favorites. I looked up at the young couple sitting across my desk and smiled. I marked places that needed initials and signatures with a yellow highlighter.

"If you'll initial here and here. Then sign at the bottom, we'll get you guys out of here." The young woman smiled. Cute little dimples formed in her cheeks.

"How much is the uninsured motorist clause going to cost us, Mike?" the man asked.

I looked into his friendly face. "Only one hundred dollars a year, but it's worth it, Ray." I knew this young couple from church. Ray leaned across the table, put his initials down in all the right places, and signed the document.

"Thank you, Michael. We checked around. I know you're giving us a good deal," the woman said. A strand of strawberry blonde hair fell into her face.

"Don't I always do right by you guys, Barb? Now, all we need is the check," I said.

"Aren't you going on vacation?" Ray asked.

I smiled. "Yep. Today's my last day. Sharon and I are taking a trip on the bike."

Ray grinned. "Man, I wish I was you. I burned up the last of my vacation three months ago." He pulled his checkbook and wrote out a check for his initial deposit on the insurance policy. I stood up, came around to the front of the desk, and stuck out my hand. Ray and Barb stood to their feet. I shook hands with Ray and Barb hugged me. I felt the pressure of her midsized breasts against my chest and breathed in the scent of her perfume. When Barb pulled away, I escorted them to the door of my office. After saying goodbye to Ray and Barb, I went back to my desk. Picking up my phone, I punched 7832 and called my boss, Adam Bullard. Adam, who occupied the office at the end of the hall, picked up the phone on the third ring.

"What can I do for you, Mike?" Adam said. His gruff, loud voice caused me to move my head away from the receiver.

"Nothing much, boss man. I thought that if you didn't mind, I'd leave early today."

There was a short pause on the line before he responded. "You start vacation tomorrow, don't you?"

"Yeah, Sharron and I are going on a trip, on the Gold Wing. I thought that if you don't mind, I'd like to get an early start."

"I don't see why not. Things are slow right now. You guys have fun and give Sharon my love."

"Will do boss. You and Marge are going to have to come over again one of these weekends for another barbeque. We had fun the last time," I said.

"Tell Sharon to give Marge a call and set it up. This time we'll have it at my place. Invite that preacher friend of yours. What was his name again? Blackwood, wasn't it? That man's a kick in the pants."

"I'll do it."

"Then goodbye. Have fun on your trip," Bullard said.

I hung up the phone, crossed the room to my refrigerator, took out my thermos, and stepped out the door. I headed down the hallway and paused in the reception area. "I'm off Louise. The boss man gave me an early quit," I said to our voluptuous secretary. The smell of her perfume drifted across the room. It was something different from what Sharon wore. I didn't like it.

Louise smiled, leaned over her desk. I noticed some cleavage and a tiny field of freckles running across the tops of her breasts. I glanced away after a fraction of a second.

"Have a good vacation, Mike. Tell Sharon I said hello. I hope you guys have a good time."

I nodded. "We will. Give Sharon a call sometime." I waved goodbye and headed out the door. My footfalls echoed off the surrounding buildings. I hurried across the marble stepping stones, on my way to the parking structure. The stones ended at the elevators and I rode an elevator up to the third floor. Whistling an old gospel tune, a big grin crossed my face. The sound of my whistling echoed through the parking garage. Halfway down the aisle, I stopped and my heart skipped a beat. There set my baby leaning on her side stand.

She was a Candy Apple red nineteen ninety Honda Gold Wing. She had an AM/FM radio, a cassette deck, and cruise control. With a full tour pack and side cases, I could carry everything but the kitchen sink. If I couldn't fit it in the tour pack, I could bungee it to the luggage rack mounted on top. I stepped up to the bike, put my key in the ignition switch, and swung to the saddle. I brought the bike off its stand, feeling its seven hundred plus pounds, and put up the side stand. Turning on the ignition, I hit the starter button and the engine purred to life. The engine idled while I took my helmet from the right side mirror and put it on. I strapped my helmet into place, put on my gloves, and backed her out of the parking spot. The transmission made an audible clunk when I mashed the shifter into gear with my foot. I let out the clutch, turned the throttle, and leaned back to enjoy the ride.

The Gold Wing glided through the parking garage like if it was floating on air. The purr of its engine resonated throughout the building. I turned on the radio to the gospel station and listened to some Christen rock. When I reached the exit, I leaned into the curve spiraling down from the third floor to the first. Giving it some throttle, I headed to the main exit. The sunburst forth when I left the parking structure and headed to the street.

Looking left and right, I waited for my break in traffic and pulled out onto E Street heading south. The buzz of traffic filled the street. I passed the mall, caught the green light, and turned right onto Fourth Street. Some gang bangers stood on the street corner and a sense of sadness shot through me. *Those guys aren't much older than the teens I teach at church. What a waste.* I said a silent prayer. Passing two more stoplights, I headed for the onramp to the interstate. An old man in raggedy clothes stood on the corner begging for change when I pulled onto the onramp. I goosed the throttle, picking up speed. The speedometer jumped up to seventy-five miles an hour and I enjoyed the feel of the wind in my face.

Worming my way through traffic, I took the I15 to the cross-town freeway. I headed toward Highland, a bedroom community of San-Bernardino California. When I reached Highland Avenue, I took the exit and headed east. Hustle and bustle filled the street as commuters made their way home from work. Passing an Arco station and Patton State Hospital, I continued east until I came to Boulder

Road. Turning right on Boulder, I headed south. At Baseline, I took a left and headed east toward East Highland. The tract homes gave way to open fields and high-dollar homes on three to five-acre lots.

I crossed the bridge spanning City Creek and listened to the water babble over the rocks. I turned left on Birch Street. A group of kids playing baseball in the street moved out of the road and let me pass. Halfway up the street, I turned into the driveway of my modest two-story raised ranch-style home.

***

I parked the bike in the front driveway, killed the motor, put the bike on its side stand, and swung from the saddle. Sharon stormed out the front door, crossing the front lawn on the run. Her long blonde hair billowed in the breeze. I stood watching her breasts bounce up and down underneath her wife-beater t-shirt. She leaped through the air, slamming into me, and wrapped her legs around my waist. Breathing in her essence, I put my hands on her bottom, concealed by her Daisy Duke shorts, and pulled her close. She smelled of soap. Something grew hard in my lower regions while she smothered me with kisses.

"Michael. You're home early! I was hoping that Adam might let you go early. I've got everything packed. You need to feed Lucky and Totem. Karen, from across the street is going to feed them while we're away and watch the house. I love you, baby," she said and kissed me again.

"I love you too, babe," I said and let her slip to the ground. She took my arm and we headed across the lawn toward the house. I enjoyed the feel of her right breast against my arm as I looked at my two-story brick house. I felt like the luckiest man alive.

"I like your sexy legs and I like the way your tight butt hangs out of those shorts. But don't you think you'd better put on a pair of long pants before we go?" I said when we stepped under the front porch awning and reached the front door.

Sharon let go of my arm and patted me on the back. "I know. I didn't expect you home so early. Take a shower, and then go feed Lucky and Totem. I'll fix you something to eat and then will get ready."

I slapped Sharon on the butt as we entered my spacious living room. She headed to the kitchen and I headed to the master bath. Stripped out of my clothes, I stepped into the shower and turned the water on as hot as I could stand it. The hot water felt invigorating.

Finished in the shower, I palmed away fog from the mirror and shaved. In our master bedroom, I dressed in a pair of jeans and a black t-shirt. I put a black skullcap over my short blond hair and put on my sunglasses.

Sharon's voice sounded musical coming from the kitchen. I crossed the living room stepped out our sliding glass door and into my three-acre backyard. My tanned German shepherd let out a loud bark, came running up onto my covered patio. He leaped upon me putting his big paws on my chest. His tail wagged and his tongue hung out.

"Hello, Lucky. How's my big guy?" I said rubbing his big furry head. "How's it going, fur face?" Lucky jumped down, I went to the steel trashcan where I kept the dog food and filled his dish. While Lucky gobbled down his food, I crossed the yard to the horse corral. Sharon's roan appaloosa gelding put his head over the top rail, so I stepped up and let the horse nuzzle me.

"Hey amigo. How are you today, Totem?" Totem let out a snort. His name was, Totem because he seemed as tall as a totem pole. White with black spots, Totem didn't look like much. He was so narrow in the chest that his front legs looked like they both came from the same hole. His back had a sharp ridge to it, but we compensated for that with a thick pad under the saddle. What Totem lacked in looks, he made up for in ability and personality. He had an easy lope that could eat up the miles. He wasn't very fast, but you could ride him all day and he wouldn't tire. He could stop on a dime, turn on his hindquarters and take off in the opposite direction at a dead run. At some time in his life, Totem had been a cow horse. If you put a set of hobbles on his front legs, he would stand still. You could leave him to go into a store or do whatever and he wouldn't move. I didn't think of Totem as him being an animal and me his master. Even though Totem was Sharron's horse, he was my buddy; I felt the same way about Lucky. I scratched Totem behind the ears and went to the hay pile. Breaking a flake off an open bale, I put it in Totem's feeder and Totem munched away. Brushing minute particles of hay off my clothes, I sneezed and went back into the house.

Sharon had a large burrito and a cold glass of Pepsi waiting for me when I came back inside. "Thanks, babe," I said, picking my burrito up off the plate. I took a bite. The food was delicious; Sharon knew how to cook. Taking a drink from my glass of Pepsi, I thought, *I could almost go for a cold beer.* I hadn't had a drink since I came back from the Gulf and started going to church. When I was in the Marines, I drank a lot, but I gave up drinking beer, for Sharon. I didn't regret it, but, I missed having a cold beer in the evening after coming home from work.

Finished eating, Sharon, pulled me into the bedroom, pushed me down on the bed, and took off her clothes. I sat back to watch the show, taking in her large voluptuous breasts, her thin waist, and her firm round hips. I gazed at her long sensual legs and her long blonde hair that swirled down the front of her breasts. My eyes widened and my heart pummeled my ribcage. She climbed onto the bed, took my clothes off, and made love to me. She had such a frenzied pace that I had trouble keeping up with her rhythm. When we finished, I felt as weak and shaky as a newborn calf, but I had a smile on my face.

We showered together and dressed. Sharon made coffee while I packed our gear and put our traveling bags inside the tour pack. I secured our tent and sleeping bags to the luggage rack. Then I put the rest of the camping gear along with our food into the side cases. We sat down in the living room to enjoy a cup of coffee before leaving. I enjoyed the rich taste of the Columbian blend.

Finished with the coffee, we went out back to say goodbye to our pets. Lucky jumped up putting his paws on Sharon's stomach.

"You be a good boy while we're gone, Lucky. Mamma's gonna miss you," Sharon said to the dog. I noticed tears in her eyes. We finished with Lucky and said our goodbyes to Totem. After locking up the house, we headed out front to the bike; I picked the bike off the stand and fired up the beast.

"I need to go across the street and give Karen the keys to the house. I'll ask her to pick up our mail, too," Sharon said. She ran across the street while I strapped on my helmet and backed the bike into the street. The warm evening sunshine felt good against my face. I waited for a few minutes while she talked to the neighbor.

"Here, put this on," I said handing Sharon her helmet when she came back. She strapped it on while I sat balancing the bike with both feet on the ground. "Get on." Sharon climbed on the back and nuzzled up against me. The firm pressure of her breasts against my back caused a thrill of arousal to shoot through me. We headed down Birch, turned right on Baseline, and headed back the way I came when I came home from work. We took the onramp heading west on the cross-town Freeway and wormed our way through traffic. I took the

I15 interchange heading north. I put my fist in the throttle and my face in the wind and settled back against Sharon's firm breasts to enjoy the ride.

The traffic slowed, I let a big rig pass, changed lanes, and took the exit to Highway 138. Putting both feet on the ground when I stopped at the stop sign, I paused, waiting for traffic. Sharon put her hand on my thigh. I turned left heading up a two-lane road that snaked its way through the mountains. Granite walls towered above us and the temperature dropped. The footpegs scraped asphalt on a couple of hairpin curves. The canyon widened with pine trees lining the road and the land opened up before us. Green lush meadows and rugged cattle ranches lined both sides of the road. I noticed horses grazing in one of the meadows. With the wind in my face, and Sharon's firm body pressed up against my back, I never felt better. I felt free and lucky to have the lovely woman on my back.

The rumble of motorcycles boomed down the canyon. I looked in my rearview mirror and saw a long line of Harley Davidson motorcycles coming up behind me fast. I felt Sharon tense up when a pack of twenty-five motorcycles blew by us. I waved, but they ignored me. Most of their bikes looked flashy with a lot of chrome, but a few looked ratty. The older bikers rode in the back of the pack. They looked like a rough bunch. Some had long beards and long hair and I noticed a few tattooed biceps. A few of the bikers wore tattered leather vests with the fronts open to expose their hairy beer bellies. I saw some type of club patch on their backs. They roared on up the road passing us like if we were standing still. An old Ford pickup truck pulling a boat blew by us heading in the opposite direction.

We went through several more curves. The road opened up and I saw a sign announcing a mom and pop store setting by the side of the road.

Sharon tapped me on the shoulder. "Stop. We need to get a bag of ice for the cooler and I need to go pee." It was hard to make out her voice over the sound of the wind, but I pulled off the road and into the parking lot. Several Harley Davidson motorcycles were parked next to the country store. A few hardcore bikers milled about out front by their motorcycles drinking beer. I parked next to a cobalt blue Pan Head. Sharon climbed off the bike and ran to the outdoor lady's room as soon as I set the bike on its stand.

Gazing about I took in the outlaw bikers in a glance. Most of them looked in their mid-forties to their early fifties and a few looked younger. They all sported tattoos. A few of the men gave me hard looks. Their women wore cut-off jean shorts and halter tops that left little to the imagination. One smiled at me.

"Damned rice poppers," one of the bikers said under his breath, but I ignored the comment. Climbing off the bike, I waited for Sharon under the awning. I noticed the patch on the back of one of the bikers going into the store. It had a top rocker that said, the Lost Souls. The main patch depicted a goulash-looking figure on a motorcycle in the middle of hell's flames. The bottom rocker said, Southern California. *The Lost Souls. That's appropriate. They're lost all right. Hell is exactly where they're bound if they don't change their ways,* I thought.

Sharon stepped up, took my arm and we stepped up on the boardwalk. Breathing in the smell of stale beer and unwashed bodies, Sharon and I entered the store. I found the ice machine, took out a small bag of ice and Sharon found a few minor things that we needed. A group of Souls sauntered down the aisle and one bumped into me.

I let out a sigh, trying not to get angry, and said, "Excuse me."

"You're excused, asshole," a big burly biker said and continued down the aisle. The men gave me hard looks and shot Sharon a few nasty leers. My hand tightened to a fist at my side.

"Ignore them," Sharon whispered, gripping my arm. I felt her hand tremble. We took our purchases to the counter, I paid the bill and the clerk seemed nervous when he handed me my change. Outside, I fired up the Gold Wing we hit the road and headed north for another half hour. Highway 138 intersected with Highway 18. I stopped at the stop sign, waited while several cars passed by, and turned right heading east on Highway 18. The road climbed heading up into the mountains and the weather cooled off. To the left, Lake Silver Wood loomed looking majestic in all her glory. A cold breeze blew off the lake and I noticed white-capped waves topping off the ocean blue water.

I took the exit for Lake Silver Wood State Recreational Area. Turning left we approached the entrance to the state park. Several vehicles set parked at the entrance waiting to gain access to the park. In the lane next to us, several people with boats set parked waiting as well. Two elderly gentlemen stood by one of the boats smoking cigars. I breathed in the rich aroma when we passed by.

"It's a little chilly up here," Sharon said putting her arms around me. The cars in front of me moved forward and I pulled up. At the park entrance, a young dark-haired woman in a park ranger's uniform stepped out of a small shack at the main gate. She had the top two buttons of her shirt undone revealing a bit of cleavage.

"Hi. Are you up here for the day or do you plan on staying the night?" She asked me, ignoring Sharon.

"We'd like to camp out overnight," I said, reaching for my wallet.

She shot me a smile and handed me some paperwork. "Go find your spot first. Fill out the paperwork and come back here to register and pay." I took the paperwork and handed it to Sharon. "After you go through the gate take the first left. That will take you to our overnight camping area," the park ranger said.

"I'll see you in a few," I said and pulled through the gate. The road snaked its way through the park; I turned left cruising through the camping area. Half of the camping spots set empty and we found a nice spot near the lake. It lay nestled among the pine trees off by itself. We unpacked the bike, I set up the tent and once we had our campsite set up, I stepped up to Sharon and put my arm around her. "I'll go back up to the ranger shack and pay."

"Let me fill out the form first. While you're up there I'll start getting things ready for supper."

"Let me get my fishing gear out. I'll see if I can catch us a couple of striped, bass to go with supper." Sharon kissed me and filled out the registration form. I headed up to the ranger's shack. A cool breeze blew through the pine trees and I saw a squirrel dart from tree to tree. At the ranger shack, I paid our entrance fee and handed the park ranger the form.

"You've got the best spot in the campground," the park ranger said. She gave me an engaging smile. The rumble of pipes bounced off the surrounding hills. A long line of Harley Davidson motorcycles pulled up to the entrance gate. I looked up recognizing the faces of several of the bikers known as the Lost Souls. The young female park ranger stepped out to greet them. Turning on my heels, I ambled back through the campground to our campsite.

"What took you?" Sharon asked when I came back.

"It's a little bit of hike up there. I saw our friends from down the road." Motorcycles thundered down the main road leading through the campground. The bikers occupied two campsites across from us. Two young women climbed off the back of a couple of the motorcycles and headed for the restrooms. One of them, the same one that smiled at me at the store, shot me another smile on the way by and they both giggled. Sharon stepped closer taking my hand and I felt a slight trimmer pass through her. "Don't worry. Go catch your fish. I'll start dinner. As long as they stay on their side of the road and we stay on ours, things will be fine," she said.

I heaved a sigh watching the crew across the road. "It's times like these that I wish that I hadn't sold my gun."

Sharon ran her hand down my back. "God will take care of us. You don't need a gun."

"I know."

"You sold the gun when we first got married because we needed the money. I never said you couldn't buy another."

I nodded. "I know. But I also know that you don't like guns."

"It's not that I don't like them. I don't see the need. God will take care of us, but if he doesn't so what? We've only got heaven to gain."

"I know," I said and kissed her. "I'm lucky to have you to keep me on track."

I strolled down toward the lake, whistling a gospel tune, and carried my fishing gear. Stepping through the pine trees, I approached the lake and glanced out at the water. The lake looked as smooth as glass. Silence floated across the water. Two other anglers stood by the shore one hundred yards up the bank. I heard a loud splash when a fish jumped out of the water. Another fish jumped making another splash. I rigged my line, baited my hook, and made my first cast. Standing on the bank, enjoying the stillness of the evening, I felt a slight tug on the line. Stepping back, I jerked the pole backward setting the hook. The bass darted back and forth fighting like a fiend.

"Come to poppa," I said and reeled him in. Putting the fish on a stringer, I cast back out and within twenty minutes, I had caught my limit. Arriving back at the campground, I noticed Sharon preparing dinner. I held up my stringer showing her my fish.

Pinching her nose and fanning the air in front of her face, Sharon said, "Cool, honey. Why don't you set them down for now and light a campfire? After you light the fire, I'll warm up the chicken while you clean the fish."

Setting the fish on a paper towel on top of the picnic table, I gathered wood and built a fire. While I cleaned the fish, Sharon wrapped barbecued chicken in tin foil. She stuck the chicken down in the coals of the fire. She wrapped a few potatoes in tinfoil and set them in the coals along with the chicken. The smell of the open fire and the cooking food caused my stomach to rumble.

Loud music blared from boom boxes across the road where the bikers camped. The sound reverberated through the campground. Greasing a pan, I sat next to the campfire and fried the fish after rolling them in breadcrumbs. Sharon and I chit-chatted, enjoying each other's company while our supper cooked. Shivering from the cold, I went to the tent, retrieved our jackets and we put them on. I heard a woman squeal and a man laugh across the road. Several of the bikers shouted back and forth using rough language. The sun went down and I lit a lantern. Sharon and I ate dinner sitting across from each other at the picnic bench. I poured us each a glass of Pepsi from a bottle I'd taken from our ice chest.

"The fish is delicious," Sharon said.

I took a bite from a chicken breast. "You know I never get tired of your chicken."

Sharon gripped my arm. "It seems like food taste better cooked on an open fire. I am so stuffed I could almost pop." A man across the way laughed and the loud music destroyed the stillness of the evening. "Do you think they'll go on like that all night?" Sharon asked.

I shrugged. "I hope not. If they do, I'll go talk to them."

Sharon caught her breath. "I wish you wouldn't."

Finished with supper, I found us each a long wooden stick and we sat next to the fire roasting marsh mellows. A log in the fire popped sending tiny embers into the sky. Sharon fed me a marsh mellow and kissed me. "You taste sweet," she said.

"Let's go into the tent and I'll show you how sweet I am."

Sharon laughed and stood up. "Lead the way, big boy," she said and took my arm. Inside the tent, I zipped up the door while Sharon undressed behind me. I turned around, my heart almost stopped; my bottom jaw dropped and a silly grin crossed my face.

Sharon laughed. "Get undressed, silly."

When I finished undressing, Sharon pushed me down onto our sleeping bags and climbed on top of me. She made love to me with such abandonment that it left me breathless. Once more, I had trouble keeping up with her rhythm. Little did I know at the time, that it would be the last time we made love. Later, while we tried to sleep, the loud music coming from across the road kept us awake. The noise seemed to pound through my brain.

"I'll get dressed and go talk to them," I said.

"Honey, don't."

"It'll be okay. I'll be nice and ask them to turn the music down." Dressed, I tucked my long blade, fishing knife in the back of my jeans and stepped into the cold night air. Crossing the road, the knife's bone handle felt good against the small of my back. The bikers sat by a roaring fire drinking beer and a few of their woman danced topless by the fire. A biker with a scruffy beard noticed me first. He sat across the fire from me when I stepped up. I noticed his hairy beer belly, the long knife scar across his cheek, and his cold bloodshot eyes. He brushed his fingers through his long black hair and shook his head as if he couldn't believe what he was seeing. The smell of marijuana smoke filled the air.

"What the hell do you want?" he asked.

I stood with one hand in my pants pocket rocking on the balls of my feet. "My wife and I are in the camp across the road. We're trying to sleep. Would you mind turning down the music?"

The biker locked onto me with his cold dark eyes. "What if we don't?"

I shrugged holding his gaze and took my hand out of my pocket. "If you don't, then you don't," I said.

"What are you gonna do? Call the ranger?" the biker said, spreading his arms apart.

I stared deep into his eyes, and a wave of anger that I hadn't felt since I came back from the gulf bubbled up inside of me. I struggled to keep it under control. "I didn't say anything about calling the ranger."

The biker broke eye contact and smiled. "Yeah, we'll turn it down. It took guts for you to come over here. Do you care for a beer?"

I paused and then shook my head. "No. I don't drink anymore," I said. Turning around, I crossed the road, headed back to our camp, climbed into our tent, and snuggled up next to Sharon. True to their word, the bikers turned down the music. Silence ebbed and flowed through the forest. A finger of moonlight stabbed through the tent's window. Two hours later, a shadow passed across the window of our tent. I thought about getting up to check it out, but the sandman grabbed me and my world went black.

***

CHAPTER 3

Sunlight streaming through the tent's window woke me at six AM the next morning. Sharon lay sleeping beside me. Rolling from my sleeping bag, I dressed and went outside. The scent of pine needles and wood smoke from last night's fire filled the air. Remembering the shadow passing across the tent's window, I checked the ground. Anger boiled up inside me when I saw two large boot prints. It looked as if someone had squatted down and looked in the window. Glancing around our campsite, the only thing I found missing was some of our firewood. I glanced across the road, but not a soul stirred in the biker camp across the way.

After rekindling last night's fire, I put a pot of water on to boil for coffee. Once I had the coffee brewing, I took a slab of bacon and a dozen eggs from our ice chest and started breakfast. Sharon awoke to the smell of frying bacon and brewing coffee.

"Something smells good out here," she said when she came out of the tent rubbing sleep from her eyes.

I looked up and smiled. "Breakfast will be ready in a few."

Sharon stepped up next to me and kissed me. "That coffee smells wonderful."

"We had visitors last night. I found some footprints. Our neighbors from across the road must have run out of firewood last night," I said and poured Sharon a cup of coffee.

Sharon glanced at the biker's camp. "There's no sign of them this morning. They must have had a rough night."

I shrugged. I bet they're hungover."

"We're only going to be here for the rest of the day. We won't need the firewood."

"I know. I don't like people creeping around our campsite," I said.

Sharon touched my arm. "I'm going to go take a shower."

"I'll have breakfast ready when you get back."

Sharon kissed me and headed up the road for the showers sipping her coffee while she strolled along. A squirrel crossed the road in her wake, while I finished breakfast. Sharon came back from the shower with her hair smelling as fresh as the morning dew, and I refilled her coffee cup. We sat down to a breakfast consisting of crispy fried bacon, eggs over easy, and fried hash browns. I used two of the potatoes from the night before.

A tent flap across the road opened, two young women stepped out and stretched. Their breasts jutted forward and their nipples stood at attention. One of them glanced our way and smiled. They giggled, put their tops on, and headed up to the showers.

Sharon noticed the direction of my gaze. "Calm down big boy," she said.

I blushed. "What? They don't hold a candle to you."

Sharon laughed and gave me a playful slap on the butt. "You should see your face. You're turning as red as that one girl's hair."

"Are you mad at me?" I asked, looking down at my feet.

Sharon leaned close to me and said, "No I'm not mad. Two young women come out of their tent with their shirts off. That's something you don't see every day. I'd wonder about you if you didn't look."

I cleaned the breakfast dishes and the hot sun beat down on me. Sweat beaded up on my forehead and dripped into my face. The two young women came back, this time with their tops on.

"What do you want to do today?" I asked and sat down on the park bench.

Sharon sat down across from me. "Let's head over to the swimming area."

"That's a good idea. I'd like to hang out here at the lake until this evening. I don't feel like crossing the desert in the heat."

"Speaking of heat," Sharon said shaking the front of her t-shirt, "Why don't we head over there now. It's starting to get hot already."

I stood up. "Do you want to take the bike?"

Sharon shook her head. "No. Let's walk. We can come back later and I'll cook lunch." After securing our campsite, I stepped out of the tent and handed Sharon a towel. She took my hand and slipped a wicker handbag over her shoulder. We headed toward the ranger shack and from there we took the trail to the daytime recreation area.

In the woods, I heard a woodpecker hammering away at a tree. Two squirrels chattered back and forth.

"It's so peaceful up here," Sharon said and took my arm.

"I know. I love Lake Silver Wood," I said.

I waved at the park ranger and we took the fork in the road heading for the swimming area. The young female park ranger smiled and waved back. Sharon elbowed me in the side.

I looked at her and grinned. "What?" I asked.

"I can't take you anywhere without the women falling all over you. Like this morning. Those young girls would not have come out this morning with their shirts off if I was by myself

I laughed. "Those two might have. Those biker chicks are wild, but I can't help it if I'm irresistible to women." Sharon elbowed me in the ribs again.

At the swimming area, Sharon headed to the women's changing room and I headed to the men's. Stepping on wet concrete, I cringed. I knew that the wet floor had to be a mixture of pee and water. Changing, I took off my jeans and t-shirt and put on my swimming trunks. Outside, I stood in shade on the grass next to the women's room waiting for Sharon. A cool breeze blew off the water offering a respite from the desert heat. When she came out of the women's room, I almost tripped over my own feet. My eyes widened and my bottom jaw sagged open. Sharon knew how to fill out a bikini. She wore a black bikini top that struggled to contain her copious breasts. The bottoms didn't even look legal. Sharon chuckled when she noticed my jaw hanging open. She ran her hand down my back and a thrill shot through me.

"Here, I'll put your clothes in my bag."

I handed Sharon my clothes and she stuffed them into her wicker handbag. "Come on silly. Let's get in the water," she said and stepped out ahead of me onto the burning sand.

"Aw, shit-I mean shoot! That sand is hot," I said, my eyes glued to the minute piece of butt floss running up the crack of Sharon's ass.

She looked over her shoulder and smiled. "Let's run," she said and took off for the lake. I took off after her, my eyes glued to her shapely bottom watching it swish back and forth, and ran after her. She stopped halfway to the beach, laid out her towel, and set down her handbag. I caught up to her, laid out my towel; she kicked sand at me and took off for the water. I followed on the run. Sharon ran into the water until it came up to her knees and then dived in. Her long lean body stretched out and disappeared underwater. I ran in after her, dived under, and came up sputtering.

"Good Lord God almighty! That water is cold! It feels like my nuts crawled up under my armpit to keep warm!" I yelled.

Sharon squealed, splashed water at me and I splashed some back in her direction. She took my arm, led me deeper into the lake and we stood with the water up to our necks. Sharon pressed her succulent body against mine and kissed me. I pulled her to me, kissed her and my hands found her shapely bottom. I felt something growing hard in my lower rejoins. Looking over Sharon's shoulder, I noticed a boat off in the distance. Two jet skis sped by and the noise from their engines destroyed the early morning serenity. Their wake caused a wave to hit my face. Sharon and I stayed in the water for an hour or so and then hit the beach. She took some suntan lotion out of her handbag and tossed it to me.

"Put some of this on my back," she said and lay down on her towel. I undid the back of her bathing suit and spared suntan lotion across her back. A sense of arousal shot through me, so I spread some on her inner thigh close to her moist center.

"Watch it stud. Not on a public beach," she said and let out a giggle.

I let out a snort. "I'm sorry. I couldn't help myself."

When I finished, I spread out on my stomach and she put some lotion on me. Forty-five minutes later, the two young women from the biker camp ran across the beach and jumped into the water. The blonde wore a wife-beater t-shirt and cut-off jeans. The redhead wore a green bikini top and a thong bikini bottom. They swam around splashing each other and giggling for a few minutes. Then they came out of the water heading for a spot on the beach not too far from where Sharon and I lay. Water glistened off their hard bodies. The blonde's t-shirt, transparent now that it was wet, clung to her ample breasts.

"That water must be cold," I said noticing the blonde's nipples pressing through the fabric of her shirt. Sharon punched me in the arm. The redhead had removed the inner lining from her bikini top and her nipples stood at attention as well. We sat up on our beach towels.

"Those girls have no shame," Sharon said. The blonde and the redhead glanced my way and I averted my eyes. They stretched out on their towels to soak up some sun. A half-hour later, their biker boyfriends came down to the beach. The bikers sat around drinking beer, talking loud and leering at the women. They gave the men on the beach hard looks.

"Those guys are looking for trouble. Let's find another spot," Sharon said.

I started to protest. I wasn't going to let a bunch of rowdy bikers chase me off, but in the end, I sighed. "Okay. Let's go." We found another spot further down the beach. We went back into the water after about a half-hour and then laid out some more. Finished at the beach, we headed back to camp at noon. Sharon fried up some cheeseburgers while I tore down the camp. The bikers packed up their gear while we were eating and roared out of the campground. The sound of their loud pipes echoed through the forest.

"I'm glad they're gone," Sharon said. I finished my burger and wiped bread crumbs from my chest. "Do you want another?"

"Yeah, you know I love your burgers. It should be a bit more peaceful now."

Sharon nodded. "You're going to miss your eye candy."

I glanced down at the ground and then looked up at Sharon and smirked. "There's always the park ranger. I could get her to take off her top for me I bet?"

Sharon snickered. "You're so bad. I bet she would too. When do you want to leave?"

"I thought we'd hang around here until the sun goes down. Don't worry about dinner. I'll stop at a restaurant along the way."

***

Finished with our lunch, we headed back to the beach. We spent the next five hours swimming and laying out on the sand. Bending down, I grabbed my towel when we were getting ready to go. Sharon looked over at me and a smile crossed her face. "Mike."

I looked up. "What?"

"I love you. I'm having a wonderful vacation."

"Me too," I said. I took her in my arms and kissed her.

Back at the campground, I packed our gear and loaded up the bike. I spread my map out on top of the tour pack and Sharon stepped up next to me. "I figured we'd head up Highway eighteen here, and take Main Street in Hesperia. We'll take Main Street to the fifteen; get on the fifteen for a few miles and then take route sixty-six."

Sharon took my arm and glanced down at the map and said, "Where to from there?"

I pointed to a thin red line on the map. "We'll take the sixty-six to Hinkley Road and head north to the fifty-eight. After that, we'll head west until we get to Four Corners and take the three ninety-five. We'll find a room somewhere along the way. Tomorrow we'll camp at Bishop and head over to the Sequoia National Park."

She let go of my arm and patted me on the back. "That sounds good to me big guy. Let's ride."

I put the map away, fired up the machine, and when I brought it off the side stand, Sharon climbed on back. I mashed the shifter into gear, turned the throttle, and headed for the exit. The Gold Wing purred along. At the ranger Shack, the young female park ranger waved and I waved back. Sharon punched me in the back. Leaving Silver Wood Lake behind, I hit the onramp and headed west on the 18. The road changed to a two-lane highway. We turned right, going through a series of tight curves, and turned left on Main Street, in Hesperia. Gunning the throttle, we topped a large hill and headed down into a small valley. Off to our right, I saw a large dam. The road passed over several large hills and dipped down into the flats. I caught air on one of the hills. We passed several two to three hundred thousand dollar homes.

A few minutes later, we buzzed past Hesperia Lakes, a local fishing spot, and entered the town of Hesperia. The suburbs gave way to city streets. We weaved our way through traffic moving from stoplight to stoplight. The setting sun shining in my eyes made me sweat. Descending a large hill, I braked at a stoplight and turned left pulling into a restaurant. I parked the bike in a dirt parking lot and Sharon climbed off. Resting the bike onto its side stand, I took off my helmet and climbed off the bike. Sharon took off her helmet and I locked both our helmets in the tour pack. She stepped up next to me and took my hand.

We ambled across the dirt lot to the quaint-looking restaurant. The wooden exterior of the building was blue with purple trim. I stepped up onto a wooden boardwalk and opened the front door. The delectable smell of cooking food filled the air when we entered the restaurant. We waited for a few seconds for the hostess to seat us. The decor inside the restaurant looked rustic. Antiques were set on display at various locations throughout the restaurant. An old-fashioned electric train set ran on a track mounted on a shelf near the ceiling. I listened to the engine's whistle blow and my mind flashed back to the train set I had when I was young. The train traversed the entire interior of the restaurant.

The hostess, a young thin girl with long black hair, showed us to a table near the rear of the building. She laid two menus down on the table, shot me a killer smile, and left. The smell of her perfume lingered in the air.

Sharon elbowed me in the ribs. "What was that for?" I said, feeling a grin spreading across my face.

"You must be doing something to make these girls flirt with you all the time."

"Who me? I didn't do anything. Besides, you know that only you hold the key to my heart." Sharon smiled, I slid the chair out for her and she sat down. I sat across from her. We chit-chatted while we waited for the waitress to come by. A brown-haired young woman stepped up to our table, batted her coal dark eyes, and gave me a pretty smile. Sharon kicked my leg underneath the table.

"Are you guys ready to order?" she said, stepping up next to where I sat. She laid her hand on my shoulder for a brief instant.

I looked up at Sharon; she looked coy and said, "I'll have the roast beef dinner."

The waitress nodded. "Soup or salad?"

"I'll have the salad with ranch dressing."

"And to drink?"

"I'll have coffee."

"And you sir?" the woman said, holding her order pad up to write on, and shot me another smile. She stepped closer to me and her thigh brushed up against my arm.

My face flushed, and Sharon gave me a kick under the table. "I'll have your T Bone steak."

The waitress backed off and said, "Baked potato, or mashed?"

"I'll take it baked with sour cream."

"And to drink?"

"Sweet tea with lemon." The waitress left taking our order to the kitchen.

"Are you happy with our life?" Sharon asked.

"What? I'm surprised you even asked me that," I said.

Sharon reached across the table and took my hand. "I know you're happy, but is there anything you would change if you could, like your job or, I don't know, anything?"

I sighed, let go of Sharon's hand, and reached across the table to caress her face. "In the first place, I have you. You are my life. Everything else is secondary. I love my job; I love our church and our friends. No. There is nothing I would change. Why aren't you happy?"

Sharon looked down at her hands. "It's not that. What if our lives were to change? Let's say I got pregnant?"

"That would only make my life better. Why are you pregnant?" I asked.

Sharon shrugged and looked away. "I was only wondering You would make a great daddy." The waitress came with our food and Sharon changed the subject. I dug into the T Bone. Sharon picked at her roast beef and it hit me like a ton of bricks. *Oh, God. She is pregnant. Only, She's not ready to tell me yet.* A sense of joy shot through me. We finished eating, I paid the fare and we went outside to the bike. The sun had gone down while we were in the restaurant. A cool breeze blew across the land making me shiver. I put on my helmet, picked the bike up off its side stand, and fired it up. The engine idled while Sharon put on her helmet.

"Are you ready?" I asked.

Yep," Sharon said and climbed on back. I mashed the shifter down with my left foot, pulled out of the parking lot and Sharon leaned against me. I enjoyed the pressure of her breasts against my back. A stirring sensation shot through my loins. My mind flashed forward and envisioned us making mad passionate love in some motel room. Waiting at the light, I watched traffic flow by and when the light turned green, I turned left. We cruised from light to light traveling for several blocks. When we reached the interstate, I took the onramp heading north onto Interstate 15. We passed an amusement park on one side of the freeway and a mall on the other.

Six miles later, I took the E Street exit in Victorville and turned left onto old Route 66. When we passed underneath the freeway, the road narrowed into a two-lane highway. We passed an Arco station on our left and went around a curve. A cement plant lit up the night sky to our right. We went through a few more curves and crossed an old

Iron bridge. The Mojave River lay off to our left, invisible in the darkness.

The Mojave River was one of the only rivers that I knew of that flowed away from the ocean. It started on the backside of the San-Bernardino Mountains and flowed into the desert. It meandered northeast, disappearing underground, and then repapered several times. It rose from the sand and headed through a scenic area known as Afton Canyon. After traversing Afton Canyon, it sank underground at the Mojave River Sink.

I slowed to Forty-Five miles an hour when we passed through a little town known as Oro Grande. The town looked quaint, a remnant of the old highway's heyday. The road curved passing under a railroad bridge, and we passed another cement plant on our right. I was approaching a bar on the left-hand side when Sharon tapped me on the back. I turned my head so I could hear.

"Pullover. I need to pee," She yelled.

I down-shifted, glancing at the motorcycles parked in front of the biker bar. An eerie feeling passed through me when I pulled into the parking lot of the rustic old tavern. An older blue Dodge pickup truck set parked under a weeping willow tree. It looked like a 65 or 66. The truck reminded me of one my dad used to own. That brought back bad memories. I pulled up to the wooden boardwalk, parked next to an old Electro Glide, and killed the engine. Sharon jumped off.

"Are you sure about this? We could find somewhere nice up the road," I said.

Sharon danced around. "No. I've got to go bad. We'll go in, I'll use the restroom and we'll leave," She said.

I climbed off the bike, we put our helmets into the tour pack and Sharon took my hand. On the boardwalk, I opened the old log door and we entered the bar. Loud rock and roll music blared from the interior of the barroom. The smell of stale beer and tobacco smoke filled the air. Bikers wearing the Lost Souls club vests filled the bar. The two young women who had come out of their tent topless earlier in the day now danced on the bar. This time they wore nothing but gee strings. Sharon looked at me and a scared look crossed her face.

"I guess this wasn't such a good idea. I'll be quick." She let go of my hand and hurried to the restroom. I wormed my way through the crowd finding an empty spot at the bar. My senses became hypersensitive and my breathing accelerated. My heart thumped inside my chest. The bar itself, made from rough mahogany, looked ancient. It had hundreds of names carved into it.

"What can I get you?" a big potbellied bartender asked. He had to yell to communicate over the loud music and the noise from the boisterous bikers. I looked up at the bartender taking in his chubby cheeks, his thinning greasy black hair, and his dark eyes.

"I'll have a Pepsi," I said.

The bartender turned and poured me a glass of Pepsi. "That will be two dollars."

I paid him. "What's with the bar?" I asked.

"It's a tradition. People who have never been here before carve their name on the bar," the bartender said. He handed me a Buck Knife. "I'll need that back." Someone from down the bar called for the bartender and he shuffled their way. I carved my name in the bar and took a drink from my Pepsi. The two women looked my way smiled and danced down the bar in my direction. I noticed the biker whom I had asked to turn down his music elbowing his way through the crowd. I stuck the buck knife in my back pocket.

"Well if it ain't our neighbor from camp? How's the rice popper running?" The man turned sideways facing me with his arm leaning on the bar. I glanced at the tattoos covering his massive biceps and looked him dead in the eyes.

"The bike runs fine!"

A cocky grin crossed the biker's face. "Are you going to tell me to turn my music down now?"

I sighed. "I didn't tell you to turn your music down last night! I asked you!" The two women danced their way down the bar until they were standing over us. A bead of sweat dripped down the red head's neck tracking down between her breasts. I looked over the biker's shoulder noticing Sharon coming out of the bathroom. The biker glanced around and an evil glint passed through his eyes. "Why are you eyeballing our women?"

My heart punched the inside of my rib cage, but I struggled to keep my voice calm. "I ain't eyeballing anybody!" I said crossing my arms in front of my chest.

"Now you're calling me a liar!" The biker glanced over his shoulder and nodded to one of his crones standing near the door. A wiry, pale-looking biker with a dirty blond goatee grabbed Sharon. He put his arms around her and lifted her off the ground. Sharon screamed. "I figure if you can eyeball our women, we can have a taste of yours!" the biker yelled. I started toward Sharon but the scar-faced biker pushed me. The wiry one with the dirty blond goatee and the pale skin pulled Sharon out the front door.

I hit the biker in front of me with a hard right-hand fist and the force knocked him back two feet. Six more bikers appeared in front of me and one had a bone-handled knife. He sliced my side; I pulled the buck knife from my pocket, snapped the blade open, and stuck him with it, low down in the belly. Seeing my way to the front door blocked, I turned and darted out the back.

Springing out the back door and around the building, I heard Sharon screaming. Looking toward the sound of her voice, I saw that a group of bikers had Sharon in the bed of the old Dodge pickup truck. They had her shirt pulled up and her pants down.

"Sharon!" I screamed and sprinted her way.

Sharon looked at me with eyes widened by fear. Blood dripped from her top lip. "Michael! Help me!" she yelled.

I ran across the dirt parking lot while the group of bikers that I had battled inside stormed out the door. The one with the scar on his face slammed into me knocking me to the ground. I landed hard on my right side. Jumping up, he hit me with his shoulder, and at the same time, I felt a blade go in. Blood dripped down my side. I jumped back and a dirty biker with long greasy black hair stepped around scarface. He pulled a revolver from his waistband and shot me. The shot spun me around, my chest went numb and I tried to recover, but six or seven of them beat me to the ground. Someone knocked over the Gold Wing and I heard somebody beating on it with what sounded like a chain. Crawling toward Sharon, I reached out my hand. The skinny pale-looking biker had his pants down leaning over Sharon and he tried to kiss her cheek. She spat, in his face, and then head-butted him. I felt a rain of blows fall on me as I tried to make it to Sharon.

"Michael!" Sharon screamed.

I tried to crawl toward her, but the biker who had been using the chain on my Gold Wing turned the chain on me. "Sharon!"

"You bitch!" the biker raping Sharon yelled. He pulled her out of the pickup bed and I saw Sharon fall. Her head hit a rock on the ground, a bone snapped, her body went limp and the world stopped for a fraction of a second.

“Sharon! No!” I shrieked feeling a sense of unadulterated rage shoot through me. I tried to stand to my feet, but someone kicked me in the side and knocked me over onto my back.

“Tell me to turn my music down, mother fucker,” Scar Face said and brought what looked like a tire iron down on my head. My vision turned white, sheering hot pain shot through my head and the world faded to black.

***

CHAPTER 4

"I have a dog named Lucky, and a horse! His name is Totem! Why didn't you tell me?" I demanded of Pastor Craig Blackwood. "Who's taking care of my animals?"

Blackwood grinned. "So you remembered. That is good. To tell you the truth, Mike, I forgot about your animals. They're okay though. The woman from across the street is taking care of them." Outside in the hallway, I heard a couple of the nurses giggling.

"I remember her name. Who's supplying the feed?"

Blackwood shrugged. "That would be me."

I leaned back and sighed. "Thanks. I owe you. I'll settle up when I get out of here."

Blackwood shook his head. "You don't owe me anything. The only thing I want is for you to get well. How much do you remember?"

"I remember everything from when I left work to go on vacation, up to the attack."

Blackwood beamed. "Then you remember Sharon?"

I nodded. "I remember what she looks like. I remember that I loved her. I remember what happened, but it's as if it happened to someone else. It's like watching a movie in my mind." The familiar anger that I'd been feeling since I woke up bubbled up inside my stomach like a boiling pot of burning oil. My hands gripped the railing at the sides of my bed. "I'm gonna get those bastards."

A disquieting look crossed the pastor's face. "Mike. I can understand your anger, but you've got to let it go. You need to get well and go on with your life. Hate is an acid that harms its container, more than what you throw it on."

I shook my head. "I don't think so reverend. Not this time. It's what keeps me warm at night inside this damned hospital."

The preacher leaned forward in his chair and looked me dead in the eyes. I could smell the mints on his breath. "Sharon would have told you, Mike, to let it go. Move on. It's what she would have wanted."

I paused. "I'll never know what Sharon would have wanted because those sons of bitches took her from me."

The pastor leaned back in his chair. "Your language, Mike. Sharon wouldn't have approved of that either. You never used to cuss like this before."

I spread my hands apart for effect. "Well excuse me Reverend. Seeing your wife raped and killed then, getting stabbed, shot, and beat half to death tends to piss you off," I said.

The preacher stood to his feet. "I know, Mike. I'm sorry. I'm happy that you came out of the coma. I want you to get over this and rebuild your life," the preacher said. A tear tracked down his face, so I reached over and touched his forearm.

"You're a good friend, Craig. I mean, I don't remember everything, but the nurses told me that you came every day while I was under. Most men wouldn't have done that. I appreciate the other things you've done for me as well. Things like making sure someone took care of my animals. Thanks for talking to my boss, and contacting my mortgage company. Because of you, my homeowner's insurance is paying my house payments. My reading is much better because of you and your cowboy books. I owe you big time."

"I told you, you don't owe me anything. You would have done the same thing for me."

I nodded. "I don't know. I can't remember. I don't think that I am a good a man like you."

The preacher laughed. "I do remember. You are a good man, Mike. You are the type of guy that would give someone the shirt off his back if you had to. Sharon saw something good in you. I saw it too when I first met you."

A young female Hispanic nurse entered the room pushing a wheelchair. I breathed in the fragrance of her perfume. It was something I didn't recognize. "Excuse me Gentlemen, but it's time for Mr. McDonald to go downstairs for his therapy session."

I looked up at her and said, "Oh Great. Another hour in the dungeon. Why don't you people shoot me and get it over with? And didn't I tell you to call me Mike?"

The nurse laughed. "I love you feisty ones."

"Why don't we walk down there? Isn't that the point of the therapy? To get me walking better?"

She stepped up next to my bed. "I don't want to tire you out along the way."

I looked at the pastor. "Are you gonna be here when I get back?"

The preacher shrugged.

"You can come with if you want," the nurse said.

The pastor nodded. "Sure I'll come."

The nurse helped me out of bed and I felt the pressure of her left breast against my arm when I stood up. A tent formed underneath my hospital gown and the nurse grinned.

"It seems that some of your parts are working fine," she said.

I felt my cheeks turn hot and I tried to keep a straight face. "It's not my fault. You make a guy parade around in nothing but a thin cotton gown with his ass hanging in the wind. Then you wonder why he gets a little wood?"

The nurse chuckled, Pastor Blackwood shook his head and I sat down in the wheelchair. I sat my hands across my lap while the nurse wheeled me out into the hallway. Pastor Blackwood ambled along behind. An elderly woman with white hair pushing a portable IV drip stand passed us in the hallway. She wore a white hospital gown. The nurse backed me into an elevator. Pastor Blackwood stepped into the elevator and turned to face the doors standing next to me.

"You'll enjoy the show, pastor. Cynthia here may look young and pretty, but she's a harsh taskmaster once we get on the ramp."

Pastor Blackwood laid a friendly hand on my arm. "She wants what is best for you. We all do."

"If you keep going the way you are, you'll be walking with a cane in a few weeks. Then you can go home. All it takes is hard work," Cynthia said patting my shoulder.

"That's all I live for: to escape from your house of pain."

"Come on Mike. It's not that bad. You know you're my favorite patient," she said.

"Be still my beating heart," I said patting my chest. "I bet you say that to all your patients."

She punched number two on the control panel and the elevator car descended. The doors slid open in front of us; she wheeled me out the door, down the hallway, and through a doorway on our right. Three tracks covered with green carpeting descended to the south end of the building. Wooden railings stood next to each lane. An indoor pool set across from the walking tack and an exam table set near the end of the room.

She wheeled me up to the first lane, so I climbed out of the wheelchair and stood holding onto the wooden railing.

"Okay Mike, let's go to work. I'd like you to walk down toward the end of the lane holding onto the railing and then come back."

"So it begins," I said and took a step down the descending ramp. Pain shot through my body, sweat beaded up on my forehead, and my head throbbed. I took a few steps putting one foot in front of the other. Stopping halfway down the lane, my legs felt like rubber and sweat rolled down my body like a river. A queasy feeling shot through the pit of my stomach.

"Come on. You only made it this far last time. Take a few more steps," she said.

Anger shot through me. My hands white-knuckled the railing, but I took another step and then another. Finally, after I'd shuffled down the lane another twenty feet, Cynthia stopped me.

"That's good. Lean on the railing and take a rest." I shook my head, took ten more steps, and stopped. Cynthia stood close to me, making sure I didn't fall.

"Good Lord Mike. I don't know how you do it. I'd have been a whimpering bowl of jelly a long time ago," Reverend Blackwood said. He stepped up to me, touched my arm and I leaned back resting on the railing.

"It makes me mad. Not being able to walk," I said.

After I rested for ten minutes, Cynthia smiled. "Now comes the hard part. Now I want you to walk back."

"You evil witch," I said and turned around facing back the way I came. Going uphill was a little harder and I had to stop to rest more often. By the time I reached my starting point, I thought I was going to collapse.

"You did well, Mike. Let's get you in the pool."

I laughed, and said, "If you want to see me naked, all you have to do is ask." I took off the hospital gown and slid into the pool. Cynthia blushed. The warm water felt invigorating. She had me walk around the edge of the shallow end of the pool for twenty minutes holding onto the side. Finished in the pool, she handed me a fresh gown and a towel. I dried off while she looked away and then put on the fresh gown. She wheeled me to the table setting at the end of the room. She asked me to lie down on the table and began to move my legs bending them in ways they didn't want to go. After three months in a coma, my muscles felt as tight as a bowstring. The muscles in my jaws clenched and I gripped the sides of the table trying to ride out the pain.

"Okay, Mike. That will be all for today," she said.

"You mean I'm done with your torture chamber for the day? I was starting to get into the pain."

"I don't want to overtax you." She helped me up off the table and back into my wheelchair.

"You can tax me all you want. Beat me hurt me talk dirty to me. Make me write bad checks," I said.

The nurse blushed and pushed me toward the exit.

"He didn't use to say things like that before," Blackwood said under his breath to the nurse.

"When patients come out of a coma, they often experience changes in their personality."

"Hey. I'm right here. You're not supposed to talk about the patient as if he isn't here," I said.

Back inside my room, Pastor Blackwood took a seat near my bed. "How do you feel?"

"Wore out and sore, but it's good pain. It feels as if I'd worked out at the gym. It's my head that's killing me."

"I don't know how you put up with it. If it were me I'd be crying like a baby."

I gave the preacher an apprising glance. "I doubt that. You look like a tough old bird," I said. "As for how I put up with it, the anger helps. When want to give up, I remember what they did."

The preacher frowned. "Don't let hate consume you."

"I'm not consumed. It helps take the edge off the pain." The preacher and I talked for another three hours. A nurse stepped in a few minutes later announcing that visiting hours were over. The preacher handed me two more cowboy books and insisted on saying a prayer for me. He stepped up to my bed and laid hands on me. After the prayer, we said our goodbyes and he went home. I watched his back when he stepped out of the room.

"No Pastor. I'm not consumed by hate. I am the consumer. It's like an old friend I keep locked in a cage. When I catch those bastards that did this to me, I'll turn it loose and set the monster free," I said to the empty room.

***

The next three weeks were brutal. Cynthia increased the intensity of my workouts. She had me lifting free weights along with my daily walks up and down the ramps. By the end of three weeks, I was able to walk the entire length of the ramp. My head still throbbed half the time, but I was able to walk on my own, using a cane. I sat on the edge of my bed waiting for Craig Blackwood to show up. Today was the big day. The doctor said that I was well enough to go home. When the doctor gave me the good news that he would sign my release papers in the morning, I phoned Blackwood.

He let out a wild whoop. "That's good news, Mike. I'll be there first thing in the morning. Is there anything I can bring you?"

I thought for a moment. "I need some clothes. They cut what I was wearing off me when the ambulance picked me up, or so they say. I don't remember any of it."

"I'll swing by your house. I know where you hide your spare key."

"Okay preacher man. Thanks a million," I said.

My mind danced back to the present. I gathered my possessions, consisting of a few cowboy books, some pain meds, my wallet, and a set of keys. A sense of unease passed through me. What would the world outside these hospital walls be like? It was a world I no longer remembered. The door swung open. Pastor Blackwood sauntered into the room wearing a black suit and white shirt. He carried a brown paper bag in one hand and a black cane with a gold eagle's head in the other. A big silly grin crossed his face. "Are you ready to go home, Mike?"

I shrugged. "I'm ready to get out of this place. As for going home, I don't know. It's a little scary. I don't remember much."

Blackwood handed me a brown paper bag. "Here's your clothes. Don't worry too much about your memory. Once you're back in familiar surroundings, you'll start to remember," he said.

I took the bag of clothes from the preacher. The preacher turned around to give me some privacy, so I stood to my feet and stripped out of my hospital gown. Goosebumps cropped up on my legs. Setting a pair of black motorcycle boots on the floor, I tossed the clothes out on the bed. I put on a pair of boxer shorts and pulled on a pair of denim jeans. The pastor turned around once I had my pants on. His eyes dropped to the scars on my upper body. My eyes dropped to the jagged scar on my side where Scar Face cut me. I had another smaller scar where he stabbed me underneath my belly. There was another small scar below my right shoulder where he shot me and scars on my side from the chain. The preacher's eyes darted away, but I looked him in the eye and smiled.

"It's all right. I didn't plan on entering any beauty contest anyway," I said.

The preacher let out a nervous laugh. "I'm sorry Mike. I shouldn't have stared. I still have a hard time getting used to what happened to you. God and I are still coming to terms with it."

"Forget about it, pastor. Shit-I, mean stuff happens. It's not your fault or God's fault. It's that scumbag that stuck me. He and his filthy band of brothers are gonna pay for what they did."

Blackwood frowned. "If not in this life, they'll answer to God. If they were smart, they would beg for his forgiveness. You should forgive them too Mike."

My face went slack. "Forgiveness is something I am fresh out of. They'll have to go to God for that. I'll make the arrangements for the meeting though," I said.

Blackwood let out a grown. "I wish you'd let that go."

I slipped on a short-sleeved black t-shirt and sat down on the bed to put on my socks and boots. "Speaking of go I'm ready," I said to change the subject after putting on my boots. I stood to my feet and the pastor handed me the cane. "Thanks," I said.

A nurse appeared at the door to my room with a wheelchair. The smell of her perfume filled the air. "Are you ready, Mr. McDonald?"

I grinned. "You know I am darlin' but what did I say about that mister stuff? Call me Mike."

She shot me a demure smile. "Okay, Mike. Your carriage awaits."

I ambled over to the wheelchair, sat down, laid the cane across my lap and she wheeled me out into the hallway. At the nurse's station, I signed my release papers and said goodbye to the daytime staff. Janet, the young dark-haired nurse that was on duty that morning wheeled me toward the exit. Pastor Blackwood ambled along beside us. When we reached the doors to the outside world, Janet pushed a black button on a control box. The glass doors slid open she pushed me outside and stopped by the edge of the curb.

"I'll go get my car," Blackwood said.

I leaned back in the chair breathing in the fresh air. A bird in a nearby tree chirped and the morning sun felt good against my face.

"I'm gonna miss you, Mike. You were one of my favorite patients," she said. She bent over, kissed me on the cheek and I felt my cheeks turn red.

"I'm gonna miss you too. Tell Cynthia and the rest of the nursing staff that I said goodbye."

"I will Mike. I am sure Cynthia wishes she could have been here. Be sure to take your pain meds, and take care of yourself," She said and laid a hand on my shoulder.

I enjoyed the soft caress, so I reached up and touched her hand. "I will. You take care, darlin'. I won't miss being in the hospital, but the girls treated me fine. I'll miss your warm smile."

Blackwood pulled up in a white Cadillac. He climbed out of the driver's side and came around to help me out of the wheelchair. The passenger side door opened. A good-looking older woman in her late forties stepped out of the car. I recognized her from the picture Blackwood showed me. She had long black hair, an hourglass figure, and a warm smile. Her ample bosom stretched the fabric of her blue sweater. The designer jeans she wore looked as if they might come apart at the seams. I breathed in the smell of expensive perfume. *Blackwood is a lucky man,* I thought.

"Hello, Mike."

I smiled. "Hello, Darlene."

"Do you remember me?"

I looked her in the eye. "Craig showed me your picture." A frown crossed her face.

"Don't worry babe. He'll remember everything soon enough." Blackwood took my right arm and the nurse took my left. I grabbed my cane and stood up. Darlene opened the back door of the Cadillac. Janet leaned against me, so I gave her a quick hug pulling her against my shoulder. I enjoyed the feeling of her left breast pressed up against my arm.

"Goodbye, Mike. Take care. If you ever get up this way stop in and see me." I saw a tear track down her cheek.

"I will," I said. She gave me another quick peck on the cheek. Inside the car, I sat down on the custom brown leather back seat and stretched out my legs. Darlene closed the door and climbed back into the passenger side of the front seat. Blackwood climbed in behind the wheel and pulled away from the curb.

"Take me there," I said to the preacher when he pulled out of the parking lot.

He turned around looking over his shoulder for a second. "What?"

"To the bar where it happened. Take me there," I said.

"Mike, are you sure? It'll bring up bad memories," Darlene said.

"That's the point. I want to see if what I remember is real. It doesn't seem real."

Blackwood sighed. "It could help you jog some other memories," he said. He turned left onto E Street in Victorville and I glanced out my window watching the scenery flash by. On the left, I saw a sign saying something about Old Town Victorville. An archway spanned a street to my left. The Street sign said Seventh Street. Railroad tracks set off the road on our right side. We passed a park and an Amtrak station. The pastor continued passing underneath the freeway. I saw a sign saying: Historic Route 66.

The scenery looked familiar. We passed a cement plant, crossed the old bridge over the Mojave River, and passed through Oro Grandee. The pastor pulled into the dirt parking lot of the rustic old tavern that haunted my dreams. A pack of Harley Davison motorcycles sped down the highway. The sound of their loud pipes caused a chill to shoot down my spine. I watched them disappear around a curve and then sat there, gazing at the old building. The place looked the same as what I remembered; only the old Dodge pickup truck was gone. I opened the passenger door. "Let's go inside."

"I don't think they're open," Blackwood said.

"There's a car in the parking lot," I said noticing an older Ford setting near the entrance. Blackwood killed the engine on the Cadillac and climbed out. A cool breeze tickled my face. Blackwood helped me out of the back seat. Using my cane, he helped me hobble across the dirt parking lot and up to the boardwalk. He kept a light hand on my arm to steady me. I stepped up on the boardwalk and paused for a moment before rapping on the door.

“We’re closed,” someone from inside, said. I knocked louder and the door banged open.

“I said we’re-oh. It’s you. Come on in,” the man said. I recognized the bartender that had been on duty that night, but he looked cleaner. He moved his big bulk aside. Breathing in the smell of stale beer and cigarette smoke, I stepped into the barroom. I glanced about. Everything looked as I remembered it, only the bar was empty. “Say, man. I’m sorry about what happened to you and your wife. Nothing like that has ever happened here before. Those guys were plain white trash. I tried to help but they held a gun on me. They robbed the place. I called the police as soon as they left.”

I nodded. “That’s all right. You couldn’t have done much. There were too many of them.” I hobbled around the bar to the place where I’d been standing that night. Glancing down at the bar, I saw my name right where I’d carved it. Mike McDonald. I ran my fingers over the carving feeling the rough texture of the wood. Memories flashed through my brain once more. I elbowed the pastor and he looked down where I’d carved my name.

“Have you seen enough?” Blackwood asked.

I took one last look. “Yeah, take me home.” We headed for the door.

“I’m sorry Mr. for what happened. If there’s anything I can do, don't be afraid to ask,” the bartender said.

I paused leaning on the doorjamb. “There’s one thing. If that bike club, the Lost Souls ever come in here again, or if you can find out about them for me give me a call.”

“Sure. We get bike clubs in here all the time. I’ll see what I can find out, or if they show up again, I’ll give you a shout if you’ll give me your number.” I looked at the pastor. He sighed and pulled a business card out of his wallet. He wrote what must have been my phone number on the back of it and handed it to the bartender. The bartender took another business card out of his shirt pocket and handed it to me. “Mr. If I were you, I’d leave those old boys alone they’re bad news.”

“Yeah, thanks,” I said and stepped out the door.

“Mike, you’re headed down the wrong road,” the pastor said while we crossed the parking lot. A cement truck blasted down the highway and blew its air horn.

“Yeah, but it’s the only one I know,” I said. The pastor looked down at his feet; I paused and laid a hand on his back. A smirk crossed my face. “Don’t worry Pastor. It will be a long time before I’m well enough to take these scumbags on. That gives you a lot of time to preach at me and pray that the good Lord will pound some sense into my brain. Who knows? I could forget about it and like you say, let the Lord handle it.”

Blackwood let out a snort. “Yeah right. Once you get something in your head, you’re like a mad dog on a bone. There’s no stopping you.” The pastor helped me back into the car. We headed back the way we came and the pastor took the interstate onramp heading south on the I15.

I watched the scenery flash by from the back seat of the Cadillac. We headed south through Victorville and down the Cajon Pass. The scenery outside my window looked familiar, yet I had no direct memory of it. In San-Bernardino, a big rig rumbled past my window. Pastor Blackwood changed lanes and took the cross-town freeway heading toward Highland. I was in familiar territory again. I remembered riding through there on my way home from work and heading back out with Sharon that same day. The pastor took an exit and we headed east on Highland Avenue. We turned right onto Boulder Road and then headed south. I noticed a country market on the right side of the road. “Could you stop here, for a moment?” I asked.

Pastor Blackwood turned right pulling into the parking lot. He started to get out and help me out of the back seat. “That’s okay preach. I can handle this on my own.” I climbed out of the back seat, using my new cane, and ambled into the store. I noticed a couple of teen-aged boys and a girl in the store. The boys had piercings on their lips and the girl, hand one in her eyebrow. The girl had pink hair. *God, do all the kids dress like that?* I wondered.

Making my way up the aisle I picked up a large bag of potato chips, some cookies and headed over to the cooler. I grabbed a two-liter of Pepsi and stopped in front of the beer section. For a moment, I stood there in indecision and then picked up a six-pack of Bud Light. Carrying my purchases under my left arm, I made my way to the front of the store trying not to drop anything. I set everything down on the counter and paused looking up at the packs of cigarettes sitting on display.

“Give me a pack of Marlboro Mediums,” I said.

The young red-headed female clerk turned around, reached up for the cigarettes. My eyes dropped to her shapely bottom. She turned back around and handed me the cigarettes. “Will there be anything else?” she asked shooting me a smile. She leaned over the counter displaying a deep valley of cleavage. I notice a field of minute freckles running across the top of her breasts. I caught a faint trace of perfume: Chanel Number Five: Sharon’s brand. A sharp pain shot through my skull, and a memory flashed through my brain like a bolt of lightning.

***

CHAPTER 5

Fresh out of the Marine Corps, I stepped off the Gray Hound in San-Bernardino California. The smell of diesel smoke filled the air and a cold breeze hit my face. A loud booming voice coming over a PA system announced the departure of a bus bound for Los Angeles. Stepping around a bum on the sidewalk, I gagged at the smell of foul whiskey and vomit coming off his unwashed body. My eyes caught a yellow taxicab parked in the corner of the parking lot, so I sauntered over.

A middle-aged Hispanic male sat behind the wheel of the taxi. He was reading a Sun Telegram newspaper. Loud Latin music blared from the interior of the taxicab. I rapped on his window, startling the man.

The taxi driver jumped. "Madre Dios! You scared the shit out of me man."

I let out a low chuckle. "Sorry about that. I need a ride." Another bus rumbled into the parking lot and I heard a hiss of air.

"Where to Amigo?"

I leaned over and looked into his window. "Right now, I could use a drink. Do you know a good bar close by? I've been away for a while."

The cabbie thought for a moment setting his newspaper down on the seat next to him. "There is the Branding Iron, on E Street. It's a gringo bar."

"How's the clientele?" I said, leaning against the cab.

The cabbie shrugged. "Shit-kicking cowboys red necks, but it's not so bad senor. They play country and Western music."

"That's good enough. Take me there," I said. I threw my seabag in the back seat and climbed in behind it. The cabbie lighted a cigarette and I breathed in the rich aroma of tobacco smoke. A loud knocking sound came from underneath the vehicle when the cabbie fired up the engine. He pulled out of the parking lot and turned left. I gazed out the window watching the scenery flash by. We passed through one of the more seedy sections of town. Bums lay on the sidewalk in front of a liquor store as we passed by. Most of the businesses had graffiti on their walls and bars on their windows. A Harley Davidson motorcycle roared by, going the opposite direction. The loud noise coming from its pipes caused me to jump in the back seat.

The cabbie turned left off Fifth Street and headed south on E Street. We passed a few used car lots and an auto parts store. I noticed the Orange Show fairgrounds a block south on the left-hand side. The cabbie turned right into the parking lot in front of a faded red brick building. The marquee above the door advertised some country band currently playing there.

"That will be six-fifty, senor," the cabbie said.

I handed him a ten. "Keep the change." Climbing out of the cab, I heaved my seabag over my shoulder. Traversing a parking lot crisscrossed with cracks, I made my way to the front entrance. I stepped up on a wooden boardwalk, opened the front door, and entered the Branding Iron. Loud country music blared from the jukebox. Pausing in the entryway, I breathed in the smell of stale beer and tobacco smoke. I let my eyes grow accustomed to the dim light inside the barroom.

Making my way across the room, I noticed three drugstore cowboys sitting on one end of the bar. Two guys that looked like working stiffs sat a few bar stools down from them. The cowboys both had black hats and boots. Noticing another Marine sitting down by the end of the bar, I made my way toward him. A barmaid that looked on the wrong side of forty stood behind the bar. She wore a low-cut black Western-style frilly dress that showed some butt cheeks in the back. A straw cowboy hat set atop her head. Dirty blonde hair sprouted from underneath the cowboy hat. When she leaned over the bar, she sported some cleavage. I gazed down the front of her dress and noticed a couple of liver spots on her sagging flesh. Discussed, I looked away ignoring the stench of her unwashed body.

"What can I get you, hun?" the barmaid asked.

"What are you drinking?" I said to the young dark-headed Marine sitting at the bar.

He pulled a pack of cigarettes from his uniform pocket. "Budweiser."

"Mind if I have one of those?" I asked.

"Sure," the young Marine said. Pulling some money out of my wallet, I tossed a ten on the bar. "Make that two Budweiser's."

The barmaid smiled, brought our drinks and the young Marine nodded his thanks. The Marine lit his cigarette and handed me his Zippo. I lighted my smoke and sat down on the barstool beside him. He blew smoke across the bar. "Thanks for the beer. Are you back from the gulf?"

I took a drag and said, "Yeah, what about you?"

The Marine sitting next to me took a pull on his beer. "I missed it. I deploy for Kuwait next week."

"You didn't miss much."

The Marine looked up at me. "What was it like?"

I paused for a couple of seconds flicking ash into the ashtray on the bar. "The first part, Desert Shield was as boring. They kept us in the desert in Saudi sitting on go for too long. The heat was a mother fucker."

"Once the fight started, it was over so fast. I was hoping I could get over there before the end. What was the war, like?" The barmaid put some quarters in the jukebox and an old country tune began to play.

"For the ground pounders, there wasn't much action, but for tankers, we saw plenty," I said.

"Yeah?"

"Yeah, I almost felt sorry for those bastards. When we went in, it was lighting quick. Some Iraqis tried to surrender, but we rolled right over them heading to Kuwait. Some got buried alive," I said.

The young Marine scooted closer to me so we could talk without having to shout over the music. "I heard their tanks weren't much."

I glanced in the mirror behind the bar. "No. They didn't have anything that could hurt us. We slaughtered them."

"You spend your whole carrier in tanks?"

I shook my head. "No. My original MOS was Scout Sniper. I went to school for that and spent some time in Columbia. By the time Saddam did his thing, they transferred me to a tank unit."

The front door squeaked open. The musical sound of girlish laughter caught my attention. I looked up in the mirror and my heart almost stopped. Three young women entered the bar and my eyes locked onto a petite young girl with long blonde hair. She stood with a redhead and a girl with dark hair and dark eyes in the entranceway.

The blonde's eyes locked with mine and she smiled. She looked familiar to me.

They stood letting their eyes grow accustomed to the light for a few seconds and moved to a table. The Marine standing next to me looked over his shoulder and his eyes widened. A few more people entered the bar.

"Talk about some trim."

I motioned to the barmaid and she stepped over. "Go tell them, ladies, that whatever they're drinking is on me." I swiveled around facing away from the bar.

The woman behind the bar smiled showing her missing front teeth. "Ain't young love grand?" The barmaid crossed the room and took their orders. The girls giggled and looked our way. On the way back to the bar, the barmaid paused standing next to me. "Hon, they said for you all to come and join them." My heart pounded inside my chest and my breathing accelerated. Grabbing my beer, I stood to my feet and stepped over to their table. The Marine that had been sitting next to me followed.

"Hey. I'm Mike. Mike McDonald," I said. I didn't know what to do with my hands so I stuck them in my pockets. The smell of their perfume filled the air.

The blonde looked up and smiled. "Don't you remember me, Mike? I'm Sharon Beasley. Why don't you guys pull up a chair?"

"Oh yeah, Sharon, from school. I remember now," I said. My face reddened as a memory flashed through my brain.

"Introduce us to your friend," the girl with the dark hair said batting her raven dark eyes.

I stood with my hands in my pockets. "We haven't got around to names yet."

The Marine standing next to me smiled. "My name is Butcher. Tom Butcher"

The dark-haired girl beamed. "I'm Connie Brooks. You've already met Sharon. It looks like she's already staked her claim. My red-headed friend here is Jenifer Cunningham."

"Hi," Jenifer said brushing back a strand of long red hair."

"Why don't you guys pull up a chair?" Connie said, so I went to an adjacent table and brought back two chairs, handing one to Butcher.

"Here, I'll make room," Sharon said and scooted over. I moved the chair between her and Jenifer and sat down. The barmaid brought the drinks. She brought mixed drinks for the other two girls but set a glass of Pepsi in front of Sharon.

Sharon looked over at me and her face lit up. "I don't drink. I'm a Christian."

I grinned. "That's all right. That means there's more for me. If you're a Christian, then why are you in a bar?"

She glanced down at the table drumming her fingers on the tabletop. "My girlfriends talked me into it."

I put my hand on her knee. "I don't think God will turn you into to stone for going out for a drink with the girls." We sat there talking and drinking for the next twenty minutes. A few more cowboys entered the bar and a band came in. They set their equipment up on a small stage. Butcher bought another round of drinks. Sharon's girlfriends talked Sharon into drinking a wine cooler. I bought another round; I had a good beer buzz going. The more I talked to Sharon, the more I liked her. We left the Branding Iron a half-hour later and lingered in the parking lot talking for a few minutes. The sun beating down on me made me sweat.

"I'm starved. Why don't we head over to Denny's and have lunch?" Connie asked.

"I don't have a ride," I said.

"We could all squeeze into mine," Connie said. I looked at her small green Toyota.

"I've got my Mustang," Butcher said. "Mike, you can ride with me. We'll meet you, girls, over there."

"That sounds like a plan," Sharon said. She hugged me and kissed me on the cheek before she climbed into the car. A thrill shot through me. Butcher and I turned around and crossed the parking lot to his yellow Mustang. I climbed in on the passenger side, Butcher climbed behind the wheel and fired up the beast. The loud shot-out glass packs growled underneath the car. We followed the girls out of the parking lot and down to Denny's on Orange Show Road.

"This car sounds healthy," I said when Butcher pulled out of the parking lot.

"Yeah, I hopped up the motor and installed a racing transmission. In my hometown back in Ohio, we like fast cars."

He pulled into Denny's parking lot following the girls in the Toyota. Butcher pulled up next to them and the girls climbed out of the car giggling. Butcher and I climbed out of the Mustang. Sharon stepped up next to me, took my arm and we hurried over to the restaurant.

Inside the restaurant, we enjoyed the air-conditioned interior. I gazed about. The restaurant seemed like your typical Denny's, trying to put on the image of a fifties diner. It had the typical serving bar and jukebox. Padded greed barstools lined the counter. Spacious booths surrounded several wooden tables. A skinny teenage girl with a pretty smile stepped up and showed us to a large booth in the back. Connie slid in next to Butcher, Jenifer slid in on the other side of him and Sharon slid in next to her. I sat down next to Sharon. We chatted, enjoying each other's company until the waitress came to take our order. The girls let out an occasional snicker.

When a young, pretty, black waitress came to take our order, I paid for Sharon and Jenifer's meal as well as my own. Butcher paid for Connie's and his.

"Would you like to go out on a date or something sometime? We could go out to dinner?" I said to Sharon. "You could give me your phone number."

Sharon patted my knee under the table, took a pen out of her purse, and wrote her phone number down on a napkin. "The only way I'd go out with you is if you come to church with me first."

I let out a snort. "Church? I haven't been to church in years."

Sharon scowled. "If you want to go out, then you'll come. It's up to you."

"What church do you go to?" I asked.

She handed me the napkin and I stuffed it into the pocket of my uniform. "Cross Roads Assembly. It's off Interstate ten in Redlands. Most people call it the church on the hill."

"What denomination is it?" I asked.

"Christian."

"I used to be Baptist when I was little, but I stopped going."

"So will you come?"

I let out a slow easy breath. "I guess I'll have to, if that's the only way I'll get you to go out to dinner with me," I said.

"Come to church first then we'll talk about dinner."

"I remember you from school now," Connie said. "Didn't you have a brother?"

I sighed. "Yeah, his name is Johnny."

"I remember Johnny. He was cute. Whatever happened to him?" Connie asked.

"He ran away from home when he was sixteen. I never saw him again."

"You never heard from him?" Sharron asked.

"My mom got a couple of postcards. The last I heard from him he was in the Army stationed in Germany," I said.

"That's a shame. You two were close," Connie said and then smiled. "Remember that day at City Creek?" All three of the women blushed and then laughed.

"Okay that's one story we don't need to relive right now," Sharron said and then changed the subject."

After we finished eating, we stood around in the parking lot for a few minutes. A cloud moved across the sky and a breeze picked up. Butcher told Jenifer that he had a buddy in his platoon that he wanted to set her up with. He got Connie's number. Sharon stepped up to me and kissed me. My heart jack-hammered inside my chest and I couldn't catch my breath. A stirring sensation passed through my lower regions.

"Will you come to church with me?" she asked after she pulled away.

I held her close for a few minutes enjoying the feel of her large breasts pressed up against my chest. "Yeah, I'll come."

"Call me on Saturday then."

I crossed my arms under my chest. "Okay. I could call you before that."

We said our goodbyes. Sharon gave me another kiss and piled into the car with her girlfriends. Butcher and I stood leaning against his car smoking after the girls pulled away.

"We got lucky tonight man," Butcher said.

"Tell me about it. I looked up when they came in. Sharon smiled and flashed those baby blues. I thought my heart was going to stop."

Butcher laughed. "I know man. You were gone there for a few seconds, but you have to tell me, what happened at City Creek when you were in school?"

I paused for a moment then said, "That's a story for another day."

"Do you need a ride somewhere?" Butcher asked.

I tossed away the butt of my cigarette. "Yeah, thanks. My folks live up on the north end. I'd appreciate it if you don't mind. I'll give you some money for gas."

"Forget about it. Let's roll," Butcher said.

We climbed into the Mustang and Butcher peeled out of the parking lot. He headed north on E Street toward the north end of San-Bernardino.

Butcher turned left on 30th Street and we passed a Seven-Eleven on the right-hand side. The neighborhood turned residential, the road curved and we stopped at a series of stop signs. A block wall set to our left when Butcher turned right onto Pico Street. The rumble of cars on the freeway provided background noise.

"What's over there on the other side of that wall?" Butcher asked.

"That's part of the cross-town freeway. On the other side is some low rent apartments. The area is ghetto. It ain't much better up here. North of Little Mountain in the North Park area, the houses are a bit ritzier." Pico Street curved and ran into Bussey Street. I told him to stop at the second house on Bussey.

"We're here man." I paused looking at the ranch-style house, with its manicured lawn and garden gnomes. A sense of unease shot through me, and a queasy feeling passed through my belly. I'd spent a lot of years growing up in that house and I wondered what it would be like, living at home again.

"Are you, getting' out man?"

"Yeah, give me a minute." I climbed out of the Mustang, took my seabag from the back seat, and said my farewells to Tom Butcher. He squealed the tires on the Mustang and headed off down the road.

***

I watched him go until he turned the corner then threw my seabag over my shoulder and crossed the lawn to the front door. Setting my seabag down on the front porch, I rapped on the door. The sound of classical music emanated from the house. I pounded harder on the door. For an instant, I felt like running away.

"Wait a minute. I'm coming," someone said from inside. The door opened. I looked into the face of a middle-aged, chunky woman with auburn hair that had the gray-washed away. Her bluish-green eyes looked puffy as though she had been crying. When she saw me, a smile shot crossed her face and she engulfed me in her arms.

"Michael! You're home! Come in! You should have called first!"

"I wanted to surprise you Mom, Mom, you're choking me." She turned me loose.

I carried my seabag inside, crossed a field of beige carpet, and sat down on an expensive black leather couch. The smell of incense permeated the room; my mother loved incense. She sat down in the matching love seat across from me.

"How are you, Michael? Do you want something to eat? Would you like some tea or a Pepsi?"

I glanced about the living room. "I'm fine Mom. I'll take a Pepsi if you don't mind."

She hurried into the kitchen. "I'm so glad you're home. We were so worried about you."

"I'm good Mom, but what about you? You look like you've been crying."

She waved her hand in the air. "It's nothing. Your father and I had a little tiff, that's all." My hands balled into fists resting on my thighs. I guess my mother must have seen the anger in my eyes, because she said, "It's not like that Michael. Your father doesn't hit anymore. He uses words now. He's slowed way down on his drinking."

I leaned back on the couch and stretched my legs. "Yeah right. Sometimes words cut worse than a knife."

"Oh, Michael. It's not like that. Your father and I say mean things to each other sometimes. It doesn't mean anything. Besides, I wasn't crying about that. I was crying, because I worry about you, and here you go and show up at the door."

I looked up. "Where is Dad, anyway?"

"He's down at the golf course. That's where he goes nowadays to cool off. He doesn't know what to do with himself now that he's retired. Why don't you walk down there and meet him? Play a few holes. It'll make his day."

I hesitated for a few seconds. "I don't know. Nothing I ever do is good enough for Dad."

"Nonsense. Your father loves you and he's proud of you, but he has a hard time showing it."

I rolled my eyes. "Yeah right. I'll go down there and see how the old goat is doing." Feeling the need for a cigarette, I stood up and stepped to the door.

My mom stopped me, taking my arm. "The problem with you and your father is that you both are too much alike."

I said goodbye to my mother and stepped out the door. The wind died down and the sun felt good against my back. Crossing the lawn, I ambled down the sidewalk passing older, but well-maintained, homes. A dog barked down the street. I noticed one of our neighbors out front in his driveway working on an old car. He looked up when he saw me and grinned.

"Hello, Mr. Stevenson. How've you been?" I asked.

"I'm fine. It's good to see you back, Mike. I expect you're going down to see your old man. I saw him head by with his golf clubs earlier."

"Yeah, I thought I would go down there and play a few holes with him." Two young girls played hopscotch on the sidewalk.

"Good luck to you, son. I'm glad to see you made it back in one piece."

At the corner, I crossed Little Mountain Drive and ambled up to the entrance to the golf course. At the clubhouse, I asked around about my dad. Someone said that he was out on the ninth hole so I rented a golf cart and headed across the golf course. When I rolled up, my dad was making a swing; I climbed out of the golf cart. After making his swing, he turned around and looked at me.

"Not bad for an old buzzard," I said. A brief smile shot across the old man's face. I looked into his bloodshot eyes taking in the lines of Crow's feet at their corners. His gray hair was starting to thin, but the mustache riding under his potato-shaped nose was as bushy as ever. The mustache was pure white, except for the yellow tobacco stains at its edges. A crow cawed overhead.

"Who you calling old? If you're so good, let me see you take a swing."

I chuckled. "I'm a bit rusty, but I'll give it a shot."

The old man handed me a ball and a tee. I stuck the tee into the ground, pulled a club from the old man's golf bag, and gave it my best shot. The ball flew true but fell way short of the old man's.

"Not bad, for being out of practice. I guess they kept you too busy over there to work on your golf game."

I shaded my eyes looking down the fairway. "They kept us busy with other things," I said. The breeze picked up again and the sun went behind a cloud.

"I'm glad you're back in one piece. I know you must have seen some horrible things."

"So you and mom were fighting?" I said to change the subject.

The old man tensed up. "No, we don't fight the way we used to. When we spend too much time together, she starts with her nitpicking until I can't take it anymore, then I come down here." There was a moment of awkward silence.

We headed down the fairway and I caught a trace of whiskey on the old man's breath. He seemed unsteady on his feet. I felt my cheeks growing hot and my hands balled into fists at my sides. "You're drunk!"

I saw a flash of anger across the old man's eyes. "No, I'm not. I'm a little tipsy, that's all. I drink to keep away the demons."

That shocked me. "What demons?" I asked.

"Oh, you'll find out about them, now that you've been to the war. I'm talking about the ones that come at night when you try to sleep." The old man paused leaning on his golf club; sweat covered his forehead. He took another shot knocking his ball onto the green and I hit, mine, coming up short of his. A shudder passed through me.

"What demons do you see at night?"

"When I was in Korea, we were up on the Chosen Reservoir. A buddy of mine and I were hiding behind a low-lying ridge when the Chinese attacked. My buddy took a bullet through the forehead. His head exploded showering me with blood and brain matter. A mortar landed next to the Marine on the other side of me and cut him in half. I see their faces when I try to sleep at night. The ones I killed too. Even in the daytime, they're in the back of my mind. I drink to keep them at bay. I expect you have a few demons of your own." The old man hit his ball into the hole, and it took me two more strokes, but I hit, mine in as well. We headed back to my golf cart.

"The Iraqi tankers didn't stand a chance. I mean, when they would hit us, it would ring our bell, but their shells wouldn't penetrate. We destroyed them. I shot one tank. The explosion blew the turret off and set it on fire. This Iraqi crawls out of it missing both of his legs. His upper half is on fire and he's screaming. He's yelling in Arabic, and then in English, he yells. 'Fuck Saddam. Fuck George Bush!' He didn't want to be there any more than me. The putrid smell of his cooking flesh is something I'll remember for the rest of my life. Then there was the highway of death when Saddam's boys tried to flee back to Iraqi with all their loot. The flyboys slaughtered those people all over a few Cadillacs. " We reached the golf cart.

"Those are things you'll have to deal with for the rest of your life. You'd better drive. I'm too drunk," the old man said, but I saw sympathy in his eyes.

Things might change between us, I thought. *At least, now I understand him.* I noticed the old man sweating more, so I took his arm. "Say, we'd better call it a day. You don't look so good."

"No, I'm tired that's all. It's hot out," he said pulling away. "You know Mike, I'm not proud of some of the things I did when I was younger: the way I treated you and your momma. Back then, I didn't know how to deal with it all. I took it out on you and your mother. I'm sorry about what happened with your brother Johnny. If I could take it all back, I would. I couldn't handle the nightmares. That's why I started drinking. I hope that someday you can forgive me."

Feeling like a horse's ass, I laid a hand on the old man's boney knee when we pulled up to the tenth hole. "It's okay pops. I'm grown up now. You made a man out of me. I got no hard feelings," I lied. The old man climbed out of the golf cart, took two steps, and collapsed.

***

CHAPTER 6

Sharon went with me to my father's funeral. I called her from the hospital that night and she came down there to be with me. They said that my father, died in hospital but I didn't believe that. I thought he died right there on the golf course. He had a massive heart attack. My mother put on a good front, but she took it hard. We stood next to the casket at the cemetery on a crisp clear morning and Sharon stood on my right holding onto my arm. A cold breeze blew leaves onto the coffin. My mother stood on my left. I gazed across the manicured cemetery grounds at the mountains in the distance. A white puffy cloud hovered over the mountain, tops.

I jumped when the funeral detail fired the twenty-one-gun salute. My mind flashed back to Kuwait. When the Marine presented my mother with the flag a tear track down her face. At the house after the funeral, my mother tried hard to keep up her front. The friends and relatives showed up with food, but later, after everyone had gone home, my mom fell apart.

Sharon was Godsend for my mother. She came over every day trying to help her through that bad time. Sharon and my mother took to each other right away and I started going to church with Sharon. I acted aloof but I enjoyed myself. I liked the pastor, Blackwood. He seemed down to Earth and he had a good sense of humor. He invited us over to his house for a barbeque one Sunday after church. He showed me his Honda Gold Wing and his hot rod setting in his garage. From my first look at the Gold Wing, I knew I had to get one.

I lived with my mother staying in her spare bedroom for a few weeks until I found a job at an insurance company. I liked the work, but I missed being outside. I put half the money from my first paycheck down on an apartment and moved out of my mother's house. Sharon helped me decorate the place. I enjoyed her bubbly laughter and her exuberance. It took her three days to decide what type of curtains I needed. I would have been happy with plain white sheets on the windows.

I started having nightmares. I remembered what my father said about his demons and I struggled with my drinking. It was on the nights when I had the nightmares that I drank. I missed my father, and I felt that if he'd only lived things would have been better between us. One night I sat out on my front porch after a particularly gruesome nightmare and drank. Up until that time, I hadn't cried for my father, but that night the tears flowed like a river over following its banks. I raged at the night cursing God, my father, and everything I could think of. The neighbors called the police. By the time they came, I had puked on myself and passed out sitting on my front porch. They helped me into my apartment, fanning the air in front of their faces, and left. Stumbling into my bedroom, I passed out on the bed.

***

One Sunday morning Pastor Blackwood stepped up on the platform. He began to preach his sermon. He strutted back and forth across the platform in his Navy blue suit like a rock star. Everything he said seemed aimed in my direction. His sermon was about people with heavy burdens. A few people in the crowd yelled, "A man!" Someone else said, "Yes Lord!"

"Jesus said, my yoke is easy and my burden is light. I don't care what your burden is. It could be drugs, booze or sexual perversions," Blackwood said. Jumping down from the platform, he slammed his Bible down on the altar. "Leave it here. The Lord will take the heavy part. You can leave this place a new man or woman, set free in Christ. Come down here to this altar. Jesus will meet you here." He paced back and forth in front of the congregation. "I don't care what demons torment your soul. I don't care what you've done or had done to you in the past. Jesus will set you free. I don't care if you've killed someone. Some of you men out there have been in the military. You've had to do terrible things. Jesus will stop the nightmares. All you have to do is get up out of that chair you're sitting in and come down here. Jesus will meet you at this altar."

I felt as if someone had shot an arrow through my heart and the wound was starting to bleed. My face flushed and tears welled up in my eyes. I felt dirty inside. All the rotten horrible things that I'd ever done flashed through my brain. I saw images of the bodies of Iraqi soldiers in their burnt-out tanks. I started to cry. Tears streamed down my face, I rose to my feet and stumbled down the aisle toward the front. Pastor Blackwood met me there. He looked into my eyes and smiled.

"Mike, let's pray." Pastor Blackwood led me in a confessional prayer. The noise from the other people standing next to me faded away. My face felt hot and the only sound I heard was the pastor's voice. "Mike, you need to surrender. Give up your burdens. It's time to lay them down."

I struggled to keep my voice from cracking. "Pastor, I've made a mess of my life so far. I had to do some terrible things in the war. I saw horrible things." Tears welled up in my eyes.

"Let them go, Mike. You didn't have a choice. Do you want Jesus in your life?"

I struggled to hold back the tears. "Yes. Yes, I do."

"Then tell him." I paused gathering my thoughts.

I let out a croak and then tried again. "Lord, I've made a terrible mess of my life. I've done terrible things. I can't do this on my own. Come into my life. Forgive me of my sins." I felt a sense of lightness and light fill my innermost being. I felt clean inside as if someone had taken a scrub brush and cleaned out all the evil things. The only thing left was love. I felt a soft hand on my back. Someone was praying for me. I turned around and Sharon stood there with tears flowing down her cheeks. Her face looked radiant and I thought *if I ever see an angel's face, this is what it will look like.*

"Oh Michael," she said and hugged me. She squeezed me so tight that I could hardly breathe. *How can such a slip of a girl be so strong,* I wondered. I felt her hot tears on my cheek. "I love you, Michael," she whispered.

***

I quit drinking after that and I quit smoking too. It was hard, but Sharon was a big help and she even got me to quit cussing. We spent all our spare time together. When we weren't attending church functions, we went out. We made out some in my apartment, but Sharon never let it go too far. She said that she was saving herself for marriage and that if I loved her, I'd have to wait. I pondered that statement for several weeks. Did I love her? I had never been in love before.

One day I went to visit my mom. After my dad died, my mom's health began to deteriorate. While my mother was sleeping, I took a walk up to the park on the next block north of her house. The warm sunshine felt good against my face. I hiked along the jogging trail oblivious to everything around me. My mind was elsewhere. *Do I love her? I enjoy her company. When I'm not with her, I can't stop thinking about her. When I am in her presence, I am whole and somehow, complete. I could see spending the rest of my life with her. Yeah, I love her. If I pop the question will she say yes?*

My mind made up, I went back to my mom's house and drove downtown to shop for an engagement ring. I had bought a beat-up old red Ford F-150 pickup truck. I still had some money saved from when I was in the service. I added to it from my paychecks from the Insurance Company. I bought the biggest diamond that I could afford. It wasn't anything fancy, but I figured Sharon would like it. When I bought the ring the young woman behind the counter smiled. "Your girlfriend will love this when you give this to her."

"I hope so," I said.

I carried the thing around in my pocket for two weeks before I, finally, built up the courage to pop the question. I asked Sharon out to dinner on a Friday night and we went to a Mexican place called Mexico's. They had some of the best enchiladas in town. I waited until we'd finished dinner and we were almost through with our desert before I asked the question. Sharon leaned back in her chair rubbing her stomach.

"I'm stuffed. I don't think I'll be able to finish my ice cream." She noticed me fidgeting. "What is it, Michael? You've been acting weird all evening. Is something wrong?"

A nervous flutter shot through my belly and my heart pounded. "I'd better do this right." I climbed out of the booth and took a knee next to Sharon's chair. Pulling the little black box out of my pocket, I opened it up and presented the engagement ring to Sharon.

"Miss Sharon, Beasley, Will you marry me?"

A smile darted across her face, tears welled up in her eyes and she let out a wild whoop. "Yes! Yes! Of course, I will, Michael, now get up!"

I stood to my feet; Sharon launched herself out of the booth and jumped up into the air slamming into me. I took an involuntary step back. She wrapped her legs and arms around me and gave me a long hard kiss on the mouth. Her lips tasted like cherry-flavored chapstick and she smelled of Chanel Number Five. A loud cheer rose from the other patrons inside the restaurant and they began to clap. Sharon came up for air and smothered my face with kisses. "I can hardly wait to start planning the wedding."

During the months that followed, my mother and Sharon started planning the wedding. They were out looking at wedding invitations, flowers, wedding dresses you name it. I put my nose to the grindstone and tucked as much money away as possible. The insurance firm where I worked handed out commissions for every policy we sold. I hit up everyone I knew trying to get them to sign up. When we weren't planning for the wedding, Sharon and I spent our time house hunting. Two months before the wedding, we found a split-level ranch-style home in East Highland. Sharon fell in love with the place and so did I. We stood holding hands on the front lawn looking at our new home.

"The first thing I want to do when we move in is to buy a horse. There are already corrals outback. Would you care if I bought a horse? I've always wanted one ever since I was a little girl," Sharon said. She was so excited that she could not stand still and a huge grin crossed her face.

I laughed. "Whatever babe. Whatever makes you happy. I'll get you a horse, as long as I can have a dog. I'd like a shepherd."

"Of course you can have a dog. I want one too. A shepherd would be wonderful," Sharon said. She turned, leaped into my arms, and kissed me. My arms circled her and my hands found her shapely bottom. I put a down payment down on the place, and we closed escrow three days before the wedding. Our friends and neighbors filled the church on the day of our wedding. Sharon looked stunning in her long white wedding gown. As we stood before the preacher, I gazed into Sharon's eyes. My heart almost stopped and felt like the luckiest man on Earth. I had on my dress blues and Tom Butcher stood next to me serving as my best man. When Sharon marched down the aisle, all my nervousness left. I stood in awe, of her beauty and I thought my heart would burst for joy.

Pastor Blackwood grinned when he stepped in front of us. "It brings me great joy, to be the one to join these two in holy matrimony. In all my years as a minister, I have never met a couple more suited for each other, or more in love. Let us begin." He turned to me and said, "Mike McDonald, do you take this woman, Sharon Beasley, to be your wedded wife?"

The church held a reception for us in their reception hall after the wedding. Sharon looked radiant and was in a playful mood, so she smashed a piece of cake into my face after we cut the cake. We received so many wedding gifts that I didn't know what we would do with them all. We headed down to San Diego for our honeymoon, I rented a motor home and we spent a week at the beach. Arriving that first evening after dark, we set up camp in an RV park near the water. I cooked dinner, barbequing some steaks, and that night when we made love for the first time. Sharon made love to me with such wild abandonment that I could hardly believe she was the same woman. I had a hard time keeping up with her energetic passion.

The first time I saw her in her bikini, I almost had heart failure. She stood there, fresh out of the water, in a white string bikini with beads of water sparkling off her bronze skin. The water caused her bikini to become transparent. Her nipples pressed against the fabric of her tiny bikini top like two twin ICBMs. The bottom, a tiny piece of cloth shaped in a V, didn't look legal. A tiny piece of string ran up between the cheeks of her ass like butt floss. My breath caught in my throat, a stirring sensation shot through me and I didn't know what to do with my hands.

"Come on Silly. Let's get wet," Sharon, said taking me by my arm and led me down to the water. One afternoon, I lay on a lounge chair in front of the motor home facing the beach. Seagulls cawed overhead and I noticed an old cabin cruiser out on the water. I drifted off to sleep and began to have strange dreams. In one dream, I crashed a motorcycle sliding off a curve on a mountain road. I had one dream where I fought for my life with a group of outlaw bikers. Another dream floated across my subconscious and I was on a boat fighting with three men. Two were Latin, and one was a black man. The younger Latin male had a missing hand and the black man shot me. I fell overboard into the water. In another dream, I stood on the bank of a murky swamp. The young Latin male stood out in the swamp; I pulled a forty-five and shot him.

Sharon's soft touch on my arm woke me with a start.

"Michael. Wake up. Supper's ready. You must have been dreaming. You were talking in your sleep."

"Yeah, I was having some crazy dreams."

"What did you dream?"

"In one dream, I got shot," I said knuckling sleep from my eyes. I followed Sharon into the motor home and sat down at the table. My stomach rumbled and I forgot all about my nightmares. Sharon set a plate load of fried chicken down on the table in front of me.

Sharon's wedding present arrived the day after we returned from our honeymoon. A pickup truck arrived pulling a horse trailer and unloaded a roan Appaloosa gelding. Sharon let out a loud squeal, ran out to the front of the house, and watched the horse's former owner unload the animal. "When did you?" She asked.

I held up my cell phone and flipped it open. "While we were at the beach you thought I was checking in at the office? I made the deal over the phone and arranged for the man to deliver the horse when we came home." A middle-aged cowboy led the animal up to where we stood. Sharon patted the side of the animal's face and the horse nuzzled her. The big horse let out a low whinny.

"He's a good old boy. He's a good horse for a beginner. He's eighteen years old. Old enough to have settled down a bit, but not too old to ride. The old boy's still got some spirit," the old cowboy said.

Sharon beamed. "What's his name?"

"I call him Totem because he's as tall as a Totem pole." I showed the man how to get into the back yard and he led the animal to the corral.

"How much did you pay for him?" Sharon asked, clutching my arm.

"Six hundred dollars. Do you like him?"

"I love him," Sharon said and kissed me. After the man who delivered the horse left, we took my pickup truck into town and bought hay at a feed store. I returned to work the following morning and put my nose back to the grindstone. That night when I came home, Sharon had a surprise waiting for me. I stepped into the living room, sat down on the couch, took off my shoes and Sharon kissed me hello. She handed me a glass of Pepsi.

"I've got someone I want you to meet," she said. "I'll go get him." She went down the hall and opened the door to our bedroom. A German shepherd puppy stormed out of the bedroom and ran into the living room. It jumped up putting its paws on my legs and wagged its tail. I felt a grin spread across my face.

"What's his name?" I asked, bending down to pet the dog.

Sharon stood next to the dog and with her hands on her hips. "That's up to you. The man at the animal shelter said that he is a full-blood shepherd. He said that they were going to put him to sleep tomorrow if no one bought him."

I picked the dog up and put him on my lap. "In that case, I'll call him Lucky."

***

The first big-ticket item we bought after our marriage was the Honda Gold Wing. When I saw it sitting on the showroom floor in the motorcycle shop, I fell in love. What caught my eye was its Candy Apple Red paint job. After I brought it home, I took Sharron for a ride. I loved the feel of Sharon's firm breasts against my back and the feel of my face in the wind. From then on, I rode the bike to work every day. During the year that followed, we went on several long rides with Pastor Blackwood and his wife. One time we went on a trip up the California coast on Coast Highway One and about froze our asses off.

On the eve of our first Christmas, I sat on the couch, while Sharon cooked dinner, thinking about my life. I had started teaching the teen class in Sunday school and I enjoyed it. When I stepped off that bus fresh from the Persian Gulf War, I was full of bitterness and despair. I had no plans for the future. I shook my head not believing my good fortune. *I am blessed,* I thought. That Christmas was one of the happiest ones of my life.

My mother passed away three weeks later, and once again, we gathered in the cemetery to say our last goodbyes. This time dark clouds covered the sky and thunder rolled across the land. I felt a raindrop hit my face. It seemed to me that my mother's death affected Sharon worse than me. During the time that they had known each other, my mother and Sharon had grown close. After the funeral, she fell into a funk and it took her three months or more to get back to her jovial self. We started making plans for my vacation. The plan was, to take the bike and go camping in the Sequoia and Yosemite National parks. The night before we left, we made love. Sharon unleashed her passion and made love to me with such intensity that it left me breathless. After, a while she lay in my arms and cried.

"What's wrong?" I asked.

Sharon wiped her tears on my arm. "I don't know. I almost feel like this is one of the last times we'll make love. That something is going to happen. There is something on the horizon."

I pulled her to me and kissed her cheek. "Nonsense. We've got our whole lives to make love to each other. Nothing is going to happen."

She smiled. "You'll still love me even when I'm old and ugly with flabby old wrinkled tits?"

I laughed. "Even then. We're both going to get old, but you'll never be ugly. You'll always be the most beautiful girl in town to me, but I could always get you a boob job," I said and then laughed.

Sharon elbowed me in the ribs and let out a chuckle. She fell asleep in my arms and I rolled over on my back but couldn't sleep. A deep sense of fear and foreboding shot through me when I thought about what Sharon had said after we made love.

***

CHAPTER 7

"Sir are you all right?" the girl behind the counter asked, a concerned look crossing her face.

I shook my head, my mind waltzing back to the present. "Yeah, I'm fine." I picked up my purchases, holding them under my left arm, and hobbled out the door leaning on the cane with my right hand. A cool breeze tickled my face. Pastor Blackwood opened the rear passenger door and helped me into the back seat. He looked inside the bag and frowned. "Mike, are you sure you want this stuff? It's not too late to take this stuff back."

I leaned back in the seat and set the bag down on the floorboard. "Pastor, I appreciate your concern but do me a favor. Don't push it."

The pastor sighed and turned his head back to the front of the vehicle. "Okay, Mike."

A tear tracked down my face and my hands gripped the arms of my chair. A vein pulsated in the side of my head and my face flushed in anger. The pastor looked in the rearview mirror and started to back up, but then he hit the brakes.

"Are you okay, Mike?" he said, looking back over his shoulder.

I glanced out the passenger side window. "Yeah, I'm okay. I had another memory."

"Was it about Sharon?" the pastor asked.

"Yeah," I said, after a second.

The pastor backed out into the parking lot. "What did you remember?"

"Everything from the day I came home from the Persian Gulf until the night before we left on vacation. This time it wasn't like before, like a movie in my mind. This time it was real. I remembered the love. It tore my guts out."

A look of trepidation passed across Blackwood's face. "Are you all right? Would you like me to say a prayer?"

I shook my head. "No. Take me home. I'm gonna kill those bastards," I said under my breath.

The pastor didn't catch the last part. He pulled out of the parking lot and headed down Boulder Avenue to Baseline. I recognized the scenery. Turning left on Baseline, we headed east and crossed the bridge spanning City Creek. I noticed several kids playing in the water. Pastor Blackwood continued east and turned left on Birch. I looked out the window noticing the well-maintained homes. A few children played on their front lawns. When he pulled up in front of my house and stopped, I sat there for a few seconds staring at the dwelling. A sense of apprehension shot through me.

Blackwood looked over his shoulder. "Do you want me to help you inside?"

I paused for a second. "No. I'll be fine."

Pastor Blackwood climbed out of the front seat opened my door and I climbed out. Taking my bag from the store out of the car, I sat it down on the walkway. Pastor Blackwood stuck out his hand and we shook. His wife Darlene stepped up next to him; I pulled the pastor close with my right arm and gave him an awkward hug. "Thank you Craig for everything you've done."

Pastor Blackwood blushed and pulled away. "What are friends for, Mike? I'm glad you're still alive. If it had been me, I know you would have been there."

Darlene hugged me. "Don't be a stranger Mike," she said.

"Yes. I want to see you at church next Sunday," Pastor Blackwood added. "If you need me you have my number."

I shrugged. "Okay, I'll call you if I need you. I ain't promising anything about church, but we'll see." A blur of dark fur shot across the street and a big German shepherd dog barked and jumped up, putting his paws on my chest. It wagged its tail and tried to lick my face.

"Lucky?" I said and reached out and scratched his ears.

Pastor Blackwood smiled. "That's right Mike. That's Lucky."

Karen, the young woman from across the street hurried over with her long black hair hanging down to her ass. She threw her arms around me, pressing her large round breasts up against my chest, and kissed my cheek.

"Mike, I'm so sorry about Sharon. Lucky, has been moping around for the past three months. I'm so glad you're all right and that you're home. If you need anything, I'm right across the street."

"Okay, Karen. Thank you," I said. All though I remembered her name, I didn't remember her face. I said my goodbyes to Pastor Blackwood and Darlene. Karen and I stood out front for a few minutes talking before she went home. Lucky and I headed to the front door.

I fumbled with my keys and opened the door. Lucky shot past me and I paused looking into the dark interior of my house. The house put off a hot musty smell and a ball of nerves bounced through my stomach when I stepped inside. Lucky came out of the kitchen with a squeaky toy. An eerie silence filled the dwelling making me feel like a stranger in my own home. Noticing the thermostat on the wall, I turned on the air conditioner and turned on the lights. Lucky dropped his squeaky toy, scampered across the living room to the sliding glass door. He let out a bark.

"Okay, boy," I said, setting my bag from the store down on the kitchen table. I crossed the living room and opened the sliding glass door. Lucky ran out into the backyard and headed over to the horse corral. I hobbled out the door, crossed the cement patio, and headed over to say hello to Totem. The horse let out a whinny, trotted over, and hung his head over the top rail of the corral. I ambled over and petted his neck. He nuzzled me.

"How're you doing old boy?" I asked. Totem let out another whinny. Taking a flake of hay from the bale, I fed the animal. Brushing tiny flakes of hay from my clothes, I found the metal trashcan near the garage where I stored the dog food. After feeding Lucky, I stepped into the garage and turned on the overhead light. My Gold Wing set parked next to my red Ford F-150 pickup truck. The bastards who attacked me smashed the tour pack along with the side cases. The tank had several dents in it and the wheels looked bent. Seeing the damage to the motorcycle made everything seem more real.

"Those sons of bitches are going to pay," I said to myself and gave one of the damaged side cases an angry kick. My stomach felt sick. When I looked at the damaged motorcycle, I thought about what they did to Sharon. I retreated into the house, took a beer from the bag and put the rest of them in the fridge. I sat down in my living room. Lucky scratched at the door and I let him in. I sat back down on the end of the couch and popped the top on a beer. Lucky let out a low melancholy whine.

"I know. I miss her too, boy." Lucky jumped up on the couch and put his head in my lap. I found the remote and turned on the boob tube. The phone on an end table next to my couch rang making me jump. I picked up the receiver. "Hello." I heard someone breathing on the other end of the line. "Is this Mr. McDonald?"

"Yeah. I'm Mike McDonald," I said recognizing the voice.

"Mr. McDonald, you were in my bar earlier today. I made some calls. I have some information on those shit bags that killed your wife."

I sat up straighter in my chair. "I'm listening."

"I take it that you know the club that was in the bar that night was the Lost Souls?"

I nodded to myself and said, "Yes."

"Yeah, well the people I talked to tell me that the ones in the bar that night were all from the LA chapter. I got a name on their president. He was the scar-faced dude with the dark hair."

"Yeah, I remember that SOB's face."

"His name is Quinn. His first name is James. They call him JD. I'm afraid, that's all I can do for you. If I dig any deeper, I'm afraid the Lost Souls will find out I've been talking. Things could get dicey for me. I get a lot of bikers in here. Word travels fast. I don't want any trouble."

I leaned back in my chair. "No, you've done enough. Thank you for your help," I said and hung up the phone. *JD Quinn.* Now I had a name to focus my anger on. I tossed back half of my beer and sat brooding on the couch for a while. Lucky let out another whine, so I reached down and stroked his fur behind his ears. Feeling restless, I went into the bedroom and breathed in the scent of a woman: Sharon's scent. Lucky followed at my heels. I stood there for a few moments gazing about the room taking in Sharon's dresser with her bottles of perfume on top. A white padded bra set next to the perfume.

I stepped up to the dresser, picked up the bra and held it to my nose. I breathed in the smell of soap and Sharon. I opened one of the perfume bottles and took a sniff. Closing the bottle, I set it back down on the dresser. Next, I opened her drawers and went through Sharon's things. I caressed the fabric of each articled of clothing. For a second I caressed a pair of black silk panties and then put them away. A tear tracked down my face and I heard a faint whisper coming from the hallway. *Michael.* Lucky's ears perked up and he glanced at the hallway. His tail began to wag. A chill shot down my spine and it felt as if someone had poured ice water down my back.

“Get a grip,” I said to myself, heading back into the living room. Lucky followed. I stood there for a few minutes feeling jumpy. The house seemed as quiet as an abandoned graveyard. Finished with the beer, I popped the top on another and headed into the kitchen. Tossing the empty in the trash can, I sat down behind my computer and logged onto the internet. I typed the words, the Lost Souls MC, into the search engine box. I looked up everything I could find on the outlaw bike club. Lucky went into the hallway sniffing around and then let out a whine. “It’s okay boy,” I said. A chill shot down my spine but I shook it off.

I discovered that the Lost Souls had four chapters, one in LA, one in Las Vegas, one in Utah, and one in Idaho. I checked out each of the chapter web pages but concentrated on the LA chapter’s web page. They didn’t provide a lot of information. I looked at a few pictures of their members, attending various functions. None of the pictures were close-ups where you could recognize any faces. A law enforcement web page was more informative. It provided a background of their sordid criminal history. It seemed that they were into drug running, guns, prostitution, and illegal gambling. Several of their members had warrants for various assaults including murder.

“These are some sweet boys,” I said to myself and ran my hands through my hair. My head was starting to hurt. I printed out everything that I found and set it aside for further study, then logged off the internet. I went through my bills expecting to be behind on everything, but much to my surprise, I wasn’t. I popped the top on another beer and went into the living room. Finding an address book next to the phone, I looked up Blackwood’s number. Craig answered on the third ring.

“Have you been paying my bills while I was in the hospital?” I asked.

“Hello, Mike. How are you? Are you having any more memories?”

“I’m okay. Nothing else since earlier today. I’m trying to get used to my house again. About those bills?”

Blackwood sighed. “Yeah. I didn’t want you to be behind on your bills when you got home.”

“How much do I owe you?” I asked, shifting my weight in my chair.

“Nothing.”

"Come on. I can't let you do that without paying you back," I said.

"Then give it to the church. So how are you? You still aren't thinking about this revenge thing, are you?"

I dodged the question. "Thanks, Craig. One of the things I remembered about Sharon was that she liked you. So do I. You're a good friend."

"You're a good friend too, Mike. That's why I worry about you."

"You don't need to. Goodbye Craig," I said and hung up the phone. Finished with my beer, I popped the top on another and sat down in front of the TV. Lucky jumped back up on the couch to join me. I had a good beer buzz going. A half-hour later, the phone rang and I picked up the receiver.

"Hello, Mike," someone said when I answered the phone.

"Hello," I said, not recognizing the voice.

"This is Bob. I heard you woke up and were out of the hospital. I'm glad to hear it."

"I'm sorry, but my memory is a little fuzzy since I woke up. Who are you?"

"Robert Donavan from the church. My friends call me Bob." I paused for a second. A fuzzy memory of a face flashed through my brain.

"You're a cop, right?" Lucky put his head in my lap and I reached down to stroke his fur.

"Yeah."

"I'm sorry, but were we, good friends? I don't remember."

"We were friends. Not what you would call best buddies, but we talked and socialized at church. I'm sorry about what those punks did to Sharon. If there's anything I can do, let me know."

I paused, thinking. "There is one thing. You could get me some INTEL on the LA chapter of the Lost Souls."

Silence filled the line for a few seconds. "I could get in trouble for that, but what the hell? If the bastards raped and killed my wife, I'd be looking for some payback too. As a law enforcement officer, I can't tell you to go after these creeps, but if it was my wife? With your military background, you could do 'em some hurt. I'll see what I can do."

"That would be great. Say, Bob. Why don't you stop by sometime for a beer?"

"I thought you didn't drink?" Bob said after a short pause.

"I do now."

"Right. Yeah, I'll stop by in a few days. By then, I'll have something for you. Take care, Mike. I'm glad you're okay."

"Thanks," I said and hung up the phone. I killed the six-pack and stumbled off to bed in an alcoholic haze. Lucky trotted along behind me and lay down on the floor next to my bed. After stripping out of my clothes, I turned out the light, crawled between the covers, but I couldn't sleep. I thought about Sharon. She wouldn't like what I was planning and I couldn't even rationalize it by telling myself that I was doing it for her. Who was I kidding? This was all about me: revenge. The thought of it tasted sweet. I, passed out a short while later.

***

A cold chill woke me sometime later. Goosebumps formed up on my arms and legs. I heard footsteps in the hallway and a chill ran down my spine. My breath fogged up in my face, my breathing accelerated and my heart thumped. The doorway to my bedroom squeaked open. Lucky let out a whine and the hackles on the back of his neck stood up. My eyes widened when I looked up and saw Sharon standing in the doorway with her arms crossed under her breasts. A stern, disapproving look crossed her face. I gazed at her for a few seconds taking in her white transparent nightgown. I could see her sensual form underneath. Her nightgown wasn't the only thing transparent. In the moonlight coming through the bedroom window, I saw right through her or her ghost if you will.

"Sharon," I whispered. She disappeared. The temperature inside the bedroom returned to normal. I heard footsteps retreating down the hallway.

"Michael." The sound of her voice in the hallway faded away with the night. Lucky jumped up on the bed and lay down by my feet. I laid back down wondering if I was hallucinating or if I'd seen the ghost of my dead wife. I finally drifted off into an uneasy sleep.

Up at six AM, I let Lucky outside to take care of his morning business and made coffee. Popping a couple of pieces of bread into the toaster, I sat down at the table to have my first cup of the morning. There's nothing like a cup of Joe in the morning to give your day a kick in the ass. I drank my second cup, ate my toast, and fed the animals. Lucky and I headed out the door. The crisp morning air felt good against my face. If I was going to hunt down the shit bags that killed my wife, I needed to be in good shape.

Lucky scampered along beside me as we headed up the road. Relying upon my cane, we went down to the corner and headed down Baseline. The muscles in my legs and back screamed out in agony. Sweat cropped up on my forehead and pain shot up my back. I walked close to a mile before turning back. Sweat drenched my shirt and upper body and my heart pounded inside my chest. Back at the house, I sat down next to the phone and found the insurance policy on the bike. I gave the broker a call and he said for me to take the bike to the dealer and have them fax an estimate. My next call was to the Honda dealership. I arranged for them to come and pick up the bike.

After talking with the people at the motorcycle shop, I called the old cowboy that I'd bought Totem from.

"Hello," a gravelly old voice said when I made the connection.

"This is Mike McDonald. I bought a horse from you a while back."

"Yes. I remember you, Mr. McDonald. I was sorry to hear what happened to your wife. I hope you're all right," the old cowboy said.

"I'm okay. I'm having problems with my memory and I'm having headaches, but I'll be all right. Could take the horse, back?

There was a pause on the line. "No. I can't afford another horse right now, but I'll ask around. I'm sure I can find a buyer for you."

"That would be great. I'd appreciate anything you can do."

We said our goodbyes and my next call was to a real estate agent. I told him that I wanted to put the house on the market. We arranged for him to come to see the house the following morning. Next, I called my boss at the insurance company. My boss wanted to know when I would come back to work, but I arranged to be off for another two weeks. Finished on the phone, I found my truck keys and headed for the door.

Pausing in the doorway, I said, "Come on Lucky. Let's go for a ride." Lucky almost knocked me down trying to get out the front door. "Easy boy." We headed for the garage. Inside the garage, I opened the passenger door to my F-150 and Lucky leaped into the cab. I closed the door and went around to the driver's side. Firing up the pickup truck, I pulled out of the garage and went back to close the garage door. Lucky stuck his head out the passenger side window. Back inside the truck, I slammed my door and pulled out onto the street. Lucky and I headed to town. We turned left at the corner and headed west. On Baseline; Lucky stuck his head out the window and let his tongue lag and his tail wag.

Turning right on Boulder Road, we headed north passing a bank and a gas station. At Highland Avenue, we took a left turn and headed west. We passed a grocery store and various other businesses. After passing Patton State Mental hospital I pulled into Galloway's Gun World. Galloway's Gun World was a combination gun store, gas station, and mini-mart. He also rented snow chains to the snowbirds in the wintertime, and he did key and lock work.

I pulled the truck around to the side of the building. A teenage boy, with short black hair, worked the island pumping gas. Galloway's Gun World was an old school where the attendant pumped gas for the customer. They washed their windshield, checked the oil, and checked the air pressure in their tires. Galloway had built a large clientele that appreciated good service. I hobbled around the corner leaning on my cane and entered the mini-mart. I bought a Pepsi, paid the kid on the island, and entered the sporting good section of Galloway's Gun World. Galloway had converted the station's backroom into his gun shop.

Popping the top on my Pepsi I bellied up to the counter. George Galloway, standing behind the counter, looked up and smiled. I took him in, in a glace. he wore a black cowboy hat, dark wraparound sunglasses, and a black cowboy shirt. The shirt had flowers embroidered on the right shoulder. Around his waist, he wore a black belt with a large silver buckle. On his feet; he wore a pair of brown custom-made cowboy boots. He had dark hair that was showing a little gray, a thick handlebar mustache, and a goatee. *Your typical drugstore cowboy.* He looked like the embodiment of cool.

"Can I help you?" Galloway said in a gruff-sounding voice.

I leaned against my cane for support. "I'm looking for some guns."

Galloway smiled. "That's good. Would you like to narrow it down a bit? I mean I'm fresh out of bazookas and machine guns," Galloway said and laughed.

I looked at the rifles he had on display. "What do you have in the way of shotguns?"

Galloway pulled a pump-action shotgun from underneath the counter and handed it to me. "I got this Remington in. It's used. I could make you a deal on it."

I checked out the shotgun and handed it back. "I'd prefer something new, and I was looking for a double barrel side by side."

"I've got a Mossberg in the back. They're good functional weapons at a reasonable price. I'll be right back." He disappeared through a door behind the counter. I heard a Harley Davidson motorcycle pulling up to the gas pump. My heart rate quickened and I glanced toward the biker pulling up to the gas pumps. He looked like your average Joe, so I turned my attention back to Galloway. He stepped from the back room carrying a long rectangular shaped box. He laid the box on the counter, opened it, and handed me the shotgun. I admired the wooden-engraved stock and put the butt plate to my shoulder. The weapon had a good feel to it. I sat it back down on the counter.

"I'll take two of them," I said.

Galloway took off his sunglasses and laid them on the counter. A nervous twitch passed across his face. "What do you plan to do with these weapons?"

I shrugged. "I'm going hunting."

"Hunting? Hunting what?"

I grinned. "Varmints. What do you have in the way of handguns?"

Galloway sighed. "What caliber were you looking for?"

"Forty-five automatic model nineteen eleven."

Galloway let out a low whistle and arched an eyebrow. "I hope these varmints need killing," he said.

"In the worst possible way." Outside, the biker fired up his Harley and sped away.

Galloway disappeared through the back door once more and came back out carrying a small box. He opened the box and handed me a Colt 45 automatic model 1911. I held the weapon, pulled back the slide, let it slip forward, and sighted down the barrel. "I'll take two," I said.

Galloway leaned forward resting his arms on the counter. "Son, I hope you're not planning anything illegal with these weapons. You know you have a ten-day waiting period and you have to pass a background check. What do you want with these weapons?" he asked.

I paused for a second and grinned. "I plan on killing the sons of bitches that murdered my wife."

Galloway pulled a pack of smokes from his front shirt pocket, shook out a cigarette, and put it in his mouth. Producing a lighter from his pants pocket, he lit his cigarette and blew smoke across the counter. "What's your name son?"

I breathed in the rich smell of tobacco smoke. "Mike. Mike McDonald."

He inhaled his smoke and said, "I remember that name. It seems like I read something about you in the paper. Didn't some gang of outlaw bikers rape and kill your wife?"

"That is correct," I said.

Galloway leaned forward resting his hands on the counter. "Can you pass the background check?"

"I got no felonies on my record."

Galloway grinned. "Is there anything else you need?"

"I could use a large caliber rifle with a scope for some long-range work," I said.

"I got a Ruger model seventy-seven, two seventy, magnum in the back with a three by nine variable scope on it."

"Let's take a look," I said.

Once more Galloway stepped through the back door, but he appeared a minute later with a hunting rifle. It had a rosewood stock with a black scope mounted to it. I held the weapon to my shoulder, looked through the scope, and handed it back to Galloway.

"Don't tell me. You want two of them," Galloway said and then laughed.

I chuckled. "No this will do, but I'd like a black carbonate stock. I'd also like five boxes of shells for each weapon."

Galloway shook his head. "I'll put the stock on for you and throw in a sling for free. I'll also throw in an extra box of shells for each weapon. I'll need a fifty percent deposit. You can pick up the hardware in ten days. If the police come nosing around, I'll tell them what you said: that you plan to do some varmint hunting. Were you in the military, son?"

I nodded. "Yeah, I fought in the gulf."

"Then you get a ten percent discount. You another five percent for buying more than one weapon." Galloway tallied my bill and another customer entered the sporting goods section. I handed him a credit card and he ran it through his machine charging me fifty percent of the total.

"You can take the ammo with you now," Galloway said. He leaned closer to me and whispered. "Son, shoot one of those scum bags for me. After it's over, stop in and see me. I'd like to hear how it turns out. I'll buy you a beer."

"I never turn down a free beer," I said.

From Galloway's Gun world, I headed to the grocery store. The cupboards at home were bare and I needed more beer. I filled my cart with groceries passing up and down the aisles. I put a jar of petroleum jelly into the cart and several boxes of wooden tipped matches. "I'm gonna have to remember how to shop all over again, now that Sharon's gone," I said to myself. When Sharon was alive, I let her handle the grocery shopping. Now, I was having a hard time finding things. Ahead of me, a man in his early forties pushed a cart loaded with beer. He had a few grocery items in the mix, but you could tell by the look that the man had a serious love for alcohol. A skinny six-year-old boy with a dirty face walked next to him. The boy wore a dirty white t-shirt and a pair of filthy blue jeans. The kid ran over to the candy display and grabbed some licorice.

"Daddy! Daddy! Can I have some-?"

"Put that back you little shithead!" the man yelled backhanding the six-year-old. The kid flew across the aisle and landed on his butt. Tears streamed down the boy's cheeks. A sheering white-hot pain passed through my head. Another memory shot through my brain like a forty-five caliber bullet.

***

CHAPTER 8

Johnny and I sat on the carpet in the living room of our shabby two-story house in Highland California. We waited for our father to get home. It was Christmas Eve and Pops was late as usual. Mom sat in her favorite chair knitting and humming a Christmas carol.

"Momma, when is Daddy coming home?" I asked. My brother Johnny sat beside me on the floor playing with a Tonka truck.

My mother sighed. "For the third time, he'll be home soon, now quit bugging me."

Johnny looked up. "He's at the bar. I hope he doesn't come home at all. He'll be drunk again."

"Johnny hush your mouth," Momma said.

"Do you think Daddy will let us open a present tonight?" I asked.

Momma paused from her knitting. "I don't know, but don't bug him if he says no. You know how he gets."

My brother made a disgusting face. "Oh yeah, Mom. We know how he gets. Believe me."

"Johnny you stop it right now. Do you think it's easy for your father taking care of us? Times are hard."

"They wouldn't be so hard if he'd quit drinking," Johnny said.

My father stumbled in two hours later reeking of alcohol and cigarettes. My mother dropped her knitting and stood to her feet.

My father stopped in the center of the living room swaying on his feet. "Where's my dinner, woman?"

"Let me warm it up. I fed the kids already." She retreated to the kitchen; I jumped up and ran over to my father. "Daddy! Daddy! Can we open one of our presents tonight?" I pleaded.

"No! Christmas ain't until tomorrow you little shit. Get away from me. Can't a man come home from a hard day's work and relax?" my father yelled pushing me away. I fell on my butt and a tear tracked down my face.

"Leave him alone!" Johnny yelled jumping in front of me.

"It's okay Johnny. Don't," I whispered. Mom came in from the kitchen in time to see my father backhand my brother. Johnny took a step back but didn't fall and he didn't cry. "Don't honey. Not tonight. It's Christmas Eve."

"You'd better get control of these kids before I give you one in the kisser." My father stumbled over to his favorite chair and fell into it. "Get me a beer, while you're in there woman!" my father yelled. Mom came in a few minutes later and handed him a plate of food and a cold beer. The smell of fried chicken filled the room

Johnny and I continued playing in front of the couch. "I'm going to kill him someday," Johnny whispered.

My eyes widened in fright. "Don't say that. He might hear you."

A scowl crossed my father's face. "What are you damned kids whispering about?" he yelled.

"We're talkin' about Christmas," I said. My father finished his meal, but then a group of Christmas carolers came to the door and sang Silent Night.

An evil frown appeared on my father's face. "Get rid of those bible thumpers, woman, before I get mad," he said.

My mom rushed to the kitchen and brought out a plate of cookies for the carolers. She stepped out into the cold night and sent them away. I stood up, crossed the living room to the Christmas tree, and touched a red ornament hanging on the tree. Its smooth glass exterior felt cold to my small hands. A golden angel with its wings spread apart adorned the front of the glass bulb. The Christmas decoration fell from the tree and landed on the floor; I backed away from the tree.

A mean look crossed my father's face. "You little shit! Can't we have anything nice without you fucking it up! You little fuck head!" he roared. He jumped out of his chair and slapped me across the face. I flew across the room landing on my behind. Tears streamed down my face and I rubbed the red handprint on my cheek. "Look at the baby crying!"

Johnny jumped to his feet. He stepped between my father and me. "You mean son of a bitch! Leave him alone!"

"What'd you call me? Why you little shit!" He pulled loose his black leather belt and swung it at my brother. The buckle caught him on the corner of his forehead causing a gash. Johnny landed on his back next to me with blood dripping down the side of his face.

"Honey! Stop!" my mother yelled, rushing in from the kitchen.

My father stood in a drunken stupor looking down at us. “Don’t start in on me woman,” he said in a cold cruel sounding voice. He noticed the Tonka truck setting on the floor and brought the heel of his boot down on it, smashing it. “If you two know what’s good for you, you little cry babies better go upstairs before I get mad.” Johnny jumped up, taking me by the arm, and we ran upstairs. My mom followed us, bringing a cold rag from the bathroom and tended to Johnny’s cut forehead.

“Why does Daddy hate us?” I sobbed.

“He doesn’t hate you. He gets mean when he’s drunk. You need to keep your distance when he’s drunk,” she said in a quiet vanquished voice.

“He’s a mean bastard even when he’s not drunk,” Johnny said. Even though my father had put a good size gash in his head, Johnny didn’t shed a tear.

“Hush. Don’t you, ever let him hear you say that.” My mom finished bandaging Johnny’s head. “You boys get dressed for bed. You want to be asleep before Santa Clause gets here.”

After we crawled between the covers and the lights were out, Johnny and I talked for a few minutes. “Why do you think Daddy’s so mean?” I asked.

“I don’t know,” Johnny said.

“He could be sad inside. He needs Jesus in his heart like, that Sunday school teacher says.”

Johnny paused and I thought for a minute that he had fallen asleep. “I don’t think that would help. I’m going to kill him someday.”

I shivered in fright. “Please don’t. Momma would be sad,” I said.

“If I don’t kill him first, I’m gonna run away, as soon as you’re big enough to take care of yourself.”

A wonderful thought flashed through my brain. “I’ll come with you! We could be pirates or join the circus!”

Johnny chuckled. “It’d be hard enough for me to take care of myself, much less a little kid like you, now go to sleep.”

I closed my eyes dreaming of pirates and circus clowns. Right before the sandman reached up and grabbed me, I wondered if other kid’s daddies were like mine.

***

My brother Johnny and I woke up at the crack of dawn and ran downstairs.

"Santa Clause came!" I yelled. "Let's open the presents!" My mom came downstairs a few minutes later but insisted that we eat breakfast first. She went into the kitchen to cook pancakes and make coffee.

"How come Daddy don't come down and open presents with us?" I asked after we finished eating.

"He's still sleeping. He'll be down later."

"I bet he's still drunk," Johnny said.

We opened most of the presents, but momma made sure that we left a few for when my father came downstairs. He came, stumbling down and plopped down on the couch around noon. He sat in his pajama bottoms and a wife-beater t-shirt with his hair in disarray. His eyes looked bloodshot and he still smelled of alcohol.

"Woman, would you get me some aspirin and a cup of coffee? My head is killing me." He looked at Johnny's bandaged forehead and a strange look crossed his face. I watched him reach out his hand and he ruffled the hair on the top of Johnny's head. Johnny flinched. "Take it, easy boy. I'm not gonna hit you again. What's the matter? Did I hit you too hard? Are you turning sissy on me? I got something that'll make you forget about that knot on your head. Go fetch that present under the tree. The one with the blue wrapping paper." Johnny did as instructed. "Go ahead, open it, boy. What'd I do, knock a screw loose?" Johnny opened his present revealing a brand new bright red Tonka truck.

"Thank you, Daddy," Johnny said and set the truck down on the couch.

My father let out a snort. "You don't sound too excited about it. That truck I smashed last night was getting old, anyway. Mike, go fetch that present in the green wrapping paper behind the tree." I jumped up and ran to the tree. Crawling behind the tree branches, I retrieved a rectangular-shaped present. When I got back to the couch, I tore into the wrapping paper and uncovered a green plastic case filled with Army men. I loved Army men. I jumped into my father's lap and hugged his neck.

"Thank you, Daddy." The next present got both my brother and me excited. Johnny opened a Hot Wheels track and I opened a box with some cars. We spent the rest of the day while Momma cooked dinner playing with the Hot Wheels. The sun went down and it was a good day. My father started drinking after supper, but he didn't get mad at anyone. He went off to bed early that night. Johnny stepped out the door into the cold night air and I followed him. He was carrying his new truck and I wondered what he was up to.

"What are you doing Johnny?" I asked when he approached the trashcan. A cloud passed across the moon and a chill shot down my back. Goosebumps cropped up on my arms and legs.

"I don't want anything that old bastard gave me. You can have the Hot Wheels track."

I stepped up next to Johnny. "He wasn't so bad today."

"It was an act," Johnny said and tossed his new truck into the trashcan.

I looked down at the shiny red truck in the bottom of the trashcan. "Why are you throwing away your new truck?"

"I don't want it. The old one was better." Johnny took his old smashed-up truck from the trashcan. "I can fix it."

"Can I have your new one?" I asked looking into the trashcan with envy.

"No. Leave it there," Johnny said and headed back into the house, so I turned around and followed him.

***

My brother Johnny and I were only two years apart age-wise and we had trouble in school. Johnny was always getting into fights because he wasn't the type of kid that would back down from anybody. I was always there to watch his back. It was the same for me. Bigger kids would pick on me and I would take their crap most of the time, but they would push me too far and I would snap. Johnny would always be there to back me up if I needed him. We spent more time in detention than we did in class. The other kids finally learned to leave us alone, but our grades suffered

Things at home were even worse than they were at school. My father was always yelling about our grades or whatever came to mind that displeased him. When we would get into trouble in school, he would whip us with his belt. When he was drunk, he would use his hands. As we grew older, his slaps with the back of his hand gave way to closed fists. We went to school several times with black eyes and bruises. After the school nurse sent the police to question him, he made sure that he never hit us in the face.

Our place of refuge from the trouble at school and the beatings at home was City Creek. City Creek was a small stream that meandered out of the San-Bernardino Mountains. Its canyon ran alongside route 330, which was the main road to Big Bear and the other mountain resorts. It was a wild area with an abundant amount of trees and wildlife such as deer and coyotes. During the summer, you had to watch out for rattlesnakes. We spent most of our spare time during the summer at City Creek.

We would pack our backpacks, head out early in the morning. We would cook our breakfast over an open fire and spend the day swimming and playing in the water. We made forts at different locations along the creek. We would dig a hole near a large rock or boulder and then cover it with fallen limbs and branches from the trees. We concealed the openings and made smoke holes at the end of the shelter to allow smoke to escape from our fire pit. We stocked these shelters with can goods and freeze-dried backpacking food. In any given shelter, we had enough food to last us for a week or more. We planned that if things got too bad at home or school, we would run away to City Creek.

During the rainy months, we moved our shelters further up into the hillside. During a rainstorm, City Creek could turn from a babbling brook to a raging torrent in an instant. There was one place near where we'd built one of the forts that we liked. During the 1930s the Army Corps of Engineers built a cement tower to measure the height of the water. They also built a cable car that stretched across the canyon for people to cross over when the water was high. Johnny and I spent many an afternoon playing in the cement tower and on the cable car.

One summer afternoon, when I was twelve and Johnny was fourteen, my mom and pop got into a fight. It was a doozy. My father came home drunk and started yelling and cursing at my mother. Johnny stepped in the middle of it and my father slammed a fist into Johnny's face knocking him out cold. He turned on my mother and beat her with his fists. I tried to pull him off her, but he knocked me aside and kept beating her.

"I'll teach you to let my dinner get cold you old bitch!" my father yelled and slammed a fist into her face. Blood flew from her nose and hit the carpet. "You need to learn some discipline, and get a handle on these kids! They're nothing but a couple of juvenile delinquents!" He beat her to the ground and the neighbors called the police. An ambulance took my mother to the hospital. Before they took her in, she told the police that she fell and she refused to press charges against my father.

I helped Johnny to his feet after he woke up, and we stood on the lawn next to the sidewalk. Sweat cropped up on my brow and ran down the side of my face. Johnny had the beginnings of a shiner. "Why don't we tell them what he did? They'll put the old son of a bitch in jail?" I whispered while the police were talking to my father. The neighbors stood in their yards watching the commotion.

Johnny shook his head trying to clear the cobwebs caused by my father's punch. "No. Don't say anything. They'd put him in jail for a little while, but then they'd let him out. After that, he'd be worse. Don't worry. After tonight, he won't beat on Mom anymore."

"What are you gonna do?" I asked.

A smirk crossed Johnny's face. "Teach that old bastard a lesson he won't forget. Do we still have those old plastic baseball bats we used to play with when we were kids?"

I nodded. "Yeah," I said. "Why don't we use the wooden ones?"

"We don't want to hurt him so bad that he can't work. We want him to think twice the next time he wants to take his fist to Mom," Johnny said.

"How are we gonna keep him from beating the shit out of us?"

"First we'll go into the hospital and see about Mom. We'll catch the bus down on the corner. Tonight he will be feeling sorry for himself and blame all his troubles on everyone else. He'll sit there drinking in his chair and later he'll stumble off to bed. We'll make ourselves scarce. Once he passes out, we'll get the baseball bats and beat the shit out of him. We'll hit him in the legs, the back of his calves, his thighs, and give him a few grand slams to the back of his head."

"What if he tries to take the bats away from us?" I asked.

Johnny laughed. "We won't let him. You'll be one side of the bed and me on the other."

"What about after?" I asked.

"Then we'll take off for City Creek. We'll lay low for a week."

The police finished talking to my father, the ambulance pulled away. A young dark-headed police officer wearing a brown suit stepped over to speak to us. He paused giving us the once over. "Tell us what happened boys," he said.

"Nothing. My mom and pop got into an argument," Johnny said.

He stepped closer to us invading our space. "Did you see your father hit your mother or abuse her in any way?"

"No. My mom fell down the stairs. She's clumsy like that," Johnny said.

The police officer rolled his eyes and his partner, an older man in his forties stepped up. He wore a white long-sleeved shirt with the sleeves rolled up. Tossing his cigarette down on the sidewalk, he killed the butt with the toe of his shoe. "Cut the crap, boys. How'd you get those bruises?"

"I got mine, fighting at school," Johnny said.

The young dark-headed police officer nodded at me. "What about you? Where'd you get those bruises?"

I put my hands in my pockets. "Like my brother said, fighting at school. When the shit goes down, I got my brother's back," I said.

The older officer shrugged. "Look, boys. I know you're trying to feed us a load of crap. Your mom told us the same BS about falling. Your pops is a drunken son of a bitch. Any man who takes his fists to his wife and kids ain't a man in my book. Tell us the truth and we'll put him behind bars where he belongs."

Johnny let out a slow breath. "And then you'll go home to your nice kids and your pretty little wife. We still have to live here. We got these bruises fighting in school." The police asked a few more questions and then left.

Johnny looked over at where my father stood in his white wife-beater t-shirt and jeans. "What?" my father asked spreading his arms apart.

"Nothing, you fat bastard! We're gonna catch the bus and go see about mom," Johnny said.

My father's eyes narrowed and I knew if the police weren't there, he would have started in on us. "Watch your mouth. None of this would have happened if she wouldn't have let my dinner get cold. All you boys ever do is whine about your mother. What about me? I work hard all day. I deserve a hot meal when I come home."

Johnny let out a distasteful laugh. "If you'd come home on time and not be drunk, your dinner wouldn't be cold."

"Yeah, yeah. Go see about your momma. You two are a couple of momma's boys anyway," my father said and stumbled inside. The screen door slammed behind him. Johnny started down the sidewalk toward the corner and I hurried to catch up with him. We caught the bus, which dropped us off at the San-Bernardino County hospital. We found our mother in the emergency room. She looked bruised and battered, but she didn't look too bad.

"You didn't say anything to the police about your father?" my mother asked.

"No, but you should have. He deserves to be in jail," Johnny said.

My mother shook her head. "That would make things worse. I shouldn't have let his dinner get cold."

"It wasn't your fault Mom," I said.

"When are they gonna let you out of here?" Johnny asked.

"The doctor said that he wants to keep me overnight to keep me under observation. I'll be okay. You boys go home now but stay away from your father. He'll be all right tomorrow." We hugged our mom goodbye and left.

That evening when we arrived back home we went to the garage and retrieve the plastic baseball bats. We entered the house through the back door and hurried upstairs. My father, who was sitting in the living room watching TV, heard us come in. "How's your mother?" my father asked.

"If you're so concerned, why don't you go see for yourself?" Johnny said.

My father turned down the TV. "Don't get smart you little shit! I'd go if I could, but I've been drinking! That's all I need is to get another DUI."

"You're always drinking. We can smell it from here. You fucking disgust me," Johnny said.

"Watch your mouth, or I finish what I started earlier. I'll put you in the room next to her since you're such a momma's boy."

We stashed the baseball bats in Johnny's bedroom. "We'll wait until he's good and drunk. When he stumbles up to go to bed, we'll give him about a half-hour to fall asleep then we'll go up there."

"What are we going to do in the meantime?" I asked.

"Pack our gear for City Creek."

We spent the next four hours packing our camping gear. We packed enough clothes for a week, and we each packed a light jacket. The weather was still warm at night, but up in the canyon that City Creek ran through, the wind could get cold. Finished packing, I laid down on the floor and read a comic book. Johnny went through his baseball card collection. We heard my father stumble up to bed at ten-thirty.

"We'll give him a half-hour," Johnny said.

I looked up from my comic. "Are you sure you want to do this?"

"Yeah, I'm sure. Don't you? We're doing it for Mom."

I glanced back at my comic book. "And a little for us," I said.

Johnny laughed. "A lot for us. I have to admit. I'll enjoy it, as much as that old bastard beats on us."

A half-hour later, we crept down the hallway to our parent's room, the floor creaked and my heart leaped into my throat. Johnny stopped, holding the baseball bat over his shoulder for a few seconds. He moved forward and I followed. At the door to my parent's bedroom, Johnny stopped and pushed on the door. The door squeaked open, and we saw my father laying on his back snoring. He smelled of alcohol, pissy underwear, and puke. Johnny stepped around to the other side of the bed. I crept up next to where my father lay, Johnny raised the bat over his head and I raised my bat over mine. My father let go with a stinky beer fart and we both giggled. "Shi. He'll wake up. Are you ready?" Johnny whispered after we got our laughter under control.

I nodded. He brought his bat down hard across my father's chest and I brought mine down crashing across his legs. The plastic bat made a loud smacking sound when it hit my father's body.

"Ouch! What the hell? You little son of a bitch!" my father yelled. He jumped up in bed and lunged toward me, I jumped back and Johnny swung his bat. Johnny loved baseball. He could knock a ball out of the park at will. He swung a grand slam connecting to the back of my father's head. The blow spun my father around and he landed on his side on the bed. Our blows rained down on him like a hailstorm. "I'll kill you, you evil little shits!" my father screamed.

"If -you-ever-hit-my-mother-again-I'm-going-to-kill-you-you.-fuckin-bastard!" Johnny yelled between blows. His breath came out in little huffs between each blow and tears ran down his face. Anger surged through me and I felt tears running down my face as well.

Choking up on the bat, I took another angry swing. We beat his chest, his sides, his arms, his legs, and his thighs until we didn't have the strength to swing anymore. By the time we were through, my father had quit screaming and he lay on the bed blubbering like a baby.

Johnny threw his baseball bat down on the floor. We stood there for a few seconds looking down at him. Disgusted, I tossed my bat in the corner. "Now you know how it feels," Johnny said. We left my father crying and blubbering in his bed.

"That's no way for a boy to treat his father," he said and continued sobbing. We stopped by Johnny's room, grabbed our backpacks, and headed out the door. Johnny hurried across the lawn, but I stopped on the sidewalk and looked back at the house. The place looked sinister in the reflected moonlight. An owl hooted in the trees near the street.

"What about Mom?" I asked.

"Oh, he'll go pick her up tomorrow when he's sober. He'll be as sweet as pie. He might be a bit sore, though," Johnny said and laughed.

I giggled releasing some pent-up adrenaline. "I imagine so. I almost felt sorry for him."

"Not me. The pitiful son of a bitch deserves what he gets," Johnny said. We tossed our backpacks onto our backs and headed down the street.

***

Chapter 9

My brother Johnny and I hiked halfway across town. Around two in the morning, an old man in an older blue Ford pickup truck picked us up. He had a mangy-looking dog sitting on the passenger seat of the pickup.

"Where are you two young fellers going?" he asked when he pulled up next to us.

"We're heading up to City Creek. We plan on camping out for a couple of days," Johnny said. The dog barked and stuck its head out the window.

The old man rubbed the gray stubble on his chin and said, "City Creek? That's that creek that runs out of the mountains by the highway to Big Bear, ain't it?"

"That's the one," Johnny said.

"You boys are in luck, then. I'm headin' up to Big Bear Lake to do some fishin'. I have to go right by there. Jump in the back."

We climbed into the back of his pickup truck and he dropped us off on the corner of Highland and Boulder Road. We jumped out of the back of the truck and put on our backpacks.

"Good luck fishing," I said to the old man.

"You boys be careful. Watch out for snakes."

I nodded.

"We will," Johnny said. The old man gave us a friendly wave and pulled away. His truck backfired putting out a belch of blue smoke. "Why can't our dad be like that?" Johnny asked.

"Yeah, that old man was cool. It would have been nice if dad took us fishing and stuff like that." I zipped up my jacket to stave off the cold night air. We headed down a narrow paved tree-lined road leading north into the canyon. We used our flashlights to guide the way being careful not to trip over broken asphalt. They hadn't maintained the road in years. The road led to an orange grove to the north that overlooked the canyon. The only vehicles using the road belonged to the farmer that owned the orange grove. Sometimes teenagers used the road to party at City Creek.

About a mile and a half up the road, we took a dirt road heading east. Tree limbs hung over the road forming a canopy above us. Our flashlights had trouble piercing the darkness. A bird screeched up in the treetops. I heard a branch snap to my left and whirled around shining my flashlight into the darkness. The hairs on the back of my neck stood up. My brother grabbed me by the shoulders from behind.

"Boo!" He yelled and I almost jumped out of my shoes.

"Damn it! Quit doing that! I almost shit myself!" Johnny started laughing and soon, we were both laughing. "Damn it's dark." We stumbled along down the road and Johnny farted. We both laughed. "Good Lord. Something must have crawled up inside you and died," I said.

Johnny couldn't stop laughing. "Yeah, and you smell like you eat and shit out of the same hole."

The sound of the stream dancing over the rocks filled our ears when we stepped out from the trees at the end of the road. The stars looked like a warm blanket up above us and off in the hills I heard a coyote howl. I tossed my backpack down on a sandy area about one hundred yards from the creek. Johnny set his backpack down next to mine. We sat down in the sand and took off our hiking boots. Once we had our boots off, we tipped toed down through the rocks to the stream and put our feet in the water. The ice-cold water from the mountain stream caused a chill to run up my spine.

"Man that feels good," I said.

"It feels bitchin'" Johnny said pulling a pack of smokes from his coat pocket.

"Can I have one of those?"

Johnny tossed me the pack. He pulled a book of matches from his pants pocket, lit his cigarette, and handed me the matches. I made a fire, lit my smoke, and listened to the coyotes yapping up in the surrounding hillside. The smell of tobacco smoke filled the air.

"I don't think I could take all this shit with Dad if we didn't have City Creek to come to," Johnny said.

"I know what you mean. It's so peaceful up here that, when we're here, I never want to leave. It's like all that stuff back home doesn't matter."

We talked until the sun came up over the eastern horizon. We lay in the sand and listened to the creek dance over the rocks.

***

The sound of girlish laughter woke me from a sound slumber and a cool breeze tickled my face. I sat up listening, heard a girl squeal and another one laughed while Johnny lay next to me snoring. There was a loud plunking sound and a girl screamed. The sound of splashing water wafted on the wind. The first girl squealed again.

"Knock it off, Jen! I'm, soaked already!" Two other girls started laughing, so I shook Johnny's shoulder.

"Knock it off asshole. I'm trying to sleep," Johnny mumbled.

"Wake up, Johnny. There are girls down by the creek," I whispered.

"What?" Johnny said, sitting up, and knuckled sleep from his eyes.

I sat down in the sand next to him. "There are some girls down by the creek playing in the water."

"Let's go down there and see what they're up to."

We stood up and goosebumps formed upon my exposed skin. I put on my shirt and my boots. I had slept in my pants, but Johnny had on only his boxer shorts. He put on his pants and his shirt and I stood waiting while he put on his boots. We headed over to the creek bank and my eyes widened when I looked down at the girls playing in the water.

A big grin crossed Johnny's face. One girl with black hair stood in waist-deep water with her arms spread apart. She wore cut-off jeans and a blue t-shirt. Her t-shirt, now soaked to the skin was transparent. My eyes tracked her petite form. Her rock-hard nipples pressed against the fabric of her shirt. A girl with long blonde hair and large breasts stood in the water. She was about to splash the dark-haired girl. She wore blue bikini bottoms and no top. Across the stream sat an older girl that looked like a junior or a senior. She had long red hair. She sat on a rock dangling her feet into the water. She wore jeans with the pant legs rolled up and was taking off her white t-shirt. My eyes darted back and forth between the three girls. They finally came to rest on the blonde's large round breasts.

My brother let out a wolf whistle and both the dark-haired girl, and the blonde looked up at the same time. Their eyes widened and they both crossed their arms across their chest. The redhead across the stream pulled her top back down real fast.

"How long have you two been standing there? You, you stalkers," the dark-haired girl said, batting her pretty brown eyes.

Johnny laughed and I noticed a red hue forming on the dark-haired girl's face. "Long enough to get an eye full. Don't stop on our account. We're enjoying the show."

I laughed. "Yeah, you've got half your clothes off. You might as well go all the way," I said.

The blonde pointed her finger at me. "I know who you guys are. I've seen you at school. You're the McDonald brothers. You're nothing but trouble."

Johnny gave her a lascivious smirk. "You got us there." Johnny sat down on a rock next to the streambed and started tossing stones into the water. I sat down next to him.

"I don't know. They don't look so bad. They're both, kind of cute," the redhead sitting across the water said. I felt the beginnings of a blush shoot across my face and something started to stir in my lower regions. Johnny raised his eyebrows and pulled a pack of smokes from his shirt pocket. The blonde and the dark-haired girl waded through the water. Johnny pulled a book of matches from his pants pocket. The blonde and the dark-haired girl turned their back to us. Johnny lit his smoke, handed me the pack and I shook out a cigarette. The blonde put on her shirt. The dark-haired girl took off her soaking wet white t-shirt and pulled a dark blue one from a knapsack. I admired her shapely back while I lighted my cigarette.

"Can I have one of those?" the redhead from across the water said. I looked at Johnny, and he nodded. The water fell over a dam of sorts forming the small pool where the girls were playing. I scampered across the stream. Stepping on the rocks above the dam, I handed the redhead girl the pack of cigarettes.

"Thank you," she said and smiled. I struck a match and held it up so she could light a cigarette. The blonde and the dark-haired girl, now dressed, sat down on a rock next to Johnny. The redhead fired up her cigarette and blew smoke across the water.

"Can we have one of those cigarettes?" the blonde asked.

Johnny nodded so I passed out the cigarettes.

After each one of the girls had a cigarette, I tucked the matches inside the cigarette pack. I wound up, like if I were throwing a fastball and threw the pack of cigarettes across the creek. It landed at Johnny's feet. He picked up the pack, tucked them into his pocket, and then crossed the stream to join us.

"I know a place upstream that is better than this. The water falls over a small waterfall and forms a big pool that is deep enough for swimming. If you girls want, we'll show you where it is," Johnny said.

"Okay, if it's not too far. We have to be home by dark." the blonde said and laughed. I enjoyed the sound of her bubbly laughter.

"It's only a couple of miles upstream. It won't take long," Johnny said.

"I know you guys are the McDonald brothers. One of you is Johnny and the other Mike, but I never knew which was which," the redhead said.

I glanced at the red-headed girl sitting next to me. "I'm Mike. That's my big brother, Johnny."

The blonde-headed girl looked up at Johnny and smiled. "I'm Sharon." She nodded to the dark-haired girl. "That's my friend, Connie, and the redhead across the stream sitting next to Mike is Jenifer." Johnny stood up, tossed his cigarette down on the bank of the stream, and stamped it out with his boot. He bent down and covered it with sand, straightened back up and his eyes darted upstream. "If you girls want to get back before dark, we'd best get going."

Johnny and I crossed the stream to retrieve our backpacks. The girls gathered their things then crossed over to join us by the road.

"Lead the way," Sharon said to Johnny.

Johnny led us down into the streambed. He made his way through some high brush and headed north into the canyon. The sound of water darting over the rocks created a constant background noise. Connie and Jenifer followed along behind Johnny giggling and laughing. Sharon fell back strolling along beside me at the rear. She looked at me and smiled. "I thought you were going to get eye strain back there for a few minutes."

I laughed feeling my cheeks turn red. "You can't blame a guy for that. It's not every day you catch three half-naked girls playing in the water."

Sharon giggled and took my arm. "Depending on how secluded this place is you might see three girls all the way naked."

I laughed feeling something rise in my britches. "Oh, it's secluded, all right. Johnny and I have a fort up by there. How come you're not up there hanging out with him? Most girls fall all over

Johnny." I noticed a small fish darting about in a shallow area near the bank of the stream.

"Oh he's cool, but he's a little rough for me. You're cuter," Sharon said, and then reached up and kissed me on the cheek. I felt my face flush I touched my cheek where she kissed me. We continued up the canyon following the creek for another hour. We took a well-used path that meandered along next to the water. Pine trees and a few scrub oaks lined the streambed. A few times, we had to cross the creek jumping from rock to rock. I saw a red-tailed hawk floating on the thermals above us. Sharon slipped off one of the rocks, fell into the stream, and let out a squeal. I held out my hand, she took it and I helped her out of the water. I enjoyed the soft feel of her skin and tried to ignore her wet shirt clinging to her young perky breasts. We continued up the canyon. The sound of the girls chatting back and forth echoed across and the water. The air smelled of sage.

The canyon snaked around a bend and widened out. Water shot over a waterfall forming a large pool below it and a cable car set suspended above the canyon to our left. A cement tower stood down near the sandy bank of the stream. "We're here," Johnny said, taking off his backpack, and set it down on a sandy area near the pool.

"It's beautiful," Sharon said, standing with her hands on her hips.

"Yeah, I like this place. It's peaceful," I said. I took off my backpack, set it down next to Johnny's. The girls set their things down next to ours and huddled to gather like a flock of hens in a chicken coop. Stepping next to Johnny, I heard them whispering back and forth, and then Connie laughed. They finally came over to where Johnny and I stood near the water and Sharon was their spokesperson.

"Look, guys. We'll go skinny dipping with you. We'll strip down to our birthday suits, but don't think you're going to get laid. We expect you to get naked too. We'll let you fool around a bit and feel us up, but that's as far as it goes."

Johnny laughed. "That's enough for me." He took off his boots and pulled off his shirt. Shucking his pants, Johnny dropped his boxer shorts and ran for the water. He dived in, making a big splash, and let out a blood-curdling scream.

"God that water is cold!" Johnny said, crossing his arms in front of his chest. His skin looked as if it was starting to turn blue.

I took my time undressing so I could watch the girls. Sharon took off her shirt, tossing it aside, to reveal her large breasts. She caught me looking and smiled. Sharon dropped her bikini bottom and ran for the water. Connie pulled off her shirt to reveal her firm midsized breasts. She tossed off her cut-off shorts, and let out a squeal when she hit the water. Jenifer tossed back her long red hair, removed her shirt and then her jeans. She wasn't wearing any underwear. I watched her shapely bottom swish back and forth, as she ran for the water. Feeling self-conscious, I bent down, took off my boots and my socks. I removed my pants and boxer shorts. Feeling my face reddening, I ran across the sand as fast as I could and jumped into the water doing a cannonball. I felt like someone had hit me in the chest with a sledgehammer when I stood up in chest-deep water sputtering.

"My balls shrunk to the size of peas and turned into ice," I said. "They feel like they're gonna fall off."

Johnny laughed. "Mine, are hiding underneath my armpit to keep warm."

Sharon giggled crossing her arms in front of her chest and said, "It is a bit nippy." The rest of the girls laughed, Johnny swam over next to the falls where the water was deep and Connie joined him. Sharon and I swam over; the water was over our heads so we clung to the rocks to keep from slipping under. A cool breeze blew across the water. Goosebumps formed upon my exposed skin. I watched Jenifer glide through the water, staying about one foot under the surface. Her long red hair flowed behind her like a long velvet mane. She popped up next to me and grabbed my arm to keep from slipping under. I felt her left breast brush up against my right arm. A stirring sensation shot through my lower regions. I noticed small fish darting about at the edge of the pool.

"Check this out," Johnny said. He dived underneath the waterfall and disappeared. The girls and I followed. A small cave had formed behind the waterfall. Johnny climbed up sitting on a rock with his legs dangling in the water, so we climbed up and joined him. I couldn't stop shaking because of the cold water. Jenifer sat down next to me on my right and Sharon on my left. Connie sat on the other side of Johnny. I felt Jenifer's hand on my leg. Johnny dived back into the water, swam underneath the falls, and headed back to the shallow end of the pool. The girls and I followed. Sharon swam up to me, pressed her firm wet body against mine, and kissed me.

We played in the water for a few hours. The weather warmed up, and then we lay out on the sand for a while on our stomachs to soak up some sun and dry off. The girls let us put suntan lotion on their backs. By noon, we had our clothes back on. Johnny and I cooked lunch, frying up some bacon and eggs that we brought with us. The smell of frying bacon caused my stomach to growl. I opened up a can of beans and heated them over a campfire that Johnny started. After lunch, we showed the girls our fort, which was set up at the base of the canyon. We sat around inside the fort talking and smoking cigarettes for most of the afternoon. We took another dip in the creek about five PM and started back downstream. Back at the bottom end of the creek, we said our goodbyes. All three of the girls each gave us a hug and a kiss. I enjoyed the taste of Sharron's raspberry-flavored lip gloss.

"Don't be a stranger at school. If you see me in the hall or something, say hi," Sharon said. "We can go out or something."

"Yeah, and as for everyone at school, the skinny dipping part never happened," Jenifer said.

I laughed, making a zipping motion across my lips, and said, "I'll never tell."

Johnny watched the girls climb into their little white car and drive away. "Damn. I can't believe that shit happened," Johnny said.

"Me neither bro. Those girls had some nice tits."

"I noticed that Sharon took a liking to you. We'd best head back upstream before it gets dark." My brother Johnny and I hiked back up to our fort further up the canyon. Johnny cooked our dinner, a can of baked beans, over an open fire. We stayed up late talking and laughing while we roasted marsh mellows over the fire. I held my hands out over the flames enjoying the warmth. I was having a good time and enjoyed Johnny's company. The problems at home were far from our minds. The week flew by; we spent our time, hiking, fishing, and playing in the water. Friday came and we decided to go home. Pitching our backpacks onto our backs, we hiked back out to the road and hitchhiked across town. When we came into the house, my parents acted as though we'd only been gone for a few minutes. My father sat in his chair smoking a cigar and drinking a beer.

"Did you boys have a fun time at City Creek?" my mom asked when we came in.

We stopped in the living room. "Yeah, Mom. We had a great time. What's for dinner?" I asked.

"I'll have some fried chicken ready in a few minutes. You boys get cleaned up."

My father looked up at Johnny and grinned. "You know those old plastic baseball bats you kids used to keep in the garage?"

"Yeah," Johnny said, and a smirk crossed his face.

"Well, I cut those things up with my band saw and threw them away."

Johnny laughed. "That's all right. We're getting too big for plastic bats anyway. The next time I need to play ball, I'll use a wooden one."

***

My father never hit my mother after that, but he slapped her now and then when he was drunk. He saved his fists for us. What he used on my mother was his tongue and it cut like a dagger. He wouldn't yell too much, he would say mean hurtful things that made her cry. Things got worse for Johnny and me; when the old man got drunk, he would turn his rage on us. We tried to stay away from home as much as possible, but things got worse at school as well. Our grades fell and we began to hang with the wrong crowd. We got into trouble a lot, but most of the time we tried to steer clear of the law.

My father seemed to have a personal vendetta against Johnny. He would start in on him for the slightest reason, even when he wasn't drunk. Johnny would stand up to him and Johnny never let my father see him cry. It came to a head one night a couple of years later when Johnny was sixteen. The police caught Johnny shoplifting and brought him home.

My father acted nice and polite to the police officers when they brought Johnny home that night. "I don't know what I'm gonna do with that boy. His mother and I worry about him. What's a hard-working man to do? We try. Believe me; we try. You won't have to pick this one up again. We'll make sure he sees the error of his way. Thank you for bringing him home, officer. You have a nice evening," my father said and closed the door. He moved the curtain aside looking out the window. When he saw the police car pull away, he whirled around and hit Johnny in the face. Blood squirted from Johnny's nose. He flew across the room and landed on my mother's glass coffee table shattering it into minute pieces.

"Now look what you did? You worthless piece of shit!" my father yelled. He strutted forward with his fists balled up, my mother screamed and Johnny jumped to his feet. He wiped the blood from his mouth and nose and went at my father with his fists. My father knocked him to the ground and began to slam his fist in his face.

"If- you-ever-come-home in the back of a police car again, I'll kill you!" my father yelled. Spittle flew into the air. Between each word, he slammed a fist into Johnny's face. I jumped onto my father's back and pummeled the back of his head. I tried to grab him around the throat and pull him off my brother, but the old man was too strong.

"James! Stop! You'll kill him!" my mother yelled. My father threw me off his back and stumbled to one knee. His left hand went to his chest. My brother's face looked like hamburger meat. He had a broken nose, his eye was turning black and he had a split lip.

Johnny, spit out a tooth. "Why don't you finish it, old man?" he whispered.

My father wheezed, huffing and puffing, and couldn't catch his breath. "You're gonna be the death of me boy. Why don't you go up to your room, before you make me, mad?" he said.

Johnny jumped up, ran upstairs and I followed him. Tears streamed down his blood-soaked face. Johnny grabbed his backpack and his jacket, but paused at the bedroom door and wiped the blood from his face. I followed Johnny down the stairs and out the front door letting the door slam behind me.

"Get back here boy!" my father yelled.

Johnny stormed across the front lawn to the sidewalk.

"Where are you going? To City Creek? Wait, I'll get my things and come with you," I said.

"No. I'm not going to City Creek. I'm getting the fuck out of here for good. That old bastard has hit me for the last time." We stood in the middle of the street under a street light. I had my arms folded across my chest due to the evening chill.

"Wait a minute. I'll get my things."

Johnny shook his head. "No. You need to stay here and protect Mom." He stepped up to me, gave me a bear hug and I felt his wet tears and warm blood against the side of my face. Johnny pulled away from me. "Don't let the old bastard beat you. Stay away from him as much as you can. After you grow up and leave home, we'll run into each other again sometime. Goodbye, little brother." With that, Johnny turned around and disappeared into the night.

***

Things got a little better at home after Johnny left. Dad received a promotion at work and bought a nicer house on the north end of San Bernardino. My father and I pretty much ignored each other. He still got drunk and flew into rages, but he never beat my mother anymore. Oh, he still gave her an occasional slap when he was drunk, but he never beat her with his fist. He treated me as if I was invisible, and that was all right with me. My mom received a postcard from Johnny about a year after he left. He said that he had hitchhiked across the country to New York City. He said that he joined a street gang, got arrested and they sent him to reform school. After that, we didn't hear from him for another year or two.

When I turned seventeen, my mom received another postcard. This time it was from Germany. Johnny said that after they let him out of reform school he joined the Army. They sent him to Germany. He said he was having the time of his life. When I turned eighteen, I joined the Marines. I kept it a secret from my mom and dad until the day came for me to leave for boot camp. I packed my bags and stepped into the living room. Mom sat on the couch knitting and watching TV. Pop sat in his favorite chair drinking a beer and smoking a cigar.

Breathing in the stink of his cheap cigar, I paused for a few moments. My eyes darted back and forth between my mother and father before I spoke.

"I'm leaving," I said.

My mother looked up from her knitting and my father glanced up from the television.

"Leaving? Where to?" my mother asked.

A nervous ball formed in my stomach. "For boot camp. I joined the Marines."

"God damn you!" my father roared jumping to his feet. He charged across the living room with his fists balled up at his sides and I took a step backward raising my hands.

"You can't talk me out of it. I've already signed the papers. I'm scheduled to catch a bus at six o'clock," I said.

"You stupid son of a bitch! You have no idea what you're in for!" my father yelled and slammed a fist into my face. The blow knocked me backward and onto the couch next to my mother. A drop of blood dripped from the corner of my mouth.

"Stop it, James! You were in the Marines! I'd think you'd be proud!" my mother screamed.

My father paused looking down at my mother in disgust. "And I suppose you want him to turn out like me?"

I wiped the blood from my mouth, jumped to my feet, and put up my fists. "That's the last time you hit me, old man. If you try it again, I'll kick your fat ass."

My father let out a sound that was half laugh and half sob. A tear tracked down his face and that was the first time I ever saw my father cry. He lifted his hand waving me off. "Oh, go ahead. They'll make a man out of you, but you don't know what you're letting yourself in for. If I were you, I'd think long and hard and go do something else. You're a smart kid. You should go to college."

That shocked me. My father never complimented anyone.

"I have thought about it. Besides, it's too late. I already signed the contract."

"When they send you halfway around the world, to some war don't blame me. When you're sitting in some rice paddy with your buddy's brains and body parts all over you, don't say I didn't warn you." After that, my father did something, unexpected. He hugged me and when he turned me loose, more tears rolled down his face. He reached into his back pocket for a handkerchief. "Mother, would you make a pot of coffee and call this boy a taxi?" We sat back down on the couch and talked while drinking coffee until the taxicab came. I stood up, hugged my mother, kissed her, my father stuck out his hand and we shook. His grip was strong for an old man. After saying our goodbyes, I stepped out the door, crossed the lawn, and climbed into the back of the taxicab. Leaning back in the seat, I took one last look at the home place. The taxicab pulled away from the curb on the first leg of my journey to my new life in the Marine Corps.

***

CHAPTER 10

I took a step back, dazed and reeling from the memories that flashed through my head. Sweat beaded on my forehead. My hands clenched into fists at my sides. My heart pounded the inside of my ribcage. The little boy in the grocery store stood up and his father jerked him by the arm pulling him back over toward his cart. He pulled his hand back and started to hit him again.

"Hey! Don't do that! You dumb son of a bitch!" I yelled and hurried over to where they stood.

The kid's father turned to face me, and I noticed his big beer gut hanging out from the bottom of his grubby t-shirt. "What did you call me? Mind your own business!" He raised his hands facing palm out. Before he could say anything more, I slammed a fist into his face putting everything I had into the punch. The boy jumped back, his eyes widened and the man flew backward landing against a shelf filled with can peas. He fell to the ground and several cans of peas fell off the shelf landing on top of him. One bounced off his head. I grabbed the man by the front of his shirt and fired off three quick punches to his face. Blood splattered against my shirt and flowed from his nose. A tiny drop leaked from the corner of his mouth.

"It doesn't feel so good does it?" I said in a cold quiet voice.

"Please don't hit me no more, Mr.," the man pleaded, raising his hands in front of his battered face. People in the store stopped and stared.

Over the PA system, a store clerk said, "Clean up on aisle number three."

"Give me your wallet," I said. I knelt over the man with my hand out.

The man's bottom jaw dropped. "What?"

"Your wallet. Give it to me!"

He reached into his back pocket and handed me his billfold. "Here I've got money. Take what you want."

I took out his driver's license. "I don't want your fucking money." I looked at his driver's license committing the name and address to memory. "Frank Bowers. Two, two, four, eight, four Vine Street. Highland California. Now I know who you are and I know where you live. I'm gonna keep track of you. If you see a strange truck out in front of your house, that will be me. If I ever hear of or see, you beating up on your kid again, I'm gonna come see you. Are you married?"

"What?" The man was almost in tears.

"I said are you married? Do you have a wife, you son of a bitch?"

"Yeah, yeah, I'm married."

"What's your wife's name?" I demanded.

"Mary."

"I assume an asshole like you that beats up on his kid beats his wife as well. If you ever hit your kid or your wife again, I'm gonna come to your house. I'm going to turn your face into hamburger meat," I said and pulled my fist back.

"No, I won't! Don't hit me again!" he said holding up his hands to protect his face.

I shoved him back to the floor, stood up, and turned to the kid. He stood looking on in blue-eyed terror. I grabbed a package of ink pens and took one out. Taking a business card from my wallet, I wrote my phone number down on the back of it. "What's your name?" I said softening my tone.

The little boy seemed to calm down. He wiped the tears from his eyes and said, "Billy."

"Billy, I'm sorry you had to see that." I put the business card inside his shirt pocket. "If your daddy ever hits you again, call me and I'll make him stop." I grabbed a handful of candy and handed it to him. The little boy's face lit up. "Here, you can have this. I'm buying." The little boy held out his hands. I filled them with candy, went back to my shopping cart, and tossed the opened package of ink pens into the basket. The boy's father was picking himself up off the floor when I passed him by heading for the checkout line.

"Thank you Mr. Thanks for the candy," Billy said.

The people in the store watching began to cheer and clap their hands. The girl at the checkout line smiled when I stepped up. "That was a good thing you did, Mr. That asshole comes in here all the time. He's always hitting that little boy."

"I can't stand rude obnoxious people. Especially people that hurt little kids. I gave that kid two dollars worth of candy. Put it on my bill."

"Okay, sir, but you'd better get out of here fast. One of the customers called the police."

"Thanks for the info," I said and paid for my groceries. She smiled and wrote her phone number down on my receipt. Outside, the sky clouded over and a cold breeze blew across the parking lot. I pushed the cart to my truck and I had finished loading the groceries when I heard a police siren. Pulling out of the parking lot, I passed a police car pulling in.

From the grocery store, I headed to the hardware store. Strolling up and down the aisles, I put some things into my shopping cart. I put in several boxes of short little nails, and I threw in several six-inch pipe nipples along with the end caps. I tossed in a soldering iron, a roll of solder, and a small propane torch. Heading for the electrical department, I put in several feet of wire. It was the copper kind with green insulation. At the checkout line, I noticed several prepaid cell phones, so I tossed four of them into my cart. I gave the pretty, young girl working at the checkout my debit card and she rang up the sale. In the parking lot, I sat behind the wheel of my truck drumming my fingers on the steering wheel.

"Where to next?" I said to Lucy. Pulling out of the parking lot, I headed west on Highland Avenue. Passing Galloway's Gun World, I pulled into a Big 5 sporting goods a few blocks down the road. The sound of loud pipes caused my hands to white knuckle the steering wheel. My pulse quickened and anger surged through me. I glanced over and watched the two bikers head down the street on their Harleys. They were regular guys and didn't sport a club patch on the back of their vests. I entered the store, snagged a cart, tossed a roll of cannon fuse into it, and headed to the area where they sold the guns. Strolling down the aisles, I put several small round cylinders filled with BBs into the cart. I stepped up to the counter where they sold the guns.

"Can I help you?" I fat balding clerk asked. He had on a wrinkled white shirt, black pants and he wore glasses with thick black frames. The glasses slipped down the bridge of his nose, so he shoved them back in place.

"I need some powder."

"You plan on doing some reloading?" the clerk said, leaning against the counter.

I nodded. "Yeah, give me a can of smokeless powder and a can of black powder. I've got an old muzzleloader that I haven't shot in a while." The clerk turned to a shelf behind him and then set two cans of gunpowder on the counter. I put them in my basket and headed to the front of the store. Later out in the parking lot, I sat behind the wheel wondering if there was anything, I forgot. I watched two teenage girls stroll by. One of them let out a giggle. Lucky stuck his head out of the passenger side window and barked.

"Oh, what a cute dog," one of the girls said. They smiled and waved, so I waved back.

"No, that about covers it," I said to myself. I fired up the truck, pulled out of the parking lot, and headed for home.

I pulled the truck into the front driveway and climbed out of the cab. Lucky jumped down from the driver's side. I crossed the front lawn, entered the house by the front door, and crossed the living room. I let Lucky out the sliding glass door and into the backyard. I went back to the kitchen, took a beer from the refrigerator, and headed for the living room. Picking up the phone, I dialed Robert Donovan's number. He picked up on the third ring. After we said our hellos, I told him about my adventure in the supermarket. The line went silent for a few seconds.

"I heard about that incident. No one wanted to give out too much information. Unfortunately, I can't do anything about him beating up on his kid. No one admitted to seeing him hit the boy. The guy refused to press charges. You're in the clear on the assault charge. You put some fear in his heart." I read off the guy's name and address. "I'll run his information through my computer and see what comes up. After that, I'll go, pay him a little visit. I'll have something for you on that other matter we discussed yesterday. I'd like to come by about six. Is that okay?"

I popped the top on my beer. "That would be great. I'll have the beer on ice."

"All right. I'll see you then," Donovan said and hung up the phone.

I headed back into the kitchen and retrieved the items I bought from the store. I headed into my garage with my beer. Inside the garage, I put the gunpowder up in a cabinet well away from my workbench. Retrieving a pipe wrench from my toolbox, I put one of the pipe nipples in the vice on my workbench. I screwed on an end cap. Opening the vice, I inserted the next pipe nipple and tightened the vice. Once I had an end cap on one end of each of the pipe nipples, I crossed the garage and took out an electric drill. I put an end cap into the vice. The whirring sound of the drill filled the interior of the garage as I drilled a hole through the center of the end cap.

I paused for a moment, taking a pull from my beer, crossed the garage, and turned on my stereo. Led Zeppelin's Stairway to Heaven blared from the speaker. I put another end cap into the vice and drilled a hole in its center. Finished with the remaining end caps, I set them aside. Bending down, I rummaged around under my workbench and found a metal bowl. I picked up one of the boxes of matches that I had bought at the store and broke the heads off the matches. I tossed them into the bowl. I used the end of a wooden-handled hammer to smash the match heads into a fine powder.

Tossing in a glob of Petroleum Jelly into the bowl, I mixed the ingredients. I added some other chemicals I had bought at the store until it formed a thin paste. Taking one of the pipe nipples from the bench, I secured it into the vice. I poured the improvised explosive into the pipe. Finished with that I threaded a piece of cannon fuse through an end cap that I had drilled a hole through earlier and stuck one end into the explosive mixture filling the pipe. I clipped off the cannon fuse leaving about six inches of space. I set the pipe nipple aside to let the explosive mixture harden. Next, I grabbed the next nipple and repeated the procedure. Once I used up all the pipe nipples I still had some of the homemade explosive left. I poured the rest of it into a small tin so it would harden into a small block. Grabbing the BBs, I poured BBs onto the hardened explosives along with some nails in each pipe nipple. I left two inches of space at the top.

Crossing the garage, I took the gunpowder from the cabinet. Using a small funnel, I poured gunpowder into each pipe. Taking a small brush, I cleaned the threads on the open end of the pipe nipples and tightened down the end caps. I took out some of the wire and my soldering iron and went to work on one of the cell phones I had bought. Taking the lid of the small tin to my vice, I drilled two holes into its top. I put the ends of the wires that I had soldered in to the cell phone through the holes and into the explosive mixture. Then I put the lid back on the tin. I put the cell phone back together and duck taped it to the tin. When I dialed the phone's number the spark would set off the explosives.

"Not perfect but it will do," I said to myself. Finished, I gathered my homemade pipe bombs and hid them inside the cabinet where I'd put the gunpowder. I headed back into the house to cook my dinner and watch some TV. Opening the sliding glass door, I let Lucky into the house and headed to the kitchen to fry up some steaks. I tossed Lucky his steak and sat down in front of the TV to watch the news while I ate. The doorbell rang.

I grabbed my cane and hobbled across the room. My back was sore and my legs felt shaky. Opening the front door, I looked at a stocky young man in his mid-thirties with coal dark hair and dark eyes. A smile crossed his face.

"It's good to see you, Mike," the man said.

"You must be Donovan. I recognize your voice from the phone. You look kind of familiar, but my memory has been a little fuzzy lately."

He shrugged. "My memory would be fuzzy too if I'd been through what you've been through," Donovan said. He held up a manila envelope. "I brought you something."

I stepped aside opening the door wider. "Come on in. I was frying up some stakes. I hope you're hungry," I said and led Donovan into my living room.

"I never turn down a good steak. They smell delicious."

"Smart man. Have a seat," I said and headed into the kitchen. I fixed him up a plate. Along with the juicy steak, I put a baked potato dripping with butter and a fresh garden salad onto his plate. I took a beer from the refrigerator, brought the meal into the living room, and set Donovan up with a TV tray. I handed him his plate along with a cold beer.

"I talked to the guy from the market. I don't think he'll be hitting his kid anymore. You scared the shit out of him."

I nodded. "Good. He deserved worse than what I gave him." I pointed my TV remote at the boob tube and changed the channel to a football game. Lucky lay down on the floor next to me.

Donovan tossed me the manila envelope. "That's everything I have on the Lost Souls. They have chapters in California, Nevada, Utah, and Idaho."

I opened up the envelope and studied photographs of various members of the bike club. Setting aside several written reports for further study, I looked at the pictures. "They don't have any chapters in Wyoming or Montana?"

Donovan shook his head.

"The Green River Boys control Wyoming and Montana. They're not as bad as some. They're a bunch of red-neck white boys. They keep to themselves but don't cross them. If you fuck with them, they can get nasty."

I looked up. "They don't get along with the Lost Souls?"

Donavan shook his head. "Nobody gets along with the Souls. They're trash."

We finished our steaks and spent the next two hours drinking beer and watching football. Donovan wasn't such a bad guy for a cop. After he left I studied the material. I thumbed through the pictures and paused looking down at the face of JD Quinn. *Mr. Scar Face himself.*

"Mr. Quinn when I'm done with you, the scars on your face will be the least of your worries. I'm coming, Mr. Quinn, and hell's coming with me," I said to myself.

***

The real estate guy came by the next morning; I showed him my house and we talked price. I signed the papers for him to list the house and he put up a real estate sign out front before he left. He said that he thought the house would sell fast enough. I set the price below market value in hopes of a quick sale. I spent two hours every morning walking and was growing stronger every day. By the end of the week, I no longer needed the cane and the headaches were lessening. I spent my days studying the material on the Lost Souls. I knew every name and could place the names with the faces. I also spent a lot of time on the internet.

The old cowboy that I had bought Totem from called me on Wednesday and said that he had a buyer for my horse. A young couple showed up the next day with a beat-up old pickup truck and a horse trailer. They paid me seven hundred dollars for the animal. I said my goodbyes to Totem. I watched them load him up into the horse trailer and haul him away. A tear tracked down my face and a lump formed in my throat. *There goes another part of my life. Sharon loved that horse.* I sat down in my living room with a bottle of beer to watch a football game when the phone rang.

I answered the phone. "This is Mike McDonald," I said.

"Mr. McDonald, this is Frank Jenson from Holliday Honda. We have your Gold Wing ready for you to pick up."

"How much do I owe you?" I asked.

"Not a thing. Your insurance covered it all. When would you like to pick it up?"

I paused for a moment, thinking. "I'd like you to keep it there at the shop. I'd like to sell it on consignment."

"We can do that. Come down and fill out the papers. I'm sure we could find you a buyer."

"I'll be right down," I said and hung up the phone. Tossing back the rest of my beer, I whistled for Lucky and we headed to the garage. Lucky jumped into the passenger side of my pickup when I opened the door and we headed to the Honda shop. I studied the new shiny motorcycles on the showroom floor. There were several brand new Honda Gold Wings. They were sleek-looking machines, but they had lost their appeal to me.

"You surprised me, Mr. McDonald, when you said that you wanted to sell your bike. I didn't figure you for the type to quit riding."

I shrugged. "I didn't say anything about wanting to quit riding, but I don't want this bike."

The sales clerk nodded. "Would you like to trade it in for a newer model?"

I sighed. "No, I don't think so." I filled out the papers agreeing to pay the shop a commission for finding a buyer and left. Outside, the warm sunshine felt good against my back. Pulling into a liqueur store, I bought a twelve-pack of beer and a Cycle Trader. After barbequing some chicken, I sat down at the kitchen table. I browsed through the Cycle Trader. Circling several ads, I called up a few. Several of the bikes had already sold, but I found an ad for a 1984 Harley Davidson Shovelhead. I dialed the number. A raspy voice answered the phone. He assured me that he still had the motorcycle, so I arranged to go look at the bike the next evening.

***

"I know it looks a little rough, but the motor is strong. It runs great," the middle-aged man who owned the Harley said the following evening. A cold breeze blew leaves into the open doorway of the garage. I squatted down in his garage looking at the motorcycle. It did look rough. It needed a paint job and new tires.

"Fire it up," I said. The man brushed a strand of gray hair out of his face and straddled the bike. He hit the starter button. The motor roared to life. He turned the throttle and the loud pipes reverberated through the garage. I stood back admiring the bike. It had potential.

"It has a kick starter as well as an electric start! It usually takes no more than three kicks!"

"Cut it off!" He killed the engine and lifted his ample bulk off the motorcycle. I crossed my arms in front of my chest. "Would you consider a trade?"

The man shrugged rubbing his chin. "That depends on what you've got."

"I have a Honda Gold Wing for sale on consignment at the Honda shop here in town."

A grin crossed the man's face. "You know, I've always wanted a Gold Wing. I'm retired now. Momma and I have been talking about doing some touring on a motorcycle. Those Honda Gold Wings are the Cadillac of motorcycles, from what I hear."

"Mine's only a couple of years old and it's in good shape. It had some damage done to it, but it's fixed now."

The old man smiled. "Come on in the house. Let's have a beer and talk. I'll have to check it out, but I'm sure we can work out a deal."

The following morning, I caught a cab to the Honda shop and canceled the consignment deal. I rode across town to the old man's house who owned the Harley. He fell in love with the Honda. "Momma will love that cushy back seat," he said. We dickered back and forth for a little while on price but, reached an agreement. I rode home on the Shovelhead with two thousand dollars cash in my pocket.

The Harley ran well and I enjoyed having my face in the wind once more, but I heard a miss inside the motor. I felt a lot of vibration coming through the bars when I rode the bike home. That night, I began to tear it down. I drained the gasoline from the tank and drained the oil from the engine and transmission. Taking the bike apart piece by piece, I gave everything a good cleaning. By the time I went to bed that night, the entire bike lay in pieces on the floor of my garage.

I had a hard time falling to sleep. The mission before me lay heavy on my mind and I had a lot of things to do before I went after the Lost Souls. I needed to be in top physical shape. I set up in bed sipping on a beer and decided to start a rigorous physical exercise program. My walks weren't enough. Oh, I could get around now without a cane, but I tired out fast and I still had a slight limp. I decided to increase the distance of my morning walks and to step up the pace to a fast jog. I kept hearing strange noises inside the house and I could smell Sharon's perfume. After my third beer, I drifted off into a sleep filled with disturbing dreams.

In one dream, a pack of evil demons on motorcycles chased me. I rode a black Harley and I couldn't seem to get away from them. I had another dream about a motorcycle crash. Then I had a dream where I laid under the cover in a large tower overlooking a city street. I looked through the scope of a rifle sighting in on some biker partying below me. I woke up as I was about to pull the trigger.

I got out of bed, padded down the hall to the bathroom, took a piss, and crawled back between the sheets. The room smelled of Chanel Number Five. Sharon stood over me. She wore a see-through white nightgown and stood looking down at me. She had he arms crossed underneath her breasts. Her long blonde hair billowed around her shoulders and she wore a stern look on her face. I bolted upright in the bed.

"Sharon," I whispered to the dark, cold room. I felt goosebumps forming up on my arms and legs. My breath fogged up in front of my face. My heart did a drum roll inside my chest. I heard her murmuring whisper retreating down the hallway fading to silence.

"Michael."

I lay back down and pulled the covers over my head.

***

The following morning, I rose at five AM, fed Lucky, and cooked a quick breakfast. I put on a pair of black sweat pants and a sweatshirt. Lucky and I hit the street at a fast jog and I managed to make three miles. When Lucky and I arrived back at the home place, I was wringing with sweat. I cooled out for five minutes, drinking a bottle of water, and started my exercise routine. I did pushups, sit-ups, leg lifts, and deep knee bends. By the time I was through, my entire body felt like jelly.

After a quick shower, I loaded the engine and transmission from my Harley into the bed of my pickup truck. I put the gas tank, the fenders, the frame, and the wheels into the pickup bed. Finished loading the pickup truck, I shook my keys at Lucky.

"Are you ready to roll buddy?" Lucky barked, wagged his tail, and danced in a small circle. I opened the passenger door of my truck and Lucky jumped in. We pulled out of the driveway heading for the Harley shop. Raindrops hit the windshield. I dropped the engine and transmission off for them to rebuild. Then I waited around for them to put new tires on both of the rims. Finished at the Harley shop, I took the gas tank, the frame and fenders across town to a custom paint shop. I unloaded everything in their office. A skinny young blond-headed man sporting tattoos looked at the parts I had set down.

"What can I do for you?" he asked, wiping his hands off with a shop rag.

"I'd like to have this frame powder coated and I'd like to have the fenders and tank painted."

"What color?"

"Vivid black." The man nodded. We discussed the price and a paint scheme for the tank and fenders. Done with our business, I shook the man's hand and left. I made a stop at an electronics store and then Lucky and I headed for home. I spent the rest of the week jogging and exercising in the morning and piddling around in my garage during the day. I went through my camping and hunting gear, making a list of things that I needed to replace. After cleaning and oiling everything, I stored my gear in a large black duffle bag.

I ordered a wiring harness, some custom pipes, and ape hanger handlebars. I also ordered some custom mirrors, but I was at a standstill until I got the parts back from the painter. On Friday, I headed back to Galloway's Gun World to pick up my guns. George smiled when I stepped up to his sporting goods counter.

"I reckon you're here to pick up your arsenal?"

I laughed. "You better believe it."

"Let's finish the paperwork first." He produced a stack of papers and I signed and initialed in all the appropriate places. Finished with the paperwork, Galloway stepped into the backroom. He came out a few minutes later carrying three long boxes and two small square ones. He set everything down on the counter and then stuck out his hand.

"Thank you for your business. If you need anything else, I'll be here."

We shook hands.

"You're welcome. Thanks."

I piled two shotguns, one rifle, and two handguns into my arms and headed for the truck. Several customers stared watching me carry the firearms away.

"Good luck on the varmint hunt," Galloway said when I stepped out the door to the service island. Back at home, I headed straight to the garage with my new toys. Setting the firearms down on my workbench, I opened the boxes. Taking some rags from underneath the workbench, I wrapped up the stock of one of the shotguns. I put it in the vice on my workbench. Rummaging around in my tool cabinet, I found a hacksaw. I began to saw off the barrels of the shotgun right at the point where they protruded from the stock. Sweat beaded up on my forehead and my arm using the hacksaw began to get sore. It was hot grueling work, cutting through the hardened steel. After that, I cut off the end of the stock forming a small pistol-like grip.

When I finished the first shotgun, I took it out of the vice to examine my work. I let out a low whistle holding a short stubby killing machine in my hands. I reduced the entire weapon to no more than two feet long. I set the weapon aside, put the other shotgun in the vice, and went to work with the hacksaw once more. By the time I finished, it was starting to get late and I was ready for a cold beer. I held both weapons in my hands. They were short and stubby and they looked deadly. The short barrels the shot would spread out in a wide pattern. They were concealable and at close range, they would most likely cut someone in two.

I nodded in satisfaction and hung the short barrels of the shotguns over my shoulders. Inside the house, I stowed the sawed offs inside a closet and brought the other weapons inside. I set the boxes containing the forty-fives and the Ruger 270 magnum onto my kitchen table. Like an excited kid on Christmas morning, I opened boxes and examined the new hardware. After inspecting and cleaning the Ruger 270 Magnum, I set it aside and cleaned the forty-fives. Finished with the forty-fives, I cleaned the shotguns and put the weapons away.

Grabbing a beer from the refrigerator, I sat down in front of the TV to watch a baseball game. I started to hear strange noises in the house again. I thought I heard the bathroom door open and the shower, turn and on by itself. I dismissed it as too much beer and my imagination. Two six-packs later, I stumbled off to bed. A loud banging on the front door woke me from a sound sleep the next morning, or I should say the next afternoon. Bleary-eyed, and hungover with my head pounding, I stumbled to the front door. I opened up the door and looked into the friendly face of a young Marine. He stood in his crisp class A uniform standing next to a young pretty brunette wearing a low-cut halter top. A sheering white-hot pain shot through my head. Another memory slammed into me like an eighteen-wheeler blasting downhill with no brakes.

***

CHAPTER 11

I boarded the bus at the depot in San Bernardino. Two Marine Corps NCOs riding along with us greeted me with a friendly smile. They asked me, what high school I went to and a score of other questions. I answered their questions and shook their hands. I found a seat in the back of the bus and found two guys I went to school with sitting back there.

"They're acting friendly now, but wait until we get to the base," a chubby young guy sitting next to me said. "It will be a whole new ball game when we get off the bus." Chubby was right. When the bus pulled to a stop on the Marine base in San Diego, they became instant assholes. They hustled us out onto the sidewalk. Sweat beaded up on my forehead as the warm sun beat down on us.

"Let's go ladies! Let's see if you can stand at attention! Put your little feet on the little yellow footprints on the sidewalk! Do you civilian pukes think you can handle that? You will not speak unless spoken to! Then the first and last thing that comes out of your mouth will be sir!" a dark-complexioned drill sergeant with a barrel chest and a mean disposition yelled. "Is that clear?" Spittle flew from his mouth.

"Sir! Yes sir!" we yelled in unison. He strutted back and forth in front of us slapping his swagger stick against the side of his leg. He stopped in front of me looking me up and down as if I were dog shit. I noticed sweat stains under the arms of his uniform blouse.

"What's your name, Shit Bird?"

"Sir! Mike McDonald, sir!" I yelled. My heart pulsated inside my chest and I felt a drop of sweat track down the side of my face.

"Where are you from, McDonald?" the drill instructor yelled.

"Sir! San Bernardino California sir!"

The drill instructor rolled his eyes. "San Bernardino? Did I hear right? Did you say, San Francisco? You look like a sissy boy to me! I'll tell you what! I won't ask if you don't tell! Get down and give me twenty, Ronald McDonald!" I dropped to the ground and did twenty pushups. A burning sensation shot through my arms before I was through. The drill instructor moved on. They marched us into the receiving barracks. They ushered us into a reception room and sat us down at several wooden tables. The sound of our footfalls echoed through the building. The room smelled of Lemon Pledge. We sat facing the front of the room.

"When the campaign hat comes around I want you pukes to put any contraband that you brought with you into the hat. That includes guns, knives, cigarettes, candy illegal drugs, or marijuana. Put your wallet, keys, and any other personnel effects into the manila envelope in front of you. Write your name and address on the envelope. The Marine Corps will mail your things home for you!" one of the drill instructors at the front of the room yelled. The NCOs at the end of the tables passed their campaign hats down the line. They had us fill out what seemed like a ton of paperwork. Finished with that, the senior drill instructor went over our general orders. Finished in the reception center, they marched us off to the barber for our haircuts.

"How would you like your hair?" a dark-headed barber asked when I sat down in his chair.

I smiled and ran my fingers through my hair. "Take a little off the back and straighten up the sideburns."

"I got ya," the barber said and proceeded to sheer me like a sheep. He took four swipes with his electric cutters taking all the hair off my head. "Let's go. Out of the chair. I got more little lambs to sheer," the barber said and laughed.

I climbed out of the chair, rubbing my chrome dome, and went outside. Glancing about at my fellow recruits, I found it hard to recognize them with all the smooth baldheads. Once everyone had their haircuts, they marched us down to a medical building. They ordered us to strip out of our clothes and gave each one of us a thorough, medical examination.

Finished with the physicals, they marched us down to another building. They gave us everything we needed in the way of clothes and equipment. The drill instructor ordered us to strip out of our civilian clothes and put on our new uniforms. The new clothes felt stiff and uncomfortable, but I figured we would get used to them. When we reached the end of the line, we received a seabag to put everything in. After we packed our gear, they marched us across the street to a three-tiered barracks. We occupied the top floor.

"You maggots find a bunk! Now let's move!" the drill instructor yelled. Once everyone found a bunk we set their seabags down on the mattress. The senior drill instructor ordered us to stand at attention. He and his assistant paced back and forth in front of us. "I am Senior Drill Instructor Shawn Casey. I am the top hat!" He motioned to a Hispanic corporal. "This is Corporal Rodriguez! He will give you a demonstration on how to make your bunk and stow your gear! There is the right way, the wrong way, and the Marine Core way! Let's do it the Marine Core way! Gather round!" We crowded around one of the bunks to watch. A big black scary-looking lance corporal stood behind us. He wore dark sunglasses, with his arms crossed. His massive biceps reminded me of tree trunks.

After the demonstration, Casey ordered us to make our bunks and stow our gear. Two footlockers were set at the end of each bunk. A set of double-sided lockers set near the bulkhead at the head of the racks. I picked a bottom bunk, made my bed as quick as I could, and stowed away my gear. All the while the drill instructors paraded up and down the aisle yelling for us to hurry. When we finished, Casey ordered us to attention once more. They inspected our bunks and our gear. When they got to my bunk, Rodriguez tossed my bedding and mattress onto the floor.

"What's wrong with you McDonald? Didn't your momma teach you anything? Get down and give me fifty pushups, and then make the bed right!" I dropped to the floor and did my pushups counting them out. By the time I finished, my arms felt like Jelly. I thought I was strong before I joined the Marines, but now I was starting to realize how weak I was. I had to redo my bunk three times and do one hundred fifty pushups before I got it right.

We finished making our bunks and stowing our gear. Washington brought in a cart carrying several mops and mop buckets. He stopped giving us an icy glare.

"You pukes have two hours! I want this squad bay clean enough to eat off of when I return!" With that, the drill instructors left us to our own devices. We stood there for a few seconds looking at each other and went to work. No one wanted to suffer the wrath of Drill Sergeant Casey. I had had a feeling that no matter how much we cleaned, we'd still feel the lash of his tongue and kiss the floor doing pushups.

I grabbed a mop bucket, opened a container of ammonia, and poured it into the bucket along with some water. Squinting, my eyes, and crinkling my nose at the smell of ammonia, I grabbed a mop and went to work. A skinny white kid standing next to me grabbed a broom.

"My name is Marshall. Damien Marshall. What yours?" the skinny kid with the broom asked.

"Mike. Mike McDonald," I said and started to swab the deck.

Marshall started to sweep. "Where you from?"

"San Bernardino California. How about you?"

"Greenwood Wisconsin."

"You're a long way from home."

"Tell me about it." I wheeled my mop bucket over to a water faucet and Marshall went to work with his broom. A beefy Hispanic guy with dark brown eyes and a fleshy face stepped up next to me with another mop bucket.

"Bro, I hope they feed us soon. I'm about starved to death."

I smiled looking up at the cubby recruit. "You don't appear to have missed too many meals. What's your name?"

"Cortez. Ruben Cortez. I'm from Silver City New Mexico. You're McDonald. I heard you talkin' with that skinny white kid down the way."

I nodded. "Well, Ruben, the sooner we get this squad bay cleaned up, the sooner it will be to, chow time."

We went to work, but of course, it wasn't good enough for our senior drill instructor. They made us hit the floor and do pushups when they returned. Finished with the pushups, they ran us through the chow hall for dinner. After evening chow, we attended night classes. We fell into our bunks at ten PM or twenty-two hundred hours. Our first day of military indoctrination left me exhausted, but at first, I couldn't sleep. I lay in a strange bed, in strange surroundings, and listened to strange sounds. The smell of ammonia and pine-scented cleaner filled the barracks. A few guys down the aisle were talking and laughing. I heard a couple of guys crying and a few snoring. Someone farted. That made me laugh. The senior drill instructor came out of the DI shack and yelled for us to be quiet. Sometime after that, I drifted off to sleep.

***

The sound of someone banging trashcan lids together woke me from a sound sleep at 04:30 the next morning. My breath caught in my throat and my heart hammered inside my chest. For a few seconds, my eyes darted back and forth and I wondered where I was and who was making all the damned noise.

"Drop your skinny little cocks and grab your socks boys! We're burning daylight! It's time for you to learn how to be Marines!" drill instructor Casey yelled. He strutted up and down the aisle, bashing a small baton against the inside of a trashcan. The other drill instructors followed along behind banging trashcan lids together. Bleary-eyed, I jumped from my bunk and stood at attention in my underwear along with the rest of the recruits. Goosebumps cropped up on my legs and arms while I stood there shivering in my boxer shorts. So began my first full day in the Marine Corps. I found boot camp both rewarding and challenging. Some of the recruits seemed intimidated and scared, but I saw it as a challenge. I wouldn't let the drill instructors get the best of me. Oh, I did my share of pushups like everyone else, but I excelled at everything we did. By the third week, the senior drill instructor made me a squad leader.

My squad consisted of a tight group of guys that were hard-chargers. We became good friends. There was Damien Marshall, Ruben Cortez, and a black dude named Guthrie. There was an Italian guy named Serrano, and a Jewish kid with a big nose named Bernstein. Out of all the guys in my squad, Cortez was the weak link. He was overweight. On the long hikes and runs, he lagged near the back of the pack. Casey put him on a diet and told me that if Cortez didn't shape up, that he would replace me as the squad leader. I made it my special duty to see to it that Cortez lost weight. I would run along beside him shouting encouragement and carry his gear for him if he got tired.

One time he almost quit on us. He stopped running and said, "I can't go on." His breathing came out wheezy and sweat flowed down his body like a river. I had two of the biggest guys in our squad grab him by the arms and carry him the rest of the way. By the end of week six, he was shaping up. Although Cortez would never be a fast runner, he quit lagging near the back of the pack. Our squad moved up closer to the middle, Cortez thinned down and began to show some muscle.

During the first weeks of training, they weeded out the trouble makers. The platoon was getting smaller. The drill instructors punished the whole group when one person did something wrong. Corporal Washington was the PT instructor. He was the one they sent you to when got into trouble. Washington would make you do pushups all day. If you weren't doing pushups, he'd make you dig ditches. Sometimes he'd make you hold buckets full of sand out from your body with your arms extended. After a day with Washington, you were ready to behave. The whole platoon began to shape up, but there was one guy who couldn't do anything right.

His name was James Blackwell. He was overweight and uncoordinated, but that wasn't his main problem. His main problem was that he wouldn't try. He wouldn't give it his best effort. One night after doing pushups and marching in circles in the rain because of one of his fuck ups, we took action. We held a blanket party. We waited until he was sound asleep and snoring away and then we struck like a ghost in the night. Two guys covered his head with his blanket and held him down. The rest of the platoon had put bars of soap inside their pillowcases. We all filed by in a line, swinging our pillowcases and struck him in his stomach, legs, and upper body. He screamed like a stuck pig.

My breathing accelerated, my hands holding the pillowcase shook and my head throbbed. "You'd better get your shit together, Blackwell, or you'll be in a world of hurt," I said. I slammed my pillowcase into his stomach several times.

"Owe! Stop!" he screamed and began to cry. We disappeared, once again like ghosts in the night, and retreated to our bunks. The only sound was the blubbering cries of James Blackwell. The senior drill instructor didn't hear a thing. Old Casey must have been sleeping well that night. The last thing I heard before I fell asleep was the sound of Blackwell crying.

***

The following morning, Blackwell was on his A-game. He began to apply himself and we quit getting into so much trouble. Someone overheard one recruit bragging saying that he planned to go AWOL. Lance Corporal Washington found out about it. The recruit's name was Jeffries.

"Mr. Jeffries seems to think that he's going to leave us tonight!" Washington said to the entire platoon. "I don't think he likes us! Mr. Jeffries, I want you to drag your mattress here into the center of the squad bay!" Washington yelled and Jeffries complied. "I want all the squad leaders to drag your mattresses out here and form a circle around Private Jefferies." We did as instructed. Corporal Washington took out several long black metal flashlights. He handed one to each squad leader. “If Private Jeffries gets itchy feet and decides to leave, I want you to beat him down with these flashlights. You might need to show him the light if you will.”

I slapped the metal flashlight against the palm of my hand and gave Jeffries a cold hard stare. Jeffries looked at the floor. I spent the night with the rest of the squad leaders on our mattresses in the center of the squad bay. Private Jeffries didn’t go anywhere.

By the time they sent us to the rifle range, the platoon was starting to shape up. There were no longer any discipline problems and our weak links were gone. We were turning into Marines. We lost most of our body fat and began to put on muscle. When we marched to the rifle range, there was a new snap in our step and a look of pride on our faces. We called cadence with gusto, held our chest out and our heads high.

We spent a week snapping in on the grass while the platoon ahead of us used the rifle range. The week we spent snapping in, had to be one of the most boring weeks of my life. It consisted of lying in the prone position and dry firing the rifle. You sighted down the barrel, practiced breath control, and squeezed the trigger. We did this in the prone position as well as in the kneeling and standing positions. The smell of grass and gun oil became my constant companion.

When our turn came to use the rifle range, we spent the first three days practicing our shooting. On Thursday and Friday, we qualified. Everyone in our platoon qualified on Thursday. On Friday, Casey let us shoot to see if we could better our score. I was the top shooter in our platoon. I fired off five aimed shots while senior drill instructor Casey stood behind me. He looked at the target through a pair of binoculars.

Casey grinned. “Damn McDonald. You must be a country boy or something. Are you sure you haven’t done this before?”

“Sir! No sir!” I yelled trying to keep a silly grin from spreading across my face.

“You finally found something you do well! Outstanding! Keep up the good work!” Overhead, thunder rolled and the sky turned overcast.

After finishing at the rifle range, we cleaned our weapons and had the rest of the evening to ourselves. The following morning, we filed out of the barracks loaded down with full combat gear. They loaded us up into Duce-and-a-half trucks and took us out into the boonies for two weeks of war games. After we bailed out of the trucks, we patrolled deeper into the bush. They made us crawl under obstacles consisting of low-strung bobbed wire. Live machine gunfire zipped overhead. Simulated explosions blew up around us. After setting up a base camp, we spent two weeks fighting war games. The brass designated our platoon as the blue Army and designated another platoon as the red Army.

Two weeks after entering the bush, we marched back to the barracks tired and dirty. After a quick shower and change of uniform, we reported to the mess hall for KP. Our two weeks in the mess hall flew by. It wasn't bad duty. I enjoyed ragging the green recruits when they came through the chow line. By now, I felt like a veteran. One fat timid recruit stuck his tray out in front of me with a hungry look on his face.

"Can I have extra potatoes please?" he whined.

I frowned. "You disgusting fat son of a bitch! You don't need extra potatoes!"

"Never mind," he said. He put his head down and started to move on.

"Get back here private!" I yelled. He stopped and I slammed an extra-large scoop of potatoes on his plate. "I expect that you'll have to do a lot of pushups! You'll need your strength! Carry on!"

A smile spread across the recruit's face. "Thank you," he said and moved down the line. The night before graduation, we were in a jubilant mood. We'd made it. We were Marines. We spent the entire evening cleaning the barracks and squaring away our gear. After lights out, I lay in my bunk, but for a while, I couldn't sleep. I couldn't believe it. I'd survived boot camp.

***

We stood in our dress blues, the following morning, for our final inspection. Senior Drill Instructor Casey swaggered down our ranks with the base commander. Before the inspection, he stood us at attention. He didn't want the base commander to find anything to criticize us for. He helped one Marine with his collar.

A trace of a smile appeared on his face. "You men make me proud! Today you are no longer maggots or worms. You are now United States Marines! Hooyah!" The platoon replied in kind. We polished our brass belt buckles and our boots until they shined. Every button on our uniforms was in place. We looked like Marines and we didn't want to get dinged, on this our last day in boot camp. After inspection, we filed out onto the parade ground for our graduation ceremony. We marched past the viewing stands filled with wives, girlfriends, and family members. The air was crisp, the American flag fluttered in the breeze, and pride, filled our hearts. After the ceremony, we had a few minutes to spend with our family. My mother was there, but my father was absent. When I stepped up to my mother, she threw her arms around me. I breathed in the smell of her perfume.

"I'm so proud of you," she said. She held me at arm's length and looked me up and down. "Look at you. You got muscles. They've gone and made a man out of you."

"Where's Dad?" I asked.

"Oh, he would have come, but you know how he is. He said that after he got out of the service that he would never go onto another military base in his life."

I nodded. "Would you like to go have lunch?"

"You bet I would," my mother said.

"I've got to square away my gear and check out of here. It should only take about an hour. Why don't you go check out the museum?"

"Okay, dear. I'll see you in a little while then."

Back in the barracks, we packed our sea bags. Sergeant Casey came into the barracks and issued us our orders. He called out our names and told us what MOS the brass assigned us to. I looked up when he called my name

"Private McDonald. I'm sorry but the Scout Sniper School up the road at Camp Pendleton is full up. The Core is sending you to Camp Ginger in North Carolina. They're going to teach you to be a life taker and a heart breaker!"

After everyone received their orders, we said our goodbyes. I met my mother at the museum, tossed my seabag into the trunk of her car and we left the base. She took me to a seafood place near the beach. Sitting across from her, I couldn't help but notice the gray in her hair. She seemed older and frailer. When the waiter came by, I ordered fish and chips along with a beer to wash it down. My mother ordered sea scallops.

"How are things between you and Dad? Has he got his drinking under control?"

My mother sighed. "Your father's fine. He has his binges now and then, but they don't come as often as they used to."

A scowl filled my face. "Is he hitting you?"

My mother shook her head. "No. He sits and broods. Let's talk about something else. What about you? Where are the Marines sending you now that your boot camp is over?"

"I'm going to scout sniper school in North Carolina."

My mother's face fell. "I was hoping you might get stationed here in California. I'm going to miss you."

I reached over and touched her hand. "I'll still be here in California for a few more weeks. We go to Advanced Infantry Training before we ship out. I'll write. I promise."

"You better, if you know what's good for you. I got a card from your brother. It was only a few lines. He's still in Germany."

"How's he doing?" I asked.

"He says everything is fine. He's taking college classes at night. He says he wants to be a lawyer when he gets out of the Army."

I let out a snort. "A lawyer? He always did try to help people. I guess he'd make a good one," I said.

My mother and I finished our lunch, she drove us down to the beach and we took a long walk on the sand. I enjoyed the sound of the waves crashing against the shore and the cool ocean breeze. A gull cawed overhead.

"I hate to cut things too short, mom, but some of the guys and I have plans for tonight," I said when we arrived back at the car.

My mother looked up. "What sort of plans?"

"Oh, we thought we'd head down to Tijuana and blow off some steam."

She laughed. "Tijuana? Be sure and wear a raincoat. I don't need any Mexican grandbabies."

I blushed. "Mom, please!"

"You think I was born yesterday or the day after?" she said.

I shook my head and climbed into the passenger side of her car. She dropped me off in front of the base, one half an hour later. Damien Marshall and Rubin Cortez met up with me a few minutes later. We caught a cab and rode down to the border. After crossing the border, the cab driver dropped us off at the nearest bar.

We stood in the middle of the noisy cantina and gazed about. The smell of tobacco smoke and stale beer filled the building. Several other groups of Marines and sailors lined the bar. They sat at tables scattered throughout the room. I noticed several tourists and a few locals. A DJ sat behind the bar playing loud Latin music. I elbowed my way through the crowd and we took up positions at the bar.

"What can I get for you senior?" a fat balding bartender asked. He wore a green apron over his ample belly.

"We'll have some of the best Mexican beer you've got," I said.

"Si senior. Coming right up."

"Where are all the women?" Marshall asked. "I am in a need of some pussy."

The bartender smiled. "It's still, early senior. When the sun goes down, the senoritas will come out to play."

"Do you have anything to eat bro? I'm starving," Cortez said.

"We have a cook in the back. I will have him make you some tacos."

"That would be great, bro."

The bartender poured us each a beer and I swiveled around in my chair so I could take in the action inside the bar. Cortez bought some tacos and shared them with the rest of us. They had to be the best-tasting tacos I'd ever eaten. A half-hour later, several good-looking young Mexican women entered the bar. I nudged Cortez's arm. "Check what's coming in the door."

"Now that's what I'm talking about," Cortez said.

"That there is some prime punting," Marshall said.

I turned back to the bar. "Pony up boys. Let's pool our resources here," I said motioning to the bartender. We ordered a round of drinks. A middle-aged sweaty Mexican woman smelling of cheap perfume, who worked as a waitress. She took the drinks over to the girl's booth when they sat down. A pretty young Mexican girl with long straight black hair locked eyes with me and smiled. She motioned us over to their table. I rose to my feet and headed over, so Marshall and Cortez followed. We stopped for a few seconds looking down at the group of young Latin ladies. The one that I'd made eye contact with looked up at me and smiled.

"I am Maria. Thank you for the drinks. These are my friends. Please sit down."

I slid in next to Maria. Marshall and Cortez slid in next to the other girls. My eyes wandered over Maria's voluptuous figure. I took in her large breasts, her high cheekbones, and her raven dark eyes.

"My name's Mike. Mike McDonald. These are my buddies, Rubin Cortez and Damien Marshall," I said. "Introduce your friends."

Maria nodded to a blonde-headed girl sitting across from her. "This is my friend, Angelina."

Angelina smiled. "I like Marines. You look so handsome in your uniforms."

Maria motioned to a heavyset girl at the end. "This is Esperanza."

Esperanza batted her eyes at me and said, "Hi."

My hand came to rest on Maria's bare thigh under the table. She wore a short dress and her legs felt smooth and soft to the touch. She looked at me and smiled. We sat at the table talking and drinking for another hour. I put my hand on Maria's leg once more.

"Would you like to do more than touch my leg under the table?"

I grinned. "Yeah."

"We live in the same hacienda. For one hundred dollars, we could have a party?"

"What? You're prostitutes?" Marshall said.

Anger flashed through Maria's eyes. "Mexico is a poor country. A girl has to have money to eat."

"I'm in," Cortez said.

"Me too. What do you say, Marshall?" I asked.

"I say hot damn! Let's go!"

We paid the bar tab, stepped outside, and flagged down a taxi. The taxi left us off in front of a large house in a rundown neighborhood. Two old men sat on the front porch drinking beer. Cans and bottles littered the front yard. Several small children played amongst the debris. The girls piled out of the taxicab giggling and led us up to the front porch. The two old men smiled and babbled back and forth to each other in Spanish. An older Mexican woman met us at the front door. She peered at us from inside and stepped out to greet us. The door squeaked on its hinges. She said something to Maria in Spanish, Maria nodded and led us through the door.

"You hombres' have a mucho grandee good time," the old woman said and laughed.

Maria led us to a stairway setting next to a large sitting room. Angelina grabbed Marshall, pulling him into the first room. Esperanza took Cortez into a room on the left side of the hallway and Maria took me to a small room at the end of the hall. I sat down on the bed and took off my boots while Maria took off her dress. I gazed up at her full round breasts. My eyes widened, my breath caught in my throat, and my heart thumped the shit out of my rib cage. She pushed me back onto the bed and climbed on top of me. Three days later and two hundred dollars lighter, I boarded a bus in San Diego. I was en route to Advanced Infantry training. After that, I would head to my duty station in North Carolina.

***

CHAPTER 12

The hot muggy air hit me like a blowtorch when I stepped off the bus in North Carolina. My uniform felt damp and clammy. Noticing a few other Marines standing next to the gray stone bus station, I sauntered over. I heard a car horn honk out on the street. The smell of diesel smoke drifted on the breeze. The Marines gathered next to the front door of the bus station talking and laughing. I stepped around a scraggly-looking bum with a long white beard sitting next to the door.

"Spare some change Mr.?" I tossed him a quarter.

"Is this where you catch the bus to Camp Ginger?" I asked. A dark-complexioned Marine who looked like a side of beef gave me the once over. He looked as if he had some Indian blood in him.

"Yep. It should be along in about fifteen minutes. Is this your first time at Camp Lejeune? Camp Ginger is part of the Lejeune complex."

I nodded and pulled a pack of cigarettes from my shirt pocket. "Yeah. It's my first time."

"I did my AIT down here. What's your MOS?"

I pulled a smoke from the pack and my Zippo from my pants pocket. "My orders are to report for Scout Sniper School." I lit a smoke, offered one up but the big guy declined with a shake of his head. The mountain of a man stuck out his hand and we shook. The bones in my hand felt as if they were going to snap. The smell of tobacco smoke filled the air.

"My name's St. Clair. Leon St. Clair. I'm headed for Scout Sniper training as well."

I flexed my hand trying to get some feeling back. "St. Clair. That sounds French, but you look Indian."

"I am. My daddy was a full-blooded Cherokee. My momma is French. I'm from down Louisiana."

I took a drag on the smoke. "My name's McDonald. Mike McDonald."

St. Clair smiled. "Oh. An Irish lad. Where you from?"

"California."

One of the other Marines standing near the building laughed. "A Hollywood Marine."

I glanced over a short stocky Marine. "They train us as hard in Dago as they do on the PI."

We boarded the bus fifteen minutes later. The floor vibrated underneath my feet as the bus left the depot. Traversing the city we headed out into the boonies. The shabby rundown buildings gave way to forest and scattered farms. Thirty miles outside of town, the bus pulled off the highway and onto the base. I glanced out the passenger window taking in the scenery. Trees lined the main road and I noticed grassy areas between the old brick buildings. A squad of Marines marched down the sidewalk heading toward the housing area. The bus pulled up in front of HQ and we disembarked. I fell into line, stepped up to the reception desk when I reached the head of the line and handed a clerk my orders.

A dark-haired female Marine looked up and smiled. My eyes dropped to her chest. "Welcome to Camp Lejeune. You'll be heading up to Camp Ginger. You'll need to catch another bus. Wait out front by the curb. It'll be along in about fifteen minutes. Your classes don't start until tomorrow. When you get up to Camp Ginger, the trainee barracks is a half-mile down the road from the HQ. Find a bunk and report to General Grant's Hall at zero seven-hundred for an orientation briefing. Dinner is at eighteen hundred hours. Breakfast is at zero six hundred. There is a map board in front of each barracks." Stepping off the bus at Camp Ginger twenty minutes later, I heaved my seabag over my shoulder. I headed down the road looking for the barracks. The humid North Carolina air caused my uniform to stick to my shirt. I gazed about, taking in my surroundings. The buildings on base looked old World War II vintage or older. Oak trees lined the main street. Gray squirrels in the trees chattered back and forth. I marched up the steps leading to the first three-tiered barracks on my right. The brass hinges on the oak doors squeaked when I pushed them open. I found an empty bunk on the ground level, stowed my gear, made my bunk, and changed into a fresh uniform.

Leon St. Clair stepped into the barracks and found a bunk across from me. A young red-headed Marine occupying the bunk above me leaned over the bunk and grinned. Freckles covered his face.

"You might as well give it up. If you change into a new uniform every time you get sweaty, you'll be changing every five minutes. It's as humid as hell here. I'm PFC Gene Walker." He stuck out his hand and we shook.

"I'm Mike McDonald and this is Leon St. Clair. Have you found the chow hall yet?"

"I was getting ready to head that way. I took a gander at the map board out front. It shouldn't be too hard to find," Walker said.

I waited for St. Clair to stow his gear and we headed for the mess hall passing several more Marines. We passed through the serving line in the mess hall and sat down to good old shit on a shingle. I dug in with gusto. Finished in the mess hall, St. Clair and I headed for the enlisted men's club. We figured to tie one on before starting sniper school. We didn't expect to have much free time once the classes started. St. Clair and I stumbled back to the barracks drunk three hours later.

***

A Remington model 700/M40 standard issue sniper rifle in 308, caliber lay on a table before me. Our first lesson was on how to clean the weapon. We would come to know these rifles as well as we knew our self. I picked up a can of gun oil, cleaned the weapon, disassembled it, and then reassembled it. It was a timed test.

"Know your weapon! I want you to become familiar with this weapon. I want you to know this weapon better than the insides of your girlfriend's silk panties!" the black baldheaded instructor said to the class. After we reassembled the weapons, the instructor had us tear them down and repeat the process.

During the weeks that followed, we spent the first four hours of the day in class. We learned about ballistics, wind effects, and wind speeds. We studied sight pictures, breath control, and urban combat. We learned every other aspect of the combat sniper's life. We spent the last four hours of our day at the rifle range becoming more than proficient with our weapons. The instructors showed us videos of sniper missions from World War Two, Korea, and Vietnam. Halfway through the course, we made our Ghillie suits in preparation for going into the field. On the range, Leon St. Clair served as my spotter half of the time and then we switched and I spotted for him.

They sent us into the field for the last three weeks of the course. For the first week, we operated in a simulated urban environment. We shot at targets from prefabricated wooden structures. The structures resembled a village in some third-world country. For the first half of the week, I spotted, for St. Clair, and the second half of the week, he spotted for me. The command staff issued us survival gear and gave us the coordinates of our objective. We were to hump our way through the woods to the target while under the pursuit of hostile forces. They ordered us not to engage, but to use stealth and evasion until we reached our target. We were to take the shot and then escape and evade the enemy forces. Instructors on the ground roll played as enemy forces.

After crawling through the woods for three days, we reached the target. We were both tired and dirty. The target was a mock-up village setting in a clearing in the woods. An officer role-playing as an enemy colonel was our target. Before heading into the bush, they issued us blank ammunition. When we fired our weapons, a beam from a small laser sight shot out from the weapon. If we scored a hit, a beeper on the colonel's uniform would beep signifying a kill. We lay in the prone position on a small hill overlooking the village. Overhead the hot sun beat down on us. I sweltered under the Ghillie suit, the humidity almost draining the life from me. Sweat soaked our bodies.

"Three hundred meters," St. Clair said calling out the yardage. "The wind is coming from the Northwest at five miles per hour."

I looked through the scope and the image of an officer in an OD green uniform came into view. "I've acquired the target," I said.

"Then take the shot." I squeezed the trigger. Down below, the trainer role-playing as the enemy colonel fell to the ground after his suit beeped." We both jumped up and headed deeper into the woods. My heart pounded in my chest and sweat poured off my body. Enemy soldiers below poured out of a grass hut and started the pursuit. We escaped. The next week, we repeated the exercise, but with St. Clair acting as the shooter and me as the spotter. St. Clair made the shot, but this time the trainer's role-playing as the enemy forces caught us in the woods. We spent the last three days of our training in a mock POW camp.

They kept us in small bamboo cages without enough room to stand up or lay down. The trainers subjected us to brutal interrogations and sleep deprivation. They would hall us into one of the grass huts, in the middle of the night, and interrogate us. They brought me in from one of the cages and tied me to a chair.

"What unit are you from? How many soldiers do you have in our area! I want answers or you die, Marine!"

I shrugged. "My name is Mike McDonald, my rank is-"

They proceeded to beat me with rubber batons on the backs of my legs and thighs. I tried not to cry out in pain, but soon I was unable to hold it in. They didn't do me any real harm, but the beatings made my legs ache. The trainers continued to ask me typical questions that a real enemy would ask. They played mind games with me trying to see how much abuse I could take before I snapped. At the end of the week, they drove us back to HQ in a duce and a half. Friday night, when we arrived back at HQ, our chief training instructor ordered us to shower and have a hot meal. After chow, we hit the rack. The field exercise had been a long grueling ordeal.

The following morning we reported to the main assembly hall for graduation ceremonies. Master Sergeant Holloway, our chief training officer stood before a podium.

He looked at the assembled Marines and grinned, clinching a large cigar between his teeth. "When I call your name step forward to receive your certificate and your orders," Holloway said. I waited, and when they called my name, I stepped forward with my chest puffed out.

"Lance Corporal McDonald, here's your certificate. Congratulations. When you get back to your barracks, pack your gear. You're going to Columbia. Your flight to Bogotá leaves the airfield at zero six hundred hours on Tuesday morning. You have a three-day pass. Make the best of it." *Colombia? What kind of shit will I get into down there?* I thought when I accepted my certificate and my orders.

***

After three days of hard drinking, Leon St. Clair and I boarded a C-130 transport. Conversation buzzed and excitement filled the airplane.

"Find a seat and secure your gear, Marine! We're due for takeoff in ten minutes!" the crew chief of the C-130 yelled.

St. Clair and I moved down to the end of a metal bench lining the right bulkhead in the cargo bay. We sat our gear at our feet. Pallets loaded down with different types of equipment set in the center of the cargo bay. Members of the flight crew tied everything down.

I sat down and pulled a pack of smokes from my pocket. "What do you think it'll be like in Columbia?" I asked St. Clair.

St. Clair paused while I lighted my cigarette. "Oh, I expect things will be routine. Our orders are to train the natives. I'm looking forward to a taste of some of that hot Latin pussy."

I laughed. Visions of Latin beauties flashed through my brain and I thought about Maria in TJ. The boarding ramp at the back of the plane closed. The C-130 taxied toward the runway. Cleared for takeoff, the plane roared down the runway and took flight. I felt the deck vibrating under my feet. The noise inside the cargo bay was so loud I thought my ears were going to bleed. Once airborne, I finished my cigarette. Then I leaned back against the bulkhead to get some sleep. We arrived in Bogotá several hours later.

The heat and humidity of North Carolina felt like baby shit compared to Columbia. The smells, the sounds, and the people all seemed different. They loaded us up in the beds of duce and a half trucks at the airfield, and we hit the road. Columbian soldiers provide security while the convoy worked its way through Bogotá. We passed through one of the better sections of town and heading through the slums. I noticed people living in cardboard and tin shanties next to stagnate streams of water. It looked to me as if they drank and shit from the same source. Everyone standing next to their hovels gave us hard looks when we passed by. I could tell that they didn't want us there any more than we wanted to be there.

We took a dirt trail at the edge of town leading into the jungle. Passing through a section of farmland, I noticed people working the fields. An older grizzled-looking NCO that met us at the airfield spoke up.

"Let's lock and load people! Keep a sharp eye out! All though we're only supposed to be serving as advisors to the Columbian Army, down here the rebels don't like us. Some of our convoys have come under attack." I put on my helmet, pulled back the charging handle on my M-16, and slid a round into the chamber. Crouching near the sidewall of the truck bed, I peered into the dense forest. A sense of unease passed through me. Branches from the trees slapped against the sides of the vehicle as we headed into the jungle. I saw something move through the forest and I wondered if someone was out trying to take a shot at me. A dark shape darted from tree to tree. I started to raise my rifle to my shoulder, but a strong hand gripped my arm.

"It's, okay son. It's a baboon. I saw it too," the NCO said. I let out a slow easy breath. "But good looking out. Stay sharp. Our rules of engagement say that we can't fire unless fired upon. But if you see some son of a bitch pointing a weapon at you, take him out."

"Roger that, Sergeant," I said and lowered my rifle. We traveled through the jungle for another two hours before reaching the base. The base, set on a high plateau in a large clearing in the jungle. The convoy stopped at the gate. The Columbian soldiers on duty pulled a string of barbed wire off the road. The convoy rumbled forward through the outer perimeter. It followed the road, which zigzagged up the side of the plateau. At the top, the convoy passed through several large Army tents. It stopped in front of a large tent that I took to be the HQ. A Columbian and American flag flew in the breeze attached to the top of two flagpoles in front of the tent. I jumped down from the truck. The rest of the Marines in the convoy jumped down to the ground and we milled about stretching our legs.

"You men work the kinks out for a few minutes. The CO will be out here shortly to brief you," the NCO who rode with us said. I took a drink from my canteen and wiped the sweat from my brow. A few minutes later, the CO stepped outside. He reminded me of Colonel Potter from the TV show, Mash. He looked tired and disheveled.

"Gentlemen, let me have your attention. I am Colonel Brian Weaver. Welcome to Camp Colina. Your duties here will be to assist the Columbian soldiers. You will instruct them in marksmanship and combat techniques. You will also go out of patrol with them. They will be on point. You are here as advisors only. If you are in the bush and the rebels engage you, you may return fire. The Columbians will carry out any attacks or ambushes upon the rebel forces. You must adhere to the rules of engagement. Chow should be about ready in the mess tent. Get some food, find a bunk and stow your gear. Relax for the rest of the evening. Have a cold beer. You start work in the morning," the colonel said, turned, and went back into his tent. St. Clair and I went looking for the mess tent.

***

I spent the first six months in Columbia training sniper teams. I went along with a few patrols to help them set up ambushes. The enemy forces engaged us in one major firefight. They attacked the base one night with rockets and mortars. Their infantry hit the wire, but we mowed them down before they reached the perimeter. St. Clair and I went to Bogotá once for R&R. We spent three days drinking in the bars and sampling the nightlife. I was developing a taste for Latin women. There was pretty much a smorgasbord of whores hanging out at the bars in the red light district of Bogotá.

One evening after we got back from Bogotá, a young private came running into our tent.

"Senor McDonald. The Hefei wants to see you. He says come now." I looked up from the newspaper I was reading.

"What's he want?"

The Columbian private shrugged. "I do not know amigo. He said for you to come. You too, Senor St. Clair." I jumped up and headed to HQ. St. Clair was hot on my heels. In the command tent, our top sergeant gathered around a table with our CO and a few other officers. They stood looking at a map and listening to the radio. The colonel looked up when St. Clair and I stepped into the tent.

"Gentlemen. We have a situation brewing here and we'll need your services. Now that everyone is here, we'll start the briefing," the colonel said standing to his feet. Everyone stepped back giving him room. "At zero eight hundred hours this morning, the rebel forces kidnapped a US diplomat. Our intelligence sources say that they are holding him at a base camp several clicks to the north of us. Mr. McDonald and Mr. St. Clair, we are going to drop you on a hillside overlooking their compound. We will insert you one-half hour before the main assault team arrives by helicopter. We want you to take out as many targets of opportunity as you can before the assault force arrives. Try to learn where they are holding the diplomat and take out any guards that might be guarding him."

"Yes sir," I said.

The colonel set his map up on an easel showing us the grid coordinates of the enemy base camp. He showed us the location of our insertion point. He went on to brief the members of the assault force.

"Are there any questions?" There was none. "Then pack your gear and be at the chopper pad in ten minutes. Good hunting. Let's bring this damned diplomat back alive."

St. Clair and I headed back to our tent. We packed our gear, put on our Ghillie suits, slung our sniper rifles, and headed for the chopper pad. The rotor blades of the chopper whirled overhead. The noise from the engine powering up was almost deafening. We jumped inside our chopper, sat down on the deck, and took off one hour ahead of the main assault force. My stomach dropped when the chopper lifted off the ground and headed north over the jungle.

The flight crew of the chopper lowered us to the ground on the backside of the hill overlooking the rebel base. I unhooked the harness and dropped six feet to the jungle floor. St. Clair unhooked his harness and landed beside me. The flight crew reeled in the cable and headed back to base. Checking my compass, I got my bearings and we began to move up the hill staying underneath the cover of the trees. We low crawled, through a couple of areas where the trees were thin. The shrill sound of a monkey screeching echoed through the jungle. The stench of rotting foliage filled the air. I stopped crawling when a snake crossed my path. Once the snake slithered on, I continued. The smell of tobacco floated through the trees.

Two rebel soldiers manned a fighting position at the top of the hill. One manned a fifty caliber and the other lay next to him to feed the gun belted ammunition. They had their backs toward us. The rebel soldier manning the gun leaned back smoking a cigarette. The other one nodded his head and looked asleep. I crept up to the edge of their foxhole with my heart pounding inside my chest. Leaping to my feet, I brought my K-Bar knife crashing down into the right side of the machine gunner's neck. Blood squirted out of his neck and soaked the front of his shirt. My left hand covered his mouth so he wouldn't scream.

His buddy looked up and was about to scream when St. Clair's massive bulk came down on top of him. He drove his K-Bar into the rebel soldier's midsection. Pulling the knife out of the rebel soldier's neck, I sliced the rest of his throat. Blood spewed onto the forest floor. His bowels voided, he kicked his feet and died. I looked over at St. Clair; he nodded and climbed off the dead body of the rebel soldier he'd killed. We moved forward to the edge of the tree line and looked down on the enemy base.

Through my scope, I saw a rebel soldier come out of what appeared to be the command tent. He carried a plate of food to a grass hut to the left of the rebel HQ. Guards with AK-47s stood guard in front of the hut.

"Contact the assault forces. Tell them that the package is in the hut next to their command tent," I whispered to St. Clair. He whispered into his handheld radio. I moved my sights to the guards in front of the grass hut. "Time to rock and roll." Bolting a round into the chamber, I let my breathing slow and then held my breath. I fired between heartbeats. The rifle roared slamming back into my shoulder. The guard's head exploded into a crimson cloud, I bolted in another round and took out the other guard. Moving to the command tent, I saw an officer run outside, so I took him out. His head exploded. Pandemonium filled the rebel camp. Enemy soldiers poured out of the shabby tents and grass huts making up the enemy base camp.

Someone below manned a machine gun. Bullets ripped through the trees. I fired off several more rounds taking out as many rebels as I could.

"Get on that fifty!" I yelled at St. Clair. "The assault forces should be here any second!" There was no response so I glanced over. "St. Clair!" I yelled looking to my right. Leon St. Clair lay dead. A small hole in the center of his forehead leaked blood. The world stopped for a fraction of a second. The sound of helicopters filled the sky. They came in from the east, the door gunners opening up on the rebel camp with fifty caliber machine guns. Hot death fell from the sky. Three choppers provided cover fire. Three more descended to insert the assault force. The assault force bailed out of their choppers. They jumped to the ground from a height of six feet, to form a defensive perimeter. Once they had their boots, on the ground, they assaulted the rebel compound. I slung my rifle, grabbed an AK, laying next to one of the dead rebels, and stormed down the hill to join the battle.

Five rebel soldiers charged up the hill trying to avoid the firestorm below. They crashed through the jungle coming straight at me and opened up on me with their AK-47s. Diving to the right, I returned fire and tossed a grenade into their midst. There was a loud explosion. Dirt and debris filled the air. Jumping to my feet, I leaped over their dead bodies and ran into the rebel encampment. Two Columbian soldiers and two USMC advisors stormed into the grass hut. A rebel colonel ran out of the back door dragging the diplomat with him. He pulled the frightened man toward the front of the hut holding a forty-five to the side of his head. He was yelling something in his native tongue. I hit the ground in the prone position. Grabbing my sniper rifle, I held my breath lining the crosshairs on the colonel's forehead and took the shot. The colonel's head exploded showering the diplomat with blood and brain matter. I jumped up, slung my sniper rifle, grabbed the AK, and charged forward firing at the few rebel soldiers left. Several bodies littered the ground. Half of the rebel commandos managed to escape, but several more lay dead on the ground. Ten of them threw their rifles on the down and raised their hands.

The gunfire tapered off and I headed over to where Sergeant Bower, stood by one of the choppers.

"How the hell are you McDonald? You did an outstanding job," Bower said.

I sighed. A tear tracked down my face. "Not worth a fuck. My spotter is dead."

Sergeant Bower's face turned grave and he took my arm. "He was that dark-skinned feller named St. Clair?"

I looked at the ground. "Yeah."

"I'll send some troops up to bring his body down. Get in the chopper and take a break. Drink some water. You did good son." Bower took a cigar from his shirt pocket and offered me one. I took it and we fired them up. Tobacco smoke drifted across the jungle.

Finished with the cigar, I climbed up into the chopper and leaned up against its right bulkhead. A skinny, middle-aged man in a blue suit with gray hair gave me a freighted, but relieved smile.

"My name is Bob Dawson. I'm the diplomat they kidnapped. I heard what you said about your friend. I'm so sorry. Thank you for coming after me." His voice sounded weak and scared.

A brief flash of mixed emotions shot through me. "Forget about it. It's what they pay me for," I said trying to let the adrenaline rush subside. I closed my eyes, leaning back against the bulkhead while the chopper lifted off the ground. Back at the base, I climbed off the chopper. The Chopper lifted off the ground taking the diplomat back to Bogotá. I headed to a tent, which they had set up as an NCO club, and had a beer. I tried to make some sense out of the mission. A half-hour later, the rest of the assault force returned.

I stood near the landing pad waiting for them to touch down. When the helicopters landed, I ran out onto the landing pad. Marines jumped to the ground. They escorted the prisoners to a wired enclosure. Two Marines lifted St. Clair's body out of a chopper and dropped it on the ground.

"Don't touch him! Leave him be!" I yelled at the Marines who had deposited the body of Leon St. Clair on the ground. The sound of the helicopter's rotor blades and its engine made it hard to hear. They stood back for a moment while I knelt next to the body. Sergeant Bower took a knee next to me and laid a hand on my shoulder.

"Son, you let these men take him to graves registration. They need to prep him for the ride back home. He did good, out there. He was a hero. So are you. He did his country proud."

"Yeah right," I said and rose to my feet. "What did we accomplish out there?"

Bower paused and shrugged his shoulders. "Not much. We saved that diplomat's ass killed some rebels and burned down their base. Most of them, scattered heading deeper into the jungle. They'll rebuild somewhere else."

I nodded, headed back to the NCO club, bought a six-pack of beer, and headed back to my tent.

***

It was after that, that I started having nightmares. During the three months that followed, I went on as many missions as possible. Although we were advisors, I went out of my way to engage the enemy. It was out there in the jungle where I felt at home. Out there, I could unleash the rage. I had no friends. One night after coming in from the bush, I was lying in my rack when a runner came looking for me. He said that the CO wanted to see me in the command tent. I crossed the base and entered the command tent. Colonel Weaver saw me come in and looked up.

"Corporal McDonald. Have a seat."

I gave him a salute and sat down in a chair across the desk from the colonel. Weaver tossed a piece of paper across the desk for me to look at. I glanced down at a flier with my picture on it. It had Spanish writing on it.

My eyes widened. "What's this?" I asked.

"Our rebel friends have put a price on your head. It seems that you've put a dent in their activities," the colonel said.

I grinned. "How much am I worth?"

"One thousand dollars American. That's worth a fortune down here."

I shrugged. "I guess I'll have to watch my back."

Weaver shook his head. "Don't worry about it. I received orders for your transfer. You're out of here at zero six hundred in the morning."

"Damn. I was starting to enjoy my work. Where am I going now?" I asked.

"You're heading to Fort Knox Kentucky. You are going to learn how to drive tanks. And by the way, they also promoted you to sergeant."

"Imagine that," I said a grin spreading across my face.

Colonel Weaver stood up and handed me my orders. I tucked them under my arm. "It's been a pleasure. You are a squared away Marine," Weaver said, extending his hand and we shook.

"Thank you, sir. I try," I said.

The following morning, I boarded a chopper, took a hop to Bogotá, and caught a flight back to the world.

***

CHAPTER 13

"Hello, we're here to have a look at the house," the young Marine standing at my front door said. Shaking off the last vestige of memory, I nodded, his pretty wife smiled and I smiled back. I breathed in the scent of her perfume. She was wearing Chanel Number Five: Sharon's brand.

"Sure. My name's Mike McDonald. Come inside and have a look," I said, extending my hand. The young Marine shook my hand.

"My name is Ron Cassidy. This is my wife Nicole."

I nodded. "It's nice to meet you, Nicole," I said shaking hands with his wife.

I led the young couple into the house and gave them a quick tour. We stepped out the back door into the warm sunshine. When I showed them the backyard, Lucky came running up wagging his tail. He jumped up on Nicole resting his paws on her stomach.

"Oh what a lovely dog," Nicole said. She bent down, petted Lucky on the head, and scratched his ears. Lucky lapped up all the attention.

"His name is Lucky. He's a big suck ass. He'll do anything for a pat on the head."

"Nicole loves animals," Tom said. Noticing the horse corrals, Nicole's face lit up.

"Oh. I see you have horse corrals. Honey if we buy this place, you've got to get me a horse," Nicole said. She went over to the corrals and leaned over the bars checking everything out. She turned, placing her hands on her shapely hips, and surveyed the entire backyard. "I love this backyard. There's room for plenty of kids."

Ron laughed and his face turned red. "Let's not rush things. We have only been married for three weeks. We still have plenty of time."

I motioned to the screen door. "If you guys have seen enough, why don't we go into the kitchen and talk," I said. They followed me inside. "Would you like a beer or a glass of iced tea?"

"I'll have some tea," Nicole said.

"I'll have a beer," Ron said. I poured Nicole an iced tea, handed Ron his beer, and popped the top on a beer for myself. Taking a pull from my beer, I sat down across from Ron.

"So what do you think?"

Ron sighed and Nicole smiled.

"I love this place," Nicole said.

"I like it too, but the price is steep. I don't know if we can afford it," Ron said.

Nicole frowned.

I shrugged. "It's priced below market value, but since you're a Marine, I'll cut you an even better deal." I wrote a figure down on a piece of paper, slid it across the table, and Ron's eyes widened.

"You'd go that low?" Nicole looked at the figure and her face beamed.

"I need out of this place," I said.

"You were in the Marines?" Ron asked.

"Yeah, I served in the gulf," I said.

"Me too. I was on a ship off the coast. We were sitting on go but they never sent us in."

"I was a tank commander," I said.

"You guys were in the shit from what I heard," Ron said. I shrugged. That part of my memory hadn't returned yet. "So why would you go so low? Is there something wrong with the house?" Ron asked.

"No I have some personal business I need to attend to and I need to get out from underneath this house. You look like a nice young couple. Do you want the place?" I asked.

Ron looked over at his wife; she grinned from ear to ear.

"Yes. Will take it. The bank approved us for a loan already. We'll stop by the bank, and see about putting it in escrow," Ron said.

"I'll call my realtor and tell him about the deal. He won't be happy about the price, but fuck 'im if he can't take a joke," I said. "Sorry about my language," I said to Nicole.

She arched her eyebrows. "I'm used to it. After all, I'm married to a Marine."

I stuck my hand across the table."Simper fi." Ron shook my hand sealing the deal. "There's one thing. I'd like a thirty-day escrow. I want to be out of here as soon as I can."

"That shouldn't be a problem," Ron said.

We sat there at the table talking and enjoying each other's company for about an hour. Ron and I swapped war stories and I enjoyed being in Nicole's presence. Her bubbly laughter reminded me of Sharon. It caused a lump to form in my throat and a bit of sorrow to shoot through my soul. Ron and I had a couple more beers, and they stood to go.

"I'm driving," Nicole, said grabbing Ron's keys.

"When you get the loan squared away and are ready to put the house in escrow, let me know. I'll set up a face-to-face with my realtor," I said at the front door.

"I'll get back with you as soon as I can," Ron said.

Nicole hugged me. "I love this house. We're going to be happy here." After seeing them out the door, I let Lucky into the house, sat down in front of the TV, and popped the top on another beer. After finishing off two six-packs, I stumbled to bed around midnight, but I had a hard time getting to sleep. Strange noises kept me awake. The temperature dropped and my breath fogged up. Once, I thought I heard a woman whispering and when I finally dropped off, the nightmares started.

***

I woke up at seven AM the next morning with a pounding headache. After chewing up five aspirin, I packed up my arsenal, plus all my ammo, and put everything into the truck.

"Let's go, Lucky," I said to my dog. Lucky charged into the garage and jumped up into the passenger seat of my pickup truck when I opened the door. We left the house, headed down the street to Baseline, and turned left heading east. An early morning mist covered the ground. The road snaked its way up a hill passing more tracked homes, which gave way to a few remaining orange groves. The road turned to dirt and orange groves lined each side of the road. A few miles later, the orange groves stopped and the road climbed into the hills and wide-open fields. We traveled through a hilly area filled with sage and creosote bushes. The road ended at El Diablo Creek: a secluded, desolate watershed.

Letting Lucky out of the truck, I retrieved the guns and hiked over to the edge of the stream. The early morning fog dissipated and the sun came out. The water whispered over the rocks. I set up some targets at the edge of the stream. First, I tried the handguns killing a few cans and bottles. After the first shot, Lucky took off for the tall uncut. Then I fired each one of the shotguns. The sawed-off monsters kicked throwing the shot out in a wide pattered. I splattered a cantaloupe to hell and gone.

"One of these could blow someone in two." I broke down the shotgun and tossed out the empties. Setting the shotgun aside, I picked up the rifle. Lying in the prone position, I looked through the scope and saw a beer can, setting up high on the bank across the stream. It had to be at least three hundred yards away. Calculating wind speed in my head, I squeezed the trigger. The rifle boomed slamming back against my shoulder. The bullet hit two inches to the left and a couple of inches high. I adjusted the scope and fired again. This time the bullet hit dead center making the can rise into the air. I spent the next hour familiarizing myself with the weapons.

"Where did my damned dog go to?" I said to myself after I tossed out a couple of empty shotgun shells. Snapping the breech shut, I ambled back to the truck looking for my wayward dog. Lucky lay in the bed of the pickup wagging his tail. He wanted no part of any gunfire.

"Okay let's go, you big chicken," I said and I opened the driver's side door. Lucky leaped into the cab ahead of me and we headed into town. At Boulder Road, I turned left heading toward Redlands, caught the 10 freeway, and headed west. I pulled off on Hospitality Lane in San Bernardino. I pulled into the parking lot of a Western supply store. Browsing amongst the saddles and bridles, I headed into the clothing section.

"Is there anything I can find for you?" a red-headed female clerk asked. She looked no more than twenty years old. The smell of her perfume filled the air around me. My eyes dropped for a fraction of a second to the tiny bit of cleavage showing at the top of her shirt.

I looked back up at her face and shot her a smile. "No thank you. I'm only looking right now." A black canvas duster caught my eye, so I took it off the rack and felt the rough fabric.

She touched my arm. "You can try it on if you want."

This could hide a lot of hardware, I thought and put on the coat. The large coat hung down with its tales stopping below my knees. *I hope this doesn't get caught in the bike's drive belt.* At the counter, I peeled off the coat and set it down.

The clerk smiled. "It looks good on you. You look handsome," she said and rung up the sale.

“Thank you,” I said returning her smile.

From the Western wear store, Lucky and I headed to a leather shop. Stepping into the store, I breathed in the smell of tanned leather. After browsing for a few minutes, I gave the clerk the dimensions of the holsters. I wanted him to make custom holsters for the two forty-fives and the sawed offs.

“I want the two holsters for the handguns on a belt at my waist. I’ll need something to connect the two large holsters to. I’ll need them further up on my sides next to my ribs,” I said to the clerk.

The blonde-headed young clerk took a pen and paper from underneath the counter and drew a diagram. “We’ll connect the two larger holsters to a shoulder rig. Then we’ll run a leather strap down your back to a cartridge belt where you’ll carry the forty-fives. What will you have in the large holsters?”

I looked him in the eye and said, “It’s better that you don’t ask.”

The clerk nodded. “A custom job like this will run you about a hundred bucks. I could have it for you in a week. If you like I can put rings on the shoulder straps for shotgun shells or whatever.”

“Do that. Make them twelve gage size,” I said taking out my wallet. I paid the clerk in advance.

“We’ll get right on it.”

After picking up a case of beer, Lucky and I headed home.

***

Another two weeks passed. The Harley shop finished the rebuild job on the motor and transmission for my Shovelhead. I picked up the powder-coated frame, plus the tank and fenders from the custom paint shop. They painted the tank black with a white iron cross on its side. White flames billowed in the background behind the cross. I put the bike back together, filled it up with gas and oil, and fired the beast up in the garage. The loud throaty rumble of the straight pipes bounced off the interior walls of the garage. I turned the motor off using the key and then tried the kick-starter. The bike fired up on the second kick. I pulled the Harley out of the garage and then headed down the street. The wind tickled my face and made me grin. I twisted the throttle and enjoyed the feel of the machine’s raw power.

After about a two-hour ride, I stopped at the leather shop on the way home and picked up my custom-made holsters. Standing in front of my bathroom mirror, I put on the holster rig. My guns fit into the holsters like if they were velvet gloves. Over this, I put on my long black duster. I wore a black Harley Davidson t-shirt, a black pair of jeans, and a black skullcap. The duster completely concealed all the hardware underneath.

"I look like some yahoo that can't figure out whether he wants to be a cowboy or a biker," I said to myself. Lucky looked up at me with his head turned and his ears cocked. "I know. I know boy. Your master is a weird duck," I said and put my gear away. Lucky looked at me and wagged his tail. Later, sitting in front of the boob tube drinking beer, I went over in my mind the things I had left to do.

"I guess that's it, Lucky," I said and reached down to scratch Lucky's ears. "All I have to do now is to wait for the house to sell and get rid of all this stuff. Then it hit me. *What am I going to do with Lucky?*

I spent the next month holding a yard sale, trying to sell everything I owned. When I wasn't sitting out in my front yard with a beer trying to sell my wares, I kept busy shooting. I tried to stay sharp with the weapons and working out. I continued with my morning walks, but by now, they had turned into runs. I worked out with the weights and kept up with my exercise routine. I did pushups, sit-ups, chin-ups, and leg lifts. By the end of the month, I was back into fighting shape. I showed little effects from my beating by the Lost Souls. My memory was still a little fuzzy, especially about my time in the Persian, Gulf.

I had the old Shovelhead dialed in; it purred like a kitten and had the power of a lion. I enjoyed taking rides on the Harley at night. As my house emptied, I allowed Ron Cassidy and his wife to move some of their things in early. The last item I sold was my pickup truck. The day we closed escrow, I put most of the money into an account, which I could access with a debit card. I kept five thousand dollars in cash. The morning I left, Ron Cassidy and his wife pulled up with the moving van. Nicole gave me a big hug when she got out of the truck.

"Where will you go?" she asked and then reached out and took my arm.

During the time I'd know them, we got close. I told them about what happened to Sharon, but not of my plans for the Lost Souls.

I paused for a few seconds. "Oh, I don't know. I have some business to take care of first, but I'll find someplace to stay."

Karen from across the street walked over. I introduced her to her new neighbors. "Are you sure you're okay with taking care of Lucky?" I asked Karen.

"Of course I'll keep Lucky for you. Lucky's a dear. When you get settled, you can come to pick him up," Karen said.

Ron Cassidy stuck out his hand and we shook. "Thanks, Mike. We would have never got into this house if you wouldn't have lowered the price."

"Forget about it," I said.

Karen hugged me, pressing her firm breasts up against my chest, and then kissed my cheek. I breathed in her essence. Her scent was a mixture of soap and perfume. "If you need anything, anything at all, you call me. I still can't get over what happened to Sharon," she whispered in my ear. I felt her salty tears on my cheek. The last goodbye I said was to my dog Lucky, but it was the hardest. I scratched his ears, a tear tracked down my face, and a lump formed in my throat.

"I'm gonna miss you old boy," I said trying to hold back the tears. Lucky licked my face. I petted him some more and stood up. With my gear bag tied on the back of the bike, I zipped up my leather jacket, threw my leg over the Harley, and fired her up. The rumble of the loud pipes boomed down the street. Lucky jumped up and I gave him another goodbye pet. *God, I'm gonna miss this damn dog*, I thought and another tear tracked down my face. Lucky jumped back to the ground, I put the Shovelhead into gear, and gave it some throttle. Waving goodbye over my shoulder, I headed down the street. Karen and the Cassidy's stood in the street talking as they watched me ride away. Taking Baseline to Boulder, I turned left and headed toward Redlands. At the Interstate 10 freeway, I hit the onramp heading toward LA and put my face in the wind.

***

James Quinn sat at an oak table in the back room of the bar where they held church. Stinky Boy and five prospects entered the bar. They had a pretty, petite-looking blonde woman with them. She looked no older than eighteen. Quinn laid a line down on the table and took a snort of coke. After enjoying the rush, he took a pull from his beer bottle.

"Who's this, Stink?" Stinky Boy, an older grubby-looking biker that had been in the club for years, smiled. He scratched his white scruffy beard.

"This prime piece of meat is Veronica. Veronica, say hi to JD." Stinky Boy said.

Veronica let out a nervous giggle and then smiled. "Hi."

"What's up?" Quinn asked.

Stinky Boy laughed. "Veronica here thinks she'd like to be a momma. I'm letting these prospects break her in. They need to earn their wings." Quinn nodded, fingering the scar on his cheek. The girl followed the prospects into a storage room. Stinky Boy stayed back for a few seconds to talk with Quinn. A few minutes later, a startled gasp came from the storage room

"What are you doing? No! Don't!" Veronica said and screamed.

Stinky Boy laughed. "I guess little Veronica there, didn't quite know what she was getting herself into."

"She'll be fine. One of the bros will snap her up pretty quick. She'll be wearing a property vest before you know it."

"Yeah. Prime stuff like that goes quick," Stinky Boy said.

"She reminds me of that blonde from a few months back. The one whose old man told me to turn down my music. Things got out of hand that night. That SOB won't be telling anybody to turn down their music anymore," Quinn said.

"Didn't you hear? He lived," Stinky Boy said.

Quinn looked up in surprise. "He lived? Are you sure?"

"It was in the paper a couple of months ago. He was in a coma, but he came out of it."

Quinn's face took on a serious cast. "Get our PI on it. I want to know where that dude lives and what he's up to."

"All right. I'll make the call," Stink Boy said.

Quinn stood up. "That can wait for a half-hour or so. Let's go in there and sample some of this prime pussy. Why let the prospects have all the fun?"

Stinky Boy let out a snort. "Yeah. I'm gonna put some of my, stink on her."

"We'll have to bathe the girl in turpentine after you're through," Quinn said. He breathed in the stench coming off Stinky Boy and chuckled. He crossed the meeting hall, stepped into the back storage room and Stinky Boy followed.

***

The Lost Souls' clubhouse laid nestled back in an industrial section of East LA. It looked like your typical biker bar. The red brick front of the building held two large windows enclosed by iron bars on each side of a set of double doors. The black wooden doors faced the sidewalk and a narrow street. Painted across the front of the building in lime green block lettering were the words: the Beaver Den. Across the street set, an abandoned two-story building with most of its windows broke out.

On my knees in the shadows, I gazed out the window from the second floor with a pair of binoculars. A light haze filled the air. Harley Davidson motorcycles lined the street. The rumble of loud pipes reverberated through the industrial park. Three more Harleys pulled up to the front of the Beaver Den. Five prospects stood out front guarding the motorcycles. I pulled my coat together and continued to study the clubhouse. In the distance, I heard the burp of a semi-truck applying his Jake brake. A white van pulled up to the front door, a young man climbed out and carried in two kegs of beer. I had been watching the clubhouse for three weeks. I took pictures and listened to the goings-on with a directional microphone. I began to notice a pattern. Every Friday, they held a party and had two kegs of beer delivered.

When I wasn't reconnoitering from above, I hit the street on my motorcycle. I followed some of the club members when they left the clubhouse. I made sure to stay a discreet distance behind them, but I managed to find out where some of them lived. Most of the regulars had established routines. They would show up at the clubhouse at certain times and leave at certain times each day.

I backed away from the window. "I've learned about as much as I can from up here," I said to myself. "I need to get inside that clubhouse. That delivery van is my ticket."

Lowering the binoculars, I retreated further into the abandoned building. I took the stairway to the ground floor where I left my Shovelhead. I parked it in the lobby of what had once been a large office complex. Firing up the motorcycle, I rode it across the glass-littered floor to the exit leading to a back alleyway. On the street, I headed north to the freeway and took interstate 10 to Santa Monica beach. So far, the Lost Souls didn't know I existed, or so I thought. I wanted to keep it that way. *I figure I'll give the recon phase of the mission one more week. After that, I go to war,* I thought.

***

I spent the next week hanging out at the beach and working on my tan. I let my beard and hair grow long. I didn't want them to find me snooping around their clubhouse, so I kept away for the most part. I did check on them, from time to time, from my hidden perch in the abandoned building across the street. On Thursday morning, I took a ride north and did some exploring in the mountains north of LA. I wore my leather jacket to ward off the cool mountain air. Pulling off Interstate 5 in Fraser Park, I took a dirt road back into the woods. I looked for secluded camping spots and places to hide. The fresh smell of the pine forest filled the air. I had to be careful on the dirt roads. Harley Davidson motorcycles aren't dirt bikes. Spending the night in the woods, I enjoyed a warm campfire and stashed some supplies. Friday morning early, I headed back to LA.

At four-thirty in the afternoon that Friday, I stood on a street corner five blocks up from the clubhouse. The weather had turned warm and sweat tracked down my face. The LA smog caused my eyes to water. The delivery van showed up like clockwork on the way to deliver the beer for the Friday night party. Luck was with me. The van's driver had to stop at a red light. I planned to step out in front of his van with my gun drawn if the light had been green. Stepping up to the passenger side door, I opened it and climbed into the van. The red-headed delivery driver looked over at me with fear in his wide eyes. I sat down on the passenger side and pointed a gun at him. He looked no more than twenty-one or twenty-two years old; he had a pocked marked face and frizzy hair. He wore a grubby tan work uniform.

"You should always lock your passenger door when you're driving. You never know who might climb into your vehicle," I said and smiled.

"What do you want man? I don't have much money, but you can have it. Take the van, if that's what you want. Please don't shoot me." Sweat flowed down the side of his face.

"See that motorcycle sitting in the parking lot of that paint supply store?" I said pointing to the side of the road. "Turn right and then turn into the parking lot. Park next to the motorcycle. Do it when the light turns green unless you want to catch a bad case of lead poisoning," I said. The light changed to green and he followed instructions. "Turn off the van and hand me the keys," I said waving the gun at him. He complied and his hands shook when he gave me the keys. "Now let's get out and climb in back to have a little talk."

"Sweet Jesus, you're gonna kill me," he said. Tears welled up in his eyes.

"Do I look like a killer? Do it."

I jumped out of the van and ran around to the driver's side before he could get out. When he stepped out of the van, I shoved the gun into his back and forced him to the rear of the vehicle. Inside the van, he dropped to his knees and raised his hands. Tears streamed down his face. "Please don't shoot me. I'll do anything you want. I'll suck your-"

"Shut the fuck up and listen, you little pussy!" I yelled.

He shut his mouth, but the tears continued to roll down his cheeks.

"How would you like to make three hundred dollars?" I said. He looked down at my crotch. "Not that way, you dumb son of a bitch!"

He stopped crying. "How?" he asked, choking back a sob.

"You deliver beer to the Lost Souls' clubhouse every Friday."

The delivery boy wiped his eyes. "Yeah. Two kegs."

"What's the layout like inside?"

He shrugged. "It's a bar. There's a door leading to their meeting hall in the back. There's a storeroom on the left where they keep the kegs."

"I'm going to make your delivery today. I'll need your clothes," I said.

He let out a frightened sigh. "My clothes?"

"Yeah strip down to your underwear," I said waving the gun at him for effect. He stripped.

"Good Lord! Don't you ever change your underwear?" I said in disgust and pulled a roll of duck tape out of my back pocket.

His eyes locked onto the Duck Tape. "What's that for?"

"To keep you honest. Rollover on your belly." He rolled over; I taped his hands together behind his back and taped his feet together. Grabbing his dirty socks, I shoved them into his mouth and taped his mouth closed. He let out a gagging sound. "This will teach you to wear clean socks next time," I said and let out a chuckle. I changed out of my jeans and t-shirt and put on the delivery uniform. "This will all be over in a half-hour or so. If you make any noise while I'm in the clubhouse, it will cause me trouble and I'll have to come out shooting. If that happens, I could put a couple of rounds in your fat ass," I said and climbed out of the van. The delivery boy shook his head indicating that he wouldn't make any noise. Behind the wheel, I pulled out of the parking lot and headed down to the Lost Souls' clubhouse.

At the clubhouse, I pulled the van up at the front door and parked. Climbing out on the driver's side, I went around to the back and unloaded two kegs of beer using a dolly. At the front door, a young prospect stopped me.

"You're new. Where's the regular guy?" he asked.

I stepped back. "He called in sick. I'm doing his route."

"Why are you wearing his shirt?" My eyes dropped to the name tag on the front of the tan shirt.

"It's my first day on the job. I'm still waiting on my uniforms. Ray let me borrow his shirt," I said.

The prospect turned around and led me into the clubhouse. I glanced about the barroom, taking in the grubby bikers along with two women dancing topless on the bar. The smell was a mixture of stale beer, cigarette smoke, and marijuana smoke. I followed the prospect to the back storage room.

"Put the kegs in here," the prospect said and left. I set the full beer kegs down. Once I was alone in the musty-smelling storage room, I left a few surprises for the boys. I unloaded the full beer kegs. Putting the empties on the dolly, and stepped out the door of the storeroom. Pausing in the doorway, I looked into the meeting hall in the back. A large oak table with the figure of a hooded demon on its top set in the center of the room. Engraved at the bottom of the tabletop were the words: the Lost Souls. Folding chairs set around the table. Leaving the beer kegs by the door, I crossed the room and stepped over to the table. I reached underneath the table and deposited another surprise for the bros. If anyone saw it, they would think it was somebody's worn-out chewing gum.

"Hey! What are you doing?" the prospect yelled.

Startled, I looked up. "I was admiring your table here. I'm into woodworking," I said.

"Well get your empty beer kegs and get the fuck out of here," the prospect said.

"Right," I said and went back to where I'd left the empty beer kegs. On the way out, I recognized a familiar face standing at the bar. One of the grubbiest looking bikers I'd ever seen stood next to him drinking a beer. My breath caught in my throat and my heart thumped in my chest. My hand moved toward the gun tucked in my jeans underneath my shirt. I choked on my anger and dropped my hand to my side.

"What'd you find out about, McDonald?" JD Quinn said to Stinky Boy.

Stinky Boy bellied up to the bar. Above him, a big-breasted redhead danced topless. Stinky Boy looked up and smirked. "Old Rachel sure has some big tits."

"About McDonald? What did our PI have to say?" Quinn asked.

"He says McDonald's dropped off the face of the Earth. The neighbors say he sold everything he owned and rode away on a Harley. He doesn't have a clue about where he is right now."

Quinn turned back to the bar. "We have problems."

Stinky Boy laughed. "Dude. The guy was ridin' a Gold Wing. The PI says that he was an insurance salesman. How much trouble can he be?"

I pulled my cap down low over my face and pushed the empty beer kegs to the door. Back down the street, I changed back into my clothes. I cut the Duck Tape binding Ray's arms and legs. Then I pulled the Duck Tape off his face, and took the socks from his mouth.

"Ouch," he said when I pulled the Duck tape loose.

I chuckled. "If the boys down the road ask questions, tell them I held a gun on you. Don't tell them about the money," I said and tossed three hundred dollars down on his chest. "If I were you, I'd get dressed and get the fuck out of here. Things are about to get bloody." Jumping back out of the van, I fired up the Harley and headed up a side street. Stopping at the corner, I turned around to see what Ray would do. Five minutes later, he jumped out of the back of the van. He climbed behind the wheel and drove off heading away from the Lost Souls' clubhouse.

"That's a good boy, Ray. I'd hate to have to put a bullet in you," I said to myself. I turned around and headed down the alley behind the building facing the clubhouse. Fifteen minutes later, I lay in my perch in the window looking down at the clubhouse below. Bikes began to arrive for the Friday night party; a band showed up and brought in their equipment while I waited. After another hour, the party started. Loud music and boisterous laughter emanated from the clubhouse. All the patched members were inside enjoying the party. Five prospects stood outside guarding the bikes.

I bolted a, round into my rifle, sighted in on the prospect that showed me to the back storeroom earlier. A streetlight illuminated his youthful face and blond goatee. The crosshairs settled on his forehead; I held my breath for an instant and squeezed the trigger. The rifle roared slamming back into my shoulder. The prospect's head exploded into a pink misty cloud.

***

CHAPTER 14

I exited interstate I 5 at two AM the next morning. Bone weary, I pulled into a twenty-four-hour gas station and mini-mart. It was right next to the freeway. Shivering from the cold, I killed the Shovelhead's engine and put the bike on its side stand. I hurried into the mini-mart.

"Can I help you?" a young pimply-faced kid behind the counter asked.

I let out a sigh. "Yeah, I'd like some gas," I said, trying to keep my eyes open. I tossed a twenty down on the counter. The kid entered the transaction into the cash register and turned on the pump. Fumbling around in my jacket pocket, I tossed a piece of paper onto the counter. "There's going to be a bunch of brain-dead bikers come in here in a half-hour or so. They might ask about me. If they do, give them this. It's a map showing the area where I'll be. Tell them I said come on out and play."

The kid glanced down at the crude map I'd drawn. "What's this all about?"

I shrugged. "Nothing you need to worry about. Tell them what I said."

I bought a cup of coffee, headed back out to the bike, and filled the gas tank. Earlier at the clubhouse, I took out the first prospect guarding bikes. I sighted in on another and fired. I hit him in the chest punching a hole through his heart. He flew back against the clubhouse wall and slid to the sidewalk. A puddle of blood pooled up beneath him. By the time, the bikers inside the clubhouse came outside all five of the prospects lay dead on the ground. Bikers came running out of the clubhouse and fired up at the windows of the abandoned building I was hiding in. Minute pieces of glass and mortar flew through the air. I slung the rifle over my shoulder, running from window to window, and fired on the bikers in the street. Hot brass from my twin forty-fives flew up into the air. Leaning against the wall, I reloaded the handguns and switched to the sawed offs.

The bikers flanked the building coming in on the ground floor. I watched them point flashlights about and firing at shadows, but I stayed in the dark and moved in for the kill. Three bikers came down the hallway and entered the room where I was hiding. A sense of calmness dropped over me. I pulled my K-Bar knife, grabbed the last guy in line, and dragged him into the stairway. Slamming the blade into the side of his neck, I clamped my hand over his mouth to stifle a scream. Blood squirted out of his neck his legs kicked and his body did its death dance. I stripped him of his colors, stuffing his vest into my duffle bag, and headed down the stairway to the second floor.

Two guys met me at the bottom of the staircase. I fired both barrels of one of the sawed-offs blowing the guts out of the biker in front of me. His bro jumped to the side and watched his buddy's body crumple to the floor. Holstering the sawed-off, I pulled its mate from the left side holster and fired. The muzzle blast lit up the dark interior of the building. The blast hit the other biker under the chin taking off his jaw and half of his head. Blood and gore splattered against the wall. I heard someone scream.

"What the fuck was that? Get that son of a bitch!" Several more bikers came charging up the stairs. Pulling my forty-fives, I ran down the staircase firing both weapons at the same time. Three bikers fell dead on the staircase and rolled back down to the ground floor. The two that remained, ran. One tripped as the body of one of the dead guys tumbled down the stairway. Bullets slammed into the bottom of the staircase pinning me down for a few seconds. Hiding in the stairwell, I fired off a shotgun blast and dived to my left. Rolling across the room, I jumped up and ran to an area across the lobby where I'd left my Harley.

Jumping into the saddle, I fired up the shovelhead and gunned the throttle. The back tire spun, kicking dirt and debris into the air, and the bike lurched forward. The smell of gun smoke and burnt rubber filled the room. I hit the door, launching the bike off a loading ramp, and landed in the asphalt. Twisting the throttle, I crossed a parking lot, slammed on the breaks, spun the bike around, and stopped. I sat there for a few seconds huffing and puffing. My heart raced, but my hands were rock steady. James Quinn and five other bikers stepped out of the building. They stood on the loading dock illuminated by a full moon.

"You shouldn't have killed my wife," I said, my voice wafting across the parking lot.

Quinn pulled a handgun. "That was a mistake. We got fucked up on meth that night. Let's finish this now."

I laughed. “You’re not getting off that easy. Your big mistake was not making sure that I was dead.”

Quinn nodded. “That is stating the obvious.”

I gunned the throttle and the bikers standing next to Quinn raised AK-47s to their shoulder.

“I’ll see you in Fraser Park, asshole,” I said and popped the clutch. The bike shot across the parking lot, and bullets tore us asphalt behind me. A bullet buzzed by my ear sounding like an angry bee. On the street, I turned a corner and headed to the interstate. With my fist in the throttle, I calculated the damage I’d done to the Lost Souls. There were the five prospects, five more out front and the one with the knife on the third floor. Then there was the three on the staircase. *Fourteen. That’s a good start*, I thought when I hit the onramp and headed north on the I5.

***

My mind danced back to the present. I fired up the Shovelhead and headed west on a two-lane road through the forest. My fingers felt numb from the cold. Three miles west of town, I pulled off onto a dirt road leading into the woods. The going was slow because of the rough, rocky dirt road. Like I said before, Harley Davidson motorcycles make shitty dirt bikes. The night seemed as black as the Devil’s heart. The only illumination was the bike’s headlight. The smell of the forest filled the air. Five miles in, I pulled the bike into the trees in a secluded area. Across the road set a clearing with a fire ring. Earlier, I’d left a surprise for the bros buried in the bottom of the fire pit. I killed the motor and concealed the bike behind a fallen pine tree. Climbing off the Harley, I took a quick piss and climbed up onto the tree to watch the road. From here on out, it was a waiting game.

Forty-five minutes later, I woke from a quick nap. I heard a pack of more than twenty Harley Davidson motorcycles coming up the road. They had a hard time keeping control of their motorcycles. One of them dumped his bike right in front of my position. I breathed in the smell of dust.

“Shit,” the guy said and didn’t even see me sitting on top of the fallen pine tree no more than ten feet away. The pack stopped and two of his bros helped him pick up his scooter. They continued up the road but came back fifteen minutes later coming to a stop right in front of me.

"He's not here. The son of a bitch led us on a wild goose chase. Let's make camp and get some rest," someone said. I smiled in the dark no more than six feet away.

"That's what he wants us to do. He could be out there watching us right now. It's kind of funny that he leads us to the only campsite on this road," someone else said.

"We could be on the wrong road," another voice added. I recognized the voice of James Quinn. "We'll camp here. I'm not gonna go out there in the dark woods looking for the cocksucker. We'll post guards until daylight. Tomorrow we'll find that fucker and kill him."

They pulled their motorcycles across the road into the clearing, but not once did they look my way. Quinn shouted orders and within a few minutes, they had a blazing fire going. Five bikers carrying AK-47s took up positions around the camp standing guard duty. I heard a few laughs and catcalls. After about an hour, the campsite quieted down as the majority of the bikers went to sleep. An owl hooted not far away and I heard a squirrel scamper up a tree. The sentries found perches on nearby rocks and logs. They were starting to fall asleep. Donning my black duster, I moved across the road using the trees for concealment.

Hitting the forest floor, I low crawled toward the nearest sentry. Pine needles clung to my clothes while I moved through the brush. At the edge of the campsite, I leaped up from behind a bush and dived upon one of the sentries. With my hand clamped over his mouth, I drove the blade of my K Bar through his breastbone. Blood spewed out of his chest and covered my hand. One of the other sentries caught the flash of movement and yelled.

"Hey!" I pulled one of my sawed offs from underneath my coat and let go with one barrel. The muzzle flash lit up the night. The blast blew his heart and a piece of his spine out his back. I used the other barrel on the third sentry. Holstering the weapon, I pulled the other sawed off. Groggy bikers jumped from their sleeping bags. I leaped over the fire and disappeared into the night. A massive explosion erupted from the campfire. The pipe bomb I'd buried in the fire ring exploded sending a deadly wall of shrapnel flying in all directions. Fiery embers and pieces of burning wood flew into the air. *God, I hope I didn't start a forest fire,* I thought while sprinting through the forest. I climbed on the Harley, fired up the motor and dirt biked it to the road keeping my feet down so I wouldn't drop the bike. I gunned the throttle heading back toward the paved road. Behind me, I heard men screaming and motorcycles starting. The roar of their pipes emanated through the woods.

A quarter-mile from the paved road, I came around a bend and pulled the Shovelhead underneath a tree. Earlier, I had tied one end of a long rope to a tree near the road and left the rest of the rope coiled behind the tree. Putting the bike on its side stand, I ran across the road and grabbed the end of the rope. With the end of the rope in hand, I ran back across the road and snubbed it around the tree setting next to my bike. I pulled the rope tight, stringing it across the road from tree to tree. It was about chest height. I tied it off, stepped back into the forest, and pulled both of my shotguns. The sound of motorcycle engines and loud pipes resonated through the forest.

The Lost Souls came around the bend in the road; the first two riders hit the rope and went down. Five or six more piled into them. The sound of crunching metal filled the air and I smelled gasoline. I opened up with the shotguns slamming a deadly wall of lead into the misfortunate bikers. The muzzle flash from the shotguns killed my night vision. The booming blast echoed through the darkness. One of the bikes caught fire and the gas tank exploded. I heard several screams and the rest of the bikers panicked. Some ran into the forest and others fired wild shots in my direction. I ambled over to my motorcycle, holstering my weapons, climbed onto the bike, and fired it up. Gunning the throttle, I peeled out showering dirt on the bikers behind me and headed for the paved road. On the pavement, I headed east, caught the interstate, and headed back to LA with my fist in the throttle and my face in the wind.

***

I spent the next two weeks watching bikinis on the beach. I wanted the LA chapter of the Lost Souls to let down their guard. I had hurt them bad. They would look for me all over LA stopping in at every biker bar or saloon there was. I rode up coast highway 1 to Morro Bay and spent the week lying out on the sand. I let my hair and beard grow longer. For the next part of my plan, I wanted to look grubby. When I headed back to East LA, I rode right down the street in front of their clubhouse. None of the Lost Souls had a real good look at my bike or me. My eyes took in the windows of the abandoned building where I'd launched my initial attack. I noticed guards with

AK-47s in the windows. On the roof of the clubhouse, two more bikers stood holding weapons. The sky was overcast and threatened rain.

I headed down the street for another three blocks and took a right turn. Coming back west, I headed back down an alley and hid my bike behind some pallets next to a loading dock. Dressed in grubby jeans and a dirty Army jacket, I had a rucksack on my back. I carried a gunnysack over my shoulder I went from dumpster to dumpster, collecting cans. When I reached the clubhouse, I camped behind a collection of trash dumpsters. The stench was overpowering. One of the bikers on the roof noticed me but paid me no mind. I guess he figured I was another bum looking for a place to sleep. I opened up the rucksack, took out my sleeping bag, spread it out, and set up my new headquarters.

From the rucksack, I took out a handheld listening device and dialed it in. When I had delivered the beer to the clubhouse, I planted a bug underneath the table in the Lost Souls' meeting room. With all the bikes lined up out front, I figured they were about to hold church. I wasn't disappointed.

The voice of James Quinn came over the speaker. "Has anybody seen or heard anything about this fucker, McDonald?" Several people spoke at once, but when the room quieted down, someone answered.

"We've looked everywhere. We've hit every bar and strip club in LA. We've scoured every abandon building and rooftop around here. There's been no sign of him. It's like he dropped off of the radar."

"I'll bet he's satisfied with his pound of flesh and called it good enough," someone said.

Quinn let out a sign. "I wish. The son of a bitch took out over twenty-five of our guys in one night. Ten out in front of the clubhouse, four more in the building across the street, and twelve up in Fraser Park. I don't think he's done. He doesn't strike me as a guy who gives up easily. Our PI did some digging in his background. He was some kind of war hero. He drove a tank in the gulf. This guy is going to be hard to kill," Quinn said.

"What do you want to do?" someone asked.

There was a pause. "Rat Man. Take Spider and Road Dog and head to Vegas in the morning. We need some help. I'll call the chapter president and have him send some of his bros our way. You guys meet them at State Line and escort them back. Tell them to bring some heavy artillery."

"What about the Christmas Party? Are we going to cancel because of this?" someone asked.

There was another pause. "No. We've had a Christmas party every year since we formed the club. I won't let this bastard ruin that."

"Interesting," I said to myself and turned down the listening device. I crawled into my sleeping bag and settled in for the night.

Early the next morning, I rolled out of my sleeping bag and packed my gear. Misty fog filled the air. Still playing the part of a vagrant, I ambled down the alley. I went from, dumpster-to-dumpster until I came to the place where I'd hidden my Harley. I fired up the machine, rode back down the alley passing the clubhouse, and headed for the freeway onramp. At a mini-mart near the freeway, I gassed up the bike and used their restroom to clean up. After shaving all the stubble from my face, I put on a clean pair of jeans and a black Harley Davidson t-shirt. Taking my weapons from my duffle bag, I put on my holster rig and put the long black duster on to conceal my hardware.

Parking the Harley behind the mini-mart, I bought a cup of coffee and a package of chocolate doughnuts. The hot liquid in the coffee cup felt good to my cold hands. The caffeine rush chased the cobwebs of sleep from my brain. Sitting on the bike, I watched the eastbound onramp to Interstate 10. Traffic in the streets buzzed by. the morning chill dissipated and the fog disappeared. Forty-Five minutes later, three motorcycles rumbled past the mini-mart. They headed up the freeway onramp. The riders wore the colors of the Lost Souls. I waited for about ten minutes and fired up the Harley. Hitting the Interstate, I put my fist in the throttle becoming one with the machine.

Somewhere between Ontario and San Bernardino, I caught up with them. They rode in a staggered formation. Pulling up next to the leader, who rode a junky-looking Fat Boy, I figured he must have been the one they called Rat Man. His face resembled a big fat rat with a mouth full of cheese. I pulled a sawed-off from underneath my coat, Rat Man's eyes widened and he hit the brakes. Letting go with both barrels, I blew the top of his head off. Blood, bits, and pieces of bone and brain matter flew through the air. It looked as if I was riding through a cloud of red mist. The rider behind him locked up his brakes hitting the downed bike in front of him and went over the handlebars. The third rider swerved to avoid both downed bikes and lost control.

His tires slid out, the bike went sideways and together they slid down the freeway. Cars behind us slammed on their brakes and blew their horns. The smell of burnt rubber filled the air.

I braked and swerved to the right, coming to a stop at the edge of the road. Traffic behind us had come to a stop. I ran into the traffic lanes. Pulling one of my forty-fives, I put two rounds each through the helmets of the two Souls that were still alive. They wouldn't have to worry about road rash. Working fast, I stripped the bodies of their vests, ran back to my bike, and stuffed my trophies into my duffle bags. Jumping into the saddle, I gunned the throttle, spinning my tires, and left the scene at a high rate of speed. I had another rendezvous with some bikers coming in from Las Vegas.

When I hit the I15-interchange I saw an ambulance and two highway patrol cars shoot by. They had their red lights flashing and their siren blaring.

I pulled over to the side of the freeway. Climbing off the bike, I stuffed my drover's coat, along with my gear inside my duffle bag. Back on the bike, I brought it up off its side stand, dropped it into gear, and headed back out into traffic. My cheeks felt numb due to a crisp breeze that buffeted the bike. I headed up the Cajon Pass keeping under the posted limit until I reached Barstow. At Barstow, I pulled off the freeway and stopped at a Chevron station. I took a piss smoked a cigarette and hit the freeway heading east on the 15.

With the throttle cranked, I rolled through Baker California thirty-five minutes later. Gazing to my left, I noticed the world's tallest working thermometer. The temperature said sixty-five degrees. A couple of miles west of Mountain Pass, I took an exit and pulled off the freeway. On the east side of the pass, lay State Line and the state of Nevada. Finding a dry brushy creek bed, fronting road, I hid the bike in the brush. I took my Ruger 270 from my duffle bag and slung it across my back. I made my way up the mountainside overlooking the freeway. When I reached the top of the ridge, I found a spot with a good field of fire that looked down on the freeway. Lying in the prone position, I took my rifle off my back and settled in to wait. A cool breeze blew across the mountain ridge and a hawk floated in the air, above me.

My mind wandered taking in past events. I'd killed a lot of men, but they needed killing. When I came back from the gulf, I didn't think I would ever have to kill again. I remembered a bible passage and ran it over in my mind. *To everything, there is a season. A time to be born a time to die, and a time to kill.*

"Killing time has come round again," I whispered to myself. Looking through the scope on my rifle, I sighted in on a big rig passing by. I adjusted the magnification on the scope bringing the trucker in crystal clear. The driver, a heavyset man with a scruffy black beard and a bad hairdo picked his nose. I laughed. Two hours later, I heard the sound of motorcycle pipes. I set the rifle down and picked up my binoculars. Twenty Harleys rolled down the highway in a column of twos and they were moving at a good clip. "These guys will never learn," I said to myself. "This is going to be like knocking down a set of dominos." Behind them, an indistinct white van chugged along. I moved the bannocks to the van. "Now that's biker trash. I bet they've got the hardware in the van," I whispered to myself. Setting aside the binoculars, I picked up my rifle and sighted in on the two bikes leading the pack. Picking the rider nearest to my side of the road, I bolted a round into the chamber.

Sighting in on the rider, I squeezed the trigger and the rifle slammed back into my shoulder. The bullet punched a hole through the rider's heart. His bike went down tangling with the bike next to it and the first next five riders in the pack went down. The sound of squealing brakes and scrapping metal filled the air. Some of the bikes high sided, launching their riders. Their bikes somersaulted down the freeway. One bike, dumped its rider, popped back up, crossed the road, and launched itself over an embankment. More bikes went down.

I moved the rifle, sighting in on the chase van, bolted in another round, and fired taking out its front left tire. Bringing up the rifle, I bolted in another round and put one through the windshield. The windshield exploded. The van swerved to the right and rolled. The five bikers at the rear of the pack managed to avoid the collision and pulled off to the side of the road. I fired at anything that moved. The sound of the injured bikers on the road drifted with the wind. One tried to crawl toward the edge of the road dragging a broken leg, but I put a round through the back of his neck. He quit crawling.

Someone crawled from the van carrying an AK. He hobbled up the embankment and dived into the prone position by the edge of the road. Slamming a magazine in the AK, he racked the top of the ridge where I lay concealed in the brush. Bullets buzzed through the creosote bush I was hiding behind. A bullet burned a path across the top of my shoulder. Glancing down, I noticed blood running down my arm from a bullet crease on my left bicep. A bead of sweat tracked down my face and my heart thumped inside my chest. I jacked another round in the chamber, sighted in on the guy with the AK, and squeezed the trigger. He flew backward off the embankment. The five bikers that avoided the crash, dived for cover. I put a round through the gas tanks on each of their motorcycles and one of the bikes caught fire. I quit firing and waited for a few seconds. Taking a water bottle from my back pocket, I took a pull. It provided a slight respite from the desert heat. Two minutes later, a biker poked his head up from behind the embankment down below. I put a round over his head and he jerked his head back down.

Hiding behind the brush, I tied up my wounded arm with a dew rag and set my rifle aside. My stomach rumbled. Feeling the need, I pulled one of the Lost Souls' vests out of my gear bag. Laying it on the ground, I pulled down my pants and took a healthy shit on the patch. Time was ticking and the cops were liable to show up. Finished with my business, I slung my rifle and grabbed my gear bag. Keeping under concealment, I made my way down the ridge to the dry creek bed where I left my motorcycle. I had to go slow to keep from slipping. At my motorcycle, I put on a leather jacket to conceal my wounded arm and fired up the bike. Hitting the freeway, I headed east to State Line. I saw three police cars and two ambulances pass by heading in the opposite direction.

Pulling off the freeway, I turned left and pulled into Whiskey Peat's Casino. After having a cold beer and eating at the buffet, I hit the freeway heading west on the 15. When I reached, the site of the shootout, the police had the five remaining Souls up against the car with the cuffs on. They had a roadblock set up and were letting cars through one at a time. When I reached the head of the line, the cop gave me the once over, taking in my new haircut and my fresh shave.

"Do you know these guys?" the cop asked.

I arched my eyebrows. "Do I look like I run with their crowd?"

"No. No, you don't. You can go," the officer said.

I pulled through the roadblock and but pulled over to the side of the road next to where the hulk of the chase van lay. The police officers were busy on the road investigating the accident. Taking a pipe bomb from my jacket pocket, I lit the cannon fuse and tossed it underneath the van.

"Hey, officer!" I yelled to the nearest cop. "That van down there looks like it is on fire. It must be leaking gas." He whirled around; I hit the throttle and headed back out on the highway. Behind me, the van exploded sending a fireball and a cloud of black smoke into the air. Cranking the throttle, I put the scene behind me, and headed to Baker. In Baker, I pulled off the freeway and found a low-rent motel. After renting a room under a false name, I pushed my bike through the front door and into the motel room. I figured to lay low for a while and give things a day or two to cool down before heading back to LA.

***

James Quinn stood on the ridge overlooking the freeway west of Mountain Pass. A cold breeze tickled his face. His mind flashed back to the face-to-face at State Line. After getting word about recent events, Quinn and twenty-five of his bro headed to State Line. They met up with their brothers from Las Vegas. Once they bailed out the five bros from the Las Vegas chapter, they met at Whiskey Pete's Casino for a sit-down. The sound of slot machines paying out filled the room and the smell of tobacco smoke filled the air.

Quinn leaned forward resting his arms on the table. "What I want to know is why in the fuck couldn't you guys, have got up on that ridge and took that son of a bitch out."

One of the remaining five looked down at his hands. "He had the high ground. We didn't even know he was there until it was too late. He took out the lead rider and everything went to shit. How are you supposed to fight back when half your crew is down on the highway? The bastard shot some of our bros who were down after they crashed. They were trying to crawl to the edge of the road."

Quinn shook his head. "You had all those guns."

The man leaned back looking Quinn in the face. "He shot the front tire out on the van and took out the driver. The van rolled. He had us pinned down with that high-powered rifle. We tried man. Mojo put some rounds up there with an AK but he took a round through the shoulder. Once he stopped shooting, my first duty was to my injured brothers. Then the cops showed up."

"What injured? I thought you five were the only ones who survived," Quinn asked.

"We were, but Charlie took a round through the calf. Mojo took one in the shoulder. We were going to go up there and look for him, but by that time, he made it back to his bike and took off. We were stuck."

Quinn's mind danced back to the present and he looked down on the pile of shit on top of a Soul's vest.

"I'll give a thousand bucks to the guy who takes out this mother fucker. I've seen enough. Let's roll." Quinn headed down the ridge and the rest of the Lost Souls followed.

Five days later, I climbed on the shovelhead and hit the freeway heading south on the 15. I rolled down the street in front of the Lost Souls' clubhouse on the day of their Christmas party. The air was chill, but the burning anger boiling up inside me made me feel nice and cozy. Motorcycles set parked against the curb lining the street. Four new prospects stood out front guarding the bikes. I pulled a sawed-off from underneath my coat and hit the throttle. The first prospect saw me rolling up and pulled a handgun. I let go with the sawed-off. The charge of buckshot hit him in the center of his chest turning his heart and upper body to mush. His body flew backward landing against the wall and he slid to the ground leaving a blood smear. His bowels voided and his legs kicked.

The second prospect tried to run out into the street to get a shot at me. I gave him the other barrel taking off the top of his head. The third prospect turned to run. Pulling my left hand sawed off, I opened up on him with both barrels. The shot hit him in the hip blowing away most of his pelvis. The last prospect made it back into the clubhouse before I could deal with him. At the end of the block, I swerved sideways in the street and brought the bike to a stop. I took a cell phone from my pants pocket. My breath formed a vapor cloud in front of my face.

"Ho, ho, ho, motherfuckers," I said and punched number one on the cell phone. A fraction of a second later, the block of home made C-4 ignited, causing a loud explosion. There was a secondary explosion when the pipe bomb under the pallet that the beer kegs were sitting on went off. The horrendous explosion sent smoke and fiery debris into the air. "So much for the LA chapter of the Lost Souls," I said to myself and hit the throttle heading for the freeway.

James Quinn and two others from the LA chapter were out back in smoking when they heard the gunfire out front. They turned to run into the clubhouse when the building exploded. The concussion knocked them to the ground. Bricks, pieces of wood, and other debris rained down on them. Shell shocked and bleeding, they stumbled to their feet.

A grin spread across my face when I hit the freeway. Finished with the LA chapter, my next mission was to exterminate the scumbags in Las Vegas. I was on the interstate where the I15 and the 215 meet and heading up the Cajon Pass when I rolled up on a military convoy. Large semi-trucks carrying military equipment occupied the slow lane. I glanced over at the camouflaged main battle tanks. Another set of memories sliced through my brain like a hot knife through butter.

***

CHAPTER 15

I climbed down from the bus at Fort Knox in Kentucky and the hot muggy air took my breath away. Sweat formed upon my brow and underneath my arms. Glancing around, I took in my surroundings. It was a large Army base and most of the buildings were brick but some of the barracks were wooden, painted OD green. I saw Quonset huts in the distance across a grassy parade ground. Hoisting my duffle bag over my shoulder, I headed toward HQ. An overhead fan osculated when I stepped into the main office complex. A second lieutenant sat at a reception desk in an outer office. Stepping up to the clerk, I fired off a salute.

"Sergeant Mike McDonald reporting for duty," I said.

The beady-eyed little clerk looked up from his desk. He wiped a bead of sweat from his face, shuffled through some paperwork, and said, "Have a seat. Colonel Jefferson will be right with you."

I sat. From inside the colonel's office, I heard a heated discussion taking place. A few minutes later a pissed-off blond-headed major exited the room. He looked like a squared away Marine. *Great. He had to go and get the CO pissed off* I thought.

The clerk looked up and smiled. "You can go in now."

Rising to my feet, I entered the colonel's office and saw the biggest black man I'd ever seen. I didn't realize they made Army uniforms that big. I stood up and fired off another salute. "Sergeant Mike McDonald reporting for duty sir."

"McDonald! Have a seat! I'm Colonel Jefferson." My breath caught in my throat and my heart pounded inside my chest. A nervous ball shot through my stomach when I sat down. I realized that the colonel wasn't yelling, earlier. I tried to relax. "Give me a minute." While he thumbed through my file, I studied the massive black man sitting across from me. He had a large bald head, sharp features, and a muscled body that strained the fabric of his uniform. There wasn't an ounce of fat on him. His eyes looked as dark as the inside of a raven's asshole. When he locked those eyes upon you, you felt as they would bore holes right through you. Finally, he tossed my file onto his desk.

"I was going over your personnel file. Impressive. If you apply yourself to tanks, like you did when you were in scout sniper school, you'll do well here. That event in Columbia was impressive as well. Tomorrow you'll start training. You'll spend six hours in class after morning PT and then you'll spend four hours on the tank range. During your final phase of training, you will spend eight hours on the range. Right now, you can head down to the barracks and stow your gear. It's down on the end of Eisenhower Boulevard. Evening, chow is at eighteen hundred hours. Welcome to Fort Knox." The colonel stood and stuck out his hand. We shook.

"Thank you, sir," I said. Trying to regain some feeling in my fingers, I snapped off another salute. He returned the courtesy.

"One more thing, Mr. McDonald You Marines that go through our tank school are our guests here. Try to get along with our soldiers."

"Yes sir," I said.

"You're dismissed." I stepped out of the room.

The clerk looked up. "Consider yourself lucky. I've never heard him comment like that on a man's record. It takes a lot to impress old Colonel JJ."

"I thought he was angry at first."

"The colonel's voice is loud. It's when he gets quiet that you have to worry."

"Could you tell me how to get to barracks?"

The clerk nodded. "Sure. Eisenhower Boulevard is the main drag out front. Follow it down to the end where it T bones into General Patton way."

"Thank you, sir," I said firing off another salute and then headed for the door. Tossing my seabag over my shoulder, I stepped outside heading down Eisenhower Boulevard.

Inside the barracks ten minutes later, I tossed my seabag down on the deck and claimed a bunk. Breathing in the smell of bleach and floor wax I glanced about. A short stocky Mexican Marine stepped up and put his gear on the bottom bunk across from mine.

"How ya doin'?" I said. "My name's McDonald. Mike McDonald."

The Mexican smiled and stuck out his hand. We shook. "I'm Gomez. Arturo Gomez. Most folks call me Art." The echo of footfalls on the hardwood floor filled the air. Other Marines entered the barracks followed by several soldiers.

"Where you from Art?"

"LA bro. How about you?"

"Ah, another California boy. I'm from San Bernardino."

Gomez grinned. "No shit?"

"Yep."

"If you waddies wouldn't mind, I'd like to lay claim on one of the top bunks," a massive corn-fed white boy said.

I looked up at his rugged-looking features. "With an accent like that, you've got to be a Texan," I said.

The big man grinned. "Born and raised."

"What you do before the Core, Tex?" Gomez asked.

"I cowboyed on my daddy's ranch among other things." Tex put his gear up on one of the top bunks and a tall skinny black Marine stepped up behind us. Another group of Marines from the bus entered the barracks. The soldiers kept to themselves.

"Say you all. Can you give a brother some room? I'd like that other top bunk if you don't mind."

I glanced up at a skinny young black Marine. "Sure. What's your name?" I asked.

"Williams, my man. Carl Williams," he said.

"I didn't get your name Tex?" I said.

"Murphy. Shawn Murphy."

After we settled in and stowed our gear, Gomez, Williams, Murphy, and I headed up to the chow hall for supper. The humidity dissipated somewhat when the sun went down. The nighttime temperature dropped. We fell into line and the soldiers on KP filled our plates. We had roast beef mashed potatoes with gravy and cornbread. The meal didn't taste bad for, mess hall fair. Finished with supper, we headed down to the enlisted men's club and partied until closing time. I fell into my rack and dropped off to sleep right away. In my dreams, I was back in Columbia and the faces of the men I'd killed appeared to haunt me. Finally, I fell into a deeper dreamless sleep.

***

Reveille came early. We dressed and met on the parade ground for our morning PT. The instructor put us through a rigorous ordeal. We did pushups, sit-ups, deep knee bends, and Jumping Jacks. After the exercises, he led us on a five-mile run. Back from the run, drenched in sweat, we hit the showers. We had fifteen minutes to change into the uniform of the day before our morning chow call. Finished with chow, we headed to our first class of the day. The class was on the maintenance and operation of the USMC M1A1 Abrams Main Battle Tank. After that, we attended a class on tank warfare and large-caliber ballistics.

After lunch, we headed out onto the tank range. The instructors went over an M1 A1 with a fine-toothed comb. They showed us how they operated and what the major maintenance concerns were. The head instructors handed out ear protection. Another group of instructors moved a tank in position on the range.

"Listen up Gentlemen! I am Major McMullan and I am in charge of the tank range! You will each get a chance to drive the tank, fire the main gun and learn how to load the shells! After three more weeks in the classroom, we will assign each of you to a tank. A tank crew consists of an operator, a gunner, a loader, and a tank commander. You will rotate through these positions so that you learn each job! The M1A1 has a fifty caliber machinegun and a 7.62-millimeter machinegun mounted on top. It can fire its main gun while on the move at over forty miles per hour. If you will put on your hearing protection, we'll let you see what these babies can do!" the large blond-headed Irish Marine yelled. He had a barrel chest and his shoulders seemed as broad as a house. He was the major who had been in the colonel's office when I reported for duty. I put on my hearing protection.

The tank fired off a round and dirt and debris flew into the air in the projectile's wake. The concussion felt like someone had punched me in the stomach. Downrange, a dilapidated old Jeep exploded. A cloud of dirt and bits of shrapnel from the jeep flew into the air. The tank fired a salvo. The concentrated fire reduced the Jeep to smoldering wreckage. I enjoyed watching the show and looked forward to driving one of those monsters. Following the fire demonstration, the instructors let us crawl through the tanks. They showed us how the tanks operated, went over the optics system, and showed us how to load and fire the main gun. That evening, we went to a class where the instructor went into detail on the main battle tank's armor. Finished with our first day of class, we headed to the chow hall for supper and hit the enlisted men's club.

***

During the weeks that followed, we learned the art of tank warfare. They issued us M-16s, and we spent time on the rifle range. We delved deeper into the ballistics of big-bore projectiles. On the tank range, we learned how to drive the vehicles. We learned how to load and fire the main gun, and how to maneuver the tanks around obstacles. The tank range consisted of a vast area that we had to plot our way through. They assigned Gomez, Murphy, Williams, and me to the same tank. On the tank course, we traversed a narrow canyon and engaged stationary and pop-up targets. On our first trip through what the instructors called, The Valley of Death. I sat in the seat operating the fifty caliber machine gun.

Targets depicting armed insurgents popped up and I opened up, on them with the fifty. Hot brass rained down around me bouncing off the floor of the tank. When we came to large stationary targets depicting enemy tanks, we engaged them with the main gun. The concussion rocked the tank each time we fired. We had to wear hearing protection to protect our ears from the loud explosion of the gun going off. The driver, traversing the tank course kept a sharp eye out for tank traps. The tank traps consisted of camouflaged trenches dug into the ground meant to stop the tanks. Sometimes, if we were only engaging one or two targets, we would fire the main gun on the move. At one point on the course, several targets representing enemy tanks blocked our way. The driver lowered the outriggers, stabilizing the tank. We opened up with concentrated fire from over a mile away.

Over several weeks, we rotated through the positions on the tank crew. I enjoyed driving the tank. During the final phase of our training, we played the aggressor force for two weeks. We built tank traps and attacked with simulated rocket and mortar fire. We mounted up in tanks and dug in ambushing the other students on the tank range. When our two weeks were up, we changed roles traveling through the range playing war games. During the final two weeks of the course, the instructors took on the role of the aggressors. The students learned how to work together fighting at company strength. The major and the rest of the brass graded our progress. When a tank took a hit, a loud beeping would sound inside the tank and its power would shut off simulating a kill.

The scenario was that of a light tank force attacking well-fortified positions. The contractors on base had created a firebase called Camp Free Bird. A ring of tanks, plus an infantry force provided security for the base. On the last day, I was driving our tank on the approach to Camp Free Bird. I slowed to a stop three hundred yards out. Williams manned the fifty; Gomez worked as the loader and Murphy as the gunner. We fired off several rounds into the base.

"Yeah! Get some!" Murphy yelled.

"Hammer the bastards!" I replied. I wiped the sweat from my forehead. The temperature inside the tank was blistering. Williams opened up with the 7.62-millimeter firing blank ammunition at the defenders.

"That's what I'm talking about!" Williams hollered. His body glistened with sweat.

"Damn bro! I'll be glad when we're done. It's hot in this damned tank!" Gomez bellowed. We had to yell to converse over the loud noise coming from the tank's engine. A loud beeping sound came from underneath my feet and the tank's engine died.

"That's all folks! Were dead!" I said.

The flowing morning was a Friday. They held the graduation ceremony in the main assembly hall at HQ. We sat at tables paralleling the stage at the front of the rectangular-shaped room. Colonel Jefferson stood with the rest of the brass on stage. When Major McMullan called our names we went forward to receive our certificates. A sense of pride shot through me when I stood up to receive mine. After everyone had received their certificate, the colonel stepped up to a microphone.

"You Gentlemen must be wondering what is next. The Marine Corps is sending half of you to tank battalions throughout the country. Most of you soldiers are going overseas. The bulk of which will go to Germany. Some of you are going to South Korea. You won't ship out until Sunday morning. We have a feast prepared for you, so enjoy. That will be all."

The brass left the stage. Caterers brought in trays filled with food and waiters served drinks. The fare was roast beef and broiled chicken. The food tasted delicious. After the banquette, Gomez, Murphy, Williams, and I headed for the enlisted men's club. We planned to spend the next two days partying until we shipped out, but we didn't have far to go. Our orders said Camp Livingston Louisiana.

At the enlisted men's club, I bought the first round of drinks and held my bottle up in a toast. "To a successful tour of duty at Camp Livingston," I said. A cloud of cigarette smoke filled the bar room.

"I'll drink to that brother," Williams replied and we clicked our glasses together.

"Shit. Livingston ain't that far from my daddy's ranch down near Nacogdoches. I'll be able to go home once in a while, I expect," Murphy said. He turned around to face the bar.

"We could go with you, man. You could teach me how to be a cowboy," Gomez said.

I laughed. "Gomez, you can't even ride on the back of a tank without falling off. What makes you think you could ride a horse?" I asked.

Gomez blushed. "Let a guy fall off a tank one time, and he's branded for life. It's in the blood amigo. I come from a long line of vaqueros."

"Vaqueros, my ass. More like strawberry pickers," I said.

Murphy put a strong arm around Gomez's shoulder. "Don't worry Gomez. There is nothing to learn about a horse that I can't teach you."

I glanced about the bar noticing a few female soldiers that worked at HQ sitting at the bar. "Tomorrow, let's head into town. I'm getting tired of seeing this Army pussy. I want some homegrown civilian pussy," I said.

"I'm with you, pard. You let me find us a cowboy bar and I'll show you how to party," Murphy said.

Williams gave Murphy a sour look. "Brother, some of us don't go for the shit kickin' two steppin' bullshit. Now if you want to head over to the black part of town, I'll show you, boys, a good time. There some black hookers over there that will curl your toes."

"I never had a black woman," Murphy said.

"Bro, you don't know what you're missing. Once you go black, you won't go back," Williams said.

I laughed. "Right about now, I don't care if it's black, red white, or blue, as long as it's pussy," I said.

"It's all pink on the inside," Gomez said. We partied for the rest of the night and closed down the enlisted men's club.

***

The next evening, we caught a bus into town. First, we hit the cowboy bars and then headed over to the black part of town. Williams took us to a blues bar on a back street and the music was phenomenal. After the blues bar, Murphy insisted on heading back to one of the cowboy places. He said that he wanted to do some line dancing. I wound up going home with a red-headed cowgirl. She was thin with an ample bosom and her long red hair cascade down her back almost to her shapely bottom. She had a musical sound to her laughter that I liked.

Waking up next to her naked body Sunday morning, I admired her sensual form while she slept. She had firm round hips, large melon-shaped breasts, and long sensual curves. Her thin waist gave her an hourglass-like figure. A strand of red hair covered half of her pretty face. I noticed a tiny birthmark underneath her left breast. Her eyes opened and she smiled. For a second, I got lost in her pale blue eyes.

"Good morning, hon," she said. I enjoyed the sound of her southern accent.

I laid my hand on her bare belly. "I need to leave. Our bus leaves at nine."

"You all ain't going nowhere until you do me one more time. A gentleman never leaves a lady's bed without leaving her satisfied," she said and climbed on top of me. Her large breasts dangled in my face.

"But I've got to find a way back to the base."

"Don't worry sugar. I'll give you a ride," she said and laughed. And, boy did she. Afterward, I enjoyed the sight of her hard body moving about the bedroom of the small rental house. She pulled me into the shower; I lathered up her wet trim body and later, she dropped me off at the base. Tired and weary with bloodshot eyes, I stood with the rest of the Marines waiting to ship out. My head throbbed, my mouth felt like I had gargled with cat piss and I reeked of alcohol, but I had a smile on my face.

Williams looked at me and grinned. "That cowgirl must have ridden you hard."

"Boy howdy," I said. A lime green military bus pulled up to the curb.

Murphy stepped up next to me and laid a friendly hand on my shoulder. "You've got to watch these Southern girls. Especially the redheads they're green broke and buck wild."

"Tell me about it," I said.

"I'll be glad when we're back on a Marine base. These soldier boys are all right, but I'll be glad to be back with our, own kind," Gomez said.

"Yeah, they're a little sissified for my taste," Murphy said. "Give me a hard-charging Marine any day."

We boarded the bus, on route to the great state of Louisiana.

***

A light rain fell from the sky when we climbed off the bus at Camp Livingston. We hurried through the storm to the HQ and reported for duty. Colonel Chambers was the exact opposite of Colonel Jefferson at Fort Knox. Their only similarities were their size. They were both big men. Chambers might have been an inch shorter than Jefferson. Where Jefferson was loud, Chambers was soft-spoken. He had a full head of salt and pepper-colored hair. When he was angry, he would dress a junior officer down in a cool quiet voice that left no doubt about who was in charge.

After processing, we headed to our barracks and settled in. We spent the next month honing our skills on the main battle tank. Although soft-spoken, Colonel Chambers demanded perfection. He could be loud if he wanted to. He didn't care much for pomp and circumstance. He demanded excellence when it came to operations of the tanks. Our training intensified. The brass promoted me to tank commander and assigned, Gomez, Williams, and Murphy as my crew. We did more live-fire exercises and more war games.

In a briefing one morning, Colonel Chambers stepped up onto a podium. "Gentlemen. I know you've been training hard and you're doing well, but you still have more to learn. As you know, our mission is to stand ready to deploy to any hot spots throughout the world. Once again, they are rattling their sabers in the Middle East. As of today, I am pulling you men in off the field. You will spend the next two weeks performing maintenance on your vehicles. We are sending you to a Marine base in the high desert of Southern California. It's in a little town called Twenty Nine Palms. They have one of the best desert training areas in the country. Its only rival is Fort Irwin. That's to the north of Twenty Nine Palms near a town called Barstow, but that's for Army pukes. The Marines send their tankers to Twenty Nine Palms for their desert training. Two weeks from now, you will ship out for three weeks of TDY. The weather will be hot, the duty rough, but you'll be better tankers when you're done," the colonel said.

A thrill shot through me. "Hot damn, Gomez. We're going to California. Twenty Nine Palms is a hop skip and a jump from home."

"Tell me about it brother. It's only three hours from LA. I'll get a chance to see some of my homies."

***

They kept us busy for the next two weeks. We spent twelve hours a day doing maintenance on our vehicles. The smell of oil and grease was our constant companion. Finished with the maintenance, we drove our tanks and support vehicles to the rail spur. We loaded them up onto rail cars and spent the next three days tying down the vehicles. A gang of railroad carmen supervised making sure we did everything right. Once we secured the vehicles to the train cars, the railroad hooked up an engine. They pulled the cars out of the rail spur on their way to California.

Shuttle buses took us to the nearest airport and we flew out to California at midnight on a Friday evening. We boarded shuttle buses at a municipal airport in Adelanto. Adelanto was a town on the high desert near an abandoned Air Force base. and they took us to the Marine base at Twenty Nine Palms. We spent three days sitting on our hands waiting for our equipment to arrive. Once the railroad set the train cars into the rail spur, we unloaded the equipment. General Patton used this base, along with Fort Irwin, to train his, tank-force during World War II.

The training at Twenty Nine Palms was some of the most realistic combat training I'd received so far. The weather was hot, not humid like in Louisiana. It was like what we would face if we deployed to the Middle East. The wide opened space of the Mojave Desert provided ample room for our tanks to maneuver. The aggressor force was good at what they did. In the war games, they spanked us, but we learned from our mistakes. By the end of two weeks in the hot desert sun, we were starting to score some hits on the aggressor. We won the last engagement. We sat around the parade ground after the final engagement. We were looking forward to a steak dinner and a beer bash to celebrate. An alert sounded. Colonel Chambers and the base commander stepped out of a Humvee.

"Gentlemen! Secure your combat gear and report back here in ten minutes! Let's move people!" We ran to our barracks and packed our gear.

"What's got their panties in a wad?" Tex said.

"It's another exercise. I was looking forward to that steak," I said.

"I don't know. The colonel looked serious. Look at all the activity on base? Something is up, bro," Williams said.

"I talked to some of my homies on the phone. They said something is going on in the Middle East," Gomez said.

Ten minutes later, we reported to the parade ground with our combat gear. The smell of cooking meat filled the air. Colonel Chambers hurried to the middle of the assembled Marines. The base commander stood next to him. The Marines stationed at the base who had acted as the aggressor force stood on the edges of the crowd watching. Colonel Chambers used a bullhorn to communicate.

"Gentlemen. During the early hours of the morning, Saddam Husain's armed forces invaded the nation of Kuwait. As we speak they are raping and pillaging a small defenseless neighbor." Colonel Chambers waited for a few seconds for the news to sink in and continued. "Our Commander and Chief, President George Bush says that this will not stand. We are deploying to Saudi Arabian. Mount your vehicles and head back to the rail spur. We'll keep your food warm! Once you load your equipment onto the train cars, you can come back here to eat. Let's go people! Let's show that bastard Saddam what a few jarheads can do!" Chambers yelled.

For once, he was loud. Forty-eight hours later, we boarded a civilian airliner on our way to Saudi Arabia.

***

CHAPTER 16

A bead of sweat dripped down the side of my face when I hit the ball. I was playing volleyball with the guys from my tank platoon in the hot scorching desert heat. A massive tent city lay sprawled out in the middle of the Saudi desert. Sand blew across the court. When the wind came up it blew sand into everything. No matter how I tried, I couldn't keep from getting minute particles of sand inside my clothes. I was always rubbing sand out of my eyes. As operation Desert Shield progressed, more soldiers and Marines arrived on base daily. The tent city exploded in size and breadth. We spent most of our time training, but you can only train so much. In our downtime, we found ways to stave off the boredom. Right now, we were in the middle of a volleyball tournament.

The shrill sound of the referee blowing his whistle filled the air. "All right people! It's half time! Let's get some water!" the referee yelled.

One of our major concerns was to stay hydrated. When we first arrived in the desert and began training, we had several heat casualties. Scorpions also bit a couple of guys. Williams and I staggered over to the water coolers. I took a bottle out of the cooler, handed one to Williams, and took one for myself. After chugalugging down a bottle of water, I took another from the cooler and poured it over my head. The cold water felt invigorating. Water dripped down the side of my face and I knuckled a few drops from my eyes.

"It's about as hot as the Devil's asshole out here," I said.

"I know man. My balls are about to swelter away," Williams said.

Murphy and Gomez stepped up next to us.

"I got a bad case of swamp ass, cuz," Gomez said.

Murphy laughed. "You boys ain't spent much time in Texas. It gets so hot down-home you can fry an ostrich egg on the sidewalk," Murphy said.

"My eggs are frying right now, bro," Williams said.

I laughed and we went back out to finish the game. After the volleyball game, we headed to the mess tent for lunch. The food wasn't bad for Marine Core slop. After lunch, we sat down under a canopy and watched CNN News. Saddam Husain was on the news and he said that if the US attacked his forces, it would be the Mother of All Battles. The sound of Marines booing the Iraqi leader filled the room.

"That guy is full of, the mother of all bullshit," Williams said.

Murphy let go with a loud fart and the smell of rotten eggs filled the air. "I may have let the mother of all farts."

Everyone laughed and I fanned the air in front of my face. "Talk about germ warfare. I need to put on my MOP suit," I said.

"Hey bro. Are you sure, that was a fart? It sounded like you launched a scud missile," Gomez said.

A puzzled look crossed Murphy's face and he said, "I don't know. Are farts wet and lumpy?" Everyone laughed.

I opened another bottle of water while the newscaster moved on to another story. An alert sounded; we scrambled outside and donned our MOP suits preparing for a gas attack. They kept us out on the parade ground simmering underneath the hot vinyl suits with our gas mask on. Inside the MOP suit, sweat flowed down my side like a river. My head felt hot and for a few seconds, I thought I was going to pass out. Thirty minutes later the all-clear whistle blew.

After lunch, we mounted up in our tanks and headed into the desert. We moved north heading closer to the Kuwaiti border. Our orders were to make an appearance near the border and watch any Iraqi activity across the line. An Army recon patrol moved on the ground ahead of us. It was a long, hot, boring day. We shut down our tanks one-half mile from the border.

"Man, I'd like to lob a few shells over the line and get this show on the road," Williams said. Murphy turned on a portable radio tuning it to an armed forces radio station. We listened to a Dodger baseball game.

"I hear yuh. I'm glad I'm not one of the ground pounders," I said and opened the top hatch. Climbing onto the tank, the burning hot desert wind made me think that my eyes were going to boil. Sweat poured down the side of my face. I took a seat on top of the tank, pulled out a pair of binoculars, and scanned the desert on the other side of the border. I saw several enemy tanks. They simmered in the heat guarding the border behind large sandy earthworks. Murphy climbed up next to me.

"The rags are making a mistake, staying bottled up in those dug-in positions. They need to be up and moving. If they're still dug in like that when we attack, we'll slaughter the bastards," I said.

Murphy studied the enemy positions for a few seconds and then lowered the binoculars. "If the rag heads were smart they'd be living in Texas and running a Seven-Eleven."

We watched the border until sundown and then turned the column around heading south. Darkness fell. The temperature outside the tank dropped. Using a pair of night-vision goggles, I sat up in the hatch behind the fifty. Murphy drove the tank. The world took on a green glow. The Saudi desert looked spooky at night. We traveled for another hour and then I saw movement to our front.

"We've got tanks to our direct front," I yelled.

"They've got to be ours," Wilson said.

"Get on the horn and give them a holler!" I yelled.

Wilson grabbed the radio, but before he could send the transmission a streak of light lit up the desert. A tank round screamed overhead and slammed into the tank behind us. A massive explosion ripped the tank apart as the projectile slammed into its turret. The guy riding up top behind the machinegun didn't stand a chance. Shrapnel rained down on us.

"Get on the horn! They think we're Iraqi!" I climbed down into the tank and buttoned up the hatch.

Another tank round flew through the air. It hit one of the tanks in the rear of the column and another explosion ripped apart the night.

"This is Echo Bravo Foxtrot. Hold your fire! We're Americans! I say again! We are U.S. Marines! Ceasefire Mother Fuckers!" Williams screamed into the radio while another tank round sailed overhead.

"Repeat that last transmission," someone said over the radio.

"We're Americans, you son of a bitch! You hit two of our tanks!"

There was a pause over the airwaves for a few seconds. "Roger that. No one said anything about having any friendly forces to our front. What company are you boys with?"

"Bravo Company USMC."

After another short pause, the guy on the radio said, "You boys are a bit off course. Your lines are over a few clicks to the east."

I climbed on top and surveyed the carnage. The putrid smell of burning human flesh wafted on the desert wind. Three tanks lay in smoldering ruins. Body parts littered the ground and one of the tanks billowed flames. Only one guy got out. His body lay on the desert sand, consumed in flames. Bile formed in my throat and my eyes widened in horror.

"God damn it!" I yelled and jumped to the ground. I went toward the smoldering wreckage searching for survivors. One guy was still alive, but he had burns over eighty percent of his body. A shell-shocked tanker popped up from his hatch. I looked up. "Get on the radio! Call a MEDEVAC!"

After seeing to the evacuation of the wounded Marine, we buttoned up our tanks and headed back to our lines. When we arrived back at our base camp, the colonel called us into the command tent. He debriefed us investigating the friendly fire incident.

"What I want to know," Colonel Chambers said, "is why you were so far to the west of our lines? The Army boys weren't to blame."

A lump formed in my throat, tears welled up in my eyes and I struggled to keep my voice from cracking when I spoke. "It was my fault, sir. My tank was on point. I was in command of the tank. When we headed south, we must have drifted too far to the west. The desert all looks the same at night."

The colonel paused and then nodded his head. "Well, these kinds of mistakes happen during a war, but when they do people die. There will be a letter in your file, but don't worry too much about that. Try not to let something like this happen again."

"I won't sir." I stood to my feet, gave the colonel a salute and he returned the courtesy. I left the command tent and tears pooled up in my eyes. *Eleven men are dead and it's my fault,* I thought. *I was in command.* I felt like someone had driven a stake through my heart.

Williams stepped up next to me and grabbed my arm. "Come on bro. One of the brothers back home smuggled me a bottle of Jack in a care package. You look like you could use a drink."

I glanced over at him. "You've got that right." Gomez and Murphy joined us; we headed behind the motor pool and held a private little party.

"Don't beat yourself up about it, homes," Gomez said and handed me the bottle of Jack Daniels. I downed a shot. The potent brew warmed my innards. I handed the bottle to Murphy.

"If I'd paid better attention, we wouldn't have strayed so far to the west."

Murphy shrugged. "I was driving. It's about as dark as an armadillo's asshole out there on that desert. Any one of us might have lost our way."

I watched Murphy. He seemed depressed before we even left for the mission, but now he looked devastated.

"What's up with you Tex? I know you're feeling bad about the mission, but you've been walking around like someone killed your best dog."

Murphy let out a slow breath. "I got a dear John letter from my girl back in Texas. Her picture goes up on the wall of shame in the morning." The wall of shame was a board where soldiers or Marines put up photos. They put up pictures of their girlfriends or wives that left them while deployed. We stayed quiet for a while listening to the night sounds. "Fuck the bitch and the pony she rode in on," Tex said breaking the silence. We squatted down behind the motor pool passing the Jack back and forth until we killed the bottle. Drunk on our asses, we stumbled back to our tent.

***

Months passed, and still, we stayed in the desert sitting on our nuts. We were waiting for the politicians to get off their asses. Finally, President Bush gave Saddam Husain an ultimatum. He gave him forty-eight hours to pull out of Kuwait or face the wrath of the US military. The time of inactivity came to an abrupt end. The entire battalion mounted up. We took our positions online and in typical military fashion, we had to hurry up and wait. All across the Saudi desert, tanks set on go. The orders finally came down and we moved forward approaching the Kuwaiti border. The service battalions formed up behind us. We moved across the desert at a high rate of speed approaching the border. Then the brass stopped our advance when we were less than a mile from the border. Tanks with large blades attached on their front ends took up the point positions. They would be the ones to plow through the earthworks opening up pathways for the rest of us to follow.

Night fell over the desert. We sat up on top of our tanks listening to portable shortwave radios to President Bush's speech. Outside a light wind blew sand against our tank. The deadline passed. The President announced the launch of Operation Desert Storm. We heard a rumble in the sky off to our left. Miles to the west of our position, we saw flashes of light low down on the horizon.

"Those planes we heard go by. Those are Navy boys. Their pounding Bagdad to hell and gone," Murphy said. He had a set of earphones on listening to the military comm-net. "They're using stealth bombers, F-16s and they're hammering the shit out of them with cruise missiles." A sense of excitement filled the air.

"It won't be long now," I said.

Murphy looked up at me. "We've got our orders. Let's button this tin can up."

We climbed back down into the tank, closed the hatch and Murphy took his seat at the controls. Tanks with blades on their fronts moved forward lowering their blades. They pushed through the bank of sand opening the path for the rest of the vehicles behind them. Hundreds of Iraqi soldiers jumped up trying to surrender but we buried them alive. When we launched the attack, we were moving so fast that we couldn't stop. The roar of the tank's engine filled our ears and the sound of artillery rounds screamed overhead. The Iraqi tanks opened up, on us from their fortified positions.

We acquired our targets and fired on the move. Williams manned the main gun and Gomez worked with him as his loader. I opened up the hatch and manned the fifty-caliber machinegun. The Iraqi tanks guarding the border didn't stand a chance. Our tanks could shoot further and we had better armor. We slaughtered them, hammering them without mercy with our main gun. Flames from the burning Iraqi vehicles lit up the night. The smell of molten metal and burnt flesh filled the air. An Iraqi tanker fell from his burning tank. His legs were missing from the knees down and half of his body was on fire. He let out a stream of words in Arabic and then switched to English.

"Fuck Saddam Husain! Fuck George Bush! Fuck USA! Fuck Iraqi!" He let out a blood-curdling scream and the putrid smell of his burning flesh floated into the air.

I opened up with my fifty, putting him out of his misery, and said, "Fuck you too." The fire from the Iraqi tankers tapered off. The infantry put down what little resistance that the Iraqi ground troops managed to put up. The Iraqi soldiers threw down their arms and surrendered by the hundreds. Passing through a graveyard of Iraqi tanks, I looked at the carnage littering the desert. Smoldering hulks that had once been Iraqi tanks lit up the night. Body parts and smoldering corpses covered the desert sand. My stomach lurched and I breathed in the rancid smell of burning flesh floating on the breeze. We continued toward Kuwait watching the Iraqi soldiers surrender in mass. The ground pounders took their weapons and sent them on foot toward the rear. Dawn spread its warm fingers across the Kuwaiti desert.

We received word of a large Iraqi tank force heading toward the Iraqi border. HQ gave our tank platoon orders to intercept them before they could escape across the border. We took point, leading the platoon west as we thundered across the desert. Crossing a sandy barren landscape, I watched helicopters buzz overhead. F-16s and fighter bombers swooped across the desert. They were heading to Bagdad to launch their missiles and drop laser-guided bombs. We caught up with the Iraqi tanks six hours later. The battle was short but deadly. The platoon spread out in, formation and hammered them with our main guns. One of the Iraqi tankers managed to score a hit on our tank. It rang our bell, but the projectile couldn't penetrate our superior armor.

Sweat beaded up on Williams' forehead when he fired the main gun. The noise inside the tank was deafening. Shirtless, with sweat pouring down his sides, Gomez loaded another shell into the gun. Tracking another enemy tank, the computer locked on the target. Williams fired the gun and the tank exploded. The turret ripped off the top of the tank. The ammo inside exploded causing a massive fireball to rise into the air. The battle over, we stopped to survey the damage. The Iraqi tanks lay in smoldering hulks on the desert sand. The burnt copses of the Iraqi tankers littered the desert floor. Body parts lay everywhere. Popping up out of the hatch, I looked about. The head of an Iraqi tanker sat on top of a burnt-out tank with a cigarette in its mouth. I saw smoke rising off the smoldering corpses.

Airplanes screamed overhead. In the distance to the north of our position, we saw explosions. I saw smoke rising into the air.

Murphy popped his head up from the hatch. "The Navy flyboys and the Air Force are hammering the Iraqis to the north of us on the main highway leading to Iraqi. I guess Saddam and his boys are trying to flee with anything they can drive. Scuttle says the flyboys are turning brand new Cadies and Lincolns into scrap metal. Our forces are entering the capital. We have orders to head north and survey the damage."

"All right then. Let's roll," I said and climbed back inside the tank.

We headed north traveling across the desert for several more hours. The bombing continued. Smoke and flames billowed into the air to the north of our positions. When we drew closer to the site the stench became overpowering and we stopped, waiting. Finally, the bombing quit and we moved forward. We brought our tanks to the top of a sandy desert ridge and looked down upon the highway of death. Murphy stopped the tank; I opened the hatch and climbed up top. The stench hit me like a brick wall.

"Good Lord," I whispered in awe of the destruction lying before me. Gomez, Murphy, and Williams climbed up behind me. They stared down at the highway in amazement. Charred remains of any type of vehicle imaginable littered the highway. They were all filled with charred human remains. Heat rose from the highway where rubber tires had melted to the roadway. The smell of burnt rubber and human flesh drifted with the wind. A flock of crows swarmed overhead. I saw one drop-down next to a corpse and pluck an eyeball from its socket.

I jumped down to the ground and headed down to the roadway. A small pickup had melted down to the frame. The driver, burnt beyond all recognition, still sat with his hands to the wheel. All the skin on his face and hands had burned away. The mouth of the skull lay open revealing a toothy, smile of death. I looked up and down the highway. For as far as I could see, burnt-out hulks of what had once been vehicles littered the highway. Smoke drifted on the wind from this unholy altar. I turned around, threw up on the side of the road, and headed back up to my tank. "Call this shit in and let's get out of here."

After reporting the carnage on the highway of death, the brass ordered us to head toward the capital. We were ninety-six hours into the war when they called a cease-fire. The commanding general held peace talks with the Iraqis. When we rolled through the streets of the capitol citizens lining the street cheered us on. Young girls ran out onto the road and handed us flowers. I was standing next to my tank when they announced that they had reached an agreement to end the war. I glanced over at Murphy. He looked shell shocked and I wondered if I looked the same way. "I've had my fill of death and violence. When I get home, I'm gonna find a good woman, and raise some kids. I am never going to lift my hand in anger toward anyone ever again," I said. Little did I know at the time how false that statement was.

***

CHAPTER 17

I sat on the balcony of a sixth-floor hotel room looking down at a topless bar. I looked through a pair of night-vision goggles. A cool breeze hit my face. The Top Heavy Tavern was the local biker hangout. It also served as the clubhouse for the Las Vegas chapter of the Lost Souls motorcycle club. I'd been in Vegas for two weeks and I'd yet to make a move on the clubhouse. I was still in reconnaissance mode. The first thing I discovered was that James Quinn and his two right-hand men were still alive.

I lowered the night vision goggles to give my eyes a rest and my mind flashed back to my trip up from LA. When I saw that military convoy heading to Fort Irwin, memories from the war slammed through my brain. I had to pull over. I took the highway 138 exit at the bottom of the Cajon Pass and pulled over at a Chevron station. Finally, I had my life back. All my memories were there without any gaps. I thought about my time in the gulf. Back then, I thought that I could put the violence behind me. For a time, I lived up to my pledge. I lived a life of peace with Sharon, but that was gone now. These scumbags stole that life from me. A time would come when I would morn for Sharon, but that time was not yet.

The knuckles on my hands gripping the binoculars began to turn white. My heart pounded and I felt my face turning hot. That old familiar rage buried deep inside of me threatened to erupt like a raging volcano.

"You boys sowed your seeds to the wind, and now you're gonna reap the whirlwind," I said to myself. I popped the top on a beer, lit a cigarette, and continued to watch the activity below. A cloud of tobacco smoke filled the air in front of my face. My hands shook, my stomach rumbled and I tried to relax. Letting out a slow breath, I stood up, headed back inside my hotel room. I put my night vision goggles away and headed for the door. I figured I'd head down to the buffet for some supper. Sticking my room key card in my coat pocket, I stepped out into the hallway. Two good-looking young women chatted back and forth, while they passed by. The scent of their perfume filled the corridor. The dark-headed one said, "Hi," and smiled.

I smiled back. "Having any luck in the casinos?"

"We're playing the one-armed bandits. They cleaned us out," the blonde said. Cute little dimples formed in her cheeks when she smiled.

"There's always tomorrow," I said and headed down the hallway to the elevators. Pausing for a few seconds, I waited for the doors to open and stepped into the elevator. I pressed the button for the casino. My stomach dropped and the elevator descended to the ground floor. The elevator doors slid open and I stepped out into the crowded casino. The sound of people talking and slot machines paying out drifted across the room. Laughter filled the air. I elbowed my way through the crowd. At the buffet, I took my place in line at the cash register. The smell of the cooking food caused my stomach to growl.

A fat woman in red sweat pants and a blue top stood in front of me. Her ample belly hung out underneath her top. I made a mental note to try to beat her to the serving line. After paying the cashier, a hostess wearing a blue top and a green apron escorted me to my table. I set my jacket down in the booth and headed for the buffet. Picking up a plate, I loaded it down with fried chicken, mashed potatoes, an ear of corn, and a fresh garden salad. The guy behind the serving counter cut me off a thick slice of roast beef. Back at my table, a young Asian waitress stepped up. She looked half-American and half Vietnamese. I like that kind of exotic look.

"What can I get you to drink, sir?" she asked holding her order pad up with a pen in her hand.

I shot her a smile. "What kind of beer do you have?"

"Budweiser, Coors, Corona. You name it, we've got it."

"Let me have a Bud Light," I said. She smiled and headed off to the kitchen. My eyes took in her slender form for a few seconds, and then I studied the people sitting about the restaurant. The waitress came back a few minutes later with my beer and I dug into my meal with gusto. The food was good and the beer refreshing; my mind wandered. I was about to go operational on the Vegas chapter of the Lost Souls and I went over my plan of attack in my mind. I had finished eating when someone wearing, a denim motorcycle vest sauntered by. My eyes shot up taking in a grubby-looking biker. He had long blond hair and a scruffy beard; my hand gripped the steak knife I was holding. The biker headed for the serving line.

"I guess I'll open the ball early," I said to myself and stood up. I hurried toward the exit and took a seat at the nearest slot machine. Tossing a few quarters into the machine, I spun the wheels keeping my eyes off the buffet. The wheels on the slot machine, spun taking my money, a waitress came by and I ordered another beer. I fed the machine more money. A half-hour later, the biker stepped from the buffet's exit and headed across the casino. I jumped up and followed him toward the elevator. I stayed a few paces behind him. He paused, standing in front of the elevator doors, and waited for them to open. I stood behind him with my hand in my coat pocket caressing my Buck Knife. The doors opened and the biker stepped inside the elevator. Pulling the knife from my pocket, I flipped open the blade and stepped in behind him. When the biker turned around, I rushed forward grabbing him by the shoulder with one hand. I stuck the blade into his belly with my other. Blood spewed out of his stomach onto my hand.

"What the fuck?" the biker said, slumping back against the wall of the elevator car. I leaned against him, breathing in his stench, with my head down to avoid the surveillance cameras.

"Don't fight it. It will only make the pain worse," I whispered. I pulled the knife upward cutting him from his navel to his breastbone.

"Why?" He was already starting to weaken from loss of blood and shock; his face turned white.

"You shit bags raped and then killed my wife."

Urine dripped down his leg. "I didn't have anything to do with that," the guy moaned. "Good Lord, I pissed myself."

"Don't worry about it. You ride with scum, you die like scum," I said and stepped away letting him slip to the floor. Blood pooled up on the elevator floor. Closing the knife, I put it back into my pocket and knelt next to the dying man. Grabbing him by the shoulders, I leaned him forward and took his vest. I draped the vest over my arm to hide the blood on my hand and my shirt. "You'll start to feel cold and then you'll get sleepy. Close your eyes and go to sleep." The biker's eyes glazed over and the doors behind me opened. Lucky for me, no one stood waiting to enter the elevator. I headed down the hall to the stairway and hurried up to my floor. Five minutes later, I checked out of the Circus, Circus and stepped out a side door by the valet parking. Two police officers and three paramedics hurried across the casino to the elevators.

Twenty minutes later, I pulled into the parking lot of Arizona Charley's on Boulder Highway. Killing the motor on the Shovelhead, I crossed the parking lot, entered the casino, and checked into a room. On the way to the elevator, I stepped into the washroom and washed spots of blood off my hands that I had missed earlier. I looked at my reflection in the mirror after I got the blood cleaned off. I had killed a man, but I didn't feel bad, but this one was up close and personal. His face. I knew I would remember it. I would see it in dreams to come.

"One more down," I said looking at my reflection. I looked haggard. This job was taking its toll. "God I'll be glad when this is over, but when it is, then what?" Pondering my future for a few seconds, I left the washroom and headed for the elevators.

***

I spent the next three days holed up in my hotel room at Arizona Charley's waiting for things to calm down. Now that I had drawn blood in Las Vegas, the Las Vegas chapter of, the Lost Souls would be on guard. Four days later, I climbed into the saddle and rumbled up and down the streets of Las Vegas. I stayed away from the Top Heavy Tavern. I wanted to catch some of the members out by themselves. I figured that the chapter president had them scouring the streets looking for me. It was only a matter of time before we met up.

It happened one night about midnight. It was a warm Friday night and everyone was on the strip. I was approaching Tropicana when I saw two motorcycles ahead of me. Traffic filled the street. Young men in cars were hollering at a group of girls on the street. I noticed the Lost Souls patch on the back of the bikers in front of me. Weaving my way through traffic, I pulled up next to them. The sound of our loud pipes echoed down the strip. The biker closest to me looked over and his eyes widened. He reached under his vest for a handgun. Pulling one of my sawed-offs from underneath my long black coat, I opened up on him with both barrels. The sound of the shotgun blast reverberated off the surrounding buildings. The shot tore out the biker's throat and his bottom jaw. Blood splattered onto the biker riding next to him. The blast knocked him sideways off the bike. His bike went down crashing into his buddy and he went down, sliding down the street. His bike tumbled along behind him. The cars behind us braked.

I hit my brakes and cut into an alley behind a casino parking garage. I heard the group of young girls scream. Parking the Shovelhead, I ran out into the street. Blood covered the asphalt. The biker I shot lay dead on the street and the other one, lay on his back holding his busted-up knee. I grabbed him by the back of his vest and dragged him into the darkness of the alley. He screamed while I dragged him across the pavement. Once I had him in the alley, I pulled my left hand sawed off and put the muzzle in his face.

"How many guys do you have left in your chapter?" I said.

The biker moaned. "I'm not telling you shit, man."

"I can make this quick and painless, or I can go the hard way," I said pressing the barrels of the sawed-off into his crotch.

His eyes shot wide open and he let out a little gasp. "Please don't. You killed Rico, and you killed Pablo. I guess that only leaves eight of us. Don't kill me, man."

I cocked the hammer on the sawed-off. "When's your next church meeting?"

"Friday at the Top Heavy."

"What's on the agenda?"

He looked at me like if I was a dumb shit. "You, of course. What do you think? The pres has us ridin' around in groups of two or three. They put a price on your head."

I nodded. "What time do you hold church?"

"Six PM. Don't kill me, man. Have mercy," he whimpered.

I shook my head. "I'm fresh out," I said and pulled a trigger. The shotgun blast boomed down the alley. Blood from his crotch splattered against my shoes. He let go with a shriek, covered his crotch with his hands, and kicked his legs. His bowels voided. I moved the barrels of the sawed-off up to his face and gave him the other barrel. The top of his head came off splattering blood, bits, and pieces of bone and brain matter against the wall. His body slumped over on the ground, convulsed, and lay still. Jumping over a pool of blood, I hit the saddle, put the Shovelhead in gear, and gunned the throttle. The sound of sirens filled the night. At the end of the alley, I turned left and headed south on the 15 freeway looking for a place to lay low for a while.

After taking an exit, I headed west on Highway 160 toward Pahrump. The cold night air caused me to shiver. Leaving the city behind, I rolled through some open spaces getting lost in the rumble of, the loud pipes. The night looked as black as the Devil's heart. I went over my progress so far adding up the people I'd killed. I was racking up quite a list. An hour later, I saw a few lights in the distance. On the outskirts of Pahrump, I took a dirt road leading off into the desert. Slowing my roll, I eased back on the throttle; I had to be careful on the sandy dirt road. The road snaked its way back into the hills. I found a camping site in the middle of a little valley setting off away from the road. Pulling over, I parked the Harley and unloaded my gear.

Someone had left a small pile of wood next to a fire ring so, I kindled a fire and spread my sleeping bag down on the ground. For a few minutes, I stood warming myself by the fire. Taking my Bible from my gear bag, I settle back to enjoy the fire's warmth and opened the Bible. Some people might have found it odd, that after all the killing I'd done, that I would sit by the fire and read the Good Book. If you've ever read the book, you know that God did his share of killing. I paused from my reading and pulled a six-pack of beer from my gear bag. I popped the top on a Bud Light, turning to the Old Testament, and read about an old boy named Samson. I paused for a moment and listened to the night.

"Sometimes God uses people to get his killing done. All those people I killed deserved what they got. When I've killed the last one, then I'll greave for you, Sharon," I whispered. The only answer was the cold desert wind. My eyes started to get heavy, so I tossed back the rest of my beer, set the Bible aside, and crawled into my sleeping bag. Out on the desert, a coyote howled making a lonely mournful sound. Depression sank into my soul. All though alive on the outside, my insides felt as dead as two-day roadkill. The only real emotion I felt anymore was hate, but it kept me warm on that cold desert night. My thoughts drifted to Sharon. Her pretty face was the last thing I remembered before falling to sleep.

***

I stayed out in the desert for the next three days, making one trip into town for beer and water. During the day, I would sit on a hill overlooking the highway watching the road with my binoculars. I had a good view of the entire town from my vantage point. The weather was warm for late January, but the nights were still cold. Things were quiet. There was no sign of the Lost Souls. The only people I saw were the town regulars and I was starting to learn their routines. One time I panned over with my binoculars scoping out a building painted bright pink. The words of the sign said the Honey Bee Ranch. Prostitution was legal in Pahrump. Several busty-looking prostitutes climbed out of a pink Cadillac and entered the building. Things looked slow at the ranch.

The next morning, I went into town and had breakfast at the diner. I parked the Harley behind the building away from the main drag and stepped inside. The bell hanging over the door dinged when I stepped inside the restaurant. A red-headed hostess showed me to a booth near the front of the building. I sat down and gazed out the window. The girls were starting to arrive at the Honey Bee.

"Can I get you something to drink, hon?" the hostess asked and smiled. I gave her the once over, taking in her thin frame, her long legs, and her pretty face. I smelled a faint trace of perfume.

I grinned. "I'll have coffee."

"Cream or sugar?"

"No, I like it hot and black." The waitress laid a menu down on the table. I thumbed through it. Country music came through the restaurant's overhead speakers. The waitress came back a few minutes later with my coffee.

"Are you ready to order?"

I nodded. "I'll have a short stack of pancakes, a side of bacon, hash browns, and scrambled eggs."

"Would you like toast with that?" she asked.

"Yeah."

"White or wheat?"

"Wheat," I said.

The waitress left taking my order to the kitchen. Gazing about the room, I took in the restaurant's patrons. Two old men who looked like ranchers sat at the breakfast bar conversing in low tones. An elderly couple sat near the back of the building. They must have been in their eighties and a young couple with four kids sat across from me. The woman looked ready to pull her hair out and the kids were cutting up and getting loud. My waitress came back a few minutes later with my food. She shot me another smile and refilled my coffee cup. I dug into my breakfast with about as much enthusiasm as an anorexic polar bear.

Halfway through my breakfast, I heard Harley Davidson motorcycles rumble up the street. They pulled into the gravel parking lot of the Honey Bee. Glancing out the window, I watched two bikers park their scooters at the whorehouse. They both wore the patch of the Lost Souls motorcycle club on their backs. Finished with my breakfast, I headed to my Shovelhead, took a Souls club vest from my duffle bag, and put it on. I fired up the Shovelhead, put it in gear, and headed down the alley. Turning onto the main drag, I pulled the bike into the parking lot of the Honey Bee and killed the motor. Leaning the bike on its side stand, I tucked one of my forty-fives into the back of my pants. Crossing the gravel parking lot of the Honey Bee, I stepped up onto the boardwalk. I opened the large oak door and entered the whorehouse.

A bell hanging over the door tinkled when I stepped inside. Loud rock music emanated from large speakers mounted near the ceiling behind the bar. A plus-size madam in a red dress with dirty blonde hair sat behind a counter to my right. "Can I help you hon?" she asked.

I smiled. "I saw two of my buddies came in here. I'd like to surprise them."

She smiled back. "They're back with a couple of the girls. I'll need to wand you first. You'll have to remove all the metal from your pockets."

I arched my eyebrows and reached for my belt buckle. "That may take a while. I've got a lot of metal on me."

The woman shrugged and then waved her hand. "Oh never mind. You can go on back but if you want to join the party you'll have to pay."

"Thank you. If you don't mind, what room are they in?"

"One's in-room thirteen and the other is in sixteen, right down the hall. Do you want me to send another one of the girls in?"

"I may do that later. Right now I want to go raze them while they got their pants off," I said and headed down the hallway. Kicking open the door of room thirteen, I looked in on a scruffy red-headed biker with a long greasy beard. He had a chunky blonde on the bed doing her from behind. The blonde's teats hung down like utters on a Guernsey cow and jiggled back and forth.

"Hey!" I yelled.

The biker pulled out of the blonde and whirled around. Seeing the forty-five in the mirror, the blonde screamed and dived off the bed to the floor. I gave the biker three hard ones with the forty-five in the center of his chest. Blood splatter against the wall and the naked biker fell over backward onto the bed. Back in the hallway, another nude biker stormed out of room sixteen. He bent over struggling to pull up his pants. I gave him a double-tap in the center of his forehead. The madam screamed from down the hallway. Nude girls stormed out of the various rooms screaming and ran for the lobby. A black woman with huge breasts ran by me. Her breasts bounced up and down like basketballs. She let out a screech and headed for the lobby. I darted for the exit at the end of the hallway.

A fat black security guard poked his head around a corner and took a shot at me. Bullets hit the doorjamb next to my head and a splinter of wood, cut my cheek. I returned fire, aiming high. He pulled his head back around the corner. Outside, I ran to the bike, fired her up, and hit the throttle. I left a rooster tail of gravel in the air when I roared out of the parking lot. Hitting Highway 160, I headed toward Las Vegas with my fist in the throttle.

***

Back in Vegas, I rolled up to the Top Heavy Tavern on my Harley. I hadn't shaved or bathed in about a week and I wore one of the Lost Souls' club vests. Noticing the patch on my back, and taking in my general appearance, the bouncer at the door let me in. Loud rock music blared from the barroom's speakers. The only light came from the center stage where two girls danced topless. Pool tables set off by themselves in a room off to the side. A stairway at the end of the room led to an upper loft where you could sit on couches overlooking the stage. I figured that was where the girls took patrons to perform lap dances. The smell of perfume, stale beer, and cigarette smoke filled the air.

Eight to ten bikers sat behind a bar facing the stage. I climbed onto a bar stool three places down and ordered a beer. *I guess the guy I killed in the ally lied,* I thought. They didn't notice me in the dim light, so I listened in on their conversation.

"The son of a bitch killed two of my guys in Pahrump. This fucker has killed more than half of my crew. This is your problem. You people need to deal with it," a burly biker with a long black beard said.

James Quinn spoke up. "You can't kill what you can't find. The guy is like a ghost. You don't see him until he's ready to kill you."

"We'll put up another grand to the guy who kills the bastard," the Vegas chapter president said.

"We'll match it," Quinn said. "What do you think Powder?" Another biker sitting closest to me spoke up.

"We'll catch him. Sooner or later, he'll make his move. He'll get careless." He produced a lighter and made flame. When he brought the lighter to his face to light his cigarette, I recognized his features. I took in his dirty blond goatee and his wiry frame. Except for his bald head, he looked the same. Anger boiled up inside me and my hands shook so bad that I spilled my beer. He was the one that grabbed Sharon and pulled her outside at that biker bar on the old Route 66. It was all I could do to keep from launching across the bar and grabbing his throat.

It'll be sooner than you think, Fuck Head. The Devil's gonna corn hole you before the sun goes down, I thought. I stood to my feet and headed for the door. Back in the parking lot, I climbed on the Harley and fired up the beast. Pulling the bike around, I braked to a stop facing the front door of the tavern. A big stocky Italian guy stood with his arms folded across his chest looking at me. I nodded with my head motioning for him to step aside. His eyes widened and he shook his head. Pulling my left hand sawed off, I gunned the throttle and the bouncer dived out of the way.

I shot across the parking lot hitting the glass front door of the Top Heavy Tavern. The door exploded into thousands of tiny pieces of glass when the Harley slammed into it. I braked inside the bar and got my bearings. Dancers screamed, diving off the stage and the bikers at the bar scrambled. I trained my sawed-off on Powder and gave him a barrel. The sound of the shotgun blast inside the confined space caused my hearing to go away. The shot took off the top of Powder's head and he flew backward and landed on the floor. I gave J D Quinn the other barrel, but he was diving behind the stage when I fired and I only got him in the shoulder.

Holstering my right hand sawed off, I pulled my left. I gave the Vegas chapter president both barrels. He flew up onto the dance floor, did a death dance, and died. Holstering the sawed offs, I leaned the Harley up against the bar and pulled one of my forty-fives. I heard some of the dancers crying. Bullets flew overhead. Picking my targets, I stood in a shooter's stance as if I was on the range, and killed five more. The big Italian bouncer crouched by the door and fired off three shots with a big bore revolver. It sounded like a forty-four magnum. The big bullets tumbling over my head reminded me of a steamroller driving by. Crouching down, I returned fire. A bullet slammed into his shoulder and he went down. *Collateral damage,* I thought. Hearing sirens in the distance, I climbed back onto the Harley and gunned the throttle. The back tire slipped on broken glass and I almost went down, but I managed to make it out the door.

Hitting the freeway, I headed east on the 15 and figured I'd about used up my good graces in Nevada. I didn't stop until I reached the state line. Pulling off in Beaver Utah, I holed up for the night in a cheap motel. The following morning, I headed north. Three hours later, I pulled off the 15 freeway, took Highway 50, cut over to Highway 89, and headed north. The Lost Souls had a chapter in a little town known as Cap Rock, up near Mount Pleasant. They were the next batch of scum that needed my attention. The road wound through the mountains like a bull snake. The cold mountain air made my cheeks feel numb. Pine trees lined the road most of the way. They gave way to open meadows. I saw a stream off to my left dancing over the rocks.

Five miles south of Cap Rock, I came round a curve when a deer darted across the road in front of me. I braked. The back tire caught gravel and the bike slid out from under me. Sliding off the road on my back, my head hit a boulder and my lights went out.

***

CHAPTER 18

My eyes fluttered open, pain shot through my head and my leg throbbed. Gazing about, I noticed the sticky pads on my chest and breathed in the sterile smell of a hospital. This time, my memory was intact. My right leg was in a cast suspended over my head by a series of cables connected to the pins in my leg. The heart machine next to my bed beeped.

"This is fucking great," I said touching my head with my right hand. I felt cloth bandages. "Another head injury?"

A good-looking nurse with long black hair and dark brown eyes sashayed into the room. I took in her hourglass figure, her large round breasts, and her sun-bronzed legs. She wore a short, white nurse's uniform. Her eyes sparkled and she gave me a killer smile.

"Oh good. You're awake." Stepping up to my bedside, she leaned over me with a digital thermometer and took my temperature. I glanced down the front of her shirt into a deep valley of cleavage. She caught me looking. Heat rose in my cheeks and my eyes darted back up to her face. After taking my temperature, she took my blood pressure reading.

"What's the verdict?" I asked.

"You're temperature and your blood pressure is fine. You had a motorcycle wreck."

"How bad am I hurt?"

"You had a minor concussion and you broke your leg."

I gave her a smirk. "I can see that."

"Other than that, you sustained some minor contusions and some road rash. I'll call the doctor and tell him you're awake. He'll be able to tell you more about your condition."

"Could I get some water? It feels like a monkey shit in my mouth."

The nurse laughed. "I can handle that." She poured me a glass of water from a pitcher on a metal cart next to my bed. I guzzled down the water, enjoying its freshness and she refilled the glass. I breathed in the smell of her perfume.

After killing the second glass of water, I let out a sigh. "That went down smooth. You don't happen to have a six-pack of beer around here anywhere, do you?"

She giggled. "I'm afraid not."

"What's your name?" I asked looking into her pretty eyes.

A nervous flutter passed through her. "I'm Nurse Muldoon. Aili Muldoon. You can call me Aili."

I grinned. "An Irish lass. My favorite kind. My name is McDonald. Mike McDonald."

She stepped back near the foot of the bed and picked up a clipboard hanging at the foot of my bed. "I know. That's what it says here on your chart." She paused, fiddling with a piece of her hair up by her forehead. Her hands trembled. "I'll tell the doctor you're awake." She retreated to the door, but paused in the doorway and looked back at me. "The police have been asking about you. They have a guard by your door. I'm sure they'll want to talk to you, now that you're awake," Aili said and disappeared into the hallway.

"Shit. This keeps getting better and better," I said to myself.

A tall dark-headed man wearing a white lab coat entered my hospital room a few minutes later. I took in his massive frame and gigantic hands. His facial features looked rock hard, but when he saw me, they softened into a smile. His breath smelled of mints.

"Hello, Mr. McDonald. How are you feeling today? I'm Doctor Murphy. Charles Murphy."

"I feel like a warm bag of horse shit."

The doctor chuckled. "Care to be a bit more specific?"

My leg hurts and my head feels like a tribe of monkeys are up there renovating the place with a sledgehammer. Other than that, I'm okay."

The doctor let out another low chuckle. He put his stethoscope up against my chest and we did the breathing bit. "How's your memory?"

"The memory's fine."

"We'll give you some medication for the headache. You suffered a mild concussion. You broke your leg in three places. We set the leg and put some pins in it. Those will come out in three weeks. We put a temporary cast on your leg. Once we remove the pins, we'll put a more permeate one on. You'll be off your feet for quite some time."

"Will I be able to walk again, Doc?" I asked.

The doctor laid a hand on my shoulder. "Sure. Don't worry about that. You'll regain full mobility, all though you might have a slight limp."

"How long until I'm able to ride my motorcycle?" I asked.

"You'll be off your feet for four weeks. After that, you'll be on crutches. I'd say at least six months. You'll need therapy. It's going to be a slow process."

"That's fucking dandy."

The doctor paused and then said, "There's an officer of the law out here that would like to speak with you. He's our town's chief of police."

I rolled my eyes. "Great, send him in."

The doctor stepped to the door of my hospital room and spoke to someone in the hallway. A middle-aged man with curly blond hair that hung over his ears, stepped into the room. The room's florissant light reflected off the bald spot on the top of his head. I noticed a liver spot on his left cheek. He looked soft around the middle, but he wore the khaki uniform well. The forty-five riding on his hip looked well used.

He glanced at the doctor. "Doc, do you mind if I have a word in private with your patient?"

"No. Of course not. Take your time." The doctor stepped out. The police chief turned to me and gave me a friendly smile. He pulled up a chair and sat down next to my bed. "Good morning Mr. McDonald. I'm Chief Shawn Brody. I'm glad to see you're awake. I hope and you are not feeling too bad."

"I'm feeling like shit. What can I do for you chief?" I asked.

He laughed. "You fit the description of someone who's been playing holy cob with a motorcycle club know as the Lost Souls."

My eyes widened and I feigned surprise. "Huh. I can't say that I know what you're referring to."

"Well, the guy almost completely wiped out the LA chapter and the Las Vegas chapter of this club. If I knew for a fact that you were this guy, then I'd have to arrest you."

I shrugged. "Do your duty then."

The police chief smiled and raised his hand. "Now hold on a minute son. The description I got was vague. To tell you the truth, it doesn't hurt my feelings any, what happened to those biker boys. The

Lost Souls are scum. Every time the ones from down south come through here, they cause trouble. We have a chapter here in Cap Rock. I've got several of, them, under investigation for unsolved murders and assaults. They run drugs and guns. It wouldn't hurt my feelings none if something were to happen to this bunch here in town either."

"You never know what might happen, chief," I said.

"So far, this guy that's become such a thorn in the side of the Lost Souls hasn't hurt any regular citizens. I'd like to keep it that way. Hell, if someone raped and killed my wife, I'd do the same thing," Brody said looking me dead in the eyes.

I paused returning his glare. "Chief, if I was this guy, I'd take every precaution to see that innocent people don't get hurt."

A grin spread across the police chief's face. "That would be good."

"Chief, what happened to my bike?"

Chief Brody stood to his feet and stepped over by the window. "It's at the Harley shop here in town. I checked your wallet when I ran your ID. I called your insurance company. The motorcycle shop will fix your bike before you're ready to ride it."

"Thank you chief," I said. I was starting to like this guy. He reminded me of Reverend Blackwood.

"I'm keeping a guard on your door, in case our local boys start thinkin' that you're the one causing them all the trouble. Here's my card. It's got my home number and my cell on there. Give me a call if you have any problems. Day or night," Brody said.

"Thank you, Chief."

"Oh, and when they spring you from the hospital, you might need a place to stay until you get your strength back. I got a cabin out in the woods that not too many people know about. You can use it until you're better."

I looked up and smiled. "Thanks again, chief. Say, why don't you stop in some time while I'm here in the hospital. We could shoot the shit. Could you bring a six-pack?"

The chief paused for a moment. "Yeah, I could do that," he said and then stepped out.

***

Time passed by slow, but Aili Muldoon kept me entertained. When she wasn't busy, she would stop by my room and we'd talk. I broke down and told her everything. I told her about what happened to

Sharon and about my war with the Lost Souls. That troubled her. She said that I needed to let it go. She said that hate was like acid. She said that sometimes it harmed the container that held it, more than what you poured it onto. That reminded me of Reverend Blackwood.

The police chief came by as promised and he brought a six-pack of Bud Light each time he came for a visit. He was a likable fellow and I enjoyed his company.

"Chief you didn't happen to find a duffle bag strapped onto the back of my bike?" I asked one time when he stopped in to chat.

A smirk crossed his face. "I did. I didn't find it strapped to your bike though. It was lying in the brush a few yards away. I figured it must have belonged to someone else."

"Why's that?" I asked.

"Well, there were some interesting things inside that bag. It held some homemade pipe bombs and some homemade C four. It also held some evil-looking weapons and a shit load of ammunition. If I knew for sure who that stuff belonged to, I'd be duty-bound to place them under arrest. I decided that I'd better take possession of that stuff for a while to keep it safe."

I laughed. "I guess that was smart thinking, Chief."

Three weeks into my hospital stay, they removed the pins from my legs and cut off my temporary cast. Doctor Murphy mixed up some plaster and put on my permanent cast. He issued me a pair of crutches and I was finally able to move around a bit. It felt like a major victory to go to the bathroom by myself. Have you ever tried pissing while standing on a pair of crutches? It ain't easy. Aili changed from the day shift to the night shift. One evening, I was sound asleep when she glided into my room. It must have been around midnight. She turned around, reached up, and pulled the privacy curtain around my bed. When she did, the back of her skirt hiked up revealing her shapely ass covered by a pair of black silk panties.

She turned back around and a big grin crossed her face. I leaned back on my elbows and my bottom jaw dropped open. Aili unbuttoned the front of her shirt and tossed the shirt aside. Unzipping the zipper on the side of her skirt, she wiggled her hips and let the skirt fall to the floor. I heard a rustle of fabric. She stood before me in a black push-up bra and black silk panties. Aili reached behind her back and unsnapped the bra. She tossed the bra into my face and slid off her panties. Cat-like, she climbed onto the bed, making a purring sound, and climbed on top of me. I breathed in her essence. A tent formed under my sheet, her large breasts dangled in my face, so I reached up and grabbed one. Her nipple hardened to my touch.

For the next twenty minutes, Aili rode me hard. I had to be careful because of my leg, and it caused me some pain, but in the end, it was worth it. When I closed my eyes that night, I felt as if I'd run the New York City Marathon and I slept like a newborn baby. I felt a spark of something good inside. My hate for the Lost Souls hadn't died, but I put it on hold for a while.

***

My time in the hospital continued to pass like a snail with a sore foot. Aili made my life a bit more interesting. She tried hard to make me give up on my plans for the Lost Souls. She said that I should quit while I was ahead and get on with my life. We spent hours in a heated discussion. She wanted a relationship, but she said that she wouldn't give herself to a man consumed by hate.

"We could have a good life here, Mike," she said one morning after I had my breakfast. She stood at the foot of my bed with her hands on her hips.

"I know, and I could take you up on that after I'm finished with the Lost Souls."

Anger flashed in her eyes. "By then it will be too late. I have an application for a job at a hospital in New York City. They're hiring RNs. I would give that up. We could get married. I would be good to you."

I let out a noisy breath. "I know you would Aili, but I can't. I have to do this. When it's finished, I'll come back."

Tears welled up in her eyes. "Don't bother," she said and stormed out of the room.

Chief Brody continued to visit me and I was beginning to consider him as a friend. Every time he came to visit, he brought a six-pack of beer. We talked about everything imaginable. We talked about politics, sports, the Lost Souls, his job, and life in Cap Rock. On one of his visits, I stuck an empty beer bottle underneath my pillow. Even though they still had a guard on the door, I couldn't shake a sense of vulnerability. I knew that any day now, the Lost Souls would find out that I was here in the hospital and try to take me out. It happened three days later. Around midnight, I heard a sound that woke me from a dead slumber. Looking up, I saw a man standing in the doorway of my hospital room pointing a gun at me.

The scruffy-looking biker fired, lighting up the room with the gun's muzzle blast. The loud bang of gunfire filled the room and a bullet caressed my cheek when I dived off the bed. Feathers flew into the air. The room stank of gunpowder. I Landed on my side next to the bed. Reaching up, I grabbed the empty beer bottle that I had stashed underneath my pillow. I scooted underneath my hospital bed. The biker ran to the side of my bed. I lunged out from under the bed and grabbed his leg. He fell knocking over the metal stand next to my bed and the glass pitcher shattered when it hit the floor. Dropping on top of the downed biker, I broke the bottle over the top of his head. Holding the jagged neck of the broken bottle in my hand, I drove it into the side of the man's neck. Blood gushed out of his neck and formed a puddle on the floor. The coppery smell of blood filled the room. The biker's legs kicked a few times and his body went limp.

Gunshots echoed through the hospital room and bullets screamed overhead. Grabbing the dead biker's handgun, I rolled over and fired three rounds into a form standing in the doorway. The man dropped to the floor and the room dropped into silence.

"Who else is out there?" I yelled. "Identify yourself or I'll shoot!" Sweat cropped up on my forehead and my heart pounded. My hands white-knuckled the grips on the handgun.

"It's me! Officer Daniels! There were only two of them! You're safe now!"

"Where the fuck were you? Why weren't you guarding the door?" I yelled.

"I stepped out to get a cup of coffee! I don't know how they got inside the hospital!"

"Turn on the light and step into the room! Do it slow, and easy! Keep your hand away from your gun!" Light exploded throughout the room and Officer Daniels stepped in with his hands up.

"This isn't necessary," he said.

"How do I know them scumbags didn't pay you to let them in here? Did you call this in?" I asked. I noticed a scared look cross Daniels' face.

"Yeah. Chief Brody is on the way right now," he said.

"I'll keep this gun on you until the chief arrives." I heard sirens outside and a few minutes later five more uniformed officers arrived.

A few minutes after that, Chief Brody himself stormed into my hospital room. His eyes twitched in anger and he gave Daniels a rock-hard stare. I lowered the weapon.

"Hugh, how in the hell did you let this happen?" Brody asked.

"It wasn't my fault chief. I stepped out for a few seconds to get a cup of coffee."

"As of now, you're relieved of duty, pending investigation. If I find out that that you've had any dealings with the Lost Souls or took their money, your job is toast. I'll see to it that you do jail time. Is that clear?" the chief demanded.

Daniels' shoulders sagged. "Yes sir."

"Then get out of my sight." Daniels left and the chief helped me to a chair. The doctor on duty and a flock of nurses rushed into the room and insisted on checking me over. The room smelled of blood, piss, and shit. They moved me along with my bed into another room while the police investigated the crime scene. A while later I saw them wheel the bodies of the bikers I killed out on a gurney.

"How are you feeling?" the doctor asked after he checked my blood pressure.

"I'm fine. My leg hurts, but other than that, I'm okay."

"I'll have one of the nurses give you some extra pain meds," the doctor said.

Chief Brody ambled over to the bed, picked up my pillow, and gave it a look. Turning around, he showed it to me. There was a bullet hole in the center of the pillow. Chief Brody smiled and said, "Another inch to the left and you'd be sprouting daises."

"I guess I'm a lucky son of a bitch," I said.

The nurses changed my bedding while I sat in a chair talking to Brody. They brought me another pillow.

"What do you call two scumbag bikers lying dead on the hospital floor?" the chief asked.

"I don't know. You tell me chief."

"A hell of a good start." We both laughed and the nurses helped me back into bed. Brody stepped up to my bedside and laid a hand on my arm. "I put two new guys outside guarding your door. This won't happen again. If Daniels is dirty, I'll make him pay."

"He's only guilty of being stupid," I said.

Brody chuckled. "Yeah, but someone had to let them in from the outside, and who told them that you were here? The hospital keeps everything locked up tight after visiting hours. The only thing they leave unlocked is the emergency room. I don't think they came in that way."

Aili Muldoon rushed into my hospital room. Her face looked flushed. "Mike! I was working in another ward across the hospital when I heard what happened! Are you all right?"

"I'm fine Aili. Some old boys tried to take a few potshots at me. That's all," I said. She leaned over, throwing herself into my arms and I felt her warm tears on my neck. Looking over my shoulder, I saw Chief Brody smile.

"Well, it looks like I'm no longer needed here. I'll see you come visiting hours tomorrow," Brody said and strolled out of the room.

During the week that followed, my relationship with Aili thawed somewhat. She came to my room in the wee hours of the morning and climbed in bed with me a couple of times when no other nurse was around. I only put half my heart into it. I was still in love with Sharon. Aili continued to try to persuade me into giving up my vendetta against the Lost Souls. Chief Brody kept double guards on my door and there were no more attempts on my life. Brody continued his visits. We shot the shit, drank some beer, and enjoyed each other's company.

***

When Doctor Murphy sprang me from the hospital, one of the nurses wheeled me out the door in a wheelchair. The early morning sunshine felt good against my face. Brody met me out front. He had my motorcycle in the bed of an old pickup truck and it looked as good as new. Two patrol cars set parked behind Brody's old beat-up Ford pickup.

Brody stepped up next to me on the curb. "The boys at the Harley shop finished your bike yesterday. Your insurance covered everything. I got your gear in the back of my truck. You can stay at my cabin as long as you need to. I don't want you going after the Souls until you're in good health."

"It's kind of hard to fight when you're on crutches."

Brody slapped me on the back. "You'll be back in the saddle before you know it. The mountain air will do you good. There's a stream behind the cabin that's chuck full of trout."

"Do you think the Lost Souls with try to cause me some trouble up there?"

Brody paused. "They might, but the cabin is pretty isolated. There's only one road leading in and out. I'll have my deputies guarding it. You should be all right up there."

"I don't know how I'll repay you for your kindness. I have money. I can pay you to rent the cabin."

An angry look crossed Brody's face. "I'm doing this out of friendship. Payment won't be necessary," he said.

"Take it easy, chief. I meant nothing by it. I appreciate everything you've done."

Chief Brody helped me into the passenger side of his pickup. I leaned my crutches up against the dashboard. He drove through town and hit the highway. Ten miles up the road, he took a dirt trail leading into the mountains. The trail traversed a narrow canyon and crossed through a thick stand of trees. The trees gave way to a grassy clearing. A rustic-looking cabin appeared setting in the center of a meadow. A small wooden shed was set to the left of the cabin. A stand of sugar pine trees surrounded the meadow where the cabin lay. The land behind the cabin slopped down to where a good-sized stream meandered across the land. The sound of the water prancing over the rocks floated on the wind. Scrub oak trees and brush lined the stream's banks.

The chief pulled up in front of the cabin and killed the truck's motor.

"It ain't much, but it's comfy," he said.

Gazing about, I took in the scenic beauty. "It'll do. It's beautiful out here."

"Yep. It's God's country." Chief Brody exited the pickup, went around to my side, and helped me out. I breathed in the crisp mountain air. "I'll have the deputies put your scooter out in that shed."

Using my crutches, I crossed the rough terrain and stepped up onto the porch. Brody hovered about making sure that I didn't fall. He opened the log door, and I hobbled inside. Standing in the small living room, I glanced about the cabin. I saw a well-used leather couch, a rocking chair, and an old TV set. The place looked a little dusty.

"There's a fireplace, a small kitchen, and a small bedroom. I've got the firewood stacked outside by the back porch. The TV only gets the local channels, but there's plenty of beer and food in the refrigerator. The fishing gear is in the bedroom closet. If you'll have a seat, I'll go fetch your gear from the truck," Brody said. I nodded and hobbled across the hardwood floor to the couch. Chief Brody came back a few minutes later. He set my gear bag down on the floor, crossed the room, and stood next to where I sat on the couch. "I put my number into your cell phone. If you have any trouble up here, don't hesitate to call. I'll keep two deputies on guard down by the main highway."

I patted the couch. "Go fetch us a beer, chief, and then have a seat. There's no sense in you running off so fast."

Chief Brody grinned, went into the kitchen, and came back with a six-pack. We shot the shit for the next hour and a half and said our goodbyes. After the chief left, I checked my gear bag. All my equipment was how I'd left it. Brody took the liberty to clean and oil my weapons. I found a crude map drawn on a piece of paper showing the location of the Lost Souls clubhouse. He drew a large box with an X in front of it depicting the clubhouse. Over the top of the box; he drew flames and debris scattering. In bold letters above this, he wrote the word, Kaboom! I laughed. Finished with my gear bag, I hobbled out to the shed on crutches. I checked out the work the boys at the Harley shop did to my scooter. I fired the beast up and it purred like a newborn kitten.

"You can't even tell that I crashed," I said to myself.

Finished in the shed, I hobbled back into the cabin. I scrounged around for something to eat and lit a fire in the fireplace. After supper, I took a six-pack of beer from the refrigerator and sat down to watch some TV. I went to bed early that night. I planned to see if I could make it down to the stream in the morning without falling on my ass.

***

During the months that followed, I spent my time watching TV, fishing, and tinkering with the bike in the shed. Chief Brody came by every morning to visit. He took me back to the hospital so they could remove my cast. I advanced from hobbling along on crutches to walking with a cane. Chief Brody took me to my weekly therapy sessions and, to me, it seemed like déjà vu. Aili came by a few times and spent the night once. She still hounded me about giving up my vendetta against the Lost Souls.

One evening she got mad and said, "It's either give up this stupid fight that you can't win or give up me." She stood there with her hands on her hips and her lip stuck out.

I shrugged. "I've done okay so far. It's something that I have to do. I'll miss you," I said.

She stormed out of the cabin in a rage and peeled out in her Jeep leaving a cloud of dust in her wake.

"Who needs all the drama?" I said to the empty room.

During the weeks that followed, my strength returned. I used the cane but began to rely on it less and less. Winter had given way to spring and spring turned to summer. I was starting to think about moving on; it was time to go back on the attack. I hadn't heard a peep from the Lost Souls since I moved into the cabin. One afternoon I was sitting in front of the TV when the front window of the cabin exploded in a hail of gunfire.

***

CHAPTER 19

I rolled on the throttle crossing over the Utah State line and into Wyoming. A pack of Harley Davidson motorcycles sped by. The bikers wore the Hell's Angels red and white patch on the back of their vests. I white-knuckled the handlebars, breathing in the smell of exhaust. My hand slipped under my coat. A hot cauldron of anger boiled up within me, but I did nothing. My war was not with them. Hundreds of bikers were on the road heading for Sturgis South Dakota. I noticed a young couple on a Honda Gold Wing. They reminded me of my past life with Sharon. Off in the distance lightning flashed and thunder rolled. A hailstorm erupted unleashing its fury. I pulled over onto the shoulder of the road and slowed down. Visibility was next to zero, but I kept my fist in the throttle until the hail stopped. My mind drifted back to my last days in Cap Rock Utah.

***

The window of the cabin exploded. I dived onto the floor and crawled across the room to my gear bag. Grabbing my sawed offs and my forty-fives, I jumped up fired a blast through the window and ran for the back door. Charging downhill, I ran flat out for the stream behind the cabin. Two bikers ran around from the front of the cabin firing at me with automatic weapons. Bullets tore up dirt in my wake and a bullet burnt my shoulder.

Huffing and puffing, I reached the streambed and used the scrub oaks and the brush lining the bank for cover. I headed east following the stream. My leg throbbed. Bullets screamed overhead and one hit a tree branch next to me making a loud cracking sound. I ran along the bank for about two hundred yards. Bullets buzzed through the brush over my head. I came to a place where the forest was no more than twenty yards from the streambed. Cutting through the scrub oaks and brush, I ran for the stand of sugar pines to the north. Bullets kicked up dirt behind me.

When I reached the safety of the forest, I stopped to take a breather. Once I had my breathing under control, I moved through the woods, making every step deliberate. I became the hunter. A camp robber Jay chirped overhead. Moving toward the northwest, I made my way toward the edge of the tree line. I heard more gunfire. A branch ahead of me snapped. I moved from tree to tree being as quiet as a whisper of death. Peering around a tree, I saw officer Hugh Daniels standing at the tree line with a rifle slung over his back. He looked through a pair of binoculars studying the cabin in the clearing.

"There's nothing I hate worse than a crooked cop," I said. Daniels whirled around. "Go ahead! Reach for the rifle! Give me an excuse!" I held one of my sawed offs on him and Daniels raised his hands. "Drop the rifle and kick it away!" I yelled. He complied. "Now lose the handgun!" He unbuckled his gun belt and let it drop to the forest floor. "Hug the tree! One false move and I'll splatter your guts all over the forest floor!" He put his arms around the tree. Taking the handcuffs from his belt, I handcuffed him to the sugar pine tree.

Grabbing, his rifle, I sighted in on the cabin front door. A grubby-looking biker stepped outside. I put the crosshairs on the center of the man's forehead and squeezed the trigger. I heard the bullet slap bone and the man's head exploded. He flew backward, slamming into the cabin and his body slid down the wall to the front porch.

"Scratch off another one of the Lost Souls." A biker ran from behind the cabin running for a beat-up red GMC pickup truck. I worked the bolt on the rifle and fired. The bullet slammed into his chest knocking him off his feet. "How many more are there?" I said to Daniels.

Daniels let out a pent-up breath. "That was it. They only sent two."

"How'd they get back here. There's only one road in and out, and the chief had that guarded?"

"There's an old four-wheel-drive trail that the chief doesn't know about," Daniels said.

"Where are all the rest of them?"

"We only had ten or twelve in our local chapter. You might have missed a couple down south. You killed two already. The rest headed up to Sturgis for the motorcycle rally. A couple of guys from down south showed up at the clubhouse and the whole pack took off."

Leaning the rifle up against a tree, I went around to where I could face Daniels. "The only other question I have is why?"

Daniels looked at the ground. "It's not personal. They offered me money. I have a wife who likes expensive things. I'm behind on my mortgage. The bank is trying to take my house away."

I shook my head in disgust. "You stupid fuck. You lost your last chance of getting caught up." Taking my cell phone from my pocket, I stepped out into the clearing and called Chief Brody. Twenty minutes later, he showed up with four more cop cars. I watched him take the handcuffs off Daniels' wrist, freeing him from the tree. Brody cuffed Daniels' hands behind his back and put him into the back of his patrol car. An ambulance showed up and carted off the bodies of the two dead bikers.

Chief Brody stepped up next to me. "Daniels said that most of the boys are on their way up to Sturgis."

Brody nodded. "No one is at home over at the clubhouse except for a couple of prospects they left to guard the place."

I picked up the rifle. "My leg's about as good as it's gonna get. I'll go have a talk with the prospects and then ride out."

"I hope you show them the error of their ways," Brody said.

"Oh, I'm sure we'll have an explosive conversation."

Brody laughed. "When you're done with this thing, come back and see me. I'll buy the first round at the bar."

"You can count on it," I said.

The chief stepped up, grabbed me in a bear hug. The excitement over, we said our goodbyes, the police left and I packed my gear. Climbing into the saddle, I fired up the Harley and headed to Cap Rock. I had a rendezvous with a couple of prospects to attend to.

Forty-five minutes later, I cruised down Baker Street, a narrow dirt road on the outskirts of Cap Rock. Warehouses and industrial buildings lined both sides of the road. I passed a dog food plant and a cannery then pulled up in front of a rustic-looking bar at the end of the street. The Lost Souls' clubhouse looked deserted except for two motorcycles parked out front. Two men sat on lawn chairs on the boardwalk by the front door. Their eyes widened when I pulled up. Overhead, the sky turned overcast and the weather turned chilly.

The older of the two had dirty-looking dark hair tied back in a ponytail and bushy black eyebrows. His hand went underneath his vest. Killing the motor on the shovelhead, I pulled my right hand forty-five out of its holster and pointed it at him.

"I'd bring that hand out from under that vest real, slow unless you want an extra hole in your head." He removed his hand from his vest and set it on his knee. I noticed a slight trimmer in his hands. It might have been fear, but it was cold outside.

"You're him aren't you? The one that's been killing all our guys," the young prospect with the babyface said.

"You got me there. I've been killing Souls from California to Utah and I plan to kill a few more before I'm through," I said.

"Our brothers will take care of you," the scruffy-looking older guy said.

"That could happen, but it won't help you two. Where is everybody anyway?"

"They all headed up to Sturgis for the rally," the younger one said.

"Shut up Baby Cakes. Don't tell this fucker nothing."

I gave the dirty biker a frown. "You boys are lucky I don't shoot you down right now like the scum you are," I said cocking the forty-five.

The dark-headed biker's face turned ashen.

"I heard some of the LA bros killed your wife. I'm sorry man, but we had nothing to do with that," the younger one said.

"Yeah! We're only prospects! They left us here to guard the clubhouse while everyone else heads up to Sturgis to party!" the older one said. He was starting to get belligerent.

"Sorry for your luck. I'll give you guys a way out of this. Take off your vests, throw them on the ground, climb on those Harleys and leave town. I'd leave the state if I were you. I hear Arizona is nice this time of year. It's warmer down there," I said.

"You can't run us out of town!" the dark-haired biker yelled.

"It's your choice. You guys need to find a better caliber of friends to ride with. You ride with shit bags, and your life turns to shit. The Lost Souls don't have a chapter in Arizona so you two might do all right down there."

"Fuck you," the dark-headed biker yelled. "The bros in the Idaho chapter will take care of you!" He jumped up, jamming his hand underneath his vest, and pulled out a stub nosed thirty-eight. I fired the forty-five splattering his brains against the wall of the clubhouse. His body fell to the boardwalk.

Baby Cakes leaped up with his hands in the air. A vein on the side of his forehead pulsated. "Don't shoot! Don't shoot! God, I almost shit myself!" he yelled.

"Take off your patch and ride, or die like him."

"I'll ride out man! I was getting tired of hanging around these bastards anyway! They're too violent! When they get spun out on drugs, there's no tellin' what they might do!"

"Get with it then. Toss your vest on the ground along with any hardware you might be packing," I said.

The young prospect tossed his vest on the ground along with a knife and a nine-millimeter handgun. "Can I leave now?"

"It'd be best before I change my mind."

The young biker ran to his Harley, fired it up, and roared down the street. The sound of his loud pipes bounced back off the surrounding buildings. I put the Shovelhead in neutral, leaned it on its side stand, and climbed off the bike. Grabbing the dead biker by the back of his vest, I drug him into the clubhouse. I picked up the young prospect's things and tossed them through the front door of the clubhouse. Stepping over to my bike, I took a pipe bomb from my gear bag. Lighting the cannon fuse, I tossed the pipe bomb through the front door of the clubhouse.

I put the Harley in gear and rolled down the street with my eye on the rearview mirror. There was a loud bang. The clubhouse exploded sending burning pieces of wood and other debris into the air. Smoke and flames billowed into the air. Chief Brody passed me with his lights and siren blaring. He looked out the driver's side window at me and gave me the thumbs up. I gave him a wave and hit the interstate.

***

The numbness in my ass from sitting too long in the saddle brought my mind back to the present. I got hit hard by hail and rain, and I was starting to get tired. I needed to piss, so I pulled off the freeway in Green River Wyoming. The clouds dissipated and the sun came out. Noticing a park down by the river, I turned in. About twenty Harleys set parked up against the curb. Gazing about the park, I noticed the bikers partying. There were some women and kids with them, plus a few citizens. That old familiar anger boiled up inside me, but I didn't see any of the Lost Souls. I headed toward the restrooms when a big burly biker coming out of the restroom smiled and said, “How ya doin’ bud?”

“I ain’t your bud,” I said under my breath, but the biker had already left the restroom and didn’t hear my reply. After pissing like a racehorse, I bought a water bottle from a vending machine and headed back to my Harley. Standing next to my bike surveying the scene, I saw a massive red-headed biker with a long red beard start my way. He reminded me of a big, bear and he had a friendly smile on his face. I reached under my coat for my forty-five.

“There’s no need to be pullin’ that piece you got under your coat. I’m trying to be friendly,” the big man said.

I shrugged with my hand still under my coat. “Why? I’m not your friend. You don’t know me. You bikers get me with your brotherhood bullshit. I may ride a motorcycle, but that doesn’t mean you’re my brother.”

The big man nodded but seemed undisturbed by my words. “True that and you’re right. I don’t know you, but I saw you ride in here on a Harley like us. I know who you are. We’ve got more in common than you think. You’re the one that’s gone on the warpath against the Lost Souls down south. Those boys are trash, pure and simple.”

“Yeah, and how is your crew is any better?” I asked.

We stood facing each other. “All bikers ain’t trash like them. I wear a patch, but that doesn’t make me pond scum. Take a look around you. We got our woman out here. We got our kids, plus friends of the club that don’t even ride motorcycles. Why don’t you come on over and have a beer? Get to know the bros. Make up your, own mind,” he said.

I paused for a moment and said, “Sure why not.” We went over to join the party.

“I heard they killed your wife.”

“Yeah. Raped and killed her.”

The big man’s eyes locked with mine and I saw genuine compassion in his eyes.

“They kidnapped one of our guys' little, sister. They took her over to Idaho and kept her in their clubhouse for over a week. They raped her and then killed her. We caught the ones that did it,” he said.

“What’d you do with ‘em?”

He glanced over at me. “We’re a family club, but when it’s time to take care of business, we go in fast and hard. We left the two that did it hanging from a bridge over a creek near the Wyoming Idaho border. We left them with their throats slit and we left them hanging by their heels.”

“What’s your name anyway?” I asked when we reached the party.

“Alan. Alan Green. They call me Big Al.” We shook and my hand felt as if it were inside a bear trap.

“I’m Mike McDonald. Why are you having a party in weather like this?”

Big Al laughed and said, “If you don’t like the weather in Wyoming, give it a minute. It’ll change.” We reached the group of bikers partying down by the river. “Boys, this here’s Mike McDonald. Mike these are the Green River Boys.”

One of the bikers looked up, gave me a friendly smile, and took a beer from an ice chest. “Care for one of these?”

“I don’t mind if I do,” I said.

The biker handed me a Budweiser and Big Al and I sat down on lawn chairs sitting on the edge of the crowd. The weather started to feel muggy after the rain.

“You’ve been lucky so far. The Lost Souls aren’t as big down south as they are up here. Their mother chapter is over in Idaho. They have a clubhouse. It’s, an old hunting lodge, off in the forest by itself at the end of a county lane known as Thunder Road.”

“How many guys do they have over there?”

Big Al paused, thinking. “A shit load. They ain’t there now. Everyone’s over at Sturgis for the rally.”

“I guess I got my work cut out for me,” I said.

Big Al gave me a serious look. “Why don’t you let us help? The Lost Souls have been trying to make inroads here in Wyoming. They’ve shot a couple of our guys on the road and did a drive-by on a chapter clubhouse up in Jackson’s Hole. It’s about time we took care of the situation.”

“How many chapters do you guys have?” I asked.

“Six in Wyoming, five in Colorado, and four up in Montana. We also have a couple down in Alabama and one in New York. After we take care of the Lost Souls, we’ll branch out over into Idaho,” Big Al said.

"What can you guys do that I can't do by myself?"

"We've got the weapons and we've got the manpower. One of our guys owns a junkyard. We've got chase vehicles to carry the hardware. Whenever we have to do some serious business, he supplies us with vehicles registered as junk. He files all the numbers off of the engine block and does away with the VINs on the body. He has a contact supply us with phony registration. When we finish a job, we drop a grenade inside the vehicle. The cops have nothing but a burning hulk when we're through."

I let out a low whistle. "Some family club."

"We're a family club, but we're not choirboys. Some of our members have kids. We don't allow any drug dealing or using, except for a little pot now and then. We try to stay peaceable with everyone, but we do take care of our own."

I noticed a ten percent patch on the vest of a biker tossing a softball to a little kid. I've heard of the so-called, one-percenter, but what's with the ten percent patch?"

"Some of our people own businesses. We work for a living. Those that chose to, donate ten percent of their income to the club. Once they've done that for the entire year, they get the ten percent patch. Our people take care of our own. If a member loses his job, those that own businesses make a place for them. If they're sick and have to miss work, the club donates money."

I took a pull on my beer; Big Al produced a cigar and fired one up. Tobacco smoke drifted with the wind. I breathed in the rich aroma. "You want one of these?"

"I'll pass. So how can you help me with the Lost Souls?" I asked.

"I know where they camp out at during the Black Hills rally. You stay the night with us at the clubhouse and we'll ride up to Sturgis in the morning. We'll hit them while they're in camp." I hesitated for a moment thinking. "You've got to trust someone sometime. You can't do this on your own. They'll kill you for sure," Big Al said.

I leaned back in my lawn chair pondering the situation before responding. "You got me there. Sure I'd appreciate all the help you could give me," I said.

Big Al laughed, slapping me on the back, and it felt like he hit me with a baseball bat. "Go mingle with the bros. Get to know them. They're good people."

Standing to my feet, I ambled down to a group of bikers down by the river. One of them handed me another beer after I killed the first one. Big Al was right; they were good people and I could tell that their bond of brotherhood was tight. They treated me like family. Some of them seemed in awe of what I had done to the Lost Souls. After mingling for a while, I went back and sat down next to Big Al. By now, Al's cigar hand burned down to the butt. He grimaced and snuffed out the cigar on the heel of his boot.

"Smoking cheap cigars is like eating pussy," he said.

"How's that?" I asked.

"The closer you get to the butt, the worse it tastes." I laughed. "They got the food ready. We got fried chicken and barbecued ribs. Why don't we head on over there and put on a feed bag?" Big Al said.

"That sounds good to me. My stomach's starting to wear a sore spot on my backbone," I said. Big Al chuckled. We headed over to where they were fixing the food and headed back to our lawn chairs with our plates. Several more of the Green River Boys and a few of their friends joined us. The food tasted delicious and I dug in. I enjoyed their company and I was starting to feel at home. While the sun went down over the Green River, I made some new friends.

***

Two hours later, we fired up the motor scooters. The sound of loud pipes resonated across the river as twenty or more motorcycles fired up. They pulled out onto the main drag and I fell in at the rear riding the next position up from their tail gunner. Big Al, rode ahead of me and to my left. We rode through downtown Green River and took a side street near the edge of town. The Green River Boys pulled up to a building setting off by itself in a small warehouse district. They parked their bikes out front. An awning covered a cement porch on the front of the clubhouse. white vinyl siding covered the exterior walls. I backed my bike up to the curb and Big Al parked next to me.

"Let me give you the grand tour," Big Al said when we stepped up onto the porch. He led me to the front door. I noticed a metal roll-up door to my right at the far end of the porch. Loud rock and roll music emanated from the clubhouse when Big Al opened the front door. He led me down a narrow hallway and pointed to a doorway on our left. Plush blue carpeting covered the floor.

"That's our office, and this room is the meeting hall where we hold church," Big Al said. we passed another doorway on our left. He motioned to an open door on our right from whence the music came. "That's the bar. If you go through the bar, there's a garage where we work on our bikes. That roll-up metal door you saw on the end of the building opens up to the garage." He led me further down the hallway passing the restrooms to a doorway at the end of the hallway. We stepped into a large bunkhouse. Bunk beds lined the walls. Pictures of motorcycles and naked women hung on the walls between the bunk beds. A card table set in the center of the hardwood floor and a woodstove set at the far end of the room. A group of bikers sat around the table playing cards. On the wall to my right, set a TV and a stereo set in a massive entertainment center. A black leather couch and a couple of Lazy Boy chairs set facing the TV.

"Make yourself at home. You can bunk down in any of these beds that you want. We'll roll out in the morning and head up to Casper. After we hook up with some of our brothers in Casper, we'll head out to Sturgis. If you want, watch some TV or go have a beer at the bar."

"I'll unpack my gear and then hit the rack," I said.

"Are you sure I can't buy you a beer? You'll love our bar."

"Okay but only, a couple," I said

Big Al slapped me on the back and we headed to the bar. A good-looking young woman wearing a beige knit top worked behind the bar. Her long black hair hung down to the top of her ass. Her large round nipples protruded through the holes in her knit top. I breathed in the smell of perfume mixed with stale beer and tobacco smoke.

"What'll it be sweetheart?" she said and gave me a pretty smile.

"Bud Light," I said reaching for my wallet.

"I got this," Big Al said. He took a five from his wallet and put it in the donation box. Green River Boys lined the bar. Two young women, one a redhead and the other a strawberry blonde, climbed up onto the bar. They both wore schoolgirl costumes with white button-up blouses and short red skirts. Dancing on the bar, they took off their tops. The Green River Boys hooted and hollered. I looked up and grinned.

"It gets pretty wild in here sometimes. The married guys usually go home early. Their old ladies don't like them seeing too much titty. The single guys have a ball. We have wet t-shirt contests once in a while," Big Al said.

"Do all these girls belong to the club?" I asked.

"Some are official mommas. Others are, hang-arounds. There's never a shortage of women for the single guys."

"What about you? What does your old lady think about all this?" A sad look shot across Big Al's face for a second.

"My old lady died last year with cancer." One of the women dancing on the bar took off her bra and tossed it across the room. I noticed her rock-hard little nipples standing at attention.

"I'm sorry to hear that," I said and put a five in the donation box for the next round of beer. One by one, the Green River Boys headed home. A few, too drunk to ride, stumbled back to the bunkhouse. Big Al and I, along with a few die-hard Green River Boys, stayed in the bar drinking until two in the morning. By that time, the two women dancing on the bar were completely naked. They stepped down from the bar and one of the bikers handed them their clothes. After retrieving my gear, I stumbled into the bunkhouse and fell out on the nearest bunk.

***

Feeling tired and weary, I knuckled sleep from my eyes when I woke at five AM that morning. I rolled over, put my feet on the floor, and stumbled out of bed. After making my way to the bathroom to take care of my morning business, I dressed and followed my nose. The smell of scrambled eggs and frying bacon floated down the main hallway from the bar. In a room off the bar set, a kitchen and a couple of prospects were busy fixing breakfast for the crew.

"Have a seat. The coffee's on and breakfast is almost ready," Big Al said. I squeezed between Al and another Green River Boy at the bar. Big Al motioned to a prospect working behind the bar.

The young dark-headed kid stepped up to me. "You like cream or sugar in your coffee?" the prospect asked.

I shook my head. "No. I like it hot and black." I glanced down the bar. Green River Boys lined the bar and several others sat at tables throughout the room. I heard the sound of motorcycles when more Green River Boys pulled up to the clubhouse. The prospect poured my coffee and I took a tentative sip.

"Now that's what I'm talkin' about," I said.

The prospects passed out the food. They loaded down the plates with scrambled eggs, fried bacon, and hash brown potatoes. Another brought in a platter filled with pancakes and set the platter down on the bar. He headed back into the kitchen for Maple syrup.

"One thing we do know how to do around here is, eat good," Big Al said and then dug into his breakfast as only a hungry man can. It was one of the best-tasting breakfast I'd ate in quite a while. More motorcycles pulled up out front. Big Al and I conversed while we ate. I was starting to like the guy. He had a friendly way about him and a good sense of humor.

"We'd best pack our shit. I want to roll out of here by seven," Big Al said and sponged up the last of the egg yolk on his plate with a piece of toast. Taking a last bite of bacon, I leaned back and rubbed my belly.

"I haven't eaten this good in months."

Finished with breakfast, I packed my gear and joined the bikers in front of the clubhouse. I noticed two vans parked near the end of the building. Behind the vans set a three-quarter-ton Ford pickup. It had an enclosed motorcycle trailer hitched up to its rear. Big Al stepped over to one of the awaiting vans with a short, stocky black biker. The black biker's most noticeable attributes were his bald head and his massive biceps. Several prospects came out of the clubhouse carrying green canvas duffel bags. Big Al glanced at me and motioned for me to come over. I sat my gloves on the Shovelhead's seat and ambled over.

"I want you to meet my VP. This is Tom Booker. We either call him Booker T or Mr. T," Big Al said. The big black biker stuck out his hand and gave me a warm smile. We shook and the bones in my hand felt like they were ready to snap.

"I heard about what you've been doing to the Lost Souls. That's righteous, man. Them redneck peckerwoods are nothing but white trash."

"They never should have hurt my wife," I said.

"I thought you might want to see some of the hardware," Big Al said and unzipped one of the duffle bags. The smell of gun oil rose into the air. M-16s, AR-15s, and AK-47s filled the duffle bag. He unzipped another bag revealing loose ammunition and loaded magazines. "We've got grenades and a few rocket launchers." The prospects put the duffle bags in hidden compartments underneath the floorboards. I watched them bring duffle bag after duffel bag from the clubhouse and put them in the awaiting vans.

"Good Lord. You got enough guns for a small war," I said.

Big Al nodded. "It's gonna take a small war to wipe out the Lost Souls, but we've got it to do. I'm tired of losing brothers to those scumbags."

A stocky little biker with short blond hair and arms covered in tattoos stepped up. "Listen up people!"

"That's Johnny B, our road captain," Big Al said. Overhead the sky clouded up.

"It looks like it might rain! Ride safe! We've got a lot of guys going on this run! We'll have even more when we meet up with our brothers in Casper! We're going to leave in groups of ten so that we won't have problems with traffic here in town! We'll leave in five-minute intervals! We have chase vehicles! If you have trouble on the road or your bike breaks down, pull over to the side of the road and wait! They'll pick you up! Let's mount up!"

"You ride in the back with me. I usually ride up front with the road captain and sergeant of arms, but this trip will be different. We'll leave with the last group and the chase vehicles," Big Al said.

"That's fine with me," I said and headed to my bike. The bikers assembled in the street and began to leave. The sound of loud pipes ricocheted off the surrounding buildings. My cheeks reddened from the crispness in the air, so I zipped up my leather jacket to ward off the chill. I watched the Green River Boys leave. A few did burnouts showing off for the crowd. There was a lot of hooting and hollering going on. Everyone seemed to be in a good mood. I formed up in the street behind the last group of bikers. Big Al set on his Harley in front of me and to my left. The tail gunner road behind me in front of the chase vehicles.

We pulled out heading through town and took I 80 east. Weaving our way through traffic, we caught up with the guys that had left earlier and formed up into one big pack. The sound of our loud pipes reminded me of the roar of a thousand horses stampeding down a narrow canyon. The sound boomed off the surrounding hillside. A cocky grin spread across my face when I turned the throttle and put my face in the wind.

***

CHAPTER 20

We crossed the South Dakota state line at five PM that evening after a long hard ride. A thunderstorm blanketed the land. Cold rain pelted both man and machine. I shivered from the cold and my hands felt like ice. A loud crack of thunder echoed off the Black Hills. The rain increased its intensity turning into hail. After a few miles, the hail turned a light rain and then stopped. Motorcycles packed the road on their annual pilgrimage to Sturgis South Dakota. I glanced about taking in the regal forest. A deer darted across the road in front of us. Some of the guys in the head of the pack had to, brake to keep from hitting the deer. We roared through Deadwood. The road snaked its way through the hills and we pulled into Sturgis that evening.

Our road captain pulled into a gas station and we tried to find places to park. I glanced about in wonder. Motorcycles lined up at the gas pumps and we sat in line waiting to fill up. Finished filling my tank, I found an empty spot near the road and parked. Big Al stepped up to me.

"This weather sucks," I said. I stuck my hands in my pants pockets, trying to regain some feeling in my numb fingers.

Big Al lit a cigar. A cloud of tobacco smoke filled the air in front of his face. Big Al smiled and I glanced around. Groups of bikers were standing everywhere engaged in lighthearted conversation. Excitement filled the air. Some bikers wore leather and some of the women wore next to nothing. I'll bet they are *frozen stiff,* I thought.

"It's par for the course up here. Summertime is the rainiest time of the year. Give it a minute though, it'll change."

I climbed off my bike shaking off the water. "How many miles do you think we put in today?"

Big Al shrugged. "About four hundred and fifty miles." Two women on Harley Davidson motorcycles pulled up to the gas pumps. I admired how they filled out their designer jeans.

"I had a blast. I've never ridden with such a large group before," I said.

"It's different. Riding in a big group keeps you on your toes," Big Al said.

"There sure are a lot of people here," I said glancing around.

"A couple hundred thousand in town and the surrounding areas. There are people here from everywhere. There's doctors, lawyers, and badass bikers like us."

I laughed. "How far to our campground?"

"Not far. We're staying at the Bull Dog campground east of town. We'll get a beer, find somewhere to eat, and head out there in a bit." Big Al and I stood by our bikes talking while the Green River Boys gassed up. Once everyone gassed up, we cruised the boulevard looking for a place to eat.

Two hours later, with our bellies full, we headed east on Interstate 90. We took an exit fifteen miles up the road and pulled into the Bull Dog campground. A young man working at the office signed us in and escorted us across the campground to an open meadow. The road captain had us park our bikes in a big circle around the clearing and we set up camp in the center of the circle. Prospects brought out lanterns and turned them on eliminating the camp.

"Once we have the camp set up, you can move your scooters over next to your tent!" the road captain yelled. The chapter officers set up a large wall tent in the center of the clearing. The Green River Boys set up their tents surrounding the officer's tent. I set up a small pup tent with the rest of the crew. Driving in a tent stake, my mind flashed back to the events of the day.

***

It rained off and on all day after we left Green River Wyoming. I saw herds of antelope grazing out on the prairie near the freeway. After a few brief hailstorms, the sun came out when we reached Rawlins Wyoming. We pulled off the freeway and cut through town. The bikes in front of me began to stop when we reached the cemetery. Gazing across the cemetery, I saw a herd of elk grazing amongst the granite tombstones. Some of the Green River Boys parked their motorcycles and took pictures.

Big Al pulled up next to me. "No matter what time you come through here, you're liable to find elk or deer in the graveyard." A big bull elk snorted and shook its horns at us.

"They know where the good grass is," I said watching them graze. Leaving the cemetery, we passed through Rawlings and took the 287 north. Ranch country spread out for miles on both sides of the road. We passed herds of cattle along with herds of antelope grazing on the same grass. I noticed a herd of deer standing next to the road. The day warmed up and I began to enjoy the ride. With my fist in the throttle, I glanced about at the wide-open prairie. We passed several rustic-looking ranches. I saw cowboys out on horses working cattle. The loud throaty growl of our pipes spooked the cattle.

At noon, we pulled into Muddy Gap, a crossroads where highways 287 and 220 merge. We pulled into a combination gas station and mini-mart. Inside the mini-mart, they sold souvenirs and grocery items. Motorcycles lined up at the gas pumps and filled the parking lot. I noticed that same young couple on the Honda Gold Wing that I saw a couple of days earlier. They were having trouble with the bike and he was busy changing a fouled plug. I helped the guy fix his bike. After taking a piss break and filling up on coffee, we headed north on highway 220.

The highway meandered northeast and ran along next to the Platte River. Several groups of kayakers floated downstream. I saw people floating in inner tubes. A few young women sported string bikinis and a few were topless. We passed a place where the river curved forming a sandy beach. A group of people laid in the sand sunbathing in the nude. Two young women rolled over off their stomachs, sat up, and waved at us when we rolled by. The Green River Boys let out a few hoots and hollers and a couple revved their pipes and honked their horns.

The Casper chapter fed us lunch when we rolled into town. Their clubhouse set off an alleyway behind a grocery store. It was set up pretty much the same way as the clubhouse in Green River, only it was a bit smaller. The prospects kept busy behind the clubhouse cooking hotdogs and hamburgers. The smell of cooking food filled the air and made my stomach rumble. For the next hour, we chowed down on burgers and dogs and drank a few beers. At one PM, we hit Interstate 25 and headed east. Outside of Douglas Wyoming, we took Highway 18 and then headed north on highway 85. Our numbers had increased to seventy-five. The boys from the Casper chapter seemed of the same caliber as the boys from Green River. My opinions of bikers were starting to change. I could see now that they all weren't the same. The Green River Boys all seemed like, good down to Earth people to me.

On the ride north, we hit some more bad weather. A thunderstorm passed through pounding us with rain and hail. A big rig rumbled by blasting us with ice and water. I hate riding near big trucks. At Newcastle, we hooked up with the Buffalo chapter and a chapter from Gillette Wyoming. A couple of chapters from Montana met up with us on the road. From Newcastle, we headed Northeast on the 85. We crossed the South Dakota state line, one hundred twenty strong.

***

Finished with my tent, I wandered over to the officer's tent and Big Al stepped out to greet me. "I had a gabfest with the rest of the national officers. They'd like to meet you. We're holding a meeting in a few minutes to plan our attack on the Lost Souls campground. The national officers want you to attend."

I shrugged. "Sure. Let's go see what they have to say."

Big Al and I stepped into the large wall tent. Several lanterns hung from metal stands illuminating the inside of the tent. A table set next to a pot-bellied stove and several Green River Boys sat around a table talking. Others stood around drinking beer. The ones at the table looked up when I entered the tent.

"Brothers, this is the guy we've been hearing about. This is Mike McDonald," Big Al said.

They stood to greet me coming up by ones and twos and shaking my hand. Each one of them congratulated me for what I was doing to the Lost Souls. The national officers took their seats at the table. An older biker with long salt and pepper-colored hair tied back in a ponytail nodded at Big Al. He wore the national VP patch on his vest.

"Al why don't you tell us your plan," he said.

Big Al sat down at the table next to the national VP It dawned on me then that he was their national president. I hadn't noticed the patch on his vest before. I stepped up to the table while the other bikers in the tent looked on. "Mike here has been waging a one-man war against the Lost Souls. He's done good, so far, but he can't do it alone. I say we give him some help. We know that those scumbags camp over in Custer State Park. I say we wait until the end of the rally and hit them hard with everything we've got," Big Al said.

"Did you bring everything we need?" the national VP asked.

"We've got all the firepower," Big Al said.

"What exactly did you have in mind?" the VP asked.

"I say we head over to the state park on the last night of the rally. We'll form up in an L-shaped ambush in the trees surrounding their camp and shoot the shit out of them. I'll send some boys over there on their scooters tomorrow morning without their vests on to do a little recon. Then I'll station a couple of others near the entrance of the park. Those sons of bitches ain't going nowhere," Big Al said.

The national officers leaned back in their chairs. One folded his arms across his chest and said, "It sounds like a good plan"

"Do you have anything you'd like to add, Mike?" Big Al asked.

I stood to my feet and glanced about the room. "First I'd like to say thank you for your help. I would have continued on my own, but I was fortunate to roll into Green River and meet you all. What happened to my wife and me should never happen to anyone. I won't stop until every patch-holding member of the Lost Souls is in the ground. You people have changed my opinion on bikers in general. I kind of lumped all you club riders together. Now I see that there are good people wearing patches on their backs. You Green River Boys have shown me nothing but friendship and I am glad I met you," I said and sat down. The tent erupted into applause.

"Thank you, Mike. All those in favor of helping Mike with his war with the Lost Souls raise your hands!" Big Al yelled. Every hand in the tent went up. Applause thundered throughout the tent. "Okay! Quiet down!" Big Al yelled. "You chapter presidents, tell your people if they go into town, go in groups. I don't want anyone getting DUIs. If you're too drunk to ride, take Da Bus and leave your bike there. We'll pick it up in the morning. The buses run every half hour. Tonight some of us are heading to the Broken Spoke. Tomorrow night ZZ Tops is playing at the Buffalo Chip. We'll ride in for that in force. Later in the week, we'll take a trip to Deadwood and Mount Rushmore. Let's have a good time. The last thing we'll do before we ride out of here is, deal with the Lost Souls. Now let's party!" The bikers standing around inside the tent cheered.

Outside, I sat down in a lawn chair next to Big Al. Booker T sat on the other side of me. A prospect went by and handed us each a beer. Someone brought out a Boom Box and started playing loud rock and roll music.

"Damn I'm glad it quit raining," I said. Overhead the clouds separated and the moon came out. The evening chill caused goosebumps to crop up on my exposed skin. I took my jacket from the back of my chair and put it on.

"Yeah, me too. Riding in the rain sucks," Big Al said. "Tomorrow's supposed to be a nice day."

Several of the guys had brought their old ladies and a group of them gathered by the bonfire dancing. Most of the women wore next to nothing on top and a few danced topless.

"It's a little nippy out," I said, admiring the female flesh.

Big Al laughed. "Yeah, when the old ladies get up here at Sturgis they tend to let their hair down," Al said. "It's almost like they have a competition going on to see who can show off the most skin."

"What happens in Sturgis stays in Sturgis," Booker T said.

"I ain't mad at 'hem," I said, watching the show. We sat drinking and talking for another hour.

Big Al looked at his watch. "Things should be hoppin' down at the Broken Spoke. Let's roll"

Fifteen minutes later, twenty-five of us hit the I 90 heading west for the short ride into Sturgis. We took the first exit heading west through downtown. Motorcycles filled the street backing the traffic up almost to the freeway. I had never seen so many motorcycles in my entire life. The smell of exhaust drifted down the street and the sound of loud pipes filled the air. A woman ambling up the sidewalk flashed her breasts and several of the bikers in the street cheered.

Big Al grinned, noticing the direction of my gaze. "If the cops see her doing that on the street, she'll get arrested! Out in the campgrounds, anything goes, but here in town they have to keep their nipples covered!" Big Al yelled across to me from his bike.

"Only their nipples?"

"Yeah! They can go topless as long as they have either body paint or pasties covering their nipples! Some people bring their kids up here! Don't ask me why!"

Traffic moved forward at a slow crawl. My hand and wrist began to ache while we moved up the street in slow motion. Thirty minutes later, we reached the end of Main Street and turned right onto Lazelle Street. People milled about on the sidewalk and some took pictures. The women on the sidewalks hooted and hollered at the guys in the street on motorcycles. A few people did burnouts at the signal lights, only to receive tickets from police on bicycles. After another half hour of stop-and-go traffic, we found a place to park our motorcycles. I set my Shovelhead on its side stand in front of a blue house with a green manicured lawn. Big Al parked his Fat Boy next to me and climbed off. A smile crossed his face. A thrill shot through me when I saw all the action on the street.

"There's nothing like downtown Sturgis at night during bike week," Big Al said.

"There must be about twenty thousand people out there on the street," I said in awe. We had to hoof it for half a block until we reached Lazelle Street. At the corner, we turned right and stepped into the Broken Spoke Saloon. It was a big wooden barn-like structure with large open windows facing the street. Loud rock music blared from a live band performing on stage. They were playing some old Led Zeppelin tunes. The bar consisted of three large adjoining rooms. Sawdust covered the floor and people stood packed together like sardines in a can. In an open area to our left, people watched a red-headed young woman ride a mechanical bull. She took off her top and put on a good show.

We wormed our way through the crowd and stepped up to where three young women sold beer from the beer garden. All three of them were in their early twenties and were topless. A blonde with large breasts wore tiny yellow happy face stickers over her nipples. A brunette with medium-sized breasts had a King Cobra airbrushed on her chest. The dark-haired girl had a tiger painted on her breasts, with the tiger's eyes covering her nipples. The blonde looked at me and smiled. I breathed in the smell of her perfume.

"What can I get you guys?" she asked. Our eyes dropped to her chest.

"I'll get this!" Big Al. He had to yell because of the noise. "What do you want?"

"I'll have a Bud Light!" I said.

After Big Al bought our drinks and we moved through the crowd to get closer to the stage. I stood on the edge of the dance floor. Several women wore cut-off t-shirts that stopped right above their nipples. One woman wearing a short leather skirt moved out onto the dance floor. When she reached the front of the stage, she pulled up her skirt shooting the lead singer the beaver. We spent a couple of hours in the Broken Spoke and had a few more beers. The noise inside was deafening.

"Why don't we head outside? The noise is starting to give me a headache!" Big Al yelled.

"Yeah, let's take a walk! I need to sober up a little before I get back on my scooter!" I said. Outside, we headed up the sidewalk. Venders had tents set up next to the sidewalk and in the parking lots of various businesses. I noticed a few outlaw bikers swaggering up the sidewalk, but none of them wore the patch of the Lost Souls. We stepped into a large white tent where they had bikes entered into the custom bike show on display. I admired the sleek-looking machines. Bending down next to a custom chopper, I admired the craftsmanship. The bike had a Confederate flag painted on its tank and depictions of Civil War battles on its fenders. A picture of General Lee adorned the back of the rear fender.

"Now this is something I would enjoy doing. Building bikes like these," I said.

"It's an art form," Big Al said.

Standing to my feet, we continued checking out the other bikes. After looking at the custom choppers, we found a hot dog stand and got a quick bite to eat. I watched two young women strut by wearing nothing but a G-string on their bottoms. The smell of their perfume filled the air in their wake. They had tiny stars painted over their nipples. Both of them wore several strings of beads around their necks. Several guys also wore beads around their necks as well.

"What's with the beads?" I asked Big Al.

"It's like Mardi Gras. Guys buy the beads. Chicks show their tits and take the beads."

"This place is wild," I said.

"Yeah, you see things here that you won't see anywhere else." We strolled the boardwalk for another half hour and headed back to our motorcycles. After working our way down Lazelle Street like a bunch of pregnant snails, we hit the freeway. We headed back to the Bull Dog campground. I stumbled off to my tent and crawled into my sleeping bag for the night.

***

I woke the next morning with a throbbing headache. Crawling from my sleeping bag, I stumbled to the fire rings. A few prospects tended the fire and cooked breakfast off barbeque grills. They had several pots of hot coffee on the fire.

“God you look like a cold bag of shit,” Big Al said. His eyes looked bloodshot and his face flushed. Wes the national VP standing next to Big Al laughed.

“You guys don’t look so great either,” I said.”

“God I am getting too old for this shit,” Wes said.

“Get this man some coffee,” Big Al said to a young prospect tending the grill.

“Here, bro,” the prospect said handing me a hot cup of coffee. A friendly grin crossed his face. “Scrambled eggs, bacon, and sausage will be ready in five.”

I reached in my pocket for a pack of smokes.

“Care for one of these?” Big Al asked handing me an expensive cigar.

“Sure,” I said.

Big Al made flame and we lit up. Bikers crawled from their tents and made their way to the fire. I glanced around at the faces of the Green River Boys gathering around the fire ring. They acted jovial, laughing and joking with each other. They all looked hungover from a hard night of partying. The prospect handed Big Al and me a plate and we found a couple of folding chairs.

“What’s on the agenda for today?” I asked between bites.

Big Al wiped a spot of ketchup from his beard. “After last night, most of the guys aren’t in the mood to do much riding. We’ll hang around here most of the day, and head into the Buffalo Chip tonight for ZZ Tops. You’ll like the Buffalo Chip. That place is crazy. But, you’re free to do whatever you want. Don’t go near Custer State Park. We’re partying first, having a good time; then we’ll take care of that bit of business and get out of town.”

I nodded. “I wouldn’t mind heading into town a little early and pick up a couple of rally t-shirts. Who knows if I’ll ever make it back?”

“Life is short, bro. You never know what’s around the corner,” Big Al said.

Finished with breakfast, someone brought out the Boom Box and started the music going. Prospects took turns handing out beer to the patched members. The weather warmed up and the air turned hot and muggy. A couple of hours later, we headed across the campground to the bandstand. We watched one of the local bands play. A couple of young women dancing in front of the stage took off their tops. A large bus pulled in every half hour unloading and loading passengers for the trip into Sturgis. Big Al noticed me watching people board the bus.

"Before we leave, you'll have to take the bus into town. They call it Da Bus, but it's not like any bus ride you've ever been on."

"Why's that?" I asked.

"It's a party bus. You can drink on board. They don't care. You can either bring your own, beer or buy it from them. They keep an ice chest loaded down with, beer on board."

"I bet that gets wild."

Big Al nodded. "Yeah. They have permanent black markers onboard. People write their names, where they're from, and what year they were at Sturgis."

The day wore on. The prospects cooked an early dinner barbequing chicken, ribs and they baked potatoes. They pitched in working hard so that the entire club could ride into town for the concert. We hit the freeway, over a hundred strong, heading west toward town at five PM that evening. When we pulled off the freeway, the traffic slowed to a crawl. My hands began to ache because of having to use my clutch and brake so much as we moved from light to light. We turned onto Lazlle Street and the traffic stayed at a slow crawl. An hour later, we reached the east end of town and headed out to the Buffalo Chip campground. The sky opened up and a gentle rain fell from the sky. After buying our way into the concert, we rolled onto the grassy arena and parked on the edge of the crowd. Two young women strutted by. They wore cut-off jeans and had several strings of beads hanging down over their bare breasts.

ZZ Tops took the stage and rocked down the house. Between songs, people revved their engines in applause. A group of women standing in front of us took off their shirts and danced topless. The cold weather caused their nipples to stand up and pay attention. The smell of marijuana smoke filled the air. Several of the Green River Boys cheered. Big Al sent several prospects to the beer garden after beer. The band opened up with another tune. For some old graybeards, they knew how to rock.

After the concert, I bought a couple of t-shirts and we headed to the Buffalo Chip Saloon. We watched two young women climb up on the mechanical bull. Their tops came off. Soon they were rubbing their bodies up against each other and French kissing. The bikers ringing the mechanical bull cheered. Outside, the rain stopped and a full moon rose into the sky.

"Damn this place is wild!" I yelled to Big Al.

"Yeah, if you've never been to Sturgis, you've never seen anything like it! They call first-timers, Sturgis Virgins!" We had to yell to communicate over the nosy crowd. Still feeling the effects of the alcohol, we rolled out heading back to the Bull Dog campground.

***

The following morning, still hungover, we ate breakfast and had several cups of coffee. Once everyone felt human again, we mounted up and hit the freeway. Heading west, we passed through Sturgis and took Highway 34 south to Deadwood. The road snaked its way down through the gulch. The sun felt warm against my back and the view was phenomenal. Motorcycles, both coming from and going to Dead Wood, filled the two-lane highway. We spent a couple of hours playing the slots in the casinos and then had a beer in the Number 10 Saloon.

From Deadwood, we rode to Keystone and had a look at Mount Rushmore. The Green River Boys had their guard up because we were too close to Custer State Park. Big Al made contact on his cell phone with the guys he had watching the entrance and exit to the park. He had them meet us at Rapid City and sent two more guys to take their place. Leaving Keystone, we rode hard and pulled into Rapid City three hours later. We had dinner at a Denny's, restaurant. The hostess, a thin Hispanic woman, set us up in a back room sitting us at several long tables. The prospects who had been keeping an eye on the Lost Souls met us there.

One of the prospects, a wiry little dark-haired guy sat across from Big Al.

"Well, Pork Chop. What have you got to report?" Big Al asked.

The little man shrugged. "Not much. They're camped over by Stockade Lake like they usually do," the wiry little biker said.

"How many?"

"I'd say eighty to a hundred guys. There's a dirt road a quarter mile to the south of the lake that we could use. We should be able to come through the forest paralleling their camp and walk right up on 'em."

“Good,” Big Al said glancing at both the prospects. “You guys did, good. After you get something to eat, head into Sturgis and have a good time.”

Finished with dinner, we hopped back on the freeway and headed west. We visited the Harley Davidson shop in Rapid City. They had a massive vendor city set up behind the shop and we spent an hour browsing. The rest of the week flew by and we spent it partying staying close to the Bull Dog campground. On the last night of the rally, we pulled out in force around ten PM and headed south on the 385 toward Custer State Park. The going was slow, once we pulled off the highway onto the dirt road south of Stockade Lake. The narrow logging road snaked its way through the forest. The chase vans with the guns pulled over to the side of the road in front of us when we parked the motorcycles. Big Al stepped up to the guy driving the lead van and I followed along beside him.

“What was the problem back there by the highway? Why’d you guys slammed on the brakes?” Big Al whispered.

“We almost hit a damn Buffalo standing in the middle of the road. It was hard to see it in this fog. It liked to give me heart failure,” the guy whispered.

Big Al let out a low chuckle. The prospect driving the chase vehicles climbed out. They opened the rear doors of the vans and handed out the guns. I glanced about at the low-lying fog covering the ground and wondered if we would be able to see our targets.

“Okay, people let’s do this right. Let’s get these vests off and put them in the back of one of these vans. If the cops stop you, you know the drill. You Montana brothers, I want you guys to head south a quarter-mile. You’ll form the bottom leg of the ambush. The rest of us will move through the woods here and attack their flank. We’ll hit them hard and fast. After you fire off three magazines, beat it back here and stow the guns. Once we're done, we’ll all meet back at the clubhouse in Casper,” Big Al whispered. An air of tense, anticipation filled the cold night. The bikers lined up stowing their club vests and picked up their weapons. The Montana brothers headed down the road and took up their positions. I slapped a magazine into an AR-15 and stepped into the dark, foreboding forest. I stood shoulder to shoulder with Big Al and the rest of the Green River Boys.

***

CHAPTER 21

The fog lifted and a full moon rose over the clearing where the Lost Souls had set up their camp. A cold breeze blew through the forest. Gunfire lit up the predawn darkness. Our muzzle flashes looked like orange blossoms in the night. I stepped forward firing at several of the Lost Souls sitting around a fire ring. Big Al opened up on the tents keeping his line of fire low trying to take out the bikers in their sleeping bags. Several bikers fell near the fire ring. The Montana boys opened up from their positions to the North. Pandemonium filled the encampment. The loud bang of gunfire blasted through the forest. Most of those not killed in the initial onslaught panicked and ran. We shot them down like rabid dogs. Bodies littered the ground, but a few kept their wits about them and returned fire. Bullets screamed through the trees around us.

Slapping in a fresh magazine, I charged forward filled with blood lust. My heart thumped inside my ribcage. One Soul took a round in the spine and fell to the ground withering in pain. I put four rounds through his forehead and then opened up on a group fleeing toward the lake. The bolt jacked open on empty. I slapped in another magazine and kept firing. The sound of gunfire and men screaming filled the night; gun smoke drifted on the wind.

Big Al grabbed my arm. "Let's get out of here bro before the park rangers get here!" he yelled. The gunfire tapered off. Turning back the way we came, we ran through the forest. Bullets zipped overhead. At the vans, we tossed the weapons in the back and jumped onto our Harleys. Once everyone was back at the rendezvous site, the Green River Boys split up. The van carrying the weapons fled south toward Nebraska. The bros on motorcycles fled in all directions. They had orders to hole up somewhere until the coast was clear. The van carrying the club vests headed north, Everyone would meet at Casper Wyoming.

Big Al and I, along with twelve other Green River Boys, headed north to Rapid City. At Rapid City, we had breakfast and headed west on I 90. We tried to blend in with the other bikers on the highway heading home from Sturgis. Five hours later, we rolled into Casper Wyoming and parked in front of the Green River Boys clubhouse.

"You look like you could use a brew. I'll buy the first round," Big Al said when we climbed off the Harleys.

"I feel like ten pounds of monkey shit in a five-pound bag. What I could use is about ten hours of sleep," I said.

We stumbled into the clubhouse, found a seat at the bar and another group of Green River boys pulled up outside. Big Al fired up a cigar and ordered us each a beer from the prospect tending bar. The smell of cigar smoke and alcohol filled the bar room.

"How bad do you think we hurt them?" I asked.

Big Al shrugged and took a pull from his bottle. He offered me a cigar and I fired one up. "Bad. We cut their numbers way down. I'd say there were one hundred guys in that camp and I bet they don't have but thirty or forty left." Someone turned on a radio and a news broadcast came on the air. The bikers lining the bar stood in silence listening.

"There was a massacre this morning at Custer State Park in South Dakota. Gunfire erupted in the pre-dawn darkness on the last day of the Black Hills motorcycle rally. A motorcycle club known as the Lost Souls took the brunt of the attack. Park rangers believe that it was retaliation by a rival motorcycle gang. The park rangers estimate that at least sixty people are dead. A spokesman for the Lost Souls refused to comment." Conversation in the clubhouse resumed.

"That's a good start," Big Al said.

I nodded. "At least none of your guys got caught. They didn't identify us."

"I hope none of our guys got pinched, but the Lost Souls know. This ain't over yet."

"When do you plan on us riding back to Green River?" I asked.

Big Al took a puff on his cigar. "I figured we'd stay here and party with the brothers from the Casper chapter and head back in the morning. After what went down last night, everyone's pooped."

We partied for the rest of the day. The prospects made lunch. After lunch, we sat around a card table in the backroom of the clubhouse drinking beer and playing cards. That night, some of the women held a wet t-shirt contest in the bar. We drank, hooted, and hollered until well after midnight. I stumbled over to a bunk about 12:30 AM and crashed. It had been a long hard day.

***

The Green River Boys began to stir around six AM. I rolled out of my sleeping bag, stumbled off to the bathroom to take care of my morning business, and dressed. The sound of conversation filtered in from the bar. Rubbing the sleep from my eyes, I crawled up onto a barstool next to Big Al. I heard a few groans from the hungover bikers lining the bar.

"Give this man a cup of coffee. He looks like one of the undead," Big Al said to the prospect working behind the bar.

The prospect set a hot cup of coffee down in front of me and I took a sip. "Ah! The elixir of the Gods," I said.

"I figured we'd rack on out of here by nine. Is that okay with you?" Big Al asked.

I took another drink from my coffee cup. "Fine by me."

"What can I get you to eat?" the young prospect standing behind the bar asked.

I pulled a pack of smokes from my shirt pocket. "What's on the menu?"

"Pancakes, eggs, bacon, you name it," the prospect said.

Pulling a cigarette from the pack, I pulled my Zippo from my pants pocket and lit the smoke. "Give me a short stack of pancakes, a side of bacon, and some scrambled eggs," I said blowing smoke across the bar.

"I do like a man with an appetite," Big Al said.

We finished breakfast, enjoying the good food and each other's company. I had finished eating and was wiping a spot of Maple Syrup from my chin when I heard motorcycles pull up out front. Someone yelled and then a prospect stuck his head in the front door. "Hey! We got company!" he yelled.

The loud explosion of gunfire erupted from the front of the building. One of the prospects screamed. We jumped to our feet. Three of the Lost Souls appeared in the doorway of the bar and opened up with AK-47s. The sound of gunfire echoed through the clubhouse. Bits and pieces of wood and broken glass flew through the air. I dived to my left and Big Al dived right. My coffee cup hit the floor shattering to pieces. The Green River Boys lining the bar dived under tables pulling their weapons. I heard more gunfire coming from outside. Lying in the prone position on the floor, I pulled my right hand forty-five. I gave one of them a double-tap in the center of his chest. He fell back into the hallway. The room stank of spent gunpowder. Big Al shot the other guy in the forehead with a snubbed nose thirty-eight he kept in his boot. The biker flew backward bouncing off the wall and fell to the floor.

"Is anyone hurt?" Big Al yelled.

Climbing to my feet, I looked over at Big Al. "Yeah. You are," I said. "You're hit in the shoulder." Offering him my hand, I helped Big Al to his feet. Blood ran down the side of his shirt and a few drops hit the floor. Several Green river Boys came running in from off the street.

"They're gone," Booker T said.

Big Al struggled to catch his breath. "Was there anyone else hit?"

"One of the prospects got hit hard. He's not going to make it. Another one took a round through the leg," Booker T said.

"Call an ambulance. We'll leave ten guys here to take care of them. How many were there?"

"Five. Three of them got away," Booker T said.

"Let's get after them," Big Al said.

"You're not going anywhere until someone has a look at that arm," I interjected.

Big Al shook his head. "It's only a crease. Booker T will fix me up and we'll ride." Hustle and bustle filled the clubhouse while the Green River Boys packed their gear. Booker T worked on Big Al's arm and I packed my duffel bag getting my things ready for the trip south. Thirty-five minutes later, we were ready to roll. The van with everyone's colors arrived ten minutes before we left and the Green River Boys put on their club vests. One of the prospects that had been outside, said that some of the Lost Souls fled toward highway 220.

"They're all heading back to Idaho. We'll try and catch this batch on the road. If we don't, we'll take them all out once they crawl back to their hideout on Thunder Road," Big Al said and fired up his Harley.

"You plan on stopping in Green River?" Booker T asked.

"Yeah. We'll stop at the clubhouse, regroup and head to Idaho."

"If J.D Quinn's with them, if he's still alive after last night, he's mine," I said.

"By all means. After what that scumbag's boys from LA did to your wife, I wouldn't deny you the pleasure," Big Al said.

We rolled out in force heading through town. The sound of our loud pipes rebounded off the surrounding buildings. After leaving Casper, we took the turn-off for Highway 220 and headed south. Halfway to Muddy Gap, we rolled up on three motorcycles parked along the side of the road. Three guys knelt, down working on one of the bikes. When they heard the rumble of our pipes, they looked up and bolted. They charged down through the brush toward the river.

Big Al pulled over and I pulled over next to him. Several more Green River Boys pulled over to the side of the road behind us. The Green River Boys began to hoot and holler at the fleeing bikers.

"Look at the little pussies run!" someone yelled.

The three Souls tossed off their vests and dived into the river trying to make it across. I guess they figured that if they made it to the other side of the river, that we would let them go.

"This is going to be like shooting fish in a barrel," Big Al said.

"It's almost un-sportsman-like, but the fish have to eat too," I said and shot one of them with my sawed-off. A chunk of his scalp and a bit of bone from the top of his head flew into the air. It turned into a turkey shoot. Big Al and I, along with several of the Green River Boys lined the eastern bank of the river. We opened up with everything we had. We fired shotguns and handguns at the men trying to swim across the river. They didn't stand a chance. Water splashed into the air and the river turned red with their blood.

"Get there scooters and dump them into the river, then let's get out of here," Big Al said after we finished shooting. Finding a clear spot, I helped push three Harleys into the river. They made a loud splash and sank to the bottom. We rolled away a few minutes later leaving three of the Lost Souls and their motorcycles for the fishes.

An hour later, we pulled into Rawlings Wyoming. This time we didn't notice the deer and elk in the cemetery, but we saw six bikes parked next to the fence. The bikers wore the Lost Souls club vests. Two of them jumped the fence and ran trying to hide behind the tombstones. The other three jumped on their scooters and rode away at a high rate of speed. Big Al and I pulled over sliding to a stop and stirring up a small dust cloud. Al waved the rest of the guys on instructing them to go after the other three bikers. Bullets whizzed overhead. My heart pounded. Using the top of the chain-link fence to rest my arm, I opened up on one of the bikers in the graveyard. My first shot ricocheted off a tombstone. The next round caught one of the bikers in the back of his shoulder and spun him around. After that, I put three more through the center of his chest. He fell backward and disappeared behind a granite tombstone.

Big Al shot the second biker hitting him in the side of his neck. The bullet exited through his throat. He grabbed his neck blood gushed through his fingers and he fell to the ground. He landed on his butt and fell up against another tombstone.

Big Al grabbed my arm. "Let's get the fuck out of here before the cops show up!" Big Al yelled.

We climbed into the saddle and raced through town heading for the interstate. On the I 80, we headed west gunning the throttle. The wind caused speed tears to form in my eyes. Weaving through traffic, I saw a group of bikers ahead of us. We cranked the throttle catching up to the Green River Boys in pursuit of the Lost Souls that fled the cemetery. When Big Al and I caught up with the pack, we took up positions in the front.

We caught up to the other four Souls halfway to Rock Springs. I pulled up to the lead rider, pulling my right hand sawed-off, and gave him both barrels. The shotgun blast took out his lower jaw. Blood and bone splattered on the guy riding next to him. The bike went sideways, he went down and slid down the asphalt. The sound of scraping metal filled the air. The guy riding behind him swerved as Big Al shot him in the head with his thirty-eight. The guy flew off his bike landing in the next lane. The bike wobbled and fell over. The fourth Soul riding tail gunner crashed into one of the bikes and went over the handlebars. The bike tumbled after him landing on his chest.

The Green River Boys swerved, passing the downed bikes on both sides, and kept rolling. A semi-truck locked up his brakes to avoid a collision. The truck jackknifed taking out the westbound lanes of the interstate. In the process, he ran over the Lost Souls lying on the freeway. The sound of squealing tires and crunching metal filled the air. The smell of burnt brakes drifted with the Wyoming wind.

***

We pulled up next to the clubhouse in Green River forty-five minutes later. I backed the Shovelhead into a parking place and killed the motor. Big Al parked his bike next to me, leaned the Harley on its side stand, and climbed off.

I stretched trying to work the kinks out of my body. "Now what?" I asked Big Al when he climbed off his bike.

"Now we get something to eat and party. I got a couple of guys staked out over on highway thirty and highway eighty-nine by the Idaho border. They'll keep me posted. We'll give these scumbags a couple of days to limp home and then hit them where they live, over on Thunder Road." Big Al stretched his tired muscles.

"Why wait?" I asked.

"Our Montana bros and the ones in the northern Wyoming chapters want in on this. After what happened at Custer State Park, they headed home. I'll call the chapter presidents to make sure, but I figure they'll head down here tomorrow. Today's Sunday. We'll roll out for Idaho on Thursday."

"Do you think we'll have any trouble with the police?" The words were no sooner out of my mouth when a Green River police car pulled up in front of the clubhouse. An older man with receding gray hair and a potbelly climbed out of the car. I noticed a mole on the side of his face. He reminded me of Chief Brody down in Utah. He wore a friendly smile on his face.

"Hello, Sarge. What can I do for you? Are some of my boys acting up?" Big Al said.

He arched his eyebrows. "I don't know. You tell me. You wouldn't happen to know anything about this big traffic tie-up on the interstate, would you?"

Big Al stepped up next to the police officer. "No. I heard some bikes went down."

The police officer looked at me. "I don't think I know you," he said.

I stuck out my hand. "I'm Mike McDonald." We shook.

"I'm police sergeant Kincaid. Dillon Kincaid. I've heard of you." I shrugged. Turning his attention back to Big Al, he said, "You wouldn't know anything about a shooting over in Rawlings?" Big Al shook his head. "Witnesses said it involved motorcycle clubs. They described a patch like yours."

"You know Sarge, the citizens out there can't tell one patch from another," Big Al said and smiled.

The police sergeant nodded. "You don't suppose these two incidents might have something to do with that shootout in Custer State Park?"

Big Al laid a friendly hand on the officer's shoulder. "Could be. You know when you get that many bikers together and they start drinking, who knows what's bound to happen."

A scowl crossed Kincaid's face. "That's for sure. Look, I'm not stupid. I know the Lost Souls have been a thorn in your side and you need to take care of things. Those Souls are pure poison and the world would be better off without them. I'll try to keep the heat off you boys with the Chief, but try to lay low for a while. Try to keep things out of this state. I hear the Lost Souls are as thick as flies on shit over in Idaho."

Big Al stepped away from the police sergeant. "I hear you. You got nothing to worry about. Thanks for stopping by," Big Al said.

"Good day to you now," Kincaid said and climbed back into his patrol car.

"That was interesting," I said watching the police sergeant drive away.

"Kincaid's a good man. I hate this kind of business. Take those guys we shot up today. They might not have been one of the bad ones. They might have been regular guys like us, but when you wear the patch, it comes with the territory. That's why when you want to join a motorcycle club, you have to be real cautious and know what you're getting into."

I gave Big Al a friendly slap on the back. "Come on. Let's go inside. I'll buy the first round," I said and turned toward the clubhouse.

"Yeah, I could use a beer right now," Big Al said.

We entered the clubhouse, climbed up on a barstool, and the prospect, tending bar, set us up with beers. More Green River boys arrived at the clubhouse rumbling in on their motorcycles. They came in groups of twos and threes. A large pack from northern Wyoming and Montana pulled in the following afternoon. We partied hard for the next three days. Thursday morning, after a hardy breakfast, we headed for the Idaho border. There were over one hundred and twenty of us. We were a hard fightin', and hard drinkin' bunch, of bikers with a score to settle with the Lost Souls.

***

CHAPTER 22

We pulled into a seedy motel in Montpelier Idaho, later that afternoon and had lunch at a local diner. Outside, the sky looked overcast and the weather was frigid. Inside the rustic diner, the potbellied stove was a welcome respite from the cold. After lunch, we stayed in our rooms for most of the day cleaning our weapons and getting our equipment ready. The smell of gun oil filled the motel room. After an early dinner, we had a few drinks at a bar across the street from the motel and hit the rack early. Up by three AM, we fired up the motorcycles and headed northwest on Highway 30. The chase van with the weapons met us at the motel and followed at the back of the pack. The crisp morning air caused my fingers and my cheeks to feel numb. We snaked our way through the forest on the curvy mountain road. I noticed a sign that said, Tight curves next sixty miles. Twenty miles further, we turned off the main highway and onto Thunder Road.

Thunder Road, was a narrow paved road, filled with potholes that descended into a rocky gorge. The road didn't even have a centerline it was so narrow. Granite cliffs towered above us, unseen in the dark. The road twisted and turned, making its way down to the bottom of the gorge. It opened up into a small tree-filled valley. At the bottom of the gorge, the road turned to dirt. The road captain led us deeper into the forest. Several dirt roads branched off, leading into the woods. The road captain stayed on the main course. A sense of unease shot through me. My breath fogged up in front of my face, I couldn't feel my fingers or toes and the woods seemed dark and ominous. A deer darted across the road in front of me, its shape looking huge and dark in my headlight; I braked to avoid hitting it.

The road ended at the edge of a meadow and we parked our bikes underneath the trees. A cold breeze blew pine needles through the forest. I pulled my coat together in the front to stave off the chill. Looking across the clearing, I saw the flickering light of a bonfire. I watched tiny embers float up into the sky. The light from the fire lit up what looked like a rustic hunting lodge. Several motorcycles set parked out front and a few tired bikers lay sleeping near the fire. I figured them for prospects sleeping on guard duty. The Green River

Boys' sergeant at arms and a couple of prospects handed out M-16s and AK-47s. I took an AK and several magazines.

Big Al stepped up to me. He took a cigar from his vest pocket and handed me one.

"Don't you think those prospects down there might smell the smoke?" I asked. "That is if they wake up."

"No, we're cool. We're downwind from them. What we'll do is wait until we have good shooting light, and then moved up, on them. We've got some sharpshooters on the edge of the clearing. They'll take out any of those bastards that try to make a run for the woods. They've got nowhere to go," Big Al whispered. Big Al lit his cigar and handed me a lighter. I fired up mine. The smell of tobacco smoke drifted into the night.

"What's behind the cabin?" I asked.

"The land slopes down to a bluff. They won't go that way; it's a three hundred foot drop." A few hours passed, the sky turned purple in the east and the sun stabbed its warm fingers across the land. I finally stopped shivering. We stepped out of the forest and moved across the meadow toward the lodge. The quiet of the early morning felt unnerving. By now, the bonfire had burned down to embers. The only sound was the snores from the prospects asleep on guard duty. My heart thumped inside my chest and my breathing became erratic. When shooting time came around, a deathly calmness dropped over me. Fifty feet from the old hunting lodge, we opened up. The roar of automatic weapons fire blasted through the forest. Bullets riddled the hunting lodge. Pieces of glass and splinters of wood flew through the air. The prospects sleeping near the bonfire jumped up into a wall of lead. I saw one of them take several rounds through the chest and land in the remains of the fire. A cloud of ash and a few dying cinders floated into the air.

Gunfire, came from the hunting lodge, the bullets zipping over our heads. One of the Green River Boys went down. We charged forward. Three Souls made a run for the forest, but the snipers at the tree line cut them down. On the front porch, I kicked open the front door and charged into the hunting lodge. Big Al and twenty-five Green River Boys charged in after me. Another group of Green River Boys kicked in the back door and stormed in. The Lost Souls had turned over furniture using it for cover. We caught them in the crossfire and riddled them with bullets. The smell of spent gunpowder filled the room. The gunfire on the bottom floor tapered off.

Someone leaned over a loft above us and fired a shotgun. The sound was deafening. One of the Green River Boys took the blast in the center of his chest and flew across the room landing on his back. His legs kicked, a pool of blood formed underneath him and he went still. We moved toward the stairs. Another group of Souls barricaded themselves in the loft, firing at us when we came up the stairs. We ducked down for a few seconds. Bullets screamed overhead. Big Al tossed a hand grenade and there was a loud explosion. Dirt and splinters of wood rained down on us. After taking out the remaining defenders in the loft, we moved down a hallway checking each room. The gunfire tapered off when the last of the Lost Souls fell. I found JD Quinn hiding in a closet. He had three bullet holes in his upper body. When I opened the door, he looked up at me and smiled.

"If it ain't the dude with the rice popper. You should have never told me to turn down my music," he said and let out a cough. Blood dripped down from the side of his mouth.

"I didn't tell you to turn down your music. I asked you to turn it down. You could have said, fuck you, and tried to kick my ass, or you could have turned the fucking music down. You didn't have to rape and kill my wife."

Quinn laughed and let out another cough. "The things some guys will do for a piece of pussy, but I don't blame you. Powder said that wife of yours was tight. He made her squeal."

Pulling my right hand forty-five, I fired a round through his left kneecap. Quinn screamed. Waiting for a few seconds, I let him have it in the other kneecap.

He screamed again. "Finish it! You son of a bitch!"

"Okay," I said in a calm quiet voice and fired three rounds through the center of his forehead. The shots splattered his brains against the back wall of the closet. Quinn's body convulsed, his bowels voided and he died. My hands shaking in anger, I fired several more rounds through his chest. The slide on the forty-five locked back on empty.

Big Al touched my arm. "He's dead, man."

"Not dead enough," I said and lowered the handgun.

"Let's go outside," Big Al said taking my arm. We headed downstairs avoiding the puddles of blood. Bodies littered the floor.

The room stank of gunpowder, shit, and blood. Green River Boys began cleaning up the mess and a few were doctoring up their fallen brothers. A group of Green River Boys stood outside talking. "Take the trash and throw it off the cliff outback," Big Al said motioning to one of the fallen Souls. "Then clean this place up, inside and out. We own this ground now. We'll start a new chapter here. This lodge would make a bitchin' clubhouse."

"I guess that's it then. My war's over. Those guys were the last of the Lost Souls," I said. I seemed lost, almost trance-like and it almost seemed like I was on the outside watching someone else.

"Not quite, killer," Big Al said giving me a friendly slap on the back.

I looked over at Big Al. "What do you mean, not quite?"

"There's one more left. His name is Lobo, but he's on death row in San-Quinton. He was the original president of the mother chapter in LA."

I shook my head. "My war's over. I'll let the state take care of him."

"Where will you go now?" Big Al asked. He handed me a cigar and we lit up. Inhaling the rich flavor, I gazed out at the forest. It looked peaceful now.

"I guess I'll head back down south and try to pick up what's left of my life."

"Why don't you ride back with us to Green River? We'll party at the clubhouse for a few days," Big Al said.

I laughed. "Don't you ever work?"

"Yeah, I work, but I'm on vacation. I take three weeks every year for Sturgis. I got one week left. What about you? How did you fund this vendetta against the Lost Souls?"

"I sold my house in Southern California. I've been living off my savings."

Big Al nodded. "So?"

"So what?"

"So do you want to head over to Green River with us?" Big Al asked.

I slapped Big Al on the back and said, "Why not? Let's party."

Big Al left half of his chapter members at the hunting lodge. They had orders to get the place cleaned up and to start recruiting new members in Idaho. The rest of us rolled out to the highway and headed back to Green River. The weather warmed up and I felt glad. I felt tired of being cold.

***

After five days of hard-partying, I stepped out the front door of the clubhouse in Green River to head south. The warm sunshine felt good against my face. It was a good day to ride. Big Al and his boys stepped out behind me to see me off.

"Are you sure I can't talk you into hanging around for a while? You could always get a job here. What did you do before you went on the warpath against the Lost Souls?"

"I sold insurance," I said.

Big Al laughed and said, "Imagine that. You could do that here."

I shook my head. "No. I'm gonna head south," I said. There was a moment of awkward silence. "You know, when we first met, I said that you weren't my brother. I said that because you ride a motorcycle, it doesn't mean that you're my brother. I was wrong. I'd be proud to call you brother." A lump formed in my throat.

"We're blood brothers now, bro. Here, take this," Big Al said, handing me a denim vest. "You're one of us now. You are an honorary member of the Green River Boys. Even if you're out there on the road by yourself, you're still family. If anybody fucks with you, or you need us, we'll be there for you bro."

"Thank you. I'm honored to wear this vest," I said and put it on. Big Al grabbed me up in a massive bear hug. After saying my goodbyes to Big Al and his boys, I climbed on the Harley, hit the freeway, and put my fist in the throttle. I felt water forming in my eyes, but I blamed it on speed tears.

Later that day, I pulled off the freeway in Cap Rock Utah. Pulling over at a gas station, I filled up the bike. I stepped up onto the sidewalk in front of the convenience store. A pickup truck on the street backfired making a loud bang. Startled, my hand moved underneath my vest stroking the butt of my forty-five. Letting out a nervous sigh I took my cell phone from my pocket and dialed a number. Karen, the neighbor across the street from my house in San Bernardino, answered on the third ring. I said, "Hello."

"Mike! It's good to hear from you, how are you? We've heard things about you on the news," she said.

I watched the traffic on the street. "Don't believe everything you hear. I'm fine. How's my dog?"

"Lucky's fine," she said. "I love him."

I waited for a few seconds before responding. "Would you mind taking care of him for a while longer? I need to find a place to stay. I should be there in a few days."

"Not a problem, Mike. It'll be good to see you."

"It'll be good to see you too, Karen. Tell Tom and Nicole across the street that I said hi. I'll talk to you when I get there," I said and cut the connection. Climbing back on the Harley, I rode over to the police station. Things seemed quiet. A big grin crossed Chief Brody's face when he saw me step through the door. He gave me a good strong hug.

"I heard about all that excitement up in Custer State Park. I figure that since you're here, you took care of business," Brody said.

I nodded. "You don't have to worry about the Lost Souls anymore. They're out of business."

"Good, good. I'm glad to hear it. How about you? How are you doing?"

"I'm fine," I said. "I guess it's time to pick up the pieces."

Brody laid a hand on my arm. "What will you do now?"

"I'm heading south," I said.

"You could always stay here. I'm sure you could find work. I could always use a good deputy," Brody said.

"I may take you up on that if things don't pan out down south. Now, what about that beer?" I asked.

"Let me hit the clock so I'm not on duty and we'll head over to the bar."

We crossed the street to one of the local drinking establishments and shot the shit for a little while. Then we stepped out to the boardwalk. After saying our goodbyes, I rode over to the hospital. Pushing through the front doors, I stepped up to the nursing station. The hospital smell caused a nervous ball to shoot through my stomach. By this time, I hated hospitals.

"Can I help you?" an elderly nurse asked.

"I'd like to speak with Nurse Muldoon."

"I'm sorry, but Aili Muldoon doesn't work here anymore. She took a job in New York City."

I let the news sink in and let out a shallow breath. "Well, good for her," I said and headed for the door. Back on the Harley, I hit the freeway heading south and worked my way up through the gears. The wind felt good against my face. I began to think about my future wondering what I would do next. Thoughts of Sharon filled my head. *Who am I kidding? There's nothing left for me in Southern California. That part of my life is dead and gone. It died with Sharon,* I thought. My thoughts shifted to Aili, in New York *City. New York City. That's another thing. Does my brother still live there?* Backing off on the throttle, I took an off-ramp. I crossed over the interstate and took the northbound onramp. A big rig thundered past blowing its air horn. Working my way up through the gears, I twisted the throttle and got lost in the wind.

####

I hope you enjoyed reading Thunder Road as much as I enjoyed writing it. If you did then you might like In the Wind, book two in the Mike McDonald action-adventure saga. Check out the two sample chapters below.

In The Wind
Sample Chapters

CHAPTER 1

I hit the onramp, pulling onto the I 15 freeway rolled on the throttle, and put my face in the wind. A few hours earlier, I had left Green River Wyoming, heading south. Later that same day, I pulled off in a little town in Utah known as Cap Rock. I had some unfinished business there. After taking care of my business, I headed south toward Southern California. About two miles down the road, I began to have second thoughts. Who the hell was I kidding? I had nothing left in Southern California. That life died over nine months ago when those bastards murdered my wife Sharon.

Sharon and I were on a vacation cruising on my Honda Gold Wing. We stopped at a bar on old Route 66 in Southern California. An outlaw biker club known as the Lost Souls attacked us. They beat me half to death, while they raped and killed Sharon. The scumbags left me for dead and sped off into the night. That was a big mistake. I woke up from a coma three months later and couldn't remember my, own name. With help of my friend and former pastor, I regained my memories and my strength. A seething cauldron of anger boiled up inside me when I thought about what they did to my wife. Once I got my strength back, I went to war taking on the Lost Souls in Las Vegas, Utah, and Idaho.

In Green River Wyoming I hooked up with a friendly bike club known as the Green River Boys. They helped me with my war against the Lost Souls. The final battle took place at an old hunting lodge at the end of a lonely mountain road, known as Thunder Road. Finished with that bloody bit of business, I partied with the Green River Boys for a couple of days. After that I headed south, figuring that I would try to put my shattered life back together. Now I was having second thoughts.

I took an exit, crossed over the freeway, took the northbound onramp, and cranked the throttle. A tiny piece of gravel kicked up from the tire of a car in front of me hit me on the forehead. I felt a stinging sensation. Letting a big rig rumble past, the sound of its Jake brake reverberating across the land, I settled in for the ride. Thunderclouds formed to the north. Goosebumps formed upon my exposed flesh and a half-hour later, a hailstorm beat the shit out of me. Shivering from the cold, I throttled on down the highway. Fifteen minutes later, the skies cleared and the sun came out. The air felt fresh. I love the smell of the countryside after it rains.

After rolling through Provo, I skirted to the east of Salt Lake and took highway 80 east. Five hours after leaving Cap Rock, I took an exit pulled into Green River Wyoming. I took a left on Main Street and headed north on a side street that traversed a warehouse district. I pulled in front of the Green River Boys clubhouse as the sun was going down over Green River. Several Harley Davidson motorcycles were parked at the curb. A few prospects stood out front on the sidewalk drinking beer. One of them, a short stocky young man with short blond hair, looked at me and grinned. The sound of loud music emanated from the clubhouse.

"Well if it ain't Mike McDonald? I thought you were heading home," he said.

I climbed off the bike and shrugged. "I thought I was too. It took me a while to figure out that I got no home to go back to."

The prospects stepped up to the curb. "You've always got a home here with us, bro," he said. He gave me a quick hug. Wait until Big Al finds out about this."

After the prospect turned me loose I looked up when the front door of the clubhouse swung open. Its hinges let out a squeak. A big bear of a man with flaming red hair stepped out of the front door. A grin spread across his face when he saw me. "Speak of the Devil," I said.

"Mike. I thought you were heading south?"

"Yeah, I did too, for a while." Big Al grabbed me up in a massive bear hug and for a second, I thought he was going to crack a rib. "Al, Al, let me go. Your about to bust some ribs."

Big Al released me. "Come on inside. I'll buy the first round while the prospects whip up some dinner. I expect you're hungry."

"I'm about as hungry as an anorexic polar bear," I said as we stepped up to the door. Big Al laughed and slapped me across the back. It felt as if someone had hit me with a two-by-four. Inside the clubhouse, Big Al led me down a hallway and into the bar. A young blond-headed prospect tending bar looked up at me and grinned. The smell of tobacco smoke and alcohol emanated from the room.

"I thought you hit the highway," he said.

"I did, but I turned around. I changed my mind. I'll stick around here for a while and then head east," I said.

"You're more than welcome here. Your one of us now," the prospect said. Before I left the last time, they gave me a vest with a Green River Boys patch on the back. Big Al said that I was an honorary Green River Boy.

"That's right, Mike. Why don't you forget about heading east and stay here? I'm sure you could find a job somewhere," Big Al said.

"Who knows? I'll give it some thought."

Glancing up at the prospect, Big Al stuffed some money into the donation box. "Bring this man a Jack and Coke and I'll have a beer. While you're at it, see if you can rustle him up some grub. He looks like he is about to dry up and blow away," Big Al said.

I laughed. "You got that right. My belly button is about to wear a hell of a sore spot on my backbone." The prospect chuckled and then retrieved our drinks. Soon the smell of cooking food drifted in from the kitchen.

"Now that you put that bit of business with the Lost Souls behind you, you need to think about sticking around. You were ruthless out there on Thunder Road. Especially when you took out JD Quinn but that's behind you now. You need to get on with your life. You could build a good life here in Wyoming. There, is great fishing and hunting. You could even sell insurance again," Big Al said. He pulled out a couple of cigars, handed one to me and we fired them up.

"I don't know. I have some unfinished business with a nurse I met down in Utah. Her name's Aili Muldoon."

Big Al laughed. "An Irish lass. They're my favorite kind."

"Mine too," I said. "They're feisty. Anyway, when I got back down to Cap Rock Utah, I stopped in at the hospital where she used to work. The head nurse told me that she quit. She took a job at a hospital in New York City and moved. I got a brother in New York City that I haven't seen since I was about fourteen years old." I took a hit on the cigar breathing in the sharp taste. A cloud of smoke hung in the air over the bar.

"If you have to roll, then roll, but you've always got a home here and if you ever need us, we're only a phone call away."

“I appreciate that,” I said.

The prospect set a Rib Eye steak down in front of me. The plate was also loaded down with fried potatoes, biscuits, and country gravy.

“Now that’s what I’m talking about,” I said and chowed down on the steak. The steak was awesome. I wiped a spot of A1 sauce from my cheek with the back of my hand.

As the night wore on, Big Al and I sat at the bar drinking. More of the Green River Boys along with some young women showed up at the bar. The Green River Boys greeted me and we did some hugging and back-slapping. They lined the bar and the party started. Two young women climbed up on the bar and held a wet t-shirt contest. The Green River Boys cheered them on and I cheered right along with them. Once the ice-cold water touched their chest, their nipples stood up at attention. The water made their white wife-beater t-shirts turn transparent. The more alcohol the young women consumed, the wilder they became. The redhead picked up the water pitcher and poured the whole container over her head. She shook her long red hair causing tiny drops of water to shoot across the room.

The next thing you know their shirts came off and they were rubbing up against each other French kissing. By the time the night was over, they were completely naked. They stumbled around on the bar drunk and trying to dance. Some of the bros were afraid they might fall off the bar, so they help them down and handed them their clothes.

“You can come crash at my place if you want, or bunk down here in the back,” Big Al said. The Green River Boys had a bunkhouse in a back room. It had a pot-bellied stove, a stereo system, and a large TV set setting in a massive entertainment center.

“I’m way too drunk to ride. I’ll crash here,” I said.

“I’m toasted as well, but I’ve got a couple of dogs I need to feed. I’m gonna catch a cab,” Big Al said.

We stepped outside and Big Al called for a ride. We stood on the sidewalk talking and smoking cigars while we waited for his cab. Off in the distance, I heard the sound of a car backfiring. My hand dropped to the butt of the forty-five riding on my hip. The cab showed up a few minutes later.

“I’ll see you in the morning, bro,” Big Al said and he gave me a quick hug.

“Don’t make it too early. I may be a bit hungover in the morning,” I said.

“You won’t catch me stirring until noon at least noon.”

Big Al climbed into the cab; I watch it pull away and then took my duffle bag with my gear from the back of my bike. I ride a 1984 Harley Davidson Shovelhead. A couple of the prospects were closing down the bar.

“Here, let me help you with your gear, bro,” one of them said. He took the duffle bag that held my clothes and an assortment of guns, knives, and homemade pipe bombs.

“God this thing is heavy. What you got in there?” the prospect asked.

“Every damn thing I own,” I said.

The blonde and the redhead, that danced on the bar earlier took me by my arms. I enjoyed the feeling of the redhead's left breast against my right bicep.

“Hey, baby. You feel up to some company tonight?” the blonde said.

The redhead giggled. They were both still drunk.

“Hell yeah,” I said. My mind was still foggy from the effects of the alcohol. We stumbled down the hallway to the bunkhouse.

***

A numbing sensation in my right arm woke me from a sound sleep the next morning. I opened my eyes to find my arm trapped underneath a voluptuous blonde’s body. Looking over her shoulder, I realized that my right hand clutched her right breast. I could feel the firm pressure of the red head’s hard, naked body pressed up against my back. A sense of guilt shot through me and the image of my dead wife Sharon shot through my brain. I paused for a moment listening to the gentle snores of the two women. My head throbbed and my mouth tasted like monkey shit. That and an urgent need to piss like a racehorse caused me to worm my way from between the two women. I stumbled to the restroom.

After emptying my bladder, I stepped into the shower and turned the water on as hot as I could stand it. The hot water caused me to feel almost human again. Stumbling back into the bunkhouse, I retrieved a fresh set of clothes and changed. Dressed, I made my way to the bar and climbed up on a barstool. Glancing down the bar, I saw only three Green River Boys.

"What can I get yuh?" the prospect behind the bar asked.

"I have a major need for caffeine," I said.

"I put on a fresh pot. I'll have breakfast ready in about ten."

"What's on the menu?" I asked, hearing someone banging some pots and pans around in the kitchen.

"Eggs, hash browns, and toast."

Glancing down the bar, I said, "Things seem a little slow. I guess most of the bros partied too hard last night."

"Today's Sunday. Most everyone's at home with their families. We're having a picnic down at the park by the river this afternoon. Big Al called in and said for me to tell you that you're invited." The smell of cooking food drifted in from the kitchen.

"I'll be there. You guys know how to put on a feed," I said and pulled a pack of smokes from my shirt pocket. I pulled out my Zippo, shook out a smoke, and fired it up. The prospect set a cup of coffee along with a plate loaded down with food on the bar, and I dug in. The food was delicious. I heard giggling coming from the bunkhouse. The blonde and the redhead from the night before sat down at the bar next to me. The prospect poured them both a cup of coffee.

The redhead leaned against me, took my arm, and said, "How are you doing this morning stud muffin." The Green River Boys down the bar laughed and the girls giggled.

"Mighty fine. Thank you very much," I said trying to ignore the redness coming to my cheeks. We chit-chatted while we ate and then the girls left.

Finished with my breakfast, I went back into the bunkhouse and sat down in a Lazy Boy chair. One of the bros that had stayed the night at the clubhouse had a football game on so I leaned back to watch it with him. After the game, they left and I found myself alone. I pulled my Bible out of my duffle bag and settled back in the chair to read.

Some people might have found it odd, that after all, I'd been through that I would sit down and read the good book. In my past life with Sharon, I was a religious man. I attended church and I even taught Sunday school. But when those bastards killed Sharon, that part of my life ended. Oh, I still believe and I still read the good book, but I'm not the same man that I was back then.

I read for a couple of hours. Somewhere around one PM, the bros showed up at the clubhouse. The prospects packed up the gear and we headed over to the park by the river. The wind felt good against my face. A couple of prospects followed along behind the motorcycles in a pickup truck. They had the barbeque grills and the food in the back of the truck. I parked the Shovelhead and headed down toward the river. When I passed the restrooms, I stopped, feeling a sense of déjàvous. The last time I was here, was a few weeks ago when I first met Big Al and the Green River Boys. At the time, I was on the hunt for the Lost Souls. I didn't trust anybody, but after meeting Big Al and his crew, I discovered that all bikers aren't the same. Some are good down to Earth working-class people like me.

I heard a few more motorcycles pull into the parking lot. A few seconds later, Big Al himself stepped up next to me.

"Hey bro. Let's go set up down by the river," Big Al said. "We've got beer on ice."

"I'm about ready for one."

We headed down by the river; the prospects set up tables and set down four ice chests loaded with beer. Big Al opened an ice chest and handed me a beer, we grabbed a couple of folding chairs and headed down to the river. The cold beer can felt good in my hand. Big Al took a couple of cigars from his vest pocket, handed me one, and brought out his lighter. We fired up the cigars, drank beer, and watched the river flow.

"How are things now that you don't have the Lost Souls to worry about," I asked blowing smoke rings into the air.

"Things are fine; peaceful in fact. I talked to the new chapter president over in Idaho. They've got the new clubhouse on Thunder Road up and running. They've recruited some prospects."

"That's good," I said.

"I heard you had some company last night at the clubhouse, stud muffin," Big Al said and grinned.

I nodded and then laughed. "Word sure gets around. Yeah, a blonde and a redhead decided to rock my world."

"Those two are hang arounds. They're looking to become official mommas."

"I ain't mad at them," I said.

Some of the bros brought their old ladies and kids; they started up a softball game. The prospects fired up the grills and started barbequing ribs and chicken. The smell of cooking food wafted down to the river where we were sitting. The sky turned overcast and thunder rolled across the land.

"That doesn't sound good," I said looking up at the sky.

"Remember what I told you last time? If you don't like the weather in Wyoming, give it a minute and it'll change."

And change it did. A thunderstorm passed through, pelting the land with cold rain. It cleared up after about ten minutes, the sun came out and the weather turned hot and muggy. A bead of sweat traced its way down the side of my face. Several of the bros along with their old ladies and kids went into the water for a swim. Some of the single guys and some of the single women-headed, upriver, and went skinny dipping. A few of the bros brought out fishing poles and went fishing. Big Al and I sat by the river talking and drinking.

One of the Green River Boys hit a pop-up flyball. There was a loud crack when the ball hit the bat and a splash when the ball hit the water. The batter looked at one of the prospects. "Hey, Prospect. Throw me another ball." The prospect tossed him another ball the batter tossed the ball to the pitcher and the game continued.

"You know, you can stay in the clubhouse as long as you want, but if you'd like I could make some calls. We could get you set up in an apartment and I know a guy who sells insurance. I'm sure he could make a place for you in his agency," Big Al said.

I shook my head. "No, I won't be here that long. I'm only staying for two or three weeks. I've been putting money in the donation box to cover my expenses."

"It's not about the money, bro. You're one of us. We'd like it if you'd stay, but if you've got to go, we understand."

I shrugged. "You never know. Things might not work out for me on the east coast, but if it does, I'll come back sometime to visit," I said.

Two hours later, the prospects finished cooking the food and we sat down to a feast. It was one of the best meals that I've eaten in quite a while. One thing about the Green River Boys is that they know how to cook and they know to eat. We hung out by the river for a few more hours and then headed back to the clubhouse as the sun went down over the prairie.

The Green River Boys held church that evening in a meeting room, across the hallway from the bar. We gathered around a large oak table. Church, is the biker term for their club meetings.

"I know we hold church on Fridays, but I called a special meeting today. After the picnic, and all the hard work that our prospects did, I figured it was about time that we patched these guys. I would like all you bros that worked the picnic to step up," Big Al said. The five prospects stepped forward with big grins on their faces. "These guys have been working hard for the last six months. They've proved themselves one hundred times over. I would like their sponsors to step up behind them."

Each sponsor stepped up behind his prospect. "Getting your patch is the first step in club membership. When a brother gets patch in it is not the time for him to think that I've made it. That he can sit on his ass and let everyone else do the work. Getting your patch is the first step on a never-ending climb to being a better brother. That's what we are: a brotherhood. We're more than that. We're a family, and I would like to be the first one to welcome these bros into the family," Big Al said. He handed each sponsor his prospect's vest. The sponsors held the vests out to their prospects and the prospects put them on. A cheer erupted throughout the room. The bros rose to their feet. Each, in turn, grabbed each prospect up in a bear hug congratulating them on getting their patch.

I took my turn, hugging each prospect, and said, "Congratulations, bro," to each one.

"This meeting is over. Now let's party," Big Al said and banged the gavel.

We moved across the hallway and entered the bar. Someone turned on the music, a couple of the old heads tended the bar and the party started. The new members bought the first round of drinks. My blonde and redhead from the night before climbed up on the bar and held another wet t-shirt contest. Not to be undone, a few of the old ladies joined in. They drafted me to be the one who iced down the dancer's chest. The bros sitting at the bar hooted and hollered.

"Come on Killer! Don't be afraid!" one of the bros yelled. *Killer? I guess that's my biker name now*, I thought. *At least it's better than stud muffin*. Thinking back on my war with the Lost Souls, I guess I earned the handle.

"It's a tough job, but someone has to do it," I said and poured ice water all over the blonde's chest. Her t-shirt turned transparent, her nipples stood at attention and she let out a squeal. I stepped back and she began to dance. We partied until the wee hours of the morning watching the women go hog wild, but one by one the bros began to leave. It was Monday, the beginning of another work week. I stumbled back to the bunkhouse and crashed, but this time, I slept alone.

***

I spent the next few weeks in Green River Wyoming partying with the Green River Boys. We went on a couple of road trips. One day we headed east and then north passing through Rawlings. From Rawlings, we headed north and hooked up with the brothers in Casper. We stayed the night at Casper, partying with the brothers in that chapter. In the morning we headed north once again. We headed northeast and did some sightseeing at the Devil's Tower.

From the tower, we headed north again and stopped at the Little Big Horn Battlefield. Being a former military man that place had a strong effect on me. Feeling a lump form in my throat, a tear tracked down the side of my face. From there we rode southwest and spent a few days in Yellowstone National Park. We took a three-day trip to Cheyenne and watched a rodeo. We partied with the bros in the Cheyenne chapter and did some bar hopping.

I left Green River Wyoming on a crisp morning, on the 1st of October. The cold air caused my cheeks to turn red. After saying my goodbyes to the bros in front of the clubhouse, I headed to the interstate. I took the I 80 East, and put my face in the wind.

***

CHAPTER 2

Christine Chandler lay on her bed on the second floor of her two-story ranch house. In the middle of an erotic dream, her hand caressed her left breast. Her nipple hardened. Tears ran down her face. Goosebumps formed upon her exposed skin. In the dream, she made mad passionate love to her husband enjoying, his rugged good looks. She also felt a sense of foreboding and despair, as if it were the last time, they would make love. The scene in the dream changed. Her husband stepped off their back porch, stepping toward a dense fog that blanketed the land. Somehow, she knew if he stepped into that fog, he would disappear forever.

"Robert! Don't go!" she called after him.

He turned and smiled. "I have to baby. I've got to check on the cows in the north pasture," he said and disappeared into the fog.

Startled, Christine bolted upright in bed wondering what woke her. She sat, holding her breath and a chill ran down her spine. Silence filled the house. It seemed as if the entire landscape outside was holding its breath. The only sound was the ticking of the clock hanging on her bedroom wall. The sound of a single gunshot, followed by several more in rapid succession split the night.

"Oh, God. Gus no," she whispered and dived off the bed. She rolled to her feet and threw on a pair of pants. Heading downstairs, she grabbed her husband's thirty-thirty from the gun cabinet. She ran for the front door. Almost as an afterthought, she stopped at the coat rack near the door. She put on a long black duster to cover her sheer nightgown.

Out the door, she ran to her husband's Dodge Ram pickup truck. She fired up the beast and peeled out shooting a rooster tail of gravel into the air. Passing through the gate in the barbed wire fence surrounding the ranch yard, she floored the accelerator. The truck's engine roared as she headed out across the north pasture.

Please God let him be all right, she prayed as she bounced over the prairie in the pickup truck. "I can't lose you too Gus," she said. Christine's mind flashed back ten years to when she first married her husband Bob. Gus McClure, already sixty-two at the time, came to work for them on the ranch as a caretaker. He was a rugged old coot, who had no backup in him. *If it weren't for Gus, I'd have never made it through these hard times after Bob died,* she thought.

Seeing Gus's old ranch truck parked by the fence, she took in everything in, in a glance. Gus's sat on the ground leaning against his truck, and the cut barbed wire next to the county road. Christine slammed on the brakes. She grabbed her rifle, threw open the driver's side door, and ran over to where Gus sat on the ground. The smell of manure filled the air and a slight breeze blew across the prairie.

"Gus, are you all right? What happened?" she asked squatting down next to the old cowboy. She tried to keep the trimmer of her voice in check.

"Damned rustlers, is what happened. I was out here checking the fence when I saw some lights. They had a semi-truck and some of those fancy four-wheeled ATVs."

"Gus, are you hurt?"

"I jumped out of the pickup truck and took a potshot at 'em and they opened up on me with a rifle. It sounded like an AR-15 or one of them, Ruger Mini-14s like Bob used to have. I took a round through the shoulder."

Christine glanced down at Gus's bloody shoulder and then ran back to her truck. She retrieved a flashlight, ran back to Gus, and knelt next to him. She moved the flannel shirt away from the wound and examined the bloody hole in his shoulder. Not worrying about modesty, Christine opened the front of her coat. She ripped away a piece of the nightgown covering her breasts. Placing the fabric against his shoulder, she wrapped up the wound. The cold night air caused her nipples to stand erect.

Gus looked away and said, "Good Lord, woman, cover yourself."

"You're, hurt Gus. We need to get the bleeding stopped and get you to a hospital," Christine said and then chuckled. "I'll bet if it was daylight, I'd see red on your face. It ain't like you never seen a pair of tits before." She closed the front of her coat, shivered from the cold, and continued to work on the wound.

"You took me by surprise, that's all little missy."

"Here, I'll help you up. We need to get you to the hospital." In the night a cow bawled, and a coyote howled in the distance.

"I ain't going nowhere until we fix that fence. We can't afford to lose any more cows."

"You crazy old coot. You know you're worth more to me than these damned cows!"

"Never the less, little sister, we've got it to do," Gus said and tried to stand. He cried out in pain and fell back to the ground.

"Sit there, you stubborn old goat. I'll do it. You should have never tried to stop them. You should have called the sheriff," Christine said. Anger surged through her.

"A lot of good that would have done. You know Sheriff Dobbs is in Tom Boxer's back pocket."

Christine bristled at the mention of their names. "I know that Boxer can't wait to get his filthy paws on my bottom land down by the river. I am of a good mind to give up and let him have it," Christine said and headed over to Gus's pickup truck.

"Don't even say that," Gus whispered, feeling weak from the loss of blood.

Christine took a tool kit from the back of the truck. She rushed over to where the pieces of barbed wire lay on the ground. A pickup truck pulled up on the county road.

The passenger window rolled down and a deep voice said, "What's wrong Chris? I heard gunshots."

Not able to see his face in the dark, Christine recognized the voice and the pickup truck. A sense of relief passed through her. Cory Blair owned the neighboring ranch to the north. He had been one of Bob's best friends. He was her friend too, but here lately it seemed like he wanted more.

"Damned rustlers took some of my cattle. They shot Gus. I got to get him to the hospital, but he refuses to go until we fix this fence."

"Don't worry about the fence. I'll take care of it," Cory said. He climbed out pickup truck, came around the front, and joined Christine in the pasture. Christine fell against his six-foot-two-inch frame and cried.

"Easy there, girl. It'll be all right," Cory said.

Christine wiped her eyes. "It's been so hard, what with Bob gone, them bastards trying to take my land and now this."

"You're not alone Chris. You need me any time day or night, call me." They headed over to where Gus sat leaning against the pickup truck and helped him to his feet.

"What you thinking old man? You think you're Jessie James or something?" Cory said as they helped him over to the Dodge Ram.

"I can't abide rustlers. I never could. In the old times, we would have found an old oak tree and left 'em swingin' in the breeze."

"Times have changed old man. Let's get you down to the sawbones," Cory said.

"Thanks, Cory," Christine said and gave him a quick kiss on the cheek.

"Why, why don't you pull through the gap here before I fix the fence and take the county road. It'll save time," Cory stammered.

"Good thinking," Christine said and ran around to the driver's side. She climbed in, fired up the truck, pulled through the gap in the fence and onto the county road.

Gus McClure glanced in the side rearview mirror watching Cory Blair go to work on the fence.

"That old boy has the hots for you," Gus said.

"He's a good friend, Gus. Now lean back and rest until we get to town," Christine said.

She pulled into the parking lot of the Mother of Hope hospital fifteen minutes later. Gus had passed out and lay slumped over in the passenger seat. She ran into the emergency room and told the admittance clerk that she had a gunshot victim in her truck. Two orderlies and a nurse rushed outside, one of which pushed a wheelchair. The two male orderlies helped Gus into the chair and the nurse pushed him toward the door.

"Someone shot him in the shoulder. Please help him," Christine said. "He's lost a lot of blood."

"Stand back ma'am. We'll do the best we can," one of the orderlies said.

They wheeled Gus into an operating room. Christine gave the clerk Gus's information. The smell of medicine filled the air. Christine had finished with the clerk and sat down in the waiting room when a deputy walked in. "Oh great. David Carlson," she said to herself. *I didn't like him in high school and I can't stand him now,* she thought. A single tear tracked down the side of her face.

"Hello, Christine. I hear you had some trouble out at your place," the deputy said, a smirk crossing his face.

She sighed. "You could say that. Some damned rustlers shot Gus," Christine said. "We didn't waste any time calling you all."

"It's standard hospital procedure when someone brings in a gunshot victim. You should have called us yourself."

"I didn't have time. I needed to get Gus to the hospital."

"You know, Christine, you should sell that place of yours. Things might not go so bad for you in this town if you did," Deputy Carlson said.

She let out an angry huff. "That damned Tom Boxer has been trying to get his grubby claws on my property since Bob died. We built that place. I'm not selling."

"Mr. Boxer wants to build a resort along the river. It would bring jobs and money to the town. Tom's not a bad man. He'd pay you a fair price."

"All I want is for people to leave me alone."

"So about these rustlers? Did you get a look at them?"

"No. By the time I made it out to the north pasture, they were gone. You'll have to talk with Gus when they bring him out of surgery," Chris said.

"I'll do that. Tomorrow I'll have dispatch send a car out to investigate the crime scene. Right now I need to get your statement," he said and sat down next to her.

After Christine gave the deputy her statement, the deputy approached the admittance clerk. He asked her about seeing Gus. The clerk told him that Gus wouldn't be out of surgery for another two hours, so the deputy told her that he would come back. Cory Blair stepped into the emergency room as the deputy was leaving.

"How's Gus?" Cory asked and then took a seat next to Christine."

"They haven't told me anything yet. He's still in surgery."

"He'll be fine. Gus is a tough old buzzard," Cory said."

"I don't know what I'd do if I lost him."

"You've got me," Cory said.

Christine cocked her eyebrow and gave him a look. "You've got your, own ranch to run."

"I know, but I'll be there if you need me."

"I don't know Cory. I'm not too popular in this town right now, what with Boxer wanting my ranch and all."

"Screw Tom Boxer and the pony he rode in on," Cory said.

Christine chuckled.

Two hours later, a doctor with salt and pepper-colored hair cast his eyes upon Christine.

"Are you here about Mr. McClure?" he asked.

"Yes I am," Christine said when the doctor stepped up.

"He's in recovery. The operation was a success. The bullet entered the fleshy part of his shoulder at a downward angle. It nicked the bottom of his shoulder blade. We have his arm bandaged and in a sling. He has to keep it immobile for six weeks."

"Can I see him?" Christine asked.

"Give him about a half-hour to get over the effects of the anesthesia."

They released Gus from the hospital at six o'clock in the morning. Christine pulled into the ranch yard and parked the truck next to the house. Across from the house set a rectangular-shaped building. It had a small apartment on the second floor. A set of wooden stairs on the outside of the building led up a small deck, where you entered the apartment. On the first floor was a small bunkhouse, a tack room, and a storage room. Christine glanced at the stairs and the second-floor deck. The morning air felt crisp.

"You won't be able to climb those stairs with that arm in a sling. Why don't you stay in the house with me?" Christine said.

"I have been meaning to talk to you about that. I'm gettin' tired of those stairs anyway. I'll move into the bunkhouse. If you'd get my bedroll, I'll head there now. I'm a bit tuckered."

Christine sighed. "Are you sure Gus? I have plenty of room."

"I'm sure darlin'."

"I don't know what I'm gonna do, with you laid up like this," she said.

"You could hire someone else. I could use the company. He could have my place, or stay in the bunkhouse," Gus said, and then glanced at the second floor of the ranch house. The curtains to Christine's room fluttered in the breeze. "Girl, you need to keep them, curtains closed."

Christine gave him a curious look. W*hy did he say that?* she thought.

"Let me get your things. You're not the only one that's tuckered," Christine said, ignoring his last comment. After helping Gus settle into the bunkhouse, Christine went into the ranch house. She climbed the stairs to her room and went over the open window.

She paused, looking out the window. She realized that from Gus's apartment you could see right into her bedroom. A tinge of red passed across her face as she closed the window and the curtains. Crossing the room to the bed, she stripped out of her clothes and crawled between the covers. She was asleep as soon as her head hit the pillow.

***

The telephone woke Christine from a sound sleep three hours later. She rolled over, grabbed the handset of the phone setting on her nightstand, and said, "Hello."

"Hello, Mrs. Chandler."

"This is she."

"This is Deputy Monroe. I'm up on the county road to investigate the report you filed last night with Deputy Carlson."

"I'll be right there," Christine said and hung up the phone. Crawling out of bed, she put on a pair of jeans and a flannel shirt. After pulling on her boots, she headed downstairs. She grabbed the truck keys hanging on the hanger by the door and stepped outside. The warm sunshine felt good against her face. She crossed the ranch yard to the pickup truck and pulled out of the ranch yard. She turned the left heading up a dirt road that traversed the pastures heading north. She found Deputy Monroe sitting in his patrol car by the side of the road. When Christine pulled up onto the county road behind him, Deputy Monroe climbed out of his patrol car.

"Good afternoon Mrs. Chandler. How's Gus?" Monroe asked.

"I expect he'll live, Mark. How's the family?"

"Mary and the kids are fine. Would you care to show me exactly where this happened?"

She showed him where, where the rustlers cut the fence. She showed him the tire tracks the rustlers left when they used ATVs to round up the cattle. After that, she showed him where she found Gus by his pickup truck. Which Was still setting in the pasture. Deputy Monroe took pictures, searched the ground, and found several empty shell casings. He took pictures of the tire tracks on the side of the road where the semi-truck had parked.

"What do you think? Are you gonna catch 'em?" Christine asked.

Deputy Monroe shrugged. "I hope so. We'll alert all the stockyards and have them keep an eye out for altered brands." Deputy Monroe took off his hat and wiped his brow. "I'll check around.

They've got to be hiding the cattle somewhere where they can change the brands."

"You know Tom Boxer hired them," Christine said.

Monroe sighed. "I'd be careful what you say, Chris. You're not the only rancher that has cattle missing. I'm not a big fan of Boxer, but you can't go throwing accusations around like that without proof."

"If I had proof, would you do anything about it, Mark?" she asked.

"If I had proof that Tom Boxer was behind the rustling in this county I'd put his sorry ass in jail. Not everyone in this town is against you, Chris. If I owned that land, I wouldn't sell either."

Christine stepped up, took the deputy's arm, and on impulse kissed his cheek.

"Thank you, Mark," she said and then pulled away.

Deputy Monroe blushed. "Shoot, Chris. You and I go way back to high school. Tom Boxer's only been here for six years, but he thinks he runs the show. If I hear anything, or I find out anything about the location of your cows, I'll let you know," Deputy Monroe said. He climbed back into his patrol car. Christine watched him pull away and then headed back to the ranch.

***

Later that evening, Christine cooked dinner and Gus joined her in the main house. The smell of cooking food filled the air. She laid out a spread consisting of, roast beef, mashed potatoes, gravy, rolls, and corn on the cob. With Gus's arm in a sling, she had to help him cut up his meat, and cut the corn from his cob.

"I swear, girl, you do know your way around a kitchen, and you don't make a bad cup of coffee either."

"Thanks, Gus. I love a man with a good apatite," she said and looked down at her plate.

"Any man would have an appetite when the food tastes this good. What's botherin' you gal?" Gus asked.

"Gus, I don't know what I'm gonna do while you're laid up. You won't be able to do much with that arm in a sling."

Gus shrugged. "We need another hand around here anyway. You and I couldn't keep up with things even before that damned rustler shot me."

Christine took his hands from across the table. "But who, Gus? Who'd come to work for me with all the BS with Tom Boxer? And where am I supposed to get the money to pay whoever takes the job?"

"Offer room and board as part of the pay. I expect you could afford to pay a small wage if we cut back on things. They didn't steal all the cows. You could sell off a couple of yearlings."

Christine nodded, returned to the kitchen, and refilled their coffee cups. "I could sell Bob's horse. I haven't ridden him since Bob died."

Gus sighed. "I'd hate to see old Starburst go, but he'd bring a good price."

***

Up at four AM, Christine dressed put on a pot of coffee and headed for the corral.

"Where you off to so early girl?" Gus said from the dark. Christine saw the glow of his cigarette as he stood in the doorway of the bunkhouse. She caught a faint trace of tobacco smoke drifting in the air.

Startled, Christine said, "Oh, I thought I'd take Starburst for a ride down by the river."

"You got some thinkin' to do, do yuh?"

"You know me too well Gus."

"You be careful with Starburst. He's got a mind of his own and he ain't been rid for a while."

"I will Gus. I got a pot of coffee going in the house. Go get yourself a cup.

She stepped past Gus, who stood wearing a pair of jeans, and the top part of his Long Johns, and headed for the tack shed. She brought out a saddle, along with a bridle, and took them out to the corral.

"If it weren't for this dad burned arm, I'd saddle that old cayuse for you."

"I know you would Gus, but what kind of horsewoman would I be if I couldn't saddle my own, mount?"

Hanging the saddle on the top rail, she went back for the saddle pad. Starburst was a black thoroughbred quarter horse mix. He had a blazing white star on his forehead. He trotted over and nuzzled her when she came back with the saddle pad. She took a few seconds to pet the horse. "I know boy. I miss him too."

Stepping through the rails of the corral, she saddled the horse and led him to the gate. Once through the gate, she closed the gate behind her, mounted up, and headed south toward the river. The early morning air caused a chill to shoot down her spine and her cheeks began to redden. A rabbit darted across the trail in front of her as she passed through the southern pasture. A few cows balled and trotted away. She reined up at the edge of a cliff, sat there atop the horse enjoying the early morning still. A flash of movement caught her eye and she noticed a couple of coyotes down by the river. "Damn, I forgot to bring my rifle," she said to herself. The sun peaked over the eastern horizon and stabbed its warm fingers across the land. The sunlight reflected over the Plate River. The warm sunshine felt good when it touched her face. She sat there for a while watching the sun come up. Glancing down at the river below, she noticed the pristine beach and the narrow stretch of land by the river. *That piece of land down there is what all this fuss is over*, she thought.

A man in a canoe paddling downriver noticed her up on the bluff and waved. Christine waved back. "Bob's great granddaddy fought off Indians to hold this land. Bob and his daddy worked their fingers to the bone to keep it. I'll be God damned if I'm gonna lose it to the likes of Tom Boxer," she said. She reined about and headed back to the ranch.

***

About the author

David Donaghe lives in the high desert of Southern California with his wife and family. In his spare time, David writes short stories and novels. David also enjoys riding his motorcycle. He rides with his brothers and sisters in the American Cruisers motorcycle club. This is where he gets some of his ideas for his writing. With the club, David sometimes volunteers at the local veteran's home. He helps the police and fire department deliver toys to children in town at Christmas. When not reading, writing, or riding his motorcycle, David enjoys practicing martial arts. Above all David loves hearing from his readers.
Mail to: dhdonaghe@earhlink.net

Friend him at Facebook:
https://www.facebook.com/david.donaghe.5?ref=bookmarks

Or follow him on Twitter:
https://wwww.twitter.com/david_donaghe

Other Books by David Donaghe

Tale Spinner
Monroe's Paranormal Investigations
In the Wind
Blood Bond
Door Number Two
The Battle for Europa
The Battle for Mars
The Battle for Planet Earth
Galactic War-Coming Soon
Tales from the Lost Highway
The House on Maple Street

Made in the USA
Middletown, DE
25 August 2022

72071944R00168